THE QUEEN'S PARDON

J.A. SUTHERLAND

DARKSPACE PRESS

THE QUEEN'S PARDON
Alexis Carew #6

by J.A. Sutherland

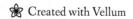 Created with Vellum

Allies and enemies are not always what they seem.

Trapped on a hostile world and abandoned by her fellow captains, Alexis Carew must lead her small band to safety, even though it seems every hand is set against her. Stalked by pirates in the skies above and shadowy, alien figures on the planet below, Alexis must convince former enemies to trust her even as she discovers where the tendrils of her true enemies lead.

ONE

O', pull me hearties, pull me mates,
And listen to the tale,
O' when that bastard Chipley
From fair Giron did sail.

"*Down!*"

Alexis Arleen Carew — once lieutenant in Her Majesty's Royal Navy, once privateer captain of the private ship *Mongoose,* and now more than a bit unsure of what she was, save in dire straits — obeyed her own order along with the nearly thirty men behind her.

The floor of the planet Erzurum's forest was dirt, turned to mud by a constant drizzle of rain, and with trees of a sort of branching needle, not unlike pine, but with long, brittle spikes off the main bit. The mud coated her as she flung herself to the ground and pulled a survival blanket over herself.

In fact, she thought, as some of the cold mud oozed around the collar of her vacsuit liner when she ducked a bit too low, *I'd call it a swamp if the planetary survey didn't insist this was a temperate forest.*

More mud oozed inside her boots, cold and squishy in a way that made her grimace at memories of unexpected things left in those boots by the Vile Creature.

Bugger the surveyors, it's a bloody swamp.

The blanket was part of their gear from *Mongoose's* crashed boat — with a mottled color pattern to hide the wearer and designed not to radiate the heat of anything inside it. The outer coating tried to match the temperature of the surroundings, rendering anything under it mostly invisible.

Alexis couldn't tell if the ship's boats that her tablet had detected coming overhead had anything in the way of gear for searching planetside at all — she thought it unlikely, as most ship's boats wouldn't — but didn't like to take the chance, no matter how much the lads might grumble at having to hunker down in the mud.

Mongoose's boat had come down away from the few parts of Erzurum controlled by the other privateers in the ad-hoc fleet she'd put together to attack the pirate stronghold here, so she knew whoever was approaching was not friendly. It would do neither her nor the other private ships' crews any good for her and her men to be captured now.

Overall, the fight for Erzurum was not going so well for her side that it could take such a blow, at least based on what few transmissions she'd had the time to listen to since leaving the crash site.

Standoff more than fight, really, for the time since her boat crashed had seen the raging battle slow, then stop entirely, settling into an uneasy quiet with both sides not moving their ships or men outside the areas they already controlled.

Those privateer ships controlled the Erzurum orbital space, with no doubt — of the six to attack the planet, only *Mongoose* had suffered major damage. The others, Captain Pennywell's *Gallion*, the injured Spensley's *Oriana*, under command of his first officer Wakeling after Alexis had run Spensley's face through in a duel over his accusations she was in league with the pirates —

And I wonder if he still believes that now I've lost my own ship and crashed outside our lines, Alexis thought, huddled under the survival blanket and hoping her men were doing the same.

— Captain Lawson's *Scorpion*, and even Kingston's little *Osprey*, which he'd done his best to keep near *Scorpion* once the fight started.

All of them were in orbit, busily repairing what damage they'd taken in the approach, and were more than enough to hold off any attack from the pirate ships holding position at Erzurum's Lagrangian points — even without the threat of their landing forces destroying what little infrastructure the pirate planet had.

Erzurum was not a wealthy world, being, first, a part of the Barbary, a stretch of space mostly barren of planets. It was hardly worth anyone's time to visit, save as a quicker route across Hanoverese space — the dearth of normal-space mass made for quick transit times between New London and *Hso-hsi*, but to achieve those times meant merchants must avoid what few planets there were, avoiding the normal-space masses that seemed to expand *darkspace*.

And, second, Erzurum was distinctly separated from other systems, even by Barbary standards. The buildup of *darkspace* shoals, an accumulation of dark matter in the space that allowed ships to travel between systems, caused these worlds in it to be left off most trade routes entirely.

Trade routes, rarely visited worlds, and governments with other battles to fight — a perfect situation for these pirates.

A check of her tablet showed the approaching ship's boats had come and gone. There were three of them up there, likely all the pirates could spare from their other efforts — the rest were busy keeping the private ships' boats penned in where they'd landed, neither side with enough force to best the other and not wanting to deplete what they had. Those three, though, were quartering and circling the space around where *Mongoose's* boat crashed, searching for Alexis' band.

Alexis pulled her blanket back and stood.

"All right, lads," she called. "They're gone and we've some time to move on."

The groans that met her words told her the lads were as tired as she was.

A hundred kilometers from where we crashed to a settlement — that's all well and good, and only a few days if it was in a straight bloody line.

It wasn't, though. The searching boats suspected they'd head for the nearest settlement and were searching along that route, and there appeared to be no straight bloody lines in Erzurum's Dark-buggered swamps.

The surface here had an odd architecture, with what Alexis would describe as rolling hills if she were a quarter of her scant meter-and-a-half height — for her and her men, it was two steps up, three steps down the entire way, with almost never a level spot more than a stride in length, and for half those strides the solid ground was covered in water and mud, so that one couldn't even tell if one was going up or down with the next step ahead of time.

That was where the land didn't drop away into a ravine or rise as a cliff from nothing — both those had to be gone around. They weren't wide or long, but they meant detouring a hundred meters, then another hundred as one met another ravine or cliff just past the first.

Water streamed down some cliffsides in waterfalls and flowed heavily amongst the hummocks of land before picking up speed to rush into a ravine. Too close to either and one was pummeled from above or in danger of having one's legs swept out from under and over the edge.

Alexis estimated the distance they'd gained toward the settlement was more than four times as much in actual walking, given their detouring around obstacles.

The men were tired, being spacers and used to walking no more than the fifty-meter length of *Mongoose's* decks. As for climbing, well, the distance of a ladder between those decks was the most they saw — climbing the masts outside *Mongoose's* hull was done in zero-g, after all.

Here they were further loaded down with packs and gear, including their vacsuits which they'd need once they contacted their allies and were back aboard a proper ship again. Some were still wearing those, taking the extra protection against the rain and mud, while others, like Alexis, had stripped out the liners to wear and bundled the bulky suit itself up into their packs.

All around her, men's heads hung low from either weariness or despair.

"Nabb! Mister Dockett!"

Her coxswain and bosun hurried over. She was glad to have them both — the chaos of abandoning *Mongoose* had sent men into the boats with little rhyme or reason, and Alexis could just as easily have wound up with no petty officers at all in hers.

Well, Nabb would always be there, she thought — the young coxswain would be by her side no matter what, having come to the Navy specifically to watch out for her. It had taken some time for her to accept that and she still felt as though she should be the one looking out for him, as she felt responsible for his father's exile from New London as one of the mutineers on the ill-fated *Hermione*.

"Aye, sir?" *Mongoose's* bosun, Dockett, asked.

"Keep an eye out for some clean source of water," Alexis said. Their supply of that was low, being only what each man could carry — and those who'd carry more had seen to the boat's spirits rations more than water. In the hurry to pack what supplies they might and be away from the crash site before the pirates came calling, there'd been little time to insist on anything else. At least discipline was still holding and those who carried the spirits weren't sampling their burdens.

Yet.

"This drizzle's not enough to fill a container and I'll not trust the groundwater, no matter our filters," Alexis went on, "but we may find some cleaner runoff on one of these cliff faces where it's coming down over rock instead of mud."

"Aye, sir."

"And keep a close eye on those carrying the spirits, will you?"

Mongoose's crew, while mostly former Navy men, had all signed aboard a private ship, a privateer, and weren't strictly bound by Naval discipline. In fact, each was free to leave at any time — sacrificing his shares in *Mongoose's* endeavors, of course, but with the ship disabled and streaking powerless through Erzurum's space there might be more than one of them wondering where his next fortune lay. Perhaps even some who wondered if those fortunes might lie with the pirates themselves, and an excess of drink would do nothing to ease those thoughts.

"I saw to it the spirits were carried by most of your boat crew, sir," Nabb said, "and made certain they knew how ill it'd go for them if they touched a drop."

That eased her mind a bit, as her boat crew were all solid men who'd stayed with her on Dalthus when *Nightingale* paid off. "Good work. We'll find a place to rest and have something to eat soon. The men are tired and we're far enough away from the boat that it should be safe for a time. Their passes overhead are coming scarcer and scarcer as they have to search farther from the crash site."

"Them pirates might start searching from the ground," Dockett said. "Be close behind us if they do — not like this lot could hide a trail."

Alexis nodded. She had three of men who'd come from more rural Fringe worlds, and gone to the Navy over ... the not entirely clear ownership of some hare or pheasant in their dinner pots, to trailing the group and doing what they might to conceal the trail. It was better than nothing, but not nearly enough if a pirate skilled in tracking were to follow them.

Or a half-blind deaf man with his head stuffed in a bucket, she mused, wincing at the noise the group was making as they milled about, leaving great tracks and prints in the muddy ground. The three poachers were staring at the space thirty men had just thrown themselves to the ground in with the same look of despair they might give the *schuffing* snout of some landowner's mastiff appearing out of the night's shadows.

"There's little more we can do about that," Alexis said, "though I think they'll not be in so much of a hurry to confront us on the ground. We're over two dozen, and they'll know we're well-armed."

One thing *Mongoose's* boats did not lack in was small arms. Every man — and Davies, her group's one other woman, Alexis reminded herself — had the short, chopping blade used in *darkspace* boarding actions, as well as a pistol of some sort, with a few rifles for those at least somewhat skilled in their use.

Two of those latter were lasers, carried by Alexis and one of the poachers who claimed great skill, while the others were chemical propellants — it was a tossup which type they had less ammunition for, though. The lasers' capacitors could be recharged with the solar panels they carried — but that required both open space and time, as well as a break in the persistent cloud cover that was sending such a miserable drizzle down on them all.

"There's a trickle runs off that cliff there," Nabb said, pointing to where he'd been walking on the other side of their column. "It's rocky, so looks clearer than most."

"Good," Alexis said, making the decision — if there was water there, then they'd break and give the men a rest now. "Set up a filter and let the men drink their fill — of the water, mind you. Announce we'll have a spirits issue after supper — quarter ration. They won't like that, but we've little enough along. And cold rations for a meal — we'll find a way to heat things when we stop for the night."

Alexis looked up at what she could see of the sky through the trees' canopy. She knew nothing about Erzurum's orbit or rotation, so couldn't yet judge how much daylight might be left and didn't relish sending her group over the edge of a ravine in darkness. The system's satellite constellation that might have given her some sort of weather report had been destroyed in their attack and she didn't dare make a transmission to contact the ships in orbit. That would just as likely be picked up by the pirates and give away her group's position.

"If we've light after all that, we'll push on a bit, if not we'll camp here for the night and give the men a rest."

"Aye, sir."

TWO

We skimmed up into Hannie space,
Ships and men both torn asunder,
But even with that butcher's bill,
Chipley'd never admit his blunder.

THEY DID NOT HAVE THE DAYLIGHT. THE GREY OVERCAST turned gradually darker, and even before the meal was finished the shadows around the cliff's base were deep enough they were forced to break out portable lights to see to the spirits issue. The drizzle deepened as well, becoming a full rain that struck the upper canopy to rain down on them in a fine mist.

The men lined up, ankle deep in mud, survival blankets draped over their shoulders and heads, for the spirits issue. Dockett showed them a full water bladder, then measured out a bit of water and replaced it with a measured bit of rum. He shook the bladder back and forth so they could all see it well-mixed, and began portioning it out.

The issue went along silently, with none of the men bothering to remind others of their debts for sippers or gulpers, as none wanted to be repaid by this weak mix.

Alexis took none, contenting herself with water that tasted dead and lifeless after passing through her canteen's filter. It was better than the recycled water aboard ship, but the advantage was not too great.

Instead, she and Nabb made their way to those too injured to stand in the issue line, bringing each a cup so he'd not have to rise. There were six of those, carried from the boat on stretchers by the others.

One, Trenten Morgan, was unconscious, which was likely a blessing given the burn across his torso and up his face. He'd been on the gundeck in *Mongoose's* approach to Erzurum and been struck down when shot splintered off a gun's barrel, sending a thin bolt of the laser's force into his vacsuit. The angle had left him alive, but horribly injured.

Alexis sat in the mud beside him for a moment and spoke, even though he probably couldn't hear.

"We'll see you to help as soon as we're able, Morgan," she said, taking up his uninjured hand in hers. "You hold fast, do you hear?"

Nabb finished passing out spirits to the other injured and returned to her side.

"He can't hear, sir," Nabb said.

"Of course he can," she said, smoothing back a bit of Morgan's hair that the rain plastered to his forehead. "You hold fast, lad." She rose. "My compliments to Mister Dockett and we'll camp here overnight. There are too many ravines for us to travel in the dark."

"Aye, sir."

Alexis moved on, visiting each of the wounded in turn. She wondered how many more there were on *Mongoose's* other boats, and who'd been left behind on the ship, hopefully dead and not abandoned in the chaos of the ship's fusion plant shutting down due to damage and the continued pounding by the pirates.

Nabb returned before she reached the last of the wounded and she was silently grateful for that.

Isom, her clerk and cabin steward for so long, lay on his stretcher, conscious, but in pain. She had no way of knowing how long he'd been in vacuum after the compartment he and the other servants sheltered in during action had been holed.

His face was swollen so that his eyes were mere slits, but less so than when she'd first seen it after exiting the boat, and he had a gash on his head that still oozed blood.

The buffeting that overtook *Mongoose's* inertial compensators during the action had thrown him against a bulkhead and knocked him unconscious. When the compartment was holed one of the others had recovered enough to seal his helmet, but only after Isom had been exposed to vacuum for so long that he'd swollen up like a balloon and his skin gone red from burst vessels.

He'd recover, but it would be a painful time for him with his skin left stretched and sensitive.

"Should be me getting you your supper, sir," he whispered, voice hoarse, as she helped him sip his weak grog.

"What? Do you think I need help unwrapping it?"

Supper, as well as breakfast and dinner, were the dense ration bars packed in each man's survival pack. Each, barely two bites, and that if one were dainty about it, was said to be a full meal. The crew swore the makers had gotten there by replacing all the flavor with solids from the recyclers of a ship that'd sat as a prison hulk for no less than a decade. They were filling, though, despite the small size — one just had to be sure to not drink too much after. The things seemed to expand once eaten and given too much moisture they'd bloat and distend one's stomach in a disturbing manner — until it came time for them to exit, which was a different sort of disturbing altogether.

It was a wonder of the Navy's ingenuity that they'd created something to make a crew yearn for their shipboard meals of vat-grown beef.

Isom raised one of the bars to his lips and nibbled at it. He chewed slowly and Alexis could see how the motion pained him.

The blanket over his midsection stirred and for a moment Alexis worried that he might have made the mistake of eating two of the bars, but a soft chitter told her it was only the Vile Creature and not Isom's insides.

The Creature's head, covered in brownish fur, poked out from under the blanket and its dark, dead, beady eyes met hers.

"At least Boots is fine as can be," Isom said.

"Indeed."

Alexis glared at the mongoose, given to her by Avrel Dansby, a rather notorious rogue, after their adventures together, as a sort of joke. She'd have disposed of the thing out an airlock if it weren't for her crews' inexplicable liking of the dirty beast.

The Creature met her gaze levelly, then seemed to dismiss her and rubbed its cheek against Isom's chest. The clerk raised his free hand to gently stroke its fur.

"He's a comfort, he is," Isom said. "Rode with me the whole walk so far."

Alexis grunted. She'd been hoping, when they opened the Creature's pressure cage back at the boat, that the thing might run off into Erzurum's forests never to be seen again. Perhaps Creasy, *Mongoose's* superstitious signalsman, could create a legend about it haunting the planet's swamps, as he had aboard ship with his talk of spirits in the Dark and the Creature's strange involvement in things.

Or I could send it back to Dansby as a sort of recompense for losing Mongoose, Alexis thought. It would be a poor trade, but serve the rogue right for saddling her with it in the first place.

"How do the others fare, sir?" Isom asked.

He was asking about the other boats from *Mongoose*, she knew, as he could see their little group well enough for himself. Their other boats and those of the other private ships — which she, Isom, and the rest of her band were now quite dependent on for getting them out of this mess.

"Mister Dockett has a man stringing an antenna up that tree as we speak, Isom, so I'll know soon enough."

THERE WAS NOT VERY much to hear from their radio, even with the better reception provided by the long antenna, than there had been back at the crash site.

A bit of a fight was still going on at the planet's main town, more an occasional skirmish than anything else — that against three boats of *Scorpion's* crew — but the rest had settled into an uneasy peace.

The private ships' crews didn't have enough men or boats to expand from their original targets against the forces of the pirates and settlers, while the pirates were spread thin keeping the attacking forces pinned down.

The lull had freed up additional boats for the pirates to search for Alexis and her band, though, and she followed that talk with interest. Luckily none were very well equipped and keeping her lads in their masking tents and blankets for the night would suffice.

Her one fear was that the pirates would put together a large enough force of men to risk following their trail on the ground — while all of her poachers assured her the rain would be helping in that respect.

"Be no trail to follow by morning, sir," Goynes said, the two with him nodding agreement. "We're getting' more rain and with little ground cover, it'll be all over mud — and this soil's such that it flows easy now. Fills in our trail, see? No more'n two hours o'backtrail, I reckon."

To demonstrate, he pressed his foot into the mud and lifted it, nodding as the mud flowed back to form a featureless surface where he'd stepped.

"Well, that's a boon, I suppose," Alexis said. Still, two hours of trail behind them was a long bit for some searcher to come across.

"Make walking a right piss, though," Warth, another of the poachers, muttered.

THREE

O', pull me hearties, pull me mates,
And hear the tale true,
When a glory-seeking admiral speaks
What's a poor spacer-man to do?

WARTH WAS RIGHT.

The next day dawned, what there was of dawn, with the rain not letting up. Alexis thought it was, indeed, a right piss to be slogging through the thick mud while the mist and droplets settled through the trees' canopy to light on them.

With no positioning satellites, she was determining how far they'd come by dead reckoning on what few maps her tablet held and a dim memory of where the nearest settlement was from before the boat crashed.

By that reckoning, they'd walked the distance between them and the settlement already, but were no more than a quarter closer to it, due to the switchbacks and false turns brought about by all the ravines and cliffs.

Alexis knew the planet was large and shouldn't be judged by only a few square kilometers — her own home world of Dalthus contained some unsettled, inhospitable regions — but she began to wonder why anyone had bothered to settle Erzurum in the first place.

They trudged on through the rain, with Alexis making occasional trips up and down the column to encourage the crew.

Column, of course, was a bit of an exaggeration.

These men weren't soldiers, trained to march in line and cadence for long distances — they were spacers, and used to going their own way, especially if that way might be a bit easier. So, many decided trudging through the mud, made muckier by the footsteps of those in front of them, might not be the easiest path and edged off to the side.

Within an hour's time, the "column" had degenerated into a group wending their way through the trees and along the ravines in near parallel.

Alexis allowed it, despite Warth's complaint that walking in line, preferably in each other's footsteps, would hide their numbers.

"But you've said this mud fills in within a few hours, so there are few tracks to follow?" she clarified when he came to argue the point again.

"Well, aye."

"And it's not as though there's any secret about how many men we might have fit aboard a ship's boat, is there?"

"I suppose."

"Was the last man in the column when we started out not trudging near knee-deep in the muck?"

"Not *knee* deep, no matter what he said."

"Still, would that not leave more of a trail in this mess than spread out as we are?"

Warth wandered off muttering about principles before Alexis could make her point that the men farther back in line had been so exhausted at the effort of lifting their feet that they'd be little use in a fight if they were located. So long as they all remained in sight of each other, which they did, none wishing to be more than an arm's length from a fellow on this hostile world, there was no harm in it.

At midday, Alexis called a halt to rest and eat what they would of the dry, tasteless ration bars. There were no streams nor cliffs that might provide water nearby, so they sufficed with filling their canteens from what trickles came down out of the trees' canopy. One of the messes rigged their blankets to catch the rainfall and funnel it, and others soon followed suit.

Alexis visited the wounded again. Morgan still showed no signs of recovery, but the others seemed in good spirits. She settled near Isom again.

The Creature came out at the crinkle of her ration's wrapper, sticking its brown head out from under Isom's blanket. Its fur was disgustingly dry when set against the drenched, bedraggled state of the crew.

"Is it quite fair to make your litter bearers haul the Creature's weight around as well, do you think?" Alexis asked.

Isom put a protective hand over the mongoose's head and offered it a bite of his ration bar with the other. The Creature sniffed, nibbled, then sneezed, sending bits of uneaten bar spraying, and bolted back under the blanket.

"The lads don't mind, sir, and I'll be on my own feet and walking soon," Isom said. "Creasy comes back and walks with us a'times — lets Boots ride on his shoulder under his blanket like a sort of hood, he does. There's a fellow or two with pockets full of better food, as well — they stop by and give Boots a bite now and again, so don't you worry about him not eating the rations. He's got his fill."

"Of course they do," Alexis muttered around a mouthful of her own ration bar, thinking the Creature had a great deal more sense than any of her men if it had managed to neither trudge through the mud nor eat the dense, tasteless ration blocks.

The private rations didn't bother her — those would be what-ever the men had managed to stuff in their pockets from their own stores as they rushed to abandon ship. Spacers had a strong view of private property and there'd be no jealous trouble from it so long as the boat's rations held out and stomachs, in general, were full —

and any with their own rations would have finished those long before.

Isom himself looked better today. The swelling was down and he was more alert. Whether he'd be walking on his own "soon" was still to be seen, but she was heartened by how he was recovering.

Taking her leave, she found a more sheltered spot and had the radio brought over to monitor things overhead. She could only hear one side of most transmissions without the larger antenna, but it was enough to know what was going on.

She heard more than one report to *Mongoose's* first officer, Whitley Villar, in command of another of the boats, from the private ships overhead, that there'd been no word from Alexis, only that the pirate boats continued to quarter the area of the crash. She longed to transmit, both to set Villar's mind at ease and for him to come pluck her and the men up from this treed swamp they'd wound up in, but that would only alert the pirates who were nearer.

The sharp *crack* of a laser split the air and Alexis' head jerked up, it was followed by another, and then a third. It was hard to tell where it had come from, but there were several men rushing in a direction, which she followed.

"Make a lane!" she yelled, coming upon a line of backs, which parted at her call to let her through.

The men were in a half circle around Veals, a topman and one of her boat crew. He was atop one of the low hummocks that surrounded some trees, providing a place out of the worst mud, but instead of resting there he was on his feet, back pressed hard to a tree's trunk, with his laser rifle aimed at the shallow water before him.

"What happened?" Alexis asked.

"Th — there!" Veals said, gesturing with his rifle's barrel. "Come straight at me!"

Warth stepped out of the crowd, a long stick in his hand and prodding before him. He went to the spot Veals indicated and probed the muck.

What came up on his stick was a bit of a nightmare and Alexis' first reaction was to join Veals on his hummock — perhaps scramble up the man himself as a start to reaching the first of the tree's branches and make her way higher from there.

The thing was not so very large, perhaps two meters long and as big around as Warth's forearm, but looking like nothing so much as a snake with hundreds — perhaps thousands, Alexis didn't even want to estimate them — of tiny legs on its underside. Its scaled body was a mottled brown and grey, closely matching the mud and leaves that covered the ground here.

Its head, though, was the true nightmare.

Disproportionately sized to three or four times the width of its body and wedge-shaped, the mouth that fell open when Warth pried at it with another stick was filled with nearly as many teeth as the thing had legs — or so it seemed — each needle-sharp and gleaming white.

Alexis couldn't blame Veals for shooting, nor for shooting again until he was certain the thing was dead. Even hanging there limp from Warth's outstretched stick, she felt the urge to draw a weapon and shoot the bloody thing again.

"Looks venomous," Warth said, eyeing the teeth.

Oh, of course, Alexis thought with a shudder, *because the writhing body, scurrying little legs, and glinting fangs weren't enough to fill the lads' nightmares already.*

She could see they were already eyeing the water warily, some sidestepping to the nearest tree and putting their backs to it.

It was likely the venom, if such it was, wouldn't kill a human any more than the thing could actually digest a bite of them — humans and most species native to the worlds they settled simply weren't compatible in that way very often — but there was a chance, still, and little comfort in the thought the thing wouldn't get any nourishment from a chunk torn off by those teeth, nor that whatever poison it carried would just scurry around their bodies with little effect.

"Good shot," Warth added, tapping the charred hole on top of the thing's skull.

It was — and the two farther back along its body. Veals had struck with all three shots, only needing to get its head to stop it.

"Veals," Alexis said, a worse thought than the snake-thing's presence striking her. "Your capacitors?"

Veals' face went white — more so than when she'd arrived — and he glanced frantically at the ground before him.

The laser rifles were powerful, the most powerful weapons their little band had, but like a ship's guns they required a great deal of power to fire. Power that was provided by a capacitor twice the size of a man's thumb, and making most such weapons single-shot. The bearer must quickly change the spent capacitor for a fresh one before firing again.

Veals' shots had come quick on each other, admirably quick, but Alexis feared too quick for him to have had a care in his panic at the snake-thing's approach for where the spent capacitors wound up.

The spacer dropped to his knees and came up with one, but the look on his face told Alexis the others were likely buried in the muck around the raised ground he stood on.

She swallowed the urge to shout — the look on Veals' face told her he knew the impact of those capacitors' loss. They could be recharged, but not if they were buried in Erzurum's muck, and they had only a half-dozen or so for each of the rifles. Barking at the man wouldn't help, and his panic at his first sight of the snake-thing was understandable.

Still, she needed to press home the need to conserve their ammunition.

"All right, Veals," she said, gesturing to the muck around his hummock. "Elbows deep and bring them up again — we've few enough to be tossing them about like that." She scanned the group, meeting the gaze of everyone with a laser weapon. "And the rest of you take note — whether it's Erzurum's buccaneers or its beasties we're after, you collect your caps or I'll know the reason why and set those weapons to one who will."

Veals looked at the muck with wide eyes, but bent to the task. "Aye, sir."

Alexis waited until they'd found and collected all of Veals' capacitors, then set the group to moving again.

The men seemed wearier now, more than should be accounted for by just the effort of walking — as though the addition of Erzurum's wildlife in opposition to them was simply one burden too many for them to carry.

She couldn't blame them, really — they'd signed up to go privateering against the easy targets of merchant ships carrying pirated goods and the occasional pirate himself, not engage in what had become a minor fleet action, crash on an inhospitable planet, and trade their ordered, controlled shipboard life for the discomforts and vagaries of Erzurum's swamp.

Their spirits were rightly low.

"Mister Dockett!" Alexis called.

"Sir?"

"What does your book say of us ever getting out of this mud and making it back aboard a proper ship?"

Dockett might have been *Mongoose's* bosun, but he was also its primary bookmaker, setting the odds on anything the crew might wish to wager a bit of coin or sip of spirits on.

The older man looked around and chuckled, seeing the need for a bit of dark humor in their situation. Privateer crew they might be, but they'd most been aboard a Navy ship at one time or another and knew the spacer's adage — you shouldn't have joined if you can't take a joke.

"Oh, sir, six-to-five against and pick-'em, if I'm any judge."

"Well, put me down for a guinea on our side, will you?"

"Aye, sir."

"And *Mongoose's* accounts will cover your book for any who take the don't."

There were chuckles all around, for they knew full well those accounts would be emptied back to *Mongoose's* owner after the loss of the ship. These men would receive their daily pay for the time they were aboard and nothing more, as the cruise had now made no profit at all — and they'd receive that pittance only if they were to make it out of this muck. Moreover, those betting against their group wouldn't make it off Erzurum anyway, so the bet was moot.

Still, she saw more than one back straighten with those chuckles, and more than a few faces firmed with resolve.

Her own did, as well — she'd see her lads home.

FOUR

Who cares for the lives of spacer-men?
The Press takes 'em two a penny.
When an admiral's glory's on the line,
It's not will some die, but how many?

WHILE THE MEN SCANNED THE SHALLOW WATER'S SURFACE FOR
more of the snake-things as they hiked, Alexis' worries were more
about the water itself and the effect it would have on her crew to walk
through it for so long. Water and mud seeped inside vacsuit liners to
soak the skin, and even those who still wore their full vacsuits —
putting up with the bulk and weight in return for a bit more protection — were damp inside from rain streaming through their
open necks.

When the rain began building she'd thought the surface water
would drain into the ravines, but it didn't — each of those had a lip of
stone around the edge, as though the collapse of the ground within
had raised it. That kept the water from draining, save for a few
trickles and streams through cracks in the resulting wall.

That must be what was keeping the water falling on the plateaus from draining down to the main surface, as well, for that came down in streams similar to those in the ravines.

Alexis measured it, and, in all, the water rose until it the space between hummocks was over the average man's calf and the sucking mud added several centimeters to that, making every step an effort of pulling one's boot from the grasping muck. As for herself, she was nearly knee deep in it at the worst, and the cold slimy feel of it seeping in through every gap in her vacsuit liner and boots made for an unpleasant day.

Effort aside, the men's boots were never made for such an environment — they were intended for shipboard life and an occasional foray into a civilized port.

Landings or crashes in uninhabited areas of a hostile planet were not something the Navy'd planned too greatly for. It was a thing that didn't happen often enough to bother with, at least not more than a few tents and blankets. If a ship were disabled in *darkspace*, they'd make due in the boats until help came along — or the food ran out, one — but crashes on planets were rare enough that there was little in the way of planetside supplies aboard the boats, save the tents, survival blankets, and the single radio.

The water and mud crept into those shipboard boots, soaking her feet and squishing mud between her toes with every step.

She'd have to find some way to let the men get their feet dry before too long — their feet and the rest of them, as well, for the constant wet had her vacsuit liner chafing at her in places and there was a danger in that too, aside from the discomfort. Most of Erzurum's bugs and germs would have no more effect on humans than its beasties could digest them, but it only took one, those things adapted quickly, and raw skin was vulnerable to such things.

The colonists here would have either adapted to it, or come up with vaccines and treatments in the colony's first few years, but she had no access to that, nor a doctor or medical lab to come up with one.

Their food was also a consideration, as the ration bars would not take them much farther. Their supply would have been adequate for the short march to a nearby settlement where she hoped they could take control and commandeer some sort of transport to get them to an area the privateers controlled, but as it was — she checked her tablet's compass, noting that they were still going nearly perpendicular to their desired direction and had been for some time. Well, as it was, there was no telling how long and far they'd have to walk.

If this went on too long, she might have to try and lure one of the searching boats into landing and attempt to take it — but how to do that without its pilot alerting his fellows to their location she hadn't come up with yet. Or risk a transmission to the rest of her forces and hope for rescue.

Or, and the possibility made her shudder, set to hunting and eating one of the snake-things in the hopes its flesh would offer some nutrition.

The problems were mounting and she saw little solution to any of them, leading her to wonder if —

A cry sounded to her right, nearer the ravine they were paralleling. At first, she thought it would be another of those snake-things, but there were no shots and the cry went on, though fading. The shouts of surrounding men confirmed her worst fears before she'd managed to half-run, half-hop through the mud to the ravine's edge.

"Look out, sir! Stay back!"

Alexis had been about to push her way through a gap in the line of staring men, for they were several meters from the ravine's edge.

"It's not stable, see?" Hickson, the one who'd warned her, said.

He pointed and she could see a seeming hole in the very ground. Here the lip of rock around the ravine's edge was wider than usual, by several meters, for a space, but some ways onto that ledge a man-sized hole had opened into empty air below.

"Who has a rope?" she asked. She'd seen to it that there were several coils of ships' line laid out in the supplies to be carried along, but couldn't tell in the constant dripping just who was nearby. The bloody rain misting down from the canopy made anything beyond a few meters a blur.

"Who was it?" she asked. "Did anyone see?" Headshakes were her answer. "Well, sound off then! Check your mates — who's missing?"

"Here, sir," Dockett said, approaching. He had two coils of light ship's line, collected from somewhere, over his shoulders, obviously having had the same thought she did. He leaned closer to her and whispered. "These ravines is steep and deep, though — I've little hope to find the man."

Alexis nodded. She'd had that same thought too, but if he were within reach, perhaps unconscious from a blow to his head, which would explain why he wasn't calling out to them for help, then she must check at least.

She took one of the coils from Dockett as they reluctantly obeyed. Bloody superstitions again, as though the longer they were unsure who had gone over the edge, the longer it might not be one of their mates.

"Here, sir, weren't thinking for you to — let me have one of the topmen do it," Dockett said, seeing her loop one end of the line around her waist.

Alexis shook her head. "No, I'm the lightest by far, so less risk of more of the edge giving way and less effort to haul me back if it does. I'm just as agile as a topman." She gave Dockett a quick grin. "Not so far removed from my midshipman days of running the yards."

The name of the missing man came back, causing Alexis' grin to fall, as everyone sounded off and checked their mates — Tubbs, able spacer, and one of her boat crew.

Hickson sighed. "I thought it'd be him, sir. Took to walking on the ledges where he could — no never mind to the drop. Said his feet was turning soft from the wet already and then that snakey-thing set him right off."

Alexis nodded, jaw tight. She should've considered the men would want to avoid the water more and warned them against trusting the edge of the ravine where they'd be out of it. Perhaps should have thought to have those who preferred to walk on the edge rope themselves together so as to provide some protection should one go over the side.

There were too many things she was ill-prepared for in the situation they found themselves in. She knew Dalthus and its backwoods well, but her homeworld was nothing like this. There were no bearcats here, which were the primary danger on Dalthus, and there was nothing on her home that told her how to keep her lads safe from what lurked in these waters.

She belted the line around her waist, noting with some satisfaction that she'd chosen the right knot and tied it properly, though it had been some time since she'd had to do that herself.

At least I still know the things I know.

Dockett sighed, but perhaps had served with her long enough to know not to argue with her about it. She handed him the rest of the coil.

"Do have them keep a tight hold on it, though, will you?" she reminded him.

ALEXIS EDGED her way out onto the ledge of stone carefully, deciding to go on hands and knees to distribute her weight more. She glanced back and saw the line held by every able-bodied man in the group.

She sighed. She'd asked Dockett to see the line well-held, but did they really think two dozen were needed to hold her up? She was only a bit over forty kilos and there must be over a ton of beefy spacers all grasping the line and —

Sweet Dark, are they bracing themselves to take my weight?

They were. Each man's hands on the line, well-apart, with legs spread wide, the one to the front straight and the back bent to take the strain and heave, as though they were set to haul the mass of a yard into place.

Or the most lop-sided tug ever.

It was enough to laugh at if the situation weren't so serious.

She crawled toward the hole, noting that the surface of the stone here wasn't solid at all. It was cracked into pieces like a puzzle or a cobbled yard. There was enough dirt and debris spread over it that it appeared solid, but she was close enough and the rain had washed enough debris away that she could see they were individual stones and not a solid whole.

Alexis paused and frowned.

Individual and not at all matched. Even wet and dirty she could tell that.

She got closer to the hole and approached slowly, inching her face over the edge to peer down.

The ledge was shockingly thin, though she supposed she should have expected that, what with a man falling through it. It seemed nothing more than the layer of individual rocks and a goodly portion of dirt held up by the gnarled, intertwined roots of the surrounding trees.

The ravine below was obscured by mist, but she was able to see that this was, indeed, a sort of ledge and not the true side of the ravine at all. Those sides were meters away, back where the lip of rock gave way to mud and water — what she was on, and what Tubbs had fallen through, was a thin facade over the depths below.

They were so far from the sides that there was no chance the man had landed on a ledge and could be got up unless the ravine itself was shallower than she thought.

Alexis lowered the end of the second line she'd dragged with her, its end weighted with a short, heavy branch.

She let out the line's full length, nearly a cable with what she held, and felt no bottom. Even if they could string two lines together and make the descent, there was no chance for Tubbs to have survived the fall.

Alexis looked back to the anxious faces, fuzzy in the mist, all hoping she'd tell them there was some sign of their mate and some way to retrieve him, and slowly shook her head. She edged her way back to what seemed more stable ground, despite the mud, and searched around the ravine's edge.

"Is there a more stable edge?" she asked. "Somewhere we might use both lines together?"

"Here, sir," Veals called, perhaps looking to make up for his near loss of their valuable capacitors.

Alexis let Dockett take the lines from her and quickly knot them together. Veals lowered the lines, hand over hand, with mates to either side grasping his waist in case this edge gave way.

Dockett caught her eye and they walked a few steps away, leaving the men to gather around and stare at the hole Tubbs had gone through.

"It's worse, sir, than just Tubbs," Dockett said quietly.

"I thought we'd accounted for everyone but him."

"Aye, sir, but —" Dockett took a deep breath. "It were Tubbs' turn on a heavy pack, sir, likely why he was so keen to stay out of the muck. Radio and antenna both today."

"No bottom!" Veals called. "No bottom with this line!"

Alexis closed her eyes. She hated the feeling that the loss of some bit of equipment struck harder than one of her lads, but there it was. That radio was their only link to the wider world, until they could get in range of some network connection and she could utilize her tablet. They were cut off, with no way of knowing how their fellows fared against the pirates, nor any way to alert those fellows that they were still alive.

FIVE

O', pull me hearties, pull me mates,
This tale's growing darker.
It's not for your bloody hair and beard
When I speak of the Barbar.

"WE THEREFORE COMMIT HIS BODY TO THE DARK, TO BE turned into corruption, looking for the resurrection of the body — when the Dark shall give up its dead — and the life of the world to come, through our Lord; who at his coming shall change our vile body, that it may be like his glorious body, according to the mighty working whereby he is able to subdue all things unto himself."

Alexis slid her tablet back into her vacsuit liner's pocket.

The crew, massed near the edge of the ravine — but not too close, as they were all wary of the edge now that Tubbs had gone in — unbowed their heads, murmured such words or made such signs as their own beliefs mandated, and stepped away.

She hoped she'd chosen the right hymn — at least Tubbs was of a religion that had one in the dozen or so contained in her tablet. This one though had variations — for burial in the Dark, on planet, and for a proper stop in normal-space to fire one's body off into a star. The one for earth hadn't seemed right to her with them being unable to recover Tubbs' remains — and the swirling mists obscuring the bottom of the ravine did, to an extent, resemble a *darkspace* storm.

Stepping back herself, she tried to judge the light. It was late in the afternoon and Erzurum had shorter than standard days, so they'd have to camp soon for the night; but not here, so near to where Tubbs had perished.

She shook her head.

Bad luck for the man, trying to avoid the mud and its perils to then fall through a spot that looked so solid but was only held up by woven roots. Bad luck for all of them he'd had the radio pack.

Alexis turned away from the ravine, then paused and frowned.

"Mister Dockett!" she called. "Bring me that line again, will you?"

It was dangerous, foolishly so, perhaps, but she wanted another look at that hole. Such a structure made little sense, now that she thought about it — roots growing straight out from the ravine's edges and then, somehow, catching rock and dirt, the rocks all different and laid like cobbles? Or, perhaps, the roots grew that way originally, there was certainly enough water near the surface here that they needn't drive too deep, and the ravine had fallen away?

That did make more sense, but it nagged at her. She'd been concentrating on any chance to save Tubbs when she looked before and hadn't truly examined the hole.

Dockett started to object, but she waved him away without explaining. There was no sense worrying the crew about phantom possibilities.

"You're not thinking of trying to retrieve the radio, are you, sir?" Nabb asked as she waited for Dockett to return.

Alexis shook her head. "No, there was no bottom with the line I tried and with so much water pouring into these ravines I'd have little hope for what the bottom's like."

"Then —"

"I just wish to examine something once more."

So once again she found herself crawling out onto the ledge of rock toward the hole Tubbs had disappeared through.

This time she took a close look at its edges and what she could see of the layers. Woven was a very good description of the roots — which she now saw had branches interwoven as well — and, while those around the hole were broken from where Tubbs went through, she could see where the others were not all long and natural. Some were cut, long ago, but with straight, sharp edges.

Alexis crawled back to solid ground — though solid under a layer of mud — and began feeling around the lip of the ravine. Where the lip of the ravine would be if the rock extended no more than was typical, and not the wide ledge. She pulled up a stone, then another, revealing the solid formation of the ravine's lip underneath, as well as the edge of the wooden lattice, its framework not growing into the ravine wall itself, but cut and formed to rest there and support the whole.

"Bloody hell," Warth muttered, peering over her shoulder.

Alexis nodded, meeting the poacher's eyes.

They were not alone in Erzurum's swampy forest, and their neighbors were ones to set traps.

"SOME SORT OF TRAP, you think sir?" Dockett asked.

They trudged on, Alexis wanting to put some distance between the false ledge and her group before stopping for the night — both to allay the memory of Tubbs and now because of what they'd found out.

"I don't know, Mister Dockett. I'm not sure what good it would do as a trap, but can think of no other purpose."

"Did well enough for Tubbs," Nabb muttered from her other side.

"It did," she agreed, "but we're alert to it now — none of the men will go walking out on a ledge like that again, I think."

"So what purpose then?"

"I cannot fathom," she admitted.

They'd examined the thing further and it seemed like only portions of it would support a man's weight. Others, by design or by poor design, would support barely anything and send a walker plummeting through.

The whole group walked more warily now, if that was possible, alert to both the snake-things in the water and to the possibility of other sorts of traps.

As Warth had pointed out, "There's more'n one sort o' way t'gig a man dishonest-like."

The decision to move on proved good, as they came upon a hummock larger than most. Large enough for all of them to get out of the muck in one spot, which was relief to those craving to have more than one or two mates about them as they slept. Though the smaller hummocks were separated only by a few meters of water and mud, the men seemed to view that as a chartless sea filled with serpents.

"Here be dragons," Alexis muttered, staring out into the mist in the last of the day's light.

———

A CRY and the *crack* of one of their rifles woke her, followed by several more and shouts of alarm.

Alexis scrambled to her feet and made her way to the commotion, the place made clear by handheld lights and the din of voices all shouting for their own explanation.

"Make a lane, damn your eyes!" she yelled, short after too little, too restless sleep and the sudden thought that she'd spent half her time in the Navy staring at the backs of those taller than she while she tried to get somewhere.

The men parted, revealing those at the fore all shining their lights out into the misty darkness.

"There's some'at out there, sir!" Hickson yelled, his rifle at his shoulder and aimed into the dark.

"One of those snakes, centipedes, whatever-beasts?" Alexis asked.

She peered at the waters then noted that the men with lights were shining them out straight, not down at the surrounding muck.

"No, it were a ... a *creature*, sir!"

"Of what sort, man? Out with it, Hickson. What happened?"

"I thort I heard a noise, sir, like a sucking sound while we're walking through that muck, y'see? Not the drips we hear, no."

Alexis nodded. There was a constant patter of drops on the water's surface as they slept, which would have been soothing if one wasn't also being dripped on and didn't know you'd spend the next day slogging through it. The wet slurp of drawing one's boot out of the muck was also well known to them all by now.

"An' so I'm thinking some fool's gone t'use the head on t'other hummock, see," Hickson went on.

The hummock they were sleeping on was large enough for that purpose, but not for so many men to use as a head as well, so they'd designated one nearby and nearly everyone had made a point of finishing their business before full dark.

"Soes I shines m'light out there, t'be sure of it, an' —"

Hickson broke off and shuddered.

"Cor', sir, it were a sight!"

"*What* was, Hickson?"

"It were all over scales, sir, like them snakeys, an' ..." Hickson swallowed hard and looked out into the darkness before meeting her gaze again. "The Dark take me if I'm lyin', sir, but it were some sort o' lizard-man, sir! Walkin' on its hind legs, standin' tall as any man, an' carrying a stick just like some sort o' spear!"

SIX

Barbary space's known far and wide
As a fine place to avoid.
With shoals and winds on every side
To leave your ship destroyed.

"THERE ARE NO LIZARD-MEN," ALEXIS WHISPERED TO DOCKETT and Nabb, not wanting the rest to hear.

"Not saying as there are, sir," Docket said. His eyes darting to the surrounding mists belied his words. "but Hickson saw something."

"He saw his imagination," Alexis said. "There are men out here, sure, as we've seen from the trap at the ravine, but they'll be as human as we are ourselves —"

She glanced over to where bloody Creasy was surrounded by nearly a third of the crew in huddled conversation.

"Though I'll grant you Creasy might be some sort of alien sent to torment me," she added.

"Creasy thinks we should turn aside," Nabb whispered. "He's saying the trap was a warning set by these alien creatures and the visit last night could be our last chance to leave their territory."

"And which way is this supposed territory?" Alexis asked. "How far does it extend, and where are we to go?"

Nabb shrugged. "Creasy's not one for details, sir — more of a big-picture sort."

"Creasy's a bloody menace," Alexis muttered. "I should have left him back on Dalthus."

Though if she had, the superstitious signalsman would likely have converted half the planet to worshiping shite-weasels, as her grandfather called the bearcats native to her home, and she'd come home to a bloody religious war.

"There *are no alien creatures*," Alexis whispered. "No aliens setting traps and warning us off. Whatever Hickson saw last night was some sort of beast. I'll grant a scaled biped of some sort, but not intelligent."

"Hickson says he saw a spear."

"Through the dark and mist with a handheld torch?" Alexis shook her head again. "No. Humanity's been traveling the galaxy for centuries now and we've found no evidence of other intelligences, not even any species with the most rudimentary communications or tool making above what's typical of animals back on Earth. Nothing to even match the tool-use of some beasts back on Earth, either. To think that there's been one on, of all places, Erzurum in the bloody Barbary all this time, and not a hundred kilometers from a human settlement, is absurd."

Dockett pursed his lips. "Not much traffic through here. Could be kept quiet, sir."

"Sweet Dark, man, the main complaint of the Barbary worlds is that they don't get *enough* merchant traffic or investment to keep their economies going — word of an intelligent alien species would have scientists from a dozen worlds pouring bloody money into the place!"

"Have the folk packed off from their homes to protect the find, though, sir, isn't that what those scientists'd do?"

"But —" Alexis paused. Dockett did have a point at that. The mere fact that humanity had encountered no other intelligent species didn't preclude the possibility of it happening — and if it did, then the impact on the world where they were discovered was more likely to be Dockett's imagining than her own. The scientists and money would descend, true, but the natives ... the *colonists* of that world would be packed off to somewhere else. There might even be a provision in the standard colony charters to specify that — buried down in the bits with the other things no one thought would ever happen.

Alexis sighed.

"The odds, though, Mister Dockett? Of intelligent aliens on this world, at this time, kept secret for so long, and now discovered by our little party?"

Dockett pursed his lips again and narrowed his eyes.

"Well, long, sir, mighty long ... but there's always some jammy bastard got to win the lotto, yes?"

THE NEXT DAY'S MARCH, and the next after that, saw a much tighter formation than the previous, with the whole crew accepting the trundled muck of their fellows in favor of proximity. Alexis would have praised their alertness, if it hadn't meant the death of so many floating branches and tree trunks.

"Looked like one o' those snakies, sir," Veals said after one such eruption of fire.

Alexis ground her teeth and took a deep breath. "Save your shots, lads," she said loudly enough for all to hear. "We've few enough chemical rounds and little chance to recharge our capacitors until these clouds have cleared, we're out from under the trees, and have clear skies for a time."

She sighed.

A platoon of ships' Marines would do her well, she thought, and have a bit of fire-discipline as well. For the common crew, being issued arms generally meant a boarding, and that meant stick the open end toward the enemy and pull the trigger as fast as one might before things came to blades.

It was no wonder they'd open fire at any perceived threat here.

She thought, as they settled in that night, that the crew should have a much larger worry — that they might never locate the settlement she sought and would have to find some other way to call for rescue. Perhaps even expose themselves to the searchers, in hopes the commotion would be picked up by the ships in orbit. That would bring down the pirate boats first — they were detecting fewer of them every day, sometimes none at all, but they'd certainly converge if given some direction — and endanger any of the private ships' boats that came to help. Unless such a large force was put together so as to overwhelm the searching pirates, which would mean abandoning the more strategic infrastructure positions they held.

Alexis thought some of the other captains would not participate in such a thing, though. Perhaps Malcomson would send a boat or two on any rescue mission, but how many of the others would risk their crew and boats for her? That would leave *Mongoose's* own boats, which Villar would certainly order come, and they'd all be overwhelmed.

Nabb came and settled next to her on her hummock, there being none about large enough for the entire crew. The crew was split up into groups of six or so each, with her given courtesy of her very own small space, which she shared with Isom who was already asleep.

"There's talk you should hear, sir," Nabb whispered.

Alexis thought it must be something like that for him to have sat unbidden. Her coxswain was well aware of protocols, but was also her eyes and ears amongst the crew. They'd tell him things they'd never tell an officer or even a master's mate, and the hearing of such things could let her stave off no end of trouble.

In truth, she'd been expecting such a conversation for a day or two already. Their winding, nonsense path amongst the ravines and cliffs must surely have the men concerned for if they'd ever reach their destination. To be fair, she had such concerns herself.

Her tablet's maps of Erzurum were old and out of date, she had no access to a positioning system, only the tablet's inertial guidance, and her sighting of the settlement on their boat's descent had been an estimate at best. It was entirely possible she had no idea where they were or where they were going — or, if she had the one, that the other was right out.

"It's Creasy, sir," Nabb said.

"*Oh, for f* —" Alexis broke off and held her breath, counting silently to calm herself and glancing about to see if any of the crew were paying particularly more attention to her after her outburst. It wouldn't do for them to see her put off her calm.

"What's the bloody fool on to now?" she whispered back once she felt she could open her mouth without calling for Mister Dockett to lay the idiot's back open. For once, she could almost feel sympathy for those captains who over-used the cat.

"The lizard-men, sir."

"*There are no bloody* —" More counting, this time with her eyes closed, allowed her to calm herself.

"As you say, sir, but —" Nabb shrugged. "— Creasy."

"Aye, Creasy. Go on — I'll try not to shout at you for bringing the news."

"Thank you, sir." Nabb looked around to see no one listening and went on. "It's all tied together for him, see? Boots, crashing on this world, that serpent Veals shot, and the liz ... whatever it was Hickson saw that night. It's Destiny he says. Can fairly hear the big letter when he says it."

Alexis cut her eyes to Isom's cot where the Vile Creature also slept, its little pointed snout poking out from under Isom's blanket and twitching to scent the air. Isom was recovering and walking some each day, but his skin was still sensitive and his joints ached.

"How in the Dark could even Creasy tie all this together into some sort of meaning?"

Nabb took a deep breath. "Well, sir, Boots, mongooses, -geeses, well, they eat snakes, and so we named the ship and then that merchant captain calls us snakeaters and then it's *him*, that very merchant captain, what gives us the word that sends us here to Erzurum, so that's connected see? And we're the only ship what's damaged, and the only boat what's crashed, and of all the planet we're crashing *here*, right in this very swamp with those snakes —"

"They're not even proper snakes," Alexis said. "They have legs — quite a lot of them in fact." She ignored the voice in her head that seemed to be chanting *It doesn't matter*, ever since she'd heard Creasy's name. There was no amount of logic that would breach the man's delusions.

"It's the scales, sir, the lads're no never mind to the legs, what with the scales ... and the fangs, those fit."

"Snakes, if I recall, have two fangs, and these have ... a great many more." *It doesn't matter.*

Nabb nodded.

"Then the liz ... whatever Hickson saw, sir, have scales, so it's all wound up in Creasy's head."

"Even if Hickson is right about what he saw, lizards are not snakes. The 'snakes', in fact, fit better as lizards, given the legs." *It doesn't matter.*

Nabb nodded. "It's the fangs —"

"The fangs, yes, I see, but —" *It doesn't matter.* "What's the rest of it, then?"

Nabb scratched at his neck. "I'm not sure I rightly understand it myself, sir. Creasy's got it all packed up tight the way he tells it and — well, a body comes away convinced, even if he don't remember all the details."

"But shouldn't one understand what —" *It doesn't matter.* "Go on, tell me what you can of it."

"Something about Boots and Destiny and lizard-alien-men — knowing as I do that there ain't none, sir, as you say — and them wanting to take over the whole universe from us and —"

"Hickson says he saw a bloody spear! How are bloody lizard-men from one planet in the bloody *Barbary*, for the Dark's sake, supposed to take over the bleeding *universe* with spears and rocks —"

It doesn't matter.

"Oh, I see it, sir, but —"

Alexis sighed. "Creasy."

"Aye, Creasy, sir."

They sat in silence for a time, contemplating the sheer volume of conviction that could be generated by how little mass of brain Alexis was certain Creasy possessed.

It doesn't matter.

"Says we're here for a Purpose, sir, and you can fairly tell he's got a right big P on that one too."

"I see. So, if I've got this straight," Alexis said, "Creasy's thought — though I hesitate to put such a word so very close to the man's mention — is that the Creature has somehow brought us here to Erzurum to save humanity from hostile lizard-men?"

"That's the size of it, sir ... well, more serpent-men — with arms and legs."

"But serpents don't have —" *It doesn't matter.*

"He's fair certain they'll have fangs, sir, and that makes all the difference."

SEVEN

O', pull me hearties, pull me mates,
And let your hearts go low.
It was deep inside the Barbary
That Chipley caught his foe.

THE NIGHT WAS COLD AND WET, AND THE GROUND UNDER
Alexis was hard and lumpy with rocks and roots. The hummocks
were mostly roots, clinging to the remnants of land that had long
since washed away into the muck and ravines, too little replenished
by any earth coming down from the cliffs above.

The survival blanket she wrapped herself in offered thin, scant
protection from any of those things. It kept a bit of the rain off, but
some still struck her exposed head and face to trickle inside. She
could cover herself entirely, but that made the air inside the blanket
stuffy and difficult to breathe.

The cold seeped in through her head, too, and with only her
vacsuit liner and the blanket between her and the roots, she could
feel every bit of the wood's grain, not least of which because the
vacsuit liner itself was growing thinner and thinner with each passing

day. Far more quickly than she could credit, in fact. Perhaps the contractor for her old one, it was from her time on *Nightingale*, after all, had cut corners, but that didn't explain why the rest of the crews' were also wearing so. Those came from dozens of different ships and systems, yet, under the persistent mud, showed the same sudden rents and patches of wear as her own had acquired.

Even whole, though, it would provide little more protection from the lumpy roots, especially with the weight bearing down on her.

Alexis shifted in her sleep, half-raising a hand to pet the Creature, as the weight on her chest made her think it had left Isom to rest on her as it was sometimes wont to do. It hadn't come to her in her sleep since they'd crashed on Erzurum, instead staying with Isom, and she hadn't begrudged that. Isom's injuries made his rest all the more important and she'd had no nightmares for the Creature to chase away with its presence, being too exhausted from the mud-slogging march.

Not that the Creature's presence actually kept the nightmares at bay, her sleepy thoughts argued, while coming a bit more awake. That was mere coincidence, and that she might — occasionally, she'd allow, and not without some reservation — like to wake with the thing's warmth on her chest was more testimony to her brain being half-addled with sleep of a morning and not that she'd come to tolerate the Creature.

Alexis grumbled and shifted.

The insulating properties of the blanket, little though she thought it did for Erzurum's cold, were doing well enough against the Creature's warmth — she felt none of that comforting sensation through it, only an oppressive weight on her chest, as though the thing had doubled in size on its new diet of emergency rations and the crew's pocket supplies instead of vat-grown beef ...

Which I'll allow may be a possibility, was the thought that ran through her head. They might all put on a few kilos if that were the case.

The image of her crew coming off a march through this swampy forest and being unable to fit through a ship's hatch came to her and she snorted. One did think the oddest things when waking.

Take the Creature, for instance.

Not only did its weight seem to have increased, but her snort disturbed its own slumber and it was now kneading her with legs that seemed to have both shrunk and multiplied. Two of its little paws normally alternated pushing at her chest as she woke, but now there were more, running the thing's full length from her chest, over her stomach, down her thigh, and even across her shin. All its tiny little legs pressing her over and over and ...

Alexis froze and her eyes snapped open to find a wedge-shaped, scale-covered head fixated on the hand she had half-raised to stroke it.

Even in the dim bits of light filtering through the canopy from Erzurum's moon the snake-thing's scales glistened and its eyes gleamed. Or perhaps the light came from the beast's eyes, for they seemed to glow all on their own.

A forked tongue ... no, triforked ... no ...

Sweet Dark, the thing's tongue has as many tips as it does legs.

The dozens of tiny tendrils tickled across her upraised palm and fingers, making her strain to keep still when she wanted nothing more than to scream and thrash about to get the thing off her.

It seemed fascinated by her hand for the moment and Alexis took the opportunity to cast her eyes about in search of anyone who might help, but she was alone on the hummock save for Isom and he was asleep. Nabb had taken up bedding down near her as well, but she couldn't see him — he also took a periodic walk about the camp with Dockett, so might not be close, or was as asleep as Isom.

But Isom was there and armed. He'd have a clear shot of the thing's head, raised as it was, if only he'd wake and act swiftly.

Alexis moved her mouth, but no sound came out. She had to tease a bit of moisture into her mouth, by licking the mist from her lips and working it about before she felt she could make a sound at all.

"Isom," she whispered. "*Is —*"

She broke off, scarcely daring to breathe as the snake, centipede, whatever it might be, spun its face to look at hers. She froze, waiting for it to dart forward and strike, but it remained as still as she.

Alexis started to lower her hand. Of course, the hand she raised to pet the damned Vile Creature when she'd thought it was that thing on her chest would be the one on the side she kept her flechette pistol while she slept. Had it been the other she might have grasped the pistol and shot while the snakipede was distracted by her other hand.

The head darted back to stare at her hand and she froze again.

Perhaps if she raised the other she might distract its gaze and reach her pistol.

She'd nearly determined to try that, thinking she'd be unable to remain still enough for much longer and must try something, when an angry, grating, chittering screech sounded from where Isom lay.

Even as the snakipede's head spun about, a blur of brown-furred motion crossed her chest, crashing into the beast and dragging it away — not off her, the snakipede was too large and the blur too small to do that, but enough that Alexis' body was reacting even before she could fully note what happened.

She rolled away, toward Isom and out from under the rest of the thing's body, scooping up her flechette pistol as she did.

Shadows fought at the edge of the hummock, one long and thick, sharp with scaled edges, thrashing from side to side and up and down in desperate motion, the other short and blurry from its bristled fur, latched onto the other's neck and being taken for a wild ride while the snakipede thrashed.

The dark night came alive with noise and light as the crew had been sleeping lightly. Every one of the crew was up at the sound of the mongoose's chittering battle cry. Hand torches sprang to life and shouts asked where the attack was.

Their lights played over Alexis' part of the hummock, illuminating the thrashing figures, as well as the snakipede's head, which Alexis fixed her flechette pistol on.

She had no clear shot, though, as the constant movement put the Creature's body in her shot as often as the snakipede's head.

Not that she cared one whit about the Creature taking a dart or two as well, she told herself, but she was certain the crew would look poorly on it, seeing how they doted on the thing.

For a moment, the mongoose was flung loose, rolling over the hummock and nearly into the surrounding water as its little jaws lost their grip on its much larger adversary.

Alexis' trigger finger tightened, ready for the opportunity, but then the stupid Creature dashed back in, barely dodging a strike of glistening fangs, and latched on under the snakipede's jaw to go for another ride.

"Damn you, get off it or I'll shoot you anyway!" Alexis yelled.

Another lost grip threw the mongoose aside, but it was back again, so fast that Alexis still couldn't get a shot off and she gnashed her teeth in frustration.

"Buggering ... *Boots! Off!*" she yelled, the command being nearly the only thing she'd ever said to the Creature, though repeatedly, as in, "Off my chair! Off my settee! Off my bunk! Off my dining table! Off my bloody dinner plate, you vile buggering thing what have you done there?!"

Whether obeying or merely flung aside again, the furred blur flew through the air to land in the swamp water with a splash many times its size.

The snakipede reared back, as though gathering itself to follow and strike, but Alexis' pistol whined.

The sharp, tiny darts of thermoplastic stripped off the pistol's magazine and propelled from its barrel were almost no match for the thing's scales. Many whined off into the surrounding space, making men duck and throw themselves into the muddy water. A few, though, made it through — a gap between scales here, one pried loose by a mongoose's tooth there.

They penetrated, making the snakipede spit and hiss with irritation, then twist to face this new attack.

That brought its eyes to face Alexis and she fired again.

"DID Y'SEE IT, LADS?" Creasy asked. "Boots takin' on that serpent ten times his size, he did!"

Alexis shook her head. The Creature wasn't even out of the bloody water yet, and Creasy was at it.

"Killed the bloody thing hisself, Boots did!"

Alexis glanced at the flechette pistol in her hand and the few darts stuck in the snakipede's head and neck, including the ones with just a bit showing where they'd penetrated the beast's left eye and found whatever it had for a brain.

"I'm quite certain it wasn't —"

"Three cheers for Boots savin' the captain!"

It doesn't matter.

"*Hip hip* —"

"*Belay that!*" Alexis ordered midway through the cheer. "There may be searchers about!"

She doubted that, and the high-pitched whine of her flechette pistol, as well as the shouts of alarm while the two animals were fighting, would likely have alerted any already, but there was no need in providing more noise if there were — nor did she particularly care to hear the crew cheering for the bloody Creature, no matter it had just saved her, if not entirely as Creasy made it out.

The Creature in question made the hummock and scrambled out of the water. Fur mud-covered and drenched, it was a bedraggled, pitiful sight.

"Boots! Here, Boots," Isom was calling, having managed to rise despite the pain of still swollen skin and joints. He was holding out a mass of cloth. "Here, come and get dry, Boots."

"Is that ..." Alexis looked closer. "Is that one of my jumpsuits?"

"An old one, sir," Isom said, kneeling down and holding it out toward the mongoose. "He likes t'have your scent near."

"If we'd had spares along, I might've liked a change, you know?"

Isom looked down at the cloth in his hands. "Old, sir, as I said, and torn —"

"Still —"

"Been in Boot's crate a time, you see."

"Bloody —"

She broke off as the Creature ignored Isom and came toward her and the hand she had outstretched to examine the snakipede's head.

Alexis sighed. She'd not normally give the thing a bit of attention, but she supposed it had earned it, what with distracting the snakipede until she could get a clear shot.

"All right, you vile thing. One head scratch then it's back to Isom and —"

The Creature knocked her hand away, actually hitched its hips to bat it aside, straddled the snakipede's head, and let loose a stream that spattered widely, including onto Alexis' boots.

EIGHT

For nigh unto a fortnight
The ships fought 'til they were hulks,
And near fifty thousand men were spilled
To the mercies of the Dark.

"It's not as though Boots did it a'purpose, sir," Isom said, his tone the one he used when he wished to admonish her for something — entirely respectful, yet carrying a clear message.

Alexis grunted, more from the effort of pulling her boot from the mud with each step than any response.

"He was more ... sending a message, like, I think. To others of those snake things."

"It's all right, Isom, I'm not angry at the Creature — over that."

In truth she wasn't. The bit of ... the stream that had spattered on her boots wasn't the worst thing the Creature'd left for her to find, after all, and it wasn't the worst she'd had on her since crashing on Erzurum, come to that.

Her vacsuit liner had split a seam as she stood from kneeling by the dead snakipede and hers wasn't the only one. While she'd noted it before, it was now clearly obvious that all their clothing was wearing at a rate she couldn't credit to anything but unnatural.

There must be something in the water.

Which would explain the chafing — which was more than chafing, when one really looked.

Under the tattered and split jumpsuits, liners, and vacsuits, all of them had red, sensitive patches on their skin, some with the start of what looked like boils. Those were tiny yet, but painful.

It was enough to make her ponder wearing the jumpsuit Isom wrapped the Creature in, no matter what the thing might have done with it in its crate.

She wondered, if it were the water, what effect it was having on their insides even with their canteens' filters.

A shout came from the edge of the group, but, thankfully, no shots.

"Passin' th'word fer the Captain!"

"It is all right, Isom," she assured her clerk with a pat on his shoulder. "For all I know, a bit of mongoose urine might be just the thing to ease whatever the mud and water here are doing to us ... *don't* repeat that, especially in Creasy's hearing."

Sweet Dark, let that idea out and his followers will be bathing in it.

"Aye, sir."

Alexis called a halt to their march — it was nearly time to rest a bit anyway — and made her way to where the shout had come from.

"What is it?"

Parke stepped aside from the group of huddled men, which included Creasy, Alexis noted, and approached. He had a rifle in hand, one of the lasers, and had been set to walking picket along their path.

He leaned close, almost closer than was appropriate, and whispered.

"T'ings in t'mist, sir. More'n one."

Alexis noted his eyes were wide and his hands shaking.

"What sort of things, Parke?"

"Only shadows, sir, but pacin' us."

"You did right to call me — and not to fire at shadows."

Parke swallowed and nodded, as though following that order had been the more difficult than pulling out on the yards with an enemy frigate ready to fire chain into them.

Alexis frowned. "'Shadows,' you say? More than one?"

Parke nodded. "Aye, sir. One a'first, din't call w'that — thort me eyes playin' tricks. Just now, tree of 'em."

"Not more snakes? Snakipedes?"

A shake of his head. "No, sir. Tall an' upright — like a man walks."

Alexis heard Creasy in the nearby group.

"Angry," he said. "Boots killed their serpent, sent to harm the captain. Probably worship it, the bloody heathen, superstitious serpent-men."

"Belay that!" Alexis turned to the larger group. "We don't know what's out there, if anything at all —"

"I saw —"

"No doubt you saw something, Parke, but there are no serpent-men. Mere shadows in the mist are —"

"Sir!"

Alexis turned, ready to snap at the man for interrupting her, but saw all eyes looking off into the misty rain.

Two hummocks away, barely visible, but clear enough it was no shadow, stood a figure.

Covered in the same sort of iridescent scales as the snakipedes, but with only two legs, its other limbs being clearly defined arms and holding a spear in what could only be hands. The torso gave way to a wide, scaled hood that hid the figure's face in shadows, like a much larger version of a cobra's hood.

They all stood still, staring for a moment, then the figure slowly backed away to disappear in the thick mists.

THEY WERE on only two hummocks tonight, having searched to find one large enough for all of them and settling for two close together. The edges of both were lined with watchers, peering out into the darkness for any sign of more of the …

Alexis sighed.

"Bloody, damned lizard-men," Alexis muttered. "I'd not have credited it, save I saw with my own eyes."

"No chance you're mistaken, sir?" Isom asked. He'd been trained as a legal clerk before being impressed into the Navy against his will and he had a sharp, skeptical mind. "Some trick of the mist?"

"I don't see how," Alexis allowed, though she longed to be able to dismiss the sight as a mistake. "Clearly arms and legs, and holding a spear — standing upright, not hunched like some ape. So much like a man, save covered in scales, and intelligent enough to make and use tools."

Aggressive tools — tools of war.

Yes, a spear could be a tool for hunting, and probably was, but she'd heard of no ancient tribe that hadn't turned those tools against their own kind — much less a group of strange invaders traipsing through their swamp.

"Do you suppose the people of Erzurum know about them?"

"I don't see how they couldn't," Alexis said. "The planet's been settled for centuries, for all it's still sparsely populated. There's sure to have been some contact."

That didn't bode well for Alexis and her group, now that she thought of it. Both that human history showed hunting tools turned to war more often than not, and the history of human colonists inter-acting with natives of their own kind — she couldn't imagine scaled aliens, a word hard to even think, would have fared better here than some primitive tribesman back on Earth.

"Kept it quiet all that time?" Isom wondered.

"They must have, or we'd be standing in the lobby of a research center right now."

"Hard to credit, sir."

Dockett and Nabb approached and sat with them.

"How are the men?" Alexis asked.

"Sore worried, sir," Dockett said. "Half're convinced Creasy's right and we've defiled some aliens' holy ground or Boots killed their bloody god last night."

"It was I who —" *It doesn't matter.* "Never mind. You made it clear they're not to fire on shadows, or even a clear sight, without we're attacked first?"

Dockett nodded. "And spread your boat crew out amongst the pickets, too. They're the steadiest and'll keep an eye on the others."

"That's good thinking."

Dockett jerked his head at Nabb. "Young Nabb's suggestion, sir."

Nabb ducked his head at the praise, then looked up. "What *will* we do if we see them again, sir?"

Alexis shrugged. "Try to communicate, I suppose. Make them understand we're only passing through and mean them no harm."

"Doubt they speak anything we'd understand," Dockett said.

"No," Alexis agreed, "but if there's been contact with Erzurum's natives — well, I suppose the lizard-folk are the natives, aren't they? If there's been contact with the human settlers, then they may understand some of the Barbary patois and my tablet's translation software may be able to sort things out for us."

DAWN CAME with no sightings of lizard-men and, more to Alexis' pleasure, no snakipedes crawling up on them in their sleep.

They ate another cold meal of ration bars and water, which the men looked on with more and more displeasure, their supply of spirits being limited to one issue a day, and that so diluted now that it was virtually indistinguishable from the water.

Lizard-men are not the worst of my worries, I think.

Alexis pondered her map as they readied to move on. By her calculations, they were actually trending farther away from the nearest settlement now, after rounding the end of a ravine in one direction and encountering another that edged them back. It might be best to reverse course and try to get around the ravine the other way, even if that took them more afield from the settlement.

It would also, though, take them back toward where they'd seen the lizard-man so clearly, and the crew might balk at that.

So, one more day on this route — if the ravine before them continued to push them away from the settlement, she'd reverse course and try getting around its other end.

She bent to ready her pack for the march to come, then froze at the sudden stillness of all those around her.

"*Hsst!* Passin' the word for the Captain," came a whispered notice.

Alexis stood and slowly made her way toward the call — across the short stretch of water and mud to the other hummock's far side.

All the men were still, but staring in a single direction, and at their edge she could see why.

Their visitor of the day before was back, or one very much like him.

Still at the edges of their vision in the mist, no clearer than the day before, but with visible scales, spear held upright, and hood fully extended.

Is that some sort of threat gesture, like a cobra, or does it mean something entirely different here?

For all she knew, an extended hood could mean a sign of friendship to these ... people. There was no way of telling, and though they might be scaled like terrestrial snakes and lizards, that didn't mean there were any other similarities. She must remember that.

Alexis stepped forward, away from the line of men. As she arrived at the hummock's edge, a second figure appeared, then another, and another.

"Belay that! Stand easy!" she shouted as the crew behind her made to raise their weapons. "Mister Dockett! I'll see the first man who fires sent to the gratings, private ship or no, do you hear me?"

"Aye, sir!"

Alexis moved a further step ahead of her crew, facing the aliens, and nearly at the water's edge. She spread her arms wide, palms open.

"We mean no harm," she said loudly and distinctly. "I have a device —" She motioned toward her pocket where her tablet was, though the material there was now so thin and frayed that she feared losing it to the swamp soon. "— it's not a weapon. No danger. It will help us talk, I think."

She didn't expect the aliens to understand her words, but hoped her tone conveyed that she and *Mongoose's* crew were no threat.

Not the most auspicious ship's name for this encounter ...

One of the lizard-men spoke, or at least made a harsh, guttural sound that she couldn't quite hear through the sound-deadening mist. It was possible her tablet's speaker wouldn't carry that far either and she might have to walk alone through the muck to get close enough to communicate.

She edged her hand toward her pocket and the aliens tensed, as though knowing humans kept weapons in such places.

One of them called out again.

"I don't understand," Alexis called back. "My device will help us!"

Suddenly more figures appeared out of the mist, on all the hummocks surrounding them. Alexis tensed along with her crew. Her thirty were suddenly facing three times that number and were surrounded.

"Sir —"

"Stand easy, Mister Dockett, but be ready. We don't know their intentions and I want no misunderstandings."

"Aye, sir."

She heard the whispered orders circulate and could sense the men's desire to raise their weapons and take aim.

"We mean no harm!" Alexis shouted, hoping to keep her tone calm and still be heard.

One of the aliens handed its spear off to another and stepped toward them, nearly into the water on its side. It raised hands to its mouth, hidden by the hood, which Alexis could see now was deeper than it was flat, not much like a cobra's at all, but more like a monk's cowl. There was something odd about the hands, as well — they didn't glint in the dim light like the scales covering the rest of the thing. No, the hands were pale, and the scales covering the arms hung loose, almost like —

The creature called out.

"*Englisch? Neuer Londoner? Warst du sklave? Warum bist du hier?*"

Alexis dropped her hands and shook her head.

"Stand the men down, Mister Dockett."

"Why, sir?"

"Because, while I've granted the possibility of alien lizard-men, Mister Dockett, alien lizard-men who speak German like a native of Hanover are right out."

NINE

O', wince me hearties, cry me mates,
Gnash your teeth and bloody gums,
For sure as shite you'd have to know
That admiral sailed on.

LIEUTENANT IAN DECKARD, ROYAL NAVY, WAS AN ODD MAN, Alexis thought.

Odd looking, odd of speech, oddly dressed, and odd to find in the company of the mostly Hanoverese group gathered about in the "lizard-men's" cave.

Like all the group, he wore the scaled skins of several snakipedes, or perhaps some other scaled creatures. Baggy scaled trousers above what amounted to scaled slippers, a similarly baggy and scaled shirt, and a hood with a short cloak that hid his features amongst the spread scales when it wasn't thrown back, as it was now, to expose his odd face.

Large ears standing nearly straight out from his head, one of them ragged around the edges as though it had been gnawed on by some beast, and a long, narrow nose above a pronounced underbite. The man looked more like a rat than any purser or chandler Alexis had ever encountered — and those were breeds known for their rat-like ways.

"That's a remarkable tale," Deckard said, "remarkable, I say, what! Yes?"

"No more than your own, I'm sure," Alexis said, hoping to prompt him into revealing how he, as a lieutenant off of *HMS Rye*, a thirty-two out of Admiral Chipley's fleet, came to be settled into an Erzurum swamp with nearly a hundred Hanoverese and a few other New Londoners, and no apparent animosity between them at all, despite no one knowing until Alexis arrived that the war wasn't still on.

She, Dockett, Nabb, and Isom were settled around a fire with Deckard and some others — those being Hanoverese officers, and Alexis lost their names nearly as soon as she was told. The shock of having accepted alien lizard-men only to find they were the very men, or at least close to the very men, she was seeking still had her befuddled.

"Oh, that, easy," Deckard said with a shrug. "A battle with ships damaged and driven onto the shoals, what? Yes! Breaking up, thought we were done for? Indeed! Set about the boats — I wasn't on *Rye*. No? I was acting as liaison to *Bouledogue*, a Berry frigate. Went to pieces with them? Absolutely. Bloody pirate gunboats come along and what? Pick us all up and make for Erzurum. Bugger it!"

"So I assumed," Alexis said, "in general, at least. But how did you all come to escape from the pirates and make your way here?"

Deckard fingered his ear, then a large, ragged scar on his neck, and translated for the surrounding Hanoverese.

Alexis edged closer to the fire, welcoming its warmth after so much time in the chill water and rain outside. No matter the efficiency of their blankets, there was something to be said about warmed air — and dry clothes, as hers were starting to become. The drying and that they were finally clean — having sluiced the mud off in a pouring waterfall outside the cave entrance, as the residents did

— showed her just what a state her vacsuit liner, and the clothing of the others, was in.

"You'll be in skins soon, too? Yes, you will," Deckard had noted right after they were introduced. "The water and mud mixed here, do you see? You do now. Something eats away at materials." He patted his scale covered leg. "Skins are the only thing for it. Yes?"

Alexis was not so very enamored of that idea, but neither would she run around Erzurum's swamp in her all-together once the last bit of liner split or frayed. Especially as Deckard told them the same combination ate away at uncovered human skin, which also explained the chafing and raw patches she and all her men had.

"And how is it that you stopped fighting each other?" she asked after he'd finished translating her last words.

Deckard rubbed his ear harder, bringing Alexis' attention to it. It was mangled, she'd thought at first it must have been in the battle, but then each of the men here had their own ears in a similar state. All around the edge the cartilage was ripped — not cut cleanly, but torn toward the edge and left in ragged strips.

Deckard translated her words and the Hanoverese beside him snorted.

"*Es gibt keinen Krieg auf der Erzurum.*"

"'There is no war on Erzurum,'" Deckard translated. "We have other enemies here, don't we? Oh, yes we do."

———

ALEXIS LISTENED as Deckard told his group's tale — which she thought took twice as long as it ought, what with half his words being to question or confirm what he'd already said once.

He started with the fleets' running battle from Giron.

A perilous, grinding, months-long chase, with Admiral Chipley never giving up on the chance to catch the Hanoverese fleet and utterly destroy it — possibly in the hopes of redeeming himself for the debacle of Giron.

The *darkspace* winds Deckard described were capricious and almost malicious, never quite allowing the two fleets to fully engage, always allowing the Hanoverese Admiral some point of sail with which to escape, yet never, quite, allowing Chipley to honestly say he could not catch them and disengage for a return to New London.

Alexis was nearly prepared to believe in Creasy's spirits of the Dark by the time the tale was half done.

The chase reached the Barbary, where the sparsity of systems opened up the winds and let the fleets travel farther and faster, yet never one enough more so than the other to end it — merely to engage and pick at one another, bleeding ships and men, leaving both to be abandoned behind and broken up by the winds.

Then came Erzurum and its shoals.

Chipley managed to get a screening wall of frigates out to windward of the Hanoverese and Erzurum, forcing the enemy into edging ever closer to the system. They could have engaged the screen, and Chipley would have lost those frigates to the larger liners of the Hanoverese, but the action would have slowed them and allowed Chipley's own liners to catch up and engage.

It was a sound tactical decision, Alexis thought, no matter the potential sacrifice of those frigates, but she couldn't help curse Chipley for doing it — had he but stayed at Giron, kept his fleet with the arriving force of Admiral Cammack, then so many men would be alive and home with their families even now, what with the cease-fire only months away from when the action at Erzurum must have occurred.

The Hanoverese admiral did not take the bait. Instead he fell to leeward, ever closer to Erzurum's dark matter shoals, and skirted the system up and over its halo, escaping with most of his fleet again and leaving Chipley to follow along.

Most of his fleet.

Chipley saw the way of it and ordered his screen of frigates to close, chipping away at the trailing Hanoverese. They weren't enough to destroy any of the big liners, but they were enough to damage the sails and rigging of a few, cutting their ability to maneuver and leaving them to drift or be driven to leeward onto Erzurum's shoals.

Not all of Chipley's ships came out of the engagement unscathed, either.

Deckard's *Bouledogue* and dozens of others were damaged by return fire and left unable to maneuver as well.

Chipley, driven himself by whatever unknown obsession had set him off after the Hanoverese in the first place, left his damaged ships behind, as the Hanoverese admiral was forced to by Chipley's pursuit, to repair and follow — or to be driven helplessly onto Erzurum's shoals and to be picked up by the system's pirate-crewed gunboats.

"How many ships in all? Too many, I think," Deckard said. "Yes, too many? Between both fleets. Frigates, sloops, more. All beat to pieces. Bloody pieces, though I think the bastards here salvaged a bit off them. Maybe. Perhaps. You faced two frigates with the pirates? You said. At least that, then. More doomed, more destroyed. Dozens? A hundred? Thousands of men, what? Oh, yes, thousands and more here on Erzurum, at least."

Alexis nodded, appalled at the destruction and loss of life. A hundred ships or more lost, and only the two pirate frigates salvaged? If thousands of men had been taken up by the pirates, how many more met their fates in *darkspace* amongst those shoals?

Despite her joy at having found these men and the thought that she might now get them home to New London and Hanover with the help of the other privateers, the scope of the destruction and loss made her wonder at the odds for her other, more personal, search.

"Do you know which ships?" Alexis asked. "There are ... some, I'd like to know the fate of more than others. The Berry March flagship, it was still with Chipley's fleet?"

Delaine Theibaud, the man who'd drawn her to privateering in the Barbary for the chance to learn his fate, had moved to that ship to assist Commodore Balestra during the operations at Giron. She couldn't be sure he hadn't been moved to another ship, but knowing Balestra was still in the fight would give her some hope.

"*La Mûre?*" Deckard shrugged. "Yes, still with Chipley. Cranky? Oh, yes, that Balestra wasn't happy with the whole lot and made no bones, did she? No. Not at all. Would've left Chipley to his bloody insanity — shouldn't say that, should I? Never mind. Balestra would have left him before the Barbary if her honor'd allow it, I think. Would she really? Oh, yes."

Alexis' shoulders relaxed. That was something, at least. The ship Delaine was on had passed Erzurum safely, so far as Deckard knew.

"Captain Theibaud had a thing or two to say about Chipley, too. Didn't he? Oh, yes, he did. Not the sort of thing I was meant to liaise on, you know? Not at all, but after dinner and wine? Oh, yes, a whinge or two can be shared."

Alexis chilled from more than Erzurum's rain and the fire's warmth was no help for it.

"Who did you say?" she asked.

"Who? What? Captain Theibaud of *Bouledogue?*" Deckard said. "That's what I said? It was, yes."

"Thcibaud? *Delaine* Theibaud?" It probably was not — she must not get her hopes up. There must be many Theibaud's in the Berry March fleet, and Delaine was lieutenant not a frigate captain. "Captain not lieutenant?"

"Delaine, yes? I think." Deckard frowned, then nodded. "Called him Captain Theibaud, so only the time or two to know his given name, but Delaine?" He shrugged. "Lieutenant on *La Mûre* — why he knew Balestra's mind to whinge on it. Yes, knew her well. She appointed him captain into *Bouledogue* when Captain Liou was injured — when was that? Six months out of Giron? Maybe. Maybe not. Could be. Eight? Perhaps, I don't —"

Alexis pulled her tablet from her pocket, ripping the last of the pocket's seam in the process and not caring. She brought up an image of Delaine and thrust the tablet at Deckard.

"Is this him?"

"Well hold it still, will you?" Deckard said, peering close. "How'm I suppose to tell with you shaking it about like that? Can't, I say. No. Yes."

"Damn your eyes, man, is it him or not?"

Deckard blinked at her while the Hanoverese captain beside him half raised a hand and scowled at her. "No need to shout, is there? No. Yes, it's him."

"I'm sorry I shouted, Lieutenant Deckard, but ... you're certain?"

"Dine with a man for months I know his face — oh, yes — even if your hand's waving like a landsman first time out on the yards. Settle down, will you? No? What's the matter there?"

Alexis couldn't stop the shaking. Couldn't even lower her tablet, she could only stare at it and Delaine's image, wondering, now she was so close, what the answer would be.

Captain of *Bouledogue*, driven onto Erzurum's shoals and left behind by the rest.

"What happened to him?"

TEN

He sailed on and left us lads,
Packed a hundred to a boat,
Like bloodied, ship-less, nomads
He valued not a groat.

Deckard shrugged.

"Same as all of us, wasn't it? Indeed." His hand went to his ragged ear. "Taken up by Erzurum's pirates and sold off as bloody slaves."

"But he's alive?" Alexis asked. "He made it through the battle? What do you mean by slaves? Sold off how? To who? Where is he? Where did you last see him?"

Deckard was silent for a moment, seeming to sink back into his baggy, scaled garb. He studied her.

"So many questions, what? What was your name again? What was it?"

"It's Carew," Alexis said, biting off the demand he answer her bloody questions without more of his own.

"You were in the Navy? Yes. Were you?"

"I am still, though a half-pay lieutenant. Look, will you please —"

Deckard squinted at her in the firelight.

"And you know Theibaud, do you? Must. I suppose. If you're asking about him, right, and have his picture? Only explanation, that."

"I do, so if you'll please —"

"Bloody Theibaud and his bloody dinners and all the bloody whinging, what? Yes. So much of it. If it wasn't whinging about Admiral Chipley it was bloody going on and on about some bloody Carew."

Alexis flushed. "Well, yes, I suppose that would —"

"Straight through the cheese, he goes on — 'great beauty' this and 'smart as a whip' that. Over and bloody over he does, right? Oh, right, yes. 'Be an admiral one day,' he says, 'and there'll be no bloody haring after fleets like stupid Chipley.' Oh, right. But he said it French, so not 'bloody,' but something worse, I think? Don't remember. Make it up yourself. Yes, do. 'Stupid' isn't right either. No? French have better insults. Take your pick."

Alexis' skin went far hotter than the fire could account for. It was all well and good for Delaine to think such things, but telling others, especially to annoyance, just wasn't done. On the other hand ... he was French, so she supposed that should excuse quite a lot of such behavior.

"I'm sorry, Lieutenant Deckard, if you felt Captain Theibaud went on too much. But will you please tell me where —"

Deckard cleared his throat and leaned nearly over the fire to squint at her.

"So you're a Carew looking for Theibaud?" He frowned and shook his head. "For your sister, right? Must."

"Why you soddin', snake-skinned, little —"

"Belay that, Mister Dockett," Alexis said. "And you, too, Nabb."

Both men had half risen at Deckard's words and Alexis herself had to push a bit of anger aside.

She had no delusions about her ability to live up to whatever description of her Delaine might have subjected Deckard to. And

Delaine *was* French, as she'd just noted. He seemed to have a cultural imperative to exaggerate such things.

Dockett and Nabb eased back into their seats, but continued to glare at the man across the fire.

"I have no sisters, Lieutenant Deckard."

She thought there might be a glint of frost on the fire's top as her words crossed it.

Deckard grunted. "Huh. Cousin?"

Alexis threw her hand out to catch Nabb by the ear as he made to rise and held him in place.

"Sweet Dark, man, I'm the one he talked about — *now where is he?*"

"What? Oh! All right. I suppose." He shrugged as if perplexed by something. "Sold off like the rest of us. Yes? Right. Haven't seen him since."

Alexis' heart fell. She was so close — she'd even entertained, for a moment, that Delaine would be right here in this cave with the rest of them and suddenly appear out of the shadows to take her up in his arms. Until the thought occurred to her, she'd not realized how much she longed for it — or any sort of human touch. She'd not had a hug since saying goodbye to her grandfather and leaving Dalthus with *Mongoose* — nor, before her time at home, since last seeing Delaine in orbit around Giron before the fleet action with Hanover. That was ... a very long time to do without such things. And others, but mostly the simple bit of human contact.

The crew could take their ease at a house each time they were given liberty, and no doubt the casino on Enclave had such places and had seen a great deal of their coin, but that wasn't really to Alexis' taste — and she felt she owed it to Delaine not to, in any case. And even the crew could clap one another on the back after a hard time on the sails or if saddening news came from a fellow's home. One's mates could always be counted on for an arm about the shoulders at such times.

For her as captain, though, there was no such release. At least aboard a Naval ship, touching the captain without permission would get one sent to the gratings, or worse, and it was a liberty that would degrade discipline if she even thought to allow it. Not even her officers would think to offer such a thing, even with the looser strictures of a private ship, as *Mongoose* was.

A dot of cold wetness nudged her hand from where it sat in her lap, lifted it and edged under. Alexis ran her hand over the warm fur that followed the nose as she thought.

The Barbary slave trade was well known but, if not entirely tolerated, then largely ignored.

Hanover was the ostensible ruler of the space and seemed not to care what the Barbary worlds did, while the other space-faring powers lacked any real power in the area. To send a Naval force would violate Hanover's borders — which was, really, why Alexis had come in command of a private ship and not as a commissioned Naval officer. No matter the involvement of the Foreign Office and its representative in Malcome Eades, the entire expedition could be effectively denied by the Crown.

And so the trade went on, with natives of the Barbary and captured spacers alike being bought and sold amongst the worlds by pirates and raiders.

It was a sad, sorry business and made little sense, as the human cargoes had less worth than machines from the more advanced and populated worlds. Such was the poverty of the region that the raiders sought to eke out the last bit of coin from their efforts, no matter how small.

She dug her fingers into the soft fur in her lap and scratched at the skin, eliciting a deep purr that seemed to shake loose some of her tension.

This news was not so bad as it first sounded, really. The odds of Delaine even having been on Erzurum were high — she should ask Dockett what the book on such a thing would be, so she could understand how lucky she was to have any word of him at all. He could have been lost aboard one of the destroyed ships or sailed on, leaving her no idea where to search next. As it was, there must be some record on Erzurum as to where he'd been sold — and he might still be on-planet, she realized.

That realization, and the vibrating purr, broke loose the last of the ice that had settled around her middle at Deckard's words. There was still a chance and she was closer.

"Why do you have a rat?" Deckard asked, peering at her lap. "I'm wondering? Yes. Strange."

"He's not a rat, he's —" Alexis stopped scratching, scooped up the Creature and dumped it back onto Isom's cot next to the fire. "Isom, will you keep control of the vile thing or not? I'll not tarry to search for it if it runs off."

ELEVEN

O', shriek me hearties, roar me mates,
Let your outrage fill the Dark.
Like the tender mercies of the Winds
Come the Brethren for their part.

THE CONVERSATION LULLED FOR A TIME AFTER ALEXIS SENT the Creature back to curl up under Isom's blanket and she took the opportunity to examine both the cave and their hosts more closely.

All of the men were clad in the same scaled skins as Deckard and armed with spears or crude bows. Her own crew had spread out amongst the fires in the cave, making what conversation they could with the primarily Hanoverese inhabitants. She was a bit surprised that things were going so well, but as Deckard had said, perhaps there was no war on Erzurum — or the word she brought of a cease-fire was just as welcome to the Hanoverese as it would be to her own crew in a similar circumstance.

The cave itself was more of a ledge set against the wall of a vast cavern, as though the inside of the plateau had been blown by a giant bubble. There was space for all, but not so much as its size might at first suggest.

Her lads stood out from their hosts, what with their proper clothes — tattered and ragged as they may be — and their pistols and few rifles in place of spears.

All of them seemed well — happy to be out of the rain and mud for a time, and to have new faces to talk to, even with the abundant language barriers. The Hanoverese seemed happy for that too, and Alexis could credit it. After months in these swamps and a year or more on Erzurum they were hungry for news from offworld, even if it was the New Londoners' side of the battles they were hearing.

Davies, one of the women Alexis had accepted aboard *Mongoose* as crew, seemed especially popular, which Alexis supposed shouldn't surprise her. She was the only one of her messmates who'd been aboard Alexis' boat, and while there were some women amongst the Hanoverese crews, as that nation didn't have the same restriction New London had, it appeared there were none with this group, and a new face was always more interesting in any case.

Yes, all was going well and the Hanoverese were friendly, but —

She glanced from the fire to the Hanoverese officers beside Deckard. There might be no war on Erzurum, but that did not mean that everyone was to be trusted.

Alexis took the distraction of someone bringing bowls of food from a communal cookpot to whisper to Dockett, "Pass the word — handsomely, mind you, so as not to arouse any comment — but I'd admire it did the lads keep their guns close and a wary eye."

"You expect trouble?"

"I do not. We're all marooned here, at least for the moment, and there's a certain code about such things, I understand."

Dockett nodded. "Once the ship's down, it's your own skin and your mates — no bloody Queen and Country then."

That's what Alexis had heard, though it didn't happen often that opposing forces were set upon the same place to await rescue — but when it did, the bare goal of survival meant more than what they'd been fighting for in the first place.

"I expect no trouble," she whispered, "but our weapons may be tempting to them. And see Davies has a man at her back, will you? The Dark knows I've seen enough of some lads walking double to know she can handle herself, but this is a different place than aboard *Mongoose*, and we're the strangers."

"Aye, sir."

Dockett whispered to Nabb, then they both rose and began making their way to the others.

"Your men go where?"

Alexis turned back, surprised that it was the Hanoverese who'd spoken and not Deckard. She hadn't been aware that he understood English, much less spoke it. Deckard had half turned from the fire and was busily scooping a thick stew from a wooden bowl with a flat of wood.

"To check on the others," Alexis said, "after such a walk I wish to know they're feeling all right. I'm sorry, but I've lost your name."

Deckard had made introductions for the three Hanoverese sharing the fire, but she hadn't been able to set them in her mind.

"*Kapitän* Kannstadt," he said, then nodded to the two others. "*Leutnant* Fischer. *Leutnant* Mayer."

Alexis nodded to each in turn. "Are you all from the same ship?"

Kannstadt shook his head. "No. From many. The slave markets scattered us widely." He frowned. "The pirates divide us."

More bowls of food arrived, served by a heavy Hanoverese whose scaled clothing fit so tightly Alexis feared a scale might pop off and strike her between the eyes at any moment.

Captain Kannstadt took two bowls and handed them to Alexis around the fire. She took them and passed one back to Isom. Kannstadt and the others took the remaining bowls.

"It is filling and will not kill you," Kannstadt said. "This is the best that can be said."

The heavyset man who'd brought the food frowned, looking from

Kannstadt to Alexis, then rattled off a string of German that Alexis couldn't hope to follow. Kannstadt answered and the man, Alexis assumed the cook, huffed and stalked off.

"Hans, our cook, tries," Kannstadt said, "but there is only so much to be done."

"You speak English very well," Alexis said. "I assumed when Lieutenant Deckard translated that it was because you didn't understand."

Kannstadt glanced at Deckard, who'd finished his own stew and was now stretched out beside the fire, eyes closed and moving his lips in his sleep. Kannstadt smiled at him almost fondly.

"Ian is not himself," Kannstadt said. "When we escaped the ... place we were held and made to work — it was so mean a place I cannot properly call it a farm or plantation — it was he who held the line with me as the others fled." His smile widened. "Not so great a battle as what brought us here — a scared family with but two rifles and some cudgels — but Ian stood." His face darkened. "And it was his hand over the controls that kept us alive, no matter how the cudgels struck his head."

"Controls?"

Kannstadt nodded.

"The pirates and slavers of Erzurum have odd traditions." He fingered his ragged ear. "Rings and studs go here — they are ..." He waved a hand, frowning. "A marker? For the cattle?"

"A brand?"

Kannstadt nodded again. "I think, yes. But more than —" He spat into the fire. "— who owns. Skills, price, other things. A tracking beacon, of course, so they must be removed."

The tattered ears of Kannstadt, Deckard, and the others suddenly made a sickening sense to her.

"And here —" Kannstadt touched his neck where there was another scar, one Alexis hadn't noted before, being too distracted by his mangled ear. "In the neck. Disobey too much and —" He chuckled and flung his fingers open. "*Poof!* A threat to keep us in behavior, *hein?*"

"I see," Alexis said, horrified.

Kannstadt's eyes turned to Deckard and softened. "So, *der Herr* comes as we fight to escape and *poof, poof, poof!*" He opened and closed his fingers near his head explosively. "A man falls, and another, and another — then, we are on him and his family, but, *poof,* another. It is expensive for him, *hein?* To destroy his property, but else he loses all, and we cannot reach him to stop. My men — they are all my men now, though from different ships, are losing heart.

"Then Ian, he leaps through them to *der Herr* —" Another gob of spit sizzled in the fire. "He cannot walk well now —" Kannstadt tapped his left side. "— a bullet to the hip as we fled and is still there, but he leapt then. He covers the box with his hands and holds it." He clutched both hands to his stomach and hunched over. "Thus. You see, *hein?*"

Alexis nodded.

Kannstadt shifted closer to Deckard and laid a hand on the now sleeping man's shoulder.

"All those blows," he murmured, "but never does Ian uncover the box."

TWELVE

So, into that, like sharks of yore,
The pirates came a' calling.
Shot boats to nothing with the men
'Til colors everywhere were falling.

Their group was silent for a time after Kannstadt told Deckard's story, and Alexis felt a bit of guilt at how she'd been thinking of the New London lieutenant. His annoying speech pattern might be related to the blows he took to ensure freedom for the others, and it seemed cold to hold that against him.

She ate silently, finding the stew at least in part what Kannstadt had claimed, filling and, she hoped, unlikely to kill her as well.

Dockett and Nabb returned from their visits to the others of their crew and brought bowls of their own, already half-eaten.

"Not the best vittles," Dockett muttered as he sat. "Ration bars almost better."

Alexis had to agree. Offended though the fat Hanoverese cook might have been at Kannstadt's words, the stew had a strong gamey taste, and not a pleasant one, even for one raised hunting wild game on Dalthus as she had been.

"Tastes like chicken," Nabb said. "Chewy, though."

Kannstadt grunted.

"I'm sorry, Captain Kannstadt," Alexis said, with a glare at Nabb and Dockett. "That's short thanks for your hospitality and we do appreciate it."

"Do not concern yourself," Kannstadt said. "Hans takes offense, but there is little he can do with *die schlange*."

Nabb and Dockett both spit mouthfuls back into their bowls.

"With what, then?" Dockett said, wiping at his mouth.

Nabb was wiping at his tongue, and never mind the mud that still permeated his sleeve.

Kannstadt frowned. "*Die schlange*, the ... snake, *hein*? There is little use we make of it, save for filling the belly, you understand? Little ... nutrient, *hein*? But it fills."

"Oh," Dockett said, then muttered and poked at the contents of his bowl, "Not sure that's better."

"Better'n what I heard," Nabb said, though he set his bowl down and scowled.

"Boots likes it," Isom said, drawing Alexis' attention to his cot where the Creature happily gnawed a piece of snakipede flesh.

"Of course it does." Alexis set her own bowl aside, the image of one of those things crouched atop her as she slept still a bit too fresh in her mind to stomach it.

"SO YOUR SHIP IS GONE?" Kannstadt asked.

Alexis nodded. She'd told the tale of their arrival in-system and the battle around the planet, including the loss of *Mongoose* and their own boat's crash.

"We were lucky to lose no one in the crash," she said, "and only one man in the swamps." The loss of Tubbs still bothered her, and the trap he'd fallen through. She met Kannstadt's eyes. "He fell through a sort of latticed trap at the edge of one of the ravines."

Kannstadt winced. "I am sorry. We have build those to hunt *die schlange*. They sun themselves when there are no rains. We tempt them to the wider space and they cannot flee to the water."

Alexis nodded. She'd thought the platform must be built by Kannstadt's men, and it was good that he'd admit it even knowing she'd lost a man. That indicated an element of honesty in the Hanoverese and eased her mind — though nothing eased that they'd lost Tubbs and their radio to a simple hunting trap.

Somewhere in the cavern, someone began playing an instrument, perhaps a harmonica, though it was hard for Alexis to tell for sure, as the instrument was either damaged or the player not quite skilled. Every so often a note would sound either too long or so off that even Alexis' ear could tell.

"*Der Musiker,*" Kannstadt muttered into his bowl.

"It's not ... bad," Alexis hazarded — and it wasn't ... quite. The tune was simply off enough that it drew one in and then gave off an eerie screech worthy of one of Creasy's Dark-haunting spirits.

"It is not good," Kannstadt said. "The boy is not without skill, but the instrument was damaged — and becomes more so with time in the swamps — yet he refuses not to play something."

Around them, Kannstadt's men, and Alexis' with them, swayed along with the tune, wincing at the off notes, but not seeming too troubled by them.

Kannstadt sighed. "And the men do like it. It is something, after all, which is better than nothing, and likely why the boy insists on playing even when he knows the instrument is beyond repair."

The Hanoverese captain resumed eating and Alexis resumed her thoughts, now buoyed along by the haunting, halting tune.

She counted her lads as she studied the cavern, spread out as they were amongst Kannstadt's. It might seem odd that they'd so readily accept their former enemies, but there were other New Londoners amongst Kannstadt's group — few, but noticeable — and they were all, after all, castaways of a sort.

There was a sort of code about such things — once a ship was disabled or struck, even enemies did not abandon each other to the Dark. And for spacers, being in-atmosphere, without a hull around them, was much the same as the void in either *darkspace* or normal-space. There were instances of enemies, in the midst of battle, caught up in a storm even while they worked the guns, then abandoning those guns to work the boats and lines and save their foes from a ship driven into dark matter shoals.

Spacers, set adrift.

Some bonds were greater than the conflicts of nations.

For Alexis, it was simply good to see her lads warmed by even the small fires here in the cave, fed even the watery, acidic soup of *schlange*, and have even a single night to sleep dry amongst, if not exactly friends, then not exactly enemies at the moment either.

Tomorrow would bring all their worries back, but for the moment they could set those aside.

Even as she did so, smiling a bit at the antics of a group of spacers attempting a dance to the butchered tune, Alexis realized that she was happy.

It might seem odd, crashed on dreary Erzurum, cut off from her fellows and the rest of her crew, and hounded by pirates, but she was happy nonetheless — or, if happy wasn't quite the right word, she no longer felt the weight of her past as she had so much and for so long.

Now she had a clear goal and a clear duty — to get her lads out of this swamp and home. To keep them safe and bring back word of the captive spacers on Erzurum so that they might be rescued as well.

The almost mercenary goals of privateering hadn't sat well with her, and neither had the tax and import duty enforcement of her time on *Nightingale*, come to that. Both were necessary, she supposed, but neither presented a worthy foe. The private ships, by their nature, went for softer targets than the pirates themselves — and retaking prizes seemed more of simply trading game tokens back and forth than really accomplishing anything, no matter the profit in it.

At least now she had a duty to her lads, and Kannstadt's, and all those others on Erzurum, to get them home.

Against a planet full of pirates, slavers, and who-knows-what sort of fleet above us, she thought. *I wonder what it says about me that the prospect of that fight leaves me with such peace?*

It was as though there were some sort of well inside her, full to overflowing like a runaway fusion plant, and now she had somewhere to direct that power so she no longer felt like she might burst at any moment.

Somewhere other than throwing hazards at the gaming table or brawling on the landing fields like some new-pressed hand, she thought, flushing at how she'd spent her time back on the planet Enclave so very recently. *Do I have some need to put myself at risk?*

Alexis pondered that possibility for a time, worrying at the train of thought until it unraveled for her. She'd noted before that she never felt so alive as when pitting her ship and crew against some foe. Just the thought of having a ship around her again, with shot flashing from the sides and her breath rasping in a vacsuit helmet, made her heart race and her lips curve in a grin.

But only a worthy foe, not some smuggler who'd strike his colors at the first shot across the bow or some ill-manned pirate prize with a handful of guns and too few crew to work them.

She glanced across the fire at Kannstadt.

What ship had he commanded? How many guns? How would *Mongoose* or *Belial* have done against him?

A sudden, flat *blat* of a mangled note in the tune drew Alexis from her thoughts.

She looked up to find that the player had come near their fire.

He was a young man, perhaps her own age, thin and with long hair bound back in a spacer's queue.

Kannstadt was glaring at him and the player alternated a

sheepish look to the Hanoverese captain with one of stern betrayal to the harmonica in his hands.

"Sorry, sir," the player said in English, a clear New Londoner, "it's only got worse." He sighed. "Might be time to retire her."

Kannstadt made a visible effort to steel his features, but Alexis noted the corners of his mouth turned up. "That is sad," he said.

"Might could get some strings from that *schlange* gut," the spacer said. "Could maybe make a sort of gittern —"

The corners of Kannstadt's mouth fell.

"— not a proper guitar, but there's some gourds in the swamp might make a body. Like to have an odd sound, but would be something."

"An odd sound?" Kannstadt asked.

The spacer scratched at his neck. "Well, no telling what the gut'll sound like, is there?"

"One of your countrymen, *Kapitän* Carew," Kannstadt said with a tone of accusation. His lip curled. "*Der Musiker.*"

"The men seem to like your playing," Alexis hazarded, though the man didn't seem to hear her.

Der Musiker, as Kannstadt named him, was staring at Alexis, first with narrowed eyes and a frown, as though pondering something, then his eyes widened and his jaw dropped.

"Carew?" He stared at her a moment. "From Dalthus?"

Now it was Alexis' turn to ponder the spacer in turn, for he seemed to know her — or of her — and she was certain they'd never met.

"I am," she hazarded. "Have we met?"

The spacer seemed to shake himself and drew his shoulders back. "No, sir — no, not met. But imagine you here." He slid the harmonica into a crude pocket sewn into the skins he wore. "Thomas Aiden, sir, off *Merlin*, but after you left her, so we've not met."

"*Merlin?* She wasn't with Chipley's fleet."

"No, sir," Aiden said. "I went aboard *Merlin* from Eidera just as the war started. Joined up, I did, then sent aboard *Cicala*, with Chipley, when she needed new men, but I was a *Merlin*-man long enough, sir — long enough to learn your name."

"I —" Alexis broke off as she caught Kannstadt looking from Aiden to her with eyebrows raised.

"Why it's like every snotty aboard — begging your pardon, sir," Aiden said, "for the term, you having been a midshipman on her and all — but the lads were forever going on about, 'Mister Carew'd not've done that' and 'Mister Carew'd've done this' and 'Mister Carew'd have a lighter hand' and 'Mister Carew'd not take such guff' and —"

"Mister Carew has the picture, Aiden," Alexis said, holding up one hand to stop the onslaught. "Vividly, I think."

"Oh. Alright then." The spacer shrugged. "Well, sir, and then word come of *Hermione*, and the lads were all more puffed up to have known you."

"*Hermione?*" Kannstadt asked. "The mutiny?"

"You know of it?" Alexis asked.

"Yes, it was made much of in Hanover that a New London crew would come to us." He frowned. "What have you to do with that?"

"I was one of her officers," Alexis said. "Only a midshipman."

"It was reported that the officers of *Hermione* were taken captive."

Alexis nodded. "We were, but we were able to take a merchant ship and escape."

Kannstadt's eyes narrowed. "This was not reported." He sighed. "Of course, it would not be."

"She's being modest, Captain Kannstadt, sir," Aiden said. "It was Mister Carew here — well, lieutenant now, is it, and well deserved from what I've heard — that broke those fellows out. *Hermione's* captain and other officers being the useless prats that they were. It was all the *Merlins* spoke of just before I transferred off."

"I think that's enough, Aiden," Alexis said. She wasn't at all sure how Kannstadt might view her for that escape. The war might be over, but they'd still been enemies only recently. His men far outnumbered hers, but Aiden was not quite finished and didn't seem to register her words as an order.

"Then that court martial'd like to have hung a few of the lads she brung out — for show — but Lieutenant Carew here, she stood up in court and says to those captains, she says, 'You harm a one of my lads and I'll cut you down where you stand, you buggers!'"

"I said no such thing!"

Alexis studied the faces around her in the next silence, even a few of the nearby groups were staring, as she'd apparently said that quite a bit louder than she'd intended. Those expectant faces demanded explanation — certainly something other than what Aiden had heard and now repeated — but she couldn't tell them the details, especially Kannstadt and the other Hanoverese. The whole of the bargain she'd made — the court determining her lads were not part of the mutiny in return for her asking Delaine to "lose" *Hermione's* log and not allow the Hanoverese access to proof of Captain Neals' abuses — was predicated on her silence. Admiralty wouldn't look kindly on her telling a cave full of Hanoverese the whole story, no matter the ceasefire.

"I convinced the court of their innocence, nothing more," she said, knowing that Aiden's tale, born in the rumor mill of ships' crews, would likely win out in the end no matter what she said. "The proceedings were sealed — I can't say more."

Aiden nodded. "Of course, sir."

Bloody hell, Alexis thought, *I've trouble enough with Admiralty in what I truly do, without adding spacers' fantasies into the mix.*

Captains heard these tales too, and she was only a lieutenant. What might await her one day serving aboard a ship whose captain thought she'd threatened the board of a court martial?

"I didn't threaten to kill anyone — I wouldn't do that." Behind her she heard a throat clear, but couldn't tell if it was Isom, Nabb, or Dockett, and flushed red. "Well, not a court martial — I've some sense."

Alexis looked from Kannstadt to Aiden to —

Was that a bloody wink?

"That will be all, I think, Aiden," she said in a voice that made certain things clear.

The spacer straightened and nodded. "Aye, sir."

He nodded to Kannstadt too and walked away, pulling the harmonica from his pocket. In a moment, the instrument's dubious tune began sounding through the cavern again.

"*Der Musiker's* approach brings us to a thing we should settle. The New Londoners among my group — I have done as I should for them, given our peril here, but even with the news of the ceasefire you bring, some have always been uncomfortable with me, I think. There are none of their own officers with our group." He patted the sleeping Lieutenant Deckard's shoulder and Alexis noted that his hand had remained there from the time Deckard had first gone to sleep. "Other than *Leutnant* Deckard, and he is too easily wearied by his injuries to see to them, you understand?"

Alexis nodded.

"They may wish, now that you are here, to look to you, *hein?*"

Alexis had been thinking that very thing, and wondering at what sort of man Kannstadt was and whether he'd object to those men who might wish to look to an officer from their own nation rather than one who had so recently been the enemy.

"I think this is best," Kannstadt said, "for those who wish it."

He watched her carefully and Alexis realized he was having those same thoughts about her, wondering if she was the sort who'd insist the New Londoners come under her command, no matter their wishes.

"Some may be more comfortable with you, Captain Kannstadt," she said, "having gone through so much with you."

Kannstadt nodded as though she'd settled something in his mind.

"We face trials here on Erzurum, *Leutnant* Carew, and the men need discipline, but also understanding." He smiled. "I think we are of the same mind on this. Those of New London who wish to join you, and I think it will be most, I will not object to."

"And the Berry March fleet," Alexis said firmly.

Kannstadt's eyes narrowed. "*Verräter*," he muttered.

Alexis wasn't sure of the meaning, but took his tone. The Berry March fleet had betrayed Hanover to join with New London and the French Republic.

"The war is over, Captain Kannstadt," she reminded him. "Those men left Hanover and are part of the New London fleet."

"We are in the Barbary, *leutnant*, and the Barbary is part of Hanover. Here they are traitors." He shrugged. "It is no matter, there are none of that fleet in this group."

Alexis frowned. His tone made her wonder if there had ever been — and what might have become of them.

"So, it is settled," Kannstadt went on in a friendlier tone. "Those of your allies who wish to look to you may do so." The sound of a damaged harmonica cut across the cavern — a note so dreadful that it stilled everyone to silent staring before Aiden resumed playing. "And *der Musiker* — yes, *der Musiker* must look to you now. *Hein?*"

THIRTEEN

O' howl me hearties, bawl me mates,
They made us slaves and chattel.
That full tale's one that I'll not tell,
But it's one to test your mettle.

ALEXIS SLEPT FITFULLY, HER MIND FULL OF PLANS — MAKING and dismissing possibilities in turn. If only their radio had not gone down into a ravine with Tubbs, then their straits would not be nearly so dire.

Definitive word, rather than a smuggler's rumor, that the spacers from the fleets were on Erzurum would surely bring a greater force to bear. If she could only get that word to the other private ship captains, then even Spensley would have to give his all toward freeing them.

"Captain Kannstadt," Alexis asked the next morning, "do you have anything in the way of communications gear? Our own was destroyed and I'd dearly wish to know what's happening with the rest of my crew and the other ships. More, word of your group's presence will certainly bring help."

Kannstadt shook his head. "*Nein.* I am sorry. We have runners from other groups in these swamps, from time to time, but little in the way of electronics. They do not fare well." His lips pursed. "I think there is a group — to the east — that has a comm, which they do not use often." He shrugged. "There is little news of importance to us out here, *hein?*"

Alexis understood that. "Would it be possible to contact them? Through these runners?"

"Yes, but a week or more to get an answer."

"That's too long — we can't wait here for that."

"Where do you intend to go? You have said there is a stalemate and the settlements your friends have taken are far from here."

"I must contact them and let them know of your presence. Unless —" They might already know. "— would there be men from the fleets at the places we hold? Might they already know and be sending word back to New London?"

Kannstadt shook his head. "The pirates kept none of us where they stay. There are slaves there, yes, but only those from merchant ships or other worlds." He shrugged. "This is not unusual in the Barbary and of no note. Those captured from the battle were spread out to the farms and villages, far from where we might be seen by visiting merchants. I think the pirates worried at a rescue, but did not wish to give up the value of so many men."

"I believe there's a settlement to the —" Alexis did her best to estimate the twists and turns of their march through the swamp. "— northwest of here? The closest, if you know it. We'll go there and attempt to steal some sort of transport or comms with which to make contact."

Kannstadt stared into the fire. "When you told your story and I heard of your ships, I too had hope. Then, with your radio lost —" He shrugged. "Do you think there is still hope? Perhaps it is best for you to wait here with us and your friends will send more help for you?"

"I'm not sure what they'll do," Alexis said. "They may think us dead. Captain Spensley is sure to lobby for escape when he's recovered. Malcomson would be set against it, I think, and he can be quite persuasive."

"Deadlocked as you say the forces were. Even a stubborn man must bow to fate," Kannstadt said.

"Malcomson is Scots."

"Oh." Kannstadt shook his head. "Even so, the settlement, Téneto, is no place for you to go. Not with thirty men, not with a hundred men. It is not large, but it is large enough, and they guard against us — escaped slaves — so you will have no more luck than we might. Even our forces combined are not enough."

"We do have more modern weapons," Alexis pointed out. "I noted your men are all armed with spears and bows."

"We have some." Kannstadt cocked his head to the rear of the cave. "The ammunition and power are limited, so we use them only when attacked by Erzurum's settlers or the pirates — and avoid that when we can. Even better armed, I would not attack Téneto."

"They can't protect everything," Alexis insisted. "These farms, like the one you escaped from, they must be more lightly manned and vulnerable."

"Surprise, desperation, and speed are what got us free," Kannstadt said. "Most escapes are not so grand as mine and Ian's. By one and two they sneak off in the night or hide in filth and garbage carted from the farm — one by one, and make their way to the swamps. Those who are not caught or die in the journey are found by groups like this — we try to search for those escaping, but not too close, so as not to reveal ourselves and our homes here to the settlers. For a group to rebel, or for you to attack, the farmers have alarms to alert their neighbors and the towns — and the pirates who will send armed boats."

Alexis considered Kannstadt's words, wondering if it were truly so hopeless or if his time in Erzurum's swamps, and what he'd experienced here before that, had simply made him not wish to try.

"Desperation we have in plenty, I think," she said finally. "Surprise may be had with a proper plan, and speed comes in its execution — do you not agree, *Kapitän* Kannstadt?"

"You are young," Kannstadt said, "and have not yet seen the cost of such actions, *leutnant*." He waved his hand around the cave. "These men are alive, they are free of Erzurum's farms and *der Herr's* lash. Most of their fellows are not so lucky — dead in *finsterweltraum*, the darkness between worlds, dead in the pirates' slave pits, dead on those farms — for not working or to show others the cost of not." He nodded toward Deckard who had woken with them, but had taken up staring into the distance. "You do not know costs, *leutnant*."

"I was at Giron. I know the costs well enough."

Kannstadt snorted. "Not aboard a ship in the battle — some officer in a *schaluppe*? Did you arrive with that fleet of reinforcements and never take a shot to your ship?"

"I was aboard *Belial*, sir." Alexis paused to control the tightness in her chest that always came with such memories. Kannstadt showed no recognition, which he shouldn't — the Hanoverese would not know the name of such a small ship in the opposing fleet. "Our task was to shepherd the transports."

Kannstadt's eyes widened. The two fleets might not have paid much attention to *Belial* and the Hanoverese frigate she fought at the time, but they'd certainly reviewed the battle's records in their running fight from Giron.

The Hanoverese captain took a deep breath and lowered his eyes to the fire.

"*Kapitän* Schäfer was not honorable," he said finally. "Your captain was a brave man. I see he taught you well, but, *fräulein*, the end is not always what you wish." He shook his head. "Better to stay safe and await a stronger force."

"There may not be a stronger force," Alexis said, ignoring for the moment that Kannstadt assumed she'd merely served aboard *Belial* and not commanded her. "If those private ship captains flee, all they know is there's a pirate base here — who will come, and why? Not to rescue you — there's no proof those captains have that anyone from the missing fleets is here. Not for me — even my own officers will have no reason to think I'm alive at this point. For all they know, we died in the boat crash. Why would they return? The private ships will seek easier loot. The Hanoverese government has shown little interest in curbing piracy in the Barbary, so there's little reason to suspect they'll change that policy now. New London will certainly not risk the current peace by sending a Naval force into the Barbary. These are Hanoverese worlds, after all." She spread her hands. "Who is it you expect to come for you, sir?"

Kannstadt made to speak but Alexis cut him off.

"I commanded *Belial* at Giron, *Kapitän* Kannstadt," Alexis said. "There were costs —" She closed her eyes and swallowed hard at the thought of those costs. "— dearer than I'd wish to pay, but I saw the soldiers and civilians on those transports safely home." She pointed to Dockett and Nabb, as they were the closest of her lads and not spread out throughout the cave. "I'll see my lads here safely home from this bit of mud, sir, because they look to me and I can do no other. These men —" She waved at the surrounding cave. "— look to you — whether they're from your ship, or your nation, or some other. These are your lads, *Kapitän* Kannstadt, will you not take them home?"

Kannstadt was still staring at her. Alexis met his eye until he grinned.

"Giron, *Hermione*." He chuckled. "I think the *Hso-hsi* have a curse about your life, *leutnant*."

"So it seems at times," Alexis allowed.

The Hanoverese captain pursed his lips and looked around the cavern. "We feel safe here, but safety is not the life we chose. I will think on your words, *Leutnant* Carew." He paused and looked around the cave again, then frowned. "No, there has been already too much thinking of home. You may be right that it is time to do."

FOURTEEN

It's after, lads, I'll tell you of,
When hope was all but lost,
Come a lass you'd not expect it of,
The only willing to bear our cost.

The farm was not what Alexis expected.

The sun was just barely up, seen only as a brightening of the ever-present cloud cover. She and Kannstadt had crept forward to the edge of the trees, leaving the bulk of their force several hundred meters back and out of sight. They each had one of the survival blankets from *Mongoose's* boat draped over them, leaving only their eyes exposed to take in the scene.

The space, cleared of trees, was perhaps ten hectares of fields with buildings in the center.

Alexis had thought Erzurum's swamps would give way to higher, drier land as they left Kannstadt's cave, but the Hanoverese captain and his men led them to what Alexis could only describe as —

Some sort of swamp-farm?

The trees had been cleared and there were crops, but the fields themselves were still the flooded muck she'd trekked through to get here. Worse, possibly, as the fields were surrounded by low dikes, apparently to both keep the water in and act as paths between them. The crop was bewildering as well.

"Cattails?" she asked, peering through the last stand of trees and some open space between their group and the fields.

Kannstadt shrugged. "There are few crops which grow on Erzurum."

"Crops?" She'd seen cattails before — there were some growing in the ponds of her grandfather's lands back on Dalthus, but the seeds for those had been imported for esthetics, not food.

"Those and the *susomun*," Kannstadt said, nodding toward another field with something growing closer to the water's surface. "A native plant, but it gives some nutrient. And the —" He pointed. "I do not know it in English."

In addition to the cattails and whatever *susomun* was, there was also a growth of water lilies in the fields.

"Few other crops grow on Erzurum," Kannstadt said. "Rice will grow, but it does not mature." He shrugged. "They make do."

Alexis stared at the fields, she'd never heard of a native plant being grown as a staple. For variety or export as a rarity, certainly, but not to sustain the world's people except in the most dire circumstances. Most plants not from Earth offered little or no nutrient value to humans at all — those that offered some often came with undesirable side effects. Never mind the cattails, that Erzurum's people were forced to grow this *susomun* for survival spoke ill of the survey company that had sold their ancestors the world in the first place.

The farm's few buildings — a long, low barn, two smaller sheds, and a small, two story house with a wing Alexis took for a bunkhouse — were built on land either diked and drained or raised a bit above the surroundings. The barn was raised on stilts about a meter above the flooded land below it.

"The slaves sleep in the barn, there," Kannstadt said, "the family in the house, and what few hired hands next to it."

Alexis nodded. "The buildings are quite small. Is the machinery kept in the barn with the slaves?"

She didn't see how that could be, with it on stilts and no visible way for farm machinery to get in and out.

Perhaps there's a ramp.

"No machines," Kannstadt said.

"But —"

"This is why they have us as slaves," Kannstadt said. "Watch."

As the light brightened, a horn sounded from the main house and men filed out of the "barn". They hopped down into the water and mud from the raised building and slogged their way to the nearest dike.

"The other buildings are on dried land, why not the barn?"

"The mud slows a man," Kannstadt said.

"What do you mean?"

"Look atop the house. Do you see that box?"

Alexis did — the farmhouse's roof had a small cupola at the center, with a commanding view of the farm. There was some movement within it.

"The overseer," Kannstadt said. "A rifle from there commands all but the farthest fields. The slave quarters are closer, and if the men are slowed they are more vulnerable, *hein?*"

"Yes, I see." Alexis had no doubt a decent marksman, especially with a good scope on the rifle, could command not only the fields but the tree line around the farm as well. "Are we safe from him here?"

Kannstadt nodded and rustled the blanket he held around himself. "With these, very, until the mist clears more. The guards will watch the workers, and this field needs no work."

On the farm, the slaves — and Alexis' stomach twisted to think of them as that, for Kannstadt had told her this and the other farms had mostly men from the missing fleets — had pulled themselves from the muck surrounding their quarters and moved onto the dikes between fields. It took a moment for Alexis to see, covered in muck as they were after their trek from the barn, but they seemed to be wearing nothing but drapes of cloth around their waists.

The light rain washed some of that muck from them as they walked, exposing bare skin covered in raw patches eaten away by the acidic mud.

They trudged off to the left of the farm buildings and spread out to begin some sort of work amongst the low-growing *susomun*, bent over and plunging their arms into the muck past their elbows.

"This is insane," Alexis muttered. "A newly settled world's economics might not support modern machinery, but Erzurum's been settled for hundreds of years. Surely they've amassed *some* capital in that time?"

Kannstadt shrugged. "All I know is from when I came here. There are few machines for the farming, and those only on the largest farms."

"No animals either?" Alexis couldn't see where they might be kept, if the slaves were in the building most resembling a barn.

"On other farms, with the men to protect them from Erzurum's *schlangen*. Here? Too small. You will see some *gänse*, geese, around the house. Chickens are taken by the *schlangen*, but they leave the *gänse* alone. I think they are afraid."

They watched the farm for a time, but nothing more happened. The house remained mostly still and silent while the slaves finished whatever it was they were about and moved to the next field. This one empty of all but water and they began moving cattail shoots from a neighboring field to form long rows in the empty one.

"Have you seen enough?" Kannstadt asked.

"More than enough," Alexis agreed.

They edged back from the tree line, turned, and stood, being sure to keep the reflective blankets between them and the farm, then headed for where they'd left the other men.

"There's no overseer out in the fields?" Alexis asked.

"The man with the rifle," Kannstadt said. "The slaves know what to do."

"Warm and dry atop the house," Alexis said, "of course." She pondered what she'd seen. "Why do they accept it? There were three dozen men in that field — surely they could come up with some way to attack the household, couldn't they? How many farmers could there be there?"

"This farm? Four hired hands, after the owner and his family — the man, his wife, two sons and three daughters, one of the sons has a wife and there is a babe."

"So —"

"There is always the man with the rifle," Kannstadt said, "and more than the rifle." He tapped his neck and the scar there.

"Yes," Alexis said. "How does that work?"

"An explosive capsule," Kannstadt said. "Enough to destroy the artery and difficult to remove without doing the same. Some farms have only a box to control them — others buy better from the pirates. Too far from the house — *poof!*" He flung his fingers wide at his throat. "Too *close* to the house — *poof! Der Herr* —" Kannstadt spat into the muck. "— presses the button — *poof!*"

"I see," Alexis said.

"Some risk it," Kannstadt said, rubbing at his throat and ear, something Alexis had noted many of his men had a habit of doing as well. "Many die."

"So if we are to take this farm and its comms," Alexis said, "we must do so quickly and by surprise, and expect no help from the prisoners."

Kannstadt nodded. "And we must be careful to not damage the transmitter. If the signal is lost before we remove the devices from those men —"

"Poof," Alexis said. "Yes, I understand."

FIFTEEN

O' look me hearties, see me mates?
Us lads were not forgotten.
Not by good Queen Annalise,
Nor by Little Bit O'Bosun.

THE FARM WAS BARELY VISIBLE AT NIGHT, WITH ONLY THE occasional sliver of one of Erzurum's moons breaking through the cloud cover.

Warth swore it was enough, though.

Alexis and the former poacher were stretched out behind one of the farm's dikes that ran parallel to the farmhouse. Covered in their survival blankets to mask their heat signatures from the guard in the cupola atop the farmhouse, legs in the cold water of the cattail field they'd crawled through to get this far.

The barrel of Warth's rifle and a bit of his face at the scope were all that was exposed.

Alexis' presence here wasn't strictly necessary, but it was as close as she could come without being with Kannstadt and the main attacking force — those were all Kannstadt's men, being more experienced at moving quickly and silently through the muddy waters. That force numbered only as many as the remaining survival blankets from Alexis' crew, to mask their heat from any scanner the guard might have, while the rest of Kannstadt's men and *Mongoose's* crew waited behind the tree line.

That decision had taken a great deal of trust on Alexis' part, because it meant turning over most of her force's small arms to Kannstadt's men. It was only the Hanoverese captain's obvious concern for Lieutenant Deckard and the good word of those few New London spacers in his group which had swayed her.

The rest of the force was to come forward once the attack started — or guard the retreat should the first force be discovered and an alert sent out to the surrounding farms.

The thin material of her masking blanket crinkled as Alexis shifted her position — there was something sharp under her left thigh.

"Best be still, sir," Warth whispered.

"Are they close, at least?" she asked.

"Middling," Warth said, which really gave Alexis no better idea than she'd had before.

"Are you certain the guard won't see us here? Or Kannstadt's men as they approach?"

Alexis couldn't see, with her head covered as it was, but she felt certain from the pause that Warth had just taken a rather large breath and held it for a time before answering.

"The Hanny captain said this farm's no motion sensors, didn't he, sir?" Warth said finally. "Think if they did, we'd've been spotted already. These blankets — they'll hide our heat from what he might have. These fields're enough to hide a man if he moves slow, an' I'll admit, though it galls me, those fellows do, for all they come off ships ... like you, sir."

Alexis suspected that was some sort of rebuke for her moving too fast or too much on their way to this spot — which had drawn more than one overly polite reminder from Warth. The truth was, if she felt a ship action in normal-space was boring compared to *darkspace*, then an action on the ground was both more boring than that and more terrifying than either.

It was quite one thing to bear a long approach in tacking to a far-off ship, or to lie in wait, sails and systems dark while one came you — but this crawling through the mud, never moving but one limb at a time, and that so slowly and only so far, so as to not alert some watcher ...

Well, she'd admire the patience and skill of a ground-fighter, she supposed, but never wished to be one.

Give her a stout hull around her and the clear surroundings of *darkspace* to be able to *see* her enemy coming, not wonder where he was in the looming darkness and whether he was a better sneak than she was. If she were ever to voluntarily fight on the ground, she'd first want an extra set of eyes or two installed to keep from constantly feeling there was someone just behind her ready to slip a knife into her back.

"And, begging yer pardon fer sayin' it, sir, but the shadows in that cupola are a right small target from here and it'd be best did my jaw not be constantly a'yammering, if you take my meaning?"

"Shut up and let you do your bloody job, is that it, Warth?"

"Wouldn't never say such, sir." There was a pause. "But if you was to watch the field behind us fer them snakes, as is why there's the two of us here, I'd be obliged, I would."

And do my bloody job, as well, though he'd never say that either.

Alexis let herself slide slowly down the side of the dike, further into the field's mud, but hidden from the farmhouse, and uncovered her face to watch the waters for any sign of the snakipedes — a designation which hadn't stuck with either her crew or the those of Kannstadt's group, who insisted on simply calling them snakes, despite the multitude of tiny legs.

I shall have to apologize to grandfather for mocking his calling those beasts on Dalthus shite-weasels when everyone else simply calls them bearcats. A thing should have a proper name, after all, and —

"No," Warth said, belying his own calm by continuing to speak. "It's not that guard up-top we have to worry about spotting us afore we're ready, it's the —"

There was a short, deep *honk* that set Alexis' every nerve on edge and seemed to hush the surrounding darkness in its wake. It was a sound she recognized well from her home, and she knew the first wouldn't be the last.

"Oh, hell," she said at the same time Warth moved to adjust his rifle.

Then the night exploded in a cacophony of *honks* that very nearly overshadowed the *crack* of Warth's laser splitting the air as he fired. Body and rifle came out of the farmhouse's cupola, rolling and clattering down the roof to land in the yard. He worked the rifle's action to set another capacitor in place even as Alexis rose to try making sense of the coming fight and direct him toward new targets.

"Bloody geese," he muttered.

ALEXIS AND WARTH had only a short time to remain in their position, as the fight for the farmhouse moved indoors without a second target presenting itself to Warth's gun — save a yard full of geese, which Alexis wouldn't at all reprimand Warth for shooting as they rushed about raising the alarm and batting at the attacking force with their wings.

More than one of Kannstadt's men was bowled over or forced to throw himself to the ground as one flew at his head. From Alexis' perspective, it even appeared the fowl had a more cohesive plan than the attacking force, which was strung out and scattered as they rushed from various points in the muddy field, up the surrounding berm and toward the farmhouse.

The inhabitants of the farm were either slow to respond, or the sound of Warth's laser had been masked enough by the bloody geese that the farmer and his family didn't rush out — perhaps they were used to the geese alerting to snakipedes and were depending on the single guard to fire if one showed itself.

In any case, as soon as the first of the attacking force made the house's door and kicked it down, Alexis and Warth moved as well. With no need for further stealth, they could stay on the dikes and not slog through the muddy field.

It was only a few meters to one of the dikes leading toward the farmyard and a hundred from there to reach the house, but Warth was wheezing and falling behind before they'd gone half the distance. The confines of shipboard life often left the men out of shape for such things, better suited to the short, steady strength tasks of hauling on a mass of sail or steadying a yard than dashing about.

She wondered if she shouldn't insist they get some small amount of other exercise once they were back aboard ship, as she did with her martial arts training. Then she wondered at the odd sorts of places one's mind went in the midst of rushing toward a fight.

It was only a thirty second run from where she'd waited to the farmhouse door, a few being added to avoid the geese which, their first targets having entered the house already, were perfectly happy to accept Alexis and Warth as substitutes.

"Bloody ... minging ... geese ..." Warth wheezed behind her, swinging his rifle like a club at any of the birds that came close.

Alexis settled for leaping over those that came for her legs and diving rolls under those in flight.

Halfway to the door those came close together and she wound up rolling right through an angry goose, opening her head up to a flurry of wing-bats and pecks that left her with a small cut on her forehead and a stinging, half-closed eye.

SIXTEEN

So landed our Alexis
On Erzurum's bloody soil.
She spurned the pirates' offers
For the lads she knew there toiled.

THE FIGHT INSIDE THE HOUSE WAS OVER EVEN AS SHE ENTERED.
Kannstadt's force, with him in the lead — something else Alexis could admire about the man, even if he was Hanoverese — had caught all but the single guard atop the house still asleep in their beds. Alexis heard a couple shouts from the connected bunkhouse as the few farmhands were subdued and the stamping of feet upstairs, but there were no shots or other sounds of fighting.

She had a moment to take in the farmhouse itself as Kannstadt and his men came downstairs with a morose farmer and his sons firmly held by two men on either side of each. She wasn't sure what she'd expected, but it had certainly been that a farmstead which worked its fields with slaves and used implanted explosives as a threat to keep them docile would not look so very much like the home she'd grown up in.

The house was small, with but a sitting room, dining room, and kitchen downstairs. The dining room was the largest, with a long table indicating the family and farmhands all ate together. The sitting room was smaller and probably just for the family, with a long couch along two walls and a pair of comfortable chairs all facing an entertainment center and the farm's data core. The decorations were different from her grandfather's house — the myriad bits and pieces that made the home this family's and not some others — but take those away and move her grandfather's in, and the place would feel like her own home.

What she could make out of the kitchen, a clean, practical space, reminded her so much of home that she could picture Julia, her grandfather's housekeeper, there even now. The bunkhouse beyond, where Kannstadt's men were busy trussing up the three remaining farmhands, was neat and tidy, not the filth and disarray she'd come to expect from pirates, much less expected from slaveowners.

In all, it was far too homey a place to reconcile with the half-naked men she'd seen working the muddy fields the day before.

Kannstadt reached the bottom of the stairs. He pointed to the dining room and barked out some German to his men, then to the front door and ordered something else, before coming up to Alexis.

"As agreed," he said, handing her the pistol he carried butt first. "My men will return their weapons to yours and arm themselves as they may from this farm."

"Thank you. It needn't have been right away."

Kannstadt shrugged. "We were once enemies and trust is hard. It is better to have no doubt."

Alexis nodded. The fact was she *would* be most relieved when all her lads had their own weapons back.

"I have sent men to the slave barracks to free them and those most experienced to begin removing the devices. We should go there — I would have you with me in case any are of New London."

The Hanoverese captain fingered his ear and neck, as he always did when he spoke of the slaves and the means of controlling them on

Erzurum. Alexis couldn't imagine how having such things in one's body, even for a short time, might affect someone.

Alexis nodded. She could see that New London spacers, held captive here for so long that they didn't know there was now a cease-fire in the war, might be wary of such a large force of Hanoverese.

"These —" Kannstadt nodded toward the dining room where his men were binding the prisoners to chairs set back against the wall. "— we will question, *hein*? Before you contact your ships, to make certain there are no tricks to guard against."

"Tricks in their comms?"

Kannstadt nodded and started for the door. "We have not seen it, but the older slaves tell of codes that must be entered, or an alert is sent to neighboring settlements."

"I see."

Alexis followed him. She wondered what other methods these small farms might use to control their workers — she disliked to even think of them as slaves.

Her own men and the rest of Kannstadt's had arrived and milled around the yard and on the dikes. Hers were tracking down the weapons they'd turned over and Kannstadt's were returning them — some of his reluctantly and hers examining the returned weapons carefully for any sign of damage. It was a wary truce, still, and she respected Kannstadt for turning the weapons back so quickly.

No dike ran directly to the slave quarters. Instead, the fields between were smaller than the others and staggered, so that one's approach was either a series of turns and walks away from the true course or a slog across those fields and up and over a series of dikes.

Alexis and Kannstadt took the dikes.

They arrived at the barracks and found five of Kannstadt's men clustered around the open door.

There was a brief exchange in German and Kannstadt explained, "They are New London and will not come out. They think we are an enemy or that the farmer will set off their explosives if they leave the building. I would have Ian speak to them first, as he did to you, but he is wearied."

Alexis nodded, the New London lieutenant in Kannstadt's band did seem worn out by his effort at talking to her that first day. He'd sat in the cave, staring into space in such a way that Alexis worried for him, but Kannstadt said this was not unusual and he would come back eventually — though he said it with such determination that Alexis wondered if the New Londoner's spells might be becoming worse and Kannstadt worried for him, as well. They'd had some success in getting him to his feet and moving with them for the attack on the farm, though he'd still moved sluggishly, as though unaware of what was happening. He was likely on his way across the fields from the tree line with the rest of Kannstadt's men even now.

They stopped a few meters from the open door, unable to see within its shadows, and Alexis cupped her hands to her mouth.

"Halloo, you in the barn! We're friends! New Londoners come to get you — you can come out!"

There was silence for a moment, then a voice called, "Who are you? I heard Hannies!"

"It's a joint force, sir," Alexis called back, assuming it was an officer speaking. "There's news of the war. A cease-fire holds, so no fears of the Hanoverese here."

"Are you in control of the farm? I'd rather keep my head attached, if it's all the same to you!"

"I understand, sir."

She shot a look to Kannstadt.

"It is safe just outside the barracks."

"I'm told the devices are still active, sir," Alexis called out, "but it's safe to come out a bit."

In trickles, twos and threes, and hesitantly, men began to emerge from the structure.

The men were as skinny and ill-kept as Kannstadt's — more so, for where Kannstadt's men had trousers and shirts of the scaled snakipede skins, these wore only bits of cloth wrapped around their

THE QUEEN'S PARDON   113

waists. They were still covered and stained with the muds of the fields, whatever the constant drizzle hadn't washed away on their way back to the barracks. Their exposed skin was red and raw in places from the corrosive effects of Erzurum's mud.

One man came to the fore — back erect, despite the filth and primitive garb.

"Who are you again?" he asked.

"Lieutenant Alexis Carew." She used her Naval rank first to give him some comfort. "Commanding the private ship *Mongoose*, in action against the pirates."

"Lieutenant? Royal Navy?" the man asked. "They've come for us."

"A certain force is here, and the battle's not done yet," she told him. "We're private ships, but we've come to get you out of this."

The man's posture eased, as though all the weight in the world had been lifted from his shoulders. He smiled and stepped forward, still not out of the building's shelter, but closer and he held out his hand.

"Private ships or no, we're bloody glad to hear a New Londoner's voice, I tell you. Captain Ellender, *Inscrutable*."

Alexis saw his wince at naming the ship he must have lost in some battle, before spending who knows how much time adrift in its dead hulk or making for safety in a boat before being taken up by the pirates. She took the offered hand.

"Bloody glad, I say," Ellender repeated. "You have these Hannies well in hand, I hope?"

"This is Captain Kannstadt. He and his men were captured by the pirates as well, and his men make up the bulk of our force. Captain Ellender, I should tell you, the war is over — a cease-fire, at least," she added quickly as Ellender started to ask a question she was certain would be about who won.

"I see," Ellender said. "Thought as much — the captives, I mean — when those blokes opened the barracks door. All snakeskin and not proper uniforms." He eyed Alexis. "Not that yours is better."

"Our boat crashed some distance from here and we had to make our way through the swamps, which is where we encountered Captain Kannstadt's group. They were instrumental in taking the farm and freeing you, Captain Ellender."

Alexis hoped that knowledge would ease any lingering tension Ellender had about the large number of Hanoverese milling about. He hadn't yet found that Alexis' New London force was outnumbered by their former enemy nearly four to one, nor truly had time to adjust to the cease-fire.

"I see, well." Ellender cleared his throat and held his hand out to Kannstadt, his other hand going to brush back his hair, which was long and unbound. The gesture uncovered his ear which, unlike Kannstadt's men, was unscarred, but instead still carried the slaver's odd assortment of rings and studs. "My thanks to you, as well, then, Captain Kannstadt, there being a cease-fire and all, yes?"

Kannstadt took the offered hand and nodded.

Ellender's free hand went from his hair to his neck. "The, ah —"

"We will work to get the codes from the farmer," Kannstadt said, "and begin removing the devices. I have a man who is experienced and the farmhouse has proper equipment." He fingered his own neck. "It will not be so ragged as some. As soon as it is safe, we will begin."

Ellender nodded and his shoulders slumped. "I suppose we must stay here until you have those codes, then."

They took their leave, assuring Ellender, and the others who'd begun to cluster nearer the door, that they'd be free as soon as possible, and started the walk back to the farmhouse.

"Captain Kannstadt," Alexis asked, something gnawing at her, "these devices — you said the items in the ear have something to do with it?"

Kannstadt nodded. "*Ja*, yes, there is one in the neck, which will explode, and these in the ears, which are — to track, to record, to give information, you understand? The patterns say a thing, too —" He spat into the muck of a nearby field. "— about who is *der Herr*."

"I didn't see any earrings or studs on the farmer and his men," Alexis said. "So, it is not some sort of Barbary custom? A fashion adapted for those things?"

Kannstadt shook his head. "They are free. It is only for slaves, and only on Erzurum."

Alexis felt a growing anger. She'd seen such things before in the Barbary, only not on Erzurum. Many of those back on Enclave, workers in Wheeley's casino, wore the same heavy assortment of rings and studs, which she'd taken for some sort of fashion there. If they were not, if such things were only done on Erzurum and only for those sold as slaves, then what did it mean?

Wheeley owned the casino there, and, now she thought about it, she'd only seen that odd ear piercing in the casino itself, not anywhere else on Enclave. Was Wheeley also a slave owner? And if he was, then he must be involved with the pirates in some way.

It would explain his seeming inability to get her any information at all on the fleets, despite Avrel Dansby's assertion that he was the man to ask. It might also explain the tainted solution for *Mongoose's* beef vats, if she wasn't rushing too far afield in her suspicions.

If the man was involved with pirates and slavers, might he not be willing to sabotage the supplies of a ship searching for those things? The other private ships had reported no problems with the supplies they purchased on Enclave, but none of them were specifically looking for news of the missing fleets and their crews. They wanted only word of pirates — or, preferably, the easier targets of merchants who dealt with pirates. Alexis and *Mongoose* had been after the source as Wheeley well knew.

"Bloody bastard," she muttered.

"What?" Kannstadt asked.

"Nothing — I've only found I must plan for a future meeting, it seems."

She and Kannstadt returned to the farmhouse and the waiting prisoners.

THE SEVEN MEN — well, six and a boy, as the farmer's youngest son was with them — were lined up against the wall, hands bound behind them and legs bound to the dining chairs' legs. Two of the farmhands were in nothing but briefs and the one Alexis took for the farmer's eldest son was naked, the others wore whatever they'd been sleeping in. All had the dark hair and brown skin she'd found common to the Barbary.

The farmer himself was older, balding in the middle, with a long mustache going grey. He was fit, but under a layer of fat, and he glared at Kannstadt with undisguised anger bordering on hatred.

Kannstadt looked at Alexis, then barked something in German and one of his men tossed a cloth from the dining table into the naked man's lap. The Hanoverese captain approached the farmer and fired off another rapid string of German that had Alexis fumbling for her tablet in order to translate it. The farmer snorted, but made no other response.

"*Sprechen sie Deutsch?*" Kannstadt demanded.

"*Ecdanını sikiyim,*" the farmer said, spitting at Kannstadt.

Kannstadt stepped back, face red as he wiped the farmer's spittle from it. "This one will claim not to speak a civilized tongue," he said, nodding to Alexis' tablet. "If you will, a translation will be easier than forcing him to admit he does."

Alexis keyed the tablet's speaker instead of her earpiece and set it on the table near Kannstadt.

"Now we have no difficulties, *hein?*" Kannstadt said.

"*Profanity filter* your ancestors," came from the tablet in response to the farmer repeating what he'd said before.

Kannstadt glanced from the tablet to Alexis and she felt her face grow hot.

"It has some settings I haven't bothered changing," she explained.

SEVENTEEN

O', shout me hearties, jump me mates,
To see her resoluteness.
No force could keep her from her path,
Nor trickery pass her shrewdness.

KANNSTADT CROUCHED IN FRONT OF THE FARMER.

"Tell us the codes to access the planet's net and it will go easier for you," he said.

"Kill me hard or easy, *racial slur on those of Hanoverese origin —* either way we are dead and we will not help you do the same to our neighbors."

"We have no interest in your neighbors," Alexis said. "We only want to contact the ships in orbit and be on our way."

It wasn't strictly true. She did intend to visit his neighbors, and every other farm, settlement, and holding on Erzurum, until all of the enslaved spacers of the fleets were freed — along with any other slaves held here. It would only be with the overwhelming force of her privateer fleet and once the pirates themselves were dealt with, or possibly a fleet brought back from New London or Hanover. A strong enough force might minimize the resistance and loss of life. Perhaps Kannstadt could take some sort of control of the system as Hanover's representative and put some official weight behind it.

All of which, though, would depend first on her being able to contact the fleet without bringing all of the neighboring farms and settlements down on them.

"Pirates," the man muttered, spitting again, but this time on the floor and not in Kannstadt's face.

"Not the pirates," Alexis said. "A privateer force out of New London."

The farmer cocked his head at her. "Those who attacked the pirates?"

Alexis smiled. If the farmer had no love for the pirates occupying Erzurum, then perhaps he'd help them with more than the communication codes for his network.

"Yes," she said. "It's a large fleet — large enough to defeat the pirates if we can fully man the ships while not giving up the targets we hold on the ground." That was probably too much information — the farmer wouldn't understand what was necessary and likely wouldn't care. "My ships are in orbit now and we hold several positions on the ground — if you help us, we can free your world from the pirates."

The farmer stared at her for a moment, then threw his head back and laughed.

"BARBARY DOG!" Kannstadt quite unexpectedly drove his fist into the farmer's gut, cutting off his laugh.

"Captain Kannstadt!" Alexis yelled.

"Fischer," he said, ignoring Alexis. "Get the men."

"*Ja.*"

One of Kannstadt's men left the dining room and then the farmhouse.

"Bauer," Kannstadt said, nodding to one of the farmhands.

Before Alexis could react, the man drove his wooden spear through a farmhand's thigh.

"What are you doing?" Alexis made to put herself between Kannstadt and the captives, but two of his men grabbed her arms.

"You will be easy to them," Kannstadt said, "because you have not been on Erzurum." He pointed to the farmhouse door. "You have not worked those fields with a knife always at your throat!" He turned back to the farmer. "You will tell us — or next it will be your boy, and it will be his belly, and you will watch him die a slow death full of pain."

Alexis struggled briefly against the men gripping her, but couldn't easily get free. She might be able to free herself, but it would mean doing them real damage, and Kannstadt had four others in the room. She had the pistol he'd returned to her, and her flechette pistol still tucked away at the small of her back, but she and her lads were still outnumbered by Kannstadt's — the New Londoners in his group would likely come over to her side, but they might not even understand what was happening until it was too late.

"Captain Kannstadt," she tried saying calmly, "this is not the way. He's a simple farmer, not one of the pirates — not some enemy."

"You do not know," Kannstadt said. "War does not choose the just or the righteous, *Kapitän* Carew. War chooses who will survive." He turned back to the farmer. "Tell us."

"Kill us now or leave us on Erzurum as you did my grandfather's grandfather, pig," the farmer yelled. "I have heard the tales of our outcast!"

"Were you told the tales of Beneschau and the *kinder* there?" Kannstadt yelled back. "For I have and we are well-rid of your kind!"

"Not all!" the farmer yelled, his face as red as Kannstadt's. "Not all of us!"

"There were more — always more! More rubble, more dead *kinder*!"

"How many children died here, do you think? Abandoned on this place where nothing grows!"

Alexis, along with all the others, had grown still, fascinated by the exchange — as though some long and bitter feud was being played out for them. Both the Hanoverese and the farmer's family seemed to understand the whole of it, but Alexis was at a loss, other than that the people of Hanover and those of Erzurum must truly hate each other, for long-past transgressions on both sides.

"We gave you your own world," Kannstadt said. "And what did you become? Pirates and slavers!"

Kannstadt was fairly screaming now, his face inches from the farmer's, who strained against his bonds as though to press his own face to that of the Hanoverese captain — or perhaps to reach his enemy with his snarling teeth.

"And where were you?" the farmer asked. "You *navy man* with your ship? Where were you when the pirates came to Erzurum? Where were you when they demanded what little food grows here? Where were you when they took the machines you left us to sell on other worlds and said, 'Here, take these men for your fields?' Always the pirates demand more food and how else are we to grow it? *What else were we to do?*"

The farmer turned his reddened face to Alexis, eyes filled with tears and anger in equal measure.

"And you, *New Londoner* —" His voice was filled with scorn. "— come to blame us for the pirates?"

He spat at her, but it fell short.

"Your New London *are* the pirates!"

EIGHTEEN

Alexis chilled at the farmer's words, no longer struggling against Kannstadt's men and their grip on her arms.

What did he mean that New London were the pirates?

She might still feel that her letter of marque and the whole privateering business was not too very far removed from piracy itself, but none of the private ships she'd encountered would stoop to raiding a poor world like Erzurum, much less making slaves of New London's own Navy spacers.

Could there be other, less scrupulous, captains working the Barbary? She'd not put such a thing past bloody Malcome Eades of the Foreign Office.

No, Eades would have warned her if he'd known, not set her after "pirates" knowing the largest group of those in the Barbary were sanctioned by his own government.

The farmer must mean something else, not the kingdom, but merely New Londoners. That was a sad thing, but not entirely unexpected — spacers from captured ships, given the choice to join or be enslaved, and even volunteers jumping their merchant ship in the Barbary and seeking out what they saw as an easier, freer life. It was disappointing to hear that her countrymen would be involved in this sort of thing, but not surprising.

"There are New Londoners among these pirates, you mean?"

"Among? Leading! And most of them!" the farmer told her.

He glared from Alexis to Kannstadt, as though torn between which he'd most like to get his hands on for a moment.

"They came in my father's time. I was just a boy," he went on, the calm translation from Alexis' tablet belied the passion and anger in his voice. "'Captain Ness' he calls himself and his crews, with so many fine ships. They waved away the troubles of the shoals like nothing, saying they wished to trade — to make Erzurum a regular stop on their routes through the Barbary. Lies! He visits the farms, he visits the towns, he buys our poor crops, and he is generous in payment — more generous than the other merchants who so rarely come."

Even Kannstadt had stilled, listening to the man, as though he wanted to understand what had happened on Erzurum as badly as Alexis did.

"Then when he has seen it all, Ness says it is his. All — our crops, our goods, the mud of Erzurum, and us." He shrugged. "Those who protested too strongly were killed and soon no one protests. And at first, there is not much change, save who claims to run Erzurum — and what have we on the farms ever cared for that, so long as we are left alone?" The farmer took a deep breath and snorted. "But then we are not left alone.

"Ness still buys our crops, but he is not so generous — then comes the 'tax' on what he does pay. Then the 'tax' on holding the land and the 'tax' for selling and the 'tax' for not selling and the 'tax' for standing in Erzurum's mud." The farmer spat to the side. "Ness, may his privates rot and burn."

"You should have sent for help," Kannstadt said. "The navy would have —"

"*Profanity filtered* your *profanity filtered*," came from the tablet as the farmer cut Kannstadt off, but it was enough to make the

Hanoverese captain turn red and square his shoulders. "How are we to ask with one of Ness' ships in orbit always? And sending honest merchants away so that all goods, all trade, comes through him and those who would trade with his ilk?" The farmer laughed. "'Oh, Mister Pirate, you will take this message to Hanover, please?' It has been my lifetime since your navy visited Erzurum, *kapitän* — *where were you?*"

Kannstadt clenched his jaw.

"What's your name, sir?" Alexis asked, realizing she had no idea and seeing him now as more than just some anonymous obstacle.

"Altu Isikli," he said, "as if you care."

"Mister Isikli, I'm sorry for your troubles, for Erzurum's troubles, but one man — one crew — is not New London, and nothing excuses what I saw in your fields. You keep slaves and —"

"Does it not? Nothing?" Isikli shrugged. "Perhaps not, but my father had machines for the fields — old, broken down, but they did the work. Now they are gone — a '*tax*,' you see? Nearly all of value on Erzurum is taken for the 'tax' and sold on other worlds — my father's machines harvest other crops there now. And Ness? He says it does not matter that we have no machines, we must still pay his 'tax' and every hectare must give food to his men or to those in the towns who service them."

Alexis was so caught up in the farmer's story that she barely noticed Fischer, the man Kannstadt had sent away earlier, had returned with a half-dozen others and went up the stairs.

"We must have his 'tax' when his men come for it, do you see? It is best it is ready and they load their shuttles quickly — if not, they search for value, without care of what they break." His eyes met Alexis' steadily. "Idle, bored, rough men search through my house, in every room and every hiding place ... and I am the father of daughters. Do you see? I must have these pirates on their way as quickly as they come, so I must have what they demand waiting for them.

"So Ness sends us men and he says, 'Here are men to work your fields.' Men from other worlds he raids, men from merchant ships, and, best of all —" He looked at Kannstadt. "— men from navies."

Isikli laughed.

"Hanover's navy put my people here. Hanover's navy promised us safety, then abandoned us. So, *Kapitän* Kannstadt, when Ness gives me men of some navy to work my fields, I touch myself and laugh."

There was a piercing scream from upstairs and Kannstadt's lips thinned in a cold smile.

"Will you laugh now, Altu Isikli, father of daughters?"

NINETEEN

"Just leave," the pirate captain said,
"And I'll let you all escape.
For when your fellows all have fled,
There'll be tuppence for your fate."

Alexis frowned, not understanding, then her blood chilled.

She'd thought Kannstadt had brought only the farm's men to the dining room to spare the women from his questioning, especially when he'd ordered Isikli's farmhand stabbed. Now, though, she knew different.

"*No!*" Alexis renewed her struggles, but even distracted as they'd been by the farmer's words, the two men holding her arms kept their grip. "Captain Kannstadt, you can't! You mustn't!"

Kannstadt let out a snort of disgust. "I had thought you knew of war," he said, "after Giron."

"I learned enough of its horror and brutality there," Alexis said. "I'd thought you had honor enough to stand against that!"

"War is brutal and horrible," Kannstadt said. "Isikli must talk or we will be doomed once we are discovered here." He shrugged. "Hanover has dealt with his kind for generations. We know what will bring his words."

"*Damn you!* In the cave, when we spoke about Giron, you said Captain Schäfer was not an honorable man for attacking the transports — is this your own honor, Captain?"

"Schäfer attacked a fleeing foe," Kannstadt said, then pointed to Isikli who closed his eyes as another scream sounded from upstairs. "*He* is a slaver and has no honor."

"Captain Kannstadt, please, those women upstairs are innocent, they've done nothing to you or your men!"

Alexis felt as though there was nothing at all stable in her world. Their enemy on this farm turned out to be a poor farmer who, perhaps, had no choice but to work the land with slaves under the direction of pirates from her own kingdom, and now Kannstadt, former enemy turned ally, yet willing to send his men to commit such atrocities.

"Your New London fleet has few women in it, *Leutnant* Carew?"

"What —"

"Hanover's does — as did the French who sailed with your own fleet — yet did you see any amongst my men? Or in this man's fields? Think on where the pirates this man supplies took the women of my ship, Carew, and then speak to me of innocence."

"Those women — those *girls* upstairs had nothing to do with what the pirates —"

Another scream sounded and Kannstadt turned his back to her, his attention once more on Isikli.

"The codes, vermin."

Alexis braced herself against the men holding her who expected her to struggle mindlessly as she had before. Then she'd only been trying to shrug off their hands and move away — she hadn't wanted to hurt them, hoping Kannstadt would see sense — but now she was determined to get loose no matter the cost.

She raised her legs, tucking them almost to her chest, and one of the men holding her laughed, as though he found it funny she might think her scant weight would bother him, then she drove her feet down.

Her shipboard boots might have been worn by Erzurum's acidic mud, but they were still sturdy enough, and their soles and heels, weighted with heavy magnets to keep contact with the deck in case her ship lost gravity, struck her captors just above the kneecaps. It was a move she'd used before to good effect and it did the same now.

The man on her left howled in pain as her heel drove solidly past, taking his kneecap part of the way with it. He released her arm and grasped at his leg.

The man on her right was luckier — her heel skipped down his leg, merely raking his shin painfully. He yelled too, but more from anger than the pain. Still, it was enough of a distraction for Alexis to plant her feet firmly, reach across him to catch and grasp his right arm, already swinging to strike her in anger, and leverage that momentum over her hip.

Her second captor rolled mid-air, the torque of her throw losing him his grip on her arm, and slammed face-first into the farmhouse's wooden floor.

Alexis reached for the pistol tucked into her belt, but the rest of Kannstadt's men reacted swiftly.

One leapt across his fallen comrade to grasp her arm and hand, forcing the pistol to point safely away. He must have had some training, for his grip on her hand pressed painfully into the joint where thumb and forefinger met, leaving her hand too numb to hold the pistol, which dropped to the floor.

Even as the pistol fell, another of Kannstadt's men struck her from behind at the knees, making her legs buckle, and a third grabbed her around the neck.

Together, the three men bore her to the floor and more than one blow landed from their free hands.

Alexis struck out in those few seconds, as well.

She ducked her head, managing to get her teeth into the forearm around her throat to clamp down hard, tasting blood, and she drove her left leg back, connecting with something that gave a quite satis-fying crunch as her heel connected.

Then she was on the floor and more blows came. Her arm was wrenched painfully behind her back, another hand grasped her jaw to clamp her mouth closed and keep it from any new target.

It all happened so quickly that it was only as that happened that Kannstadt shouted something — or only then that she heard it. Then more shouts as the rest of his men reacted to the fight.

A sudden, unexpected *crack* cut off their shouts and brought abrupt silence, as well as a stilling of the men atop her. The sharp smell of ozone came to her, that and the sound meaning someone had fired a laser — which made little sense to her, since she was still alive and left not much visible as a target beneath her three captors.

"There'll be a general an' complete lettin' go o' our captain, now, if you please," came Dockett's welcome voice.

———

"OFF HER!" Nabb was shouting. "Off! You bloody Hannie scum! *Offen dur captainen*, damn your Dark-buggered windwards to rotting Hell!"

Alexis was torn between relief as the pressure on her arm eased and the weights on her lifted, and dismay at Nabb's language — both his execrable attempt at German and the curse. Perhaps he was spending too much time with Dockett.

She shook her head to clear it of the odd thoughts that seemed to come with a blow. Her forehead hurt, but she didn't remember it striking the floor when she was taken down, though it must have. A moment's pause brought the situation back to her and she was off, shrugging off the last of Kannstadt's men — who was carefully getting off her legs in the face of Dockett's laser rifle — to dash for the stairs.

She had the briefest glimpse of the situation as she did so. Dockett and Nabb at the fore and six or more of her lads in the doorways, all armed now that they'd retrieved their weapons from Kannstadt's men.

"Nabb, you and two men with me!" she yelled. "Keep the peace, Mister Dockett!"

She had to trust that Dockett hadn't killed one of the Hanoverese spacers with his shot and wouldn't do so with her gone — that would be something their brittle alliance couldn't come back from, she thought. Assuming of course, it could come back from what Kannstadt had ordered happen upstairs — and she was certain it had been on his order, even if unspoken. A captain was responsible for what he allowed of his crew, just as much as what was spoken in orders.

It heartened her that there wasn't a bit of question called out after her, only the two men's "Aye, sirs," and the sound of Nabb's feet following her.

"Veals! Aiden!" Nabb called, even as he ran after her.

TWENTY

ALEXIS REACHED THE TOP OF THE STAIRS AND SAW ONE OF Kannstadt's men dragging a woman — a girl, one of Isikli's daughters probably — down the hallway.

"You! Stop! *Halt!*" She had her flechette pistol in hand and pointed, not really remembering drawing it from the concealed pocket in her suit liner as she raced up the stairs.

The man stopped, puzzled — probably wondering at what had happened to turn Alexis and her men from allies after they'd successfully taken the farm. He frowned and his mouth formed a question.

"Away from her," Alexis said, gesturing with the pistol. That was enough for him to understand what she wanted, if not the reasons. He let go and held his hands up putting his back to the wall. "Nabb, see to the girl! They're still captives, so watch for tricks."

"Aye, sir — Aiden see to it."

Alexis had a moment's pause to wonder at the young man from Kannstadt's group in the cave being among the first Nabb called on, but assumed her coxswain saw something in the lad to take him on so quickly, then she was off again, down the hall from where the man had come. Behind her, the girl screamed again, but Nabb's footsteps didn't falter so she assumed it was just from Aiden taking the situation in hand. From the girl's perspective, one foreign spacer grabbing her must be much like another and Alexis didn't have time to explain — nor the ability, for she'd left her tablet and its translating behind in the dining room.

The girl's scream set off another from the direction Alexis was going, so at least she was moving in the right direction. There were only two rooms off this hallway, and two on the other.

She burst through the door at the end where she thought the scream had come from and found herself in what must be the farmer's bedroom — roughly appointed, it still had a bed big enough for the man and his wife, and two bureaus of what appeared to be wood along with a chest or two. The bed had been shoved against one wall to make more room and one of the chests moved nearly to the center. The room was crowded with a dozen men.

Of the four remaining women on the farm, three were crouched in a corner, guarded by one of Kannstadt's men, while one, maybe one of the farmer's other daughters, stood on the chest. Kannstadt's man, Fischer, was gesturing at the girl.

"*Sieben,*" one of Kannstadt's men said.

Another countered, "*Acht!*"

Sweet Dark, they're auctioning them.

It made a perverse sort of sense, she supposed, if it wasn't so horrifying — the former slaves taking and auctioning their captors. It was odd there were so few of Kannstadt's men there — perhaps only those who'd take part in such a thing? Or, more likely given the small numbers she heard tossed out, only those privileged enough to be the first. And odder still, the sorts of thoughts that went through one's head when presented with a scene so unbelievable.

"*Halt!*" Alexis yelled, aiming her flechette pistol and stepping to the side to make way for Nabb and Veals.

"Oh, no y'don't, y'bloody buggers," Nabb muttered, raising his rifle to his shoulder.

She'd definitely have to talk to the young man about his language, else she'd hear from his mother when next they were on Dalthus.

The rifle was long for such close quarters and nearly touched the back of the nearest of Kannstadt's men. They were outnumbered, too, and she wished she'd called for Nabb to bring more, but most of her men were still spread out amongst Kannstadt's on the farm and were busy freeing the slaves. There hadn't been enough come back with Dockett to both hold Kannstadt downstairs and accompany her.

"Nabb, Veals, if a man so much as twitches burn him down."

That would likely end their alliance, she thought, but better to end it now than to risk being overwhelmed by the Hanoverese and see this horror go on.

"Aye, sir."

Kannstadt's men might not understand English, but they understood her tone and the steady aim of the rifles' barrels — and Alexis' pistol. A bit of space had opened in the line of men, for Alexis had hers trained on Fischer and those between wanted no part of it.

"Away from her," Alexis said to Fischer, gesturing with her pistol. What was the German? "*Ab ... weg ...* whatever it is, move your bloody arse over there!"

Fischer frowned. "*Kapitän Kannstadt —*"

Alexis lowered her aim to Fischer's waist and then below.

Fischer raised his hands and moved aside.

"All of you," Alexis said, keeping her pistol trained on Fischer, but taking in the rest of the men with her free hand and pointing at the farmer's bed. "Get on it."

Fischer seemed to understand best and crawled up onto the bed. It was silly, but it was also the most free space in the room, and with a dozen men to contend with, having them kneeling on the mattress instead of standing was to her advantage. The other Hanoverese followed.

"Watch them close, but the women, too," Alexis said.

"Aye, sir."

"Stay put," she said to Fischer, and backed slowly through the doorway, keeping her pistol trained on them, but turning her head toward the stairs. "Mister Dockett! I'd admire an extra man or two up here!"

"Aye, sir — I would, as well, for where I stand! There's a fair party brewin' in the yard, sir, and a bit of your own attention might be warranted!"

"Bloody buggering hell," Alexis muttered.

She looked around. Aiden was in the hall with the first girl and her buyer. "Aiden, put that one and the girl in here with the rest and stay with Nabb."

"Aye, sir."

That would put three guns on the Hanoverese atop the bed.

"Nabb, watch them —" She lowered her voice. "— but try not to shoot any of them dead, if you have the choice. We're outnumbered, still."

"Aye, sir."

Alexis went downstairs.

A glance through the open door showed her there was, indeed, Mister Dockett's fair-party brewing in the yard.

It seemed the shouts and clamor from the farmhouse had brought everyone to see what was the matter, both her men and Kannstadt's as well as the farm's slaves. Those last were milling about in the mud just short of the yard's dike, not wanting to risk coming closer until they were certain the farmer's transmitter for those things in their necks was off.

Kannstadt was still standing where she'd left him under the aim of Dockett's rifle, but looking more amused than angry now.

"Will you kill us all, *Leutnant* Carew, to save your enemy?"

"You and your men were my enemy not so very long ago, Captain Kannstadt. The question is, what are you now?"

"You are too soft for this sort of war, I think," Kannstadt said.

"Perhaps," Alexis said. "But I'm hard enough for this moment. I'll not have it, Captain Kannstadt, no matter Hanover's history with the people of Erzurum, no matter your own thoughts on what's proper in war — I'll not stand by and see these people harmed."

Kannstadt's face darkened. "You are a fool."

"Perhaps. In the cave, Captain Kannstadt, you said there was no war between our nations on Erzurum — should one of your men lay hands on an innocent again, there will be."

"You and your men will die, even with more guns."

Alexis nodded. "Should it come to that."

Kannstadt stared at her for a moment. "I do not see how you can be so hard and so soft."

"It's because she's standing for what's right, Wendale," Deckard's voice sounded from the farmhouse doorway.

The New London lieutenant limped into view, moving slowly as though greatly wearied by the trek from cave to farm. He edged his way between the tense, still men of Alexis' and Kannstadt's crews as though they weren't there.

"The right often appears soft until you've felt the steel within. We've spoken of this more than once, haven't we?" He blinked, alternating between focusing on Kannstadt and seeming to stare into some vast distance. "Yes. Have."

Kannstadt shook his head. "We must have the codes, Ian, or this has been for nothing and we are doomed." He sighed. "You have not faced the things Hanover has. We have learned to deal with his sort."

Deckard made his way to Kannstadt's side. He laid one hand on the Hanoverese's shoulder, then his face contorted as though he were clenching every muscle for a moment. When he opened his eyes, they were clearer than Alexis could remember them.

"You've never been comfortable with that sort of dealing, Wendale," he said. "You told me so. Don't do this. It's wrong, and you know it."

"Hanover —"

"Whatever's built up in Hanover is not the whole of its people — you said that. It is not the whole of you, either, Wendale." Deckard's face clenched again. "You know what's right."

"Ian —"

Deckard's eyes clouded and he looked around blankly. His hand dropped from Kannstadt's shoulder. "Terrible lot of guns out for having won, isn't there? Right. What?"

Kannstadt's face fell and his shoulders slumped.

TWENTY-ONE

O', pull me hearties, haul me mates,
And listen why I'm here.
If it weren't for Queen and Little Bit,
You'd have to mourn me in your beer.

DECKARD'S WORDS, OR HIS REVERSION TO THE HALF-PRESENT husk he was so much of the time, seemed to pull Kannstadt's resolve from him.

His shoulders slumped and he waved his own men to stand down before going to Deckard's side. Heedless of the wary looks Alexis' crew gave him, Kannstadt led Deckard from the dining room to the farmhouse's living area and settled him in a corner chair.

Alexis followed. Kannstadt squatted beside the chair, his hand on Deckard's forearm, and seemed to stare off into vacant space just as the New London lieutenant did.

"He was not always so," Kannstadt said, though not looking at Alexis.

She squatted near the chair and said nothing, not wanting to disturb whatever the Hanoverese might say next. Though she still burned with anger at what had almost happened upstairs, she needed Kannstadt and his men. If he revealed something, anything, in his concern over Deckard that might allow their alliance to continue, she must have it.

"He and I were the only officers, you see?" Kannstadt said. "In our group, *hein?* I think our ships did not fight each other, we —" He smiled sadly. "That is the one thing we never spoke of, I think. To be sure that we did not know if we had ever truly tried to kill one another." He looked down at the floor, or rather through it.

"After the battle, we all tried to make our way, but ship's boats?" He sighed. "Erzurum's winds are so strong, and the *der heiligenschein* —" He looked up to frown at her. "The —" He formed his hands in a globe, fingers spread.

"The halo," Alexis supplied. "The shell of dark matter around the system."

Kannstadt nodded.

"*Ja*, it is so strong here."

Alexis pictured it in her head. Small boats, not meant to travel far in *darkspace*, driven by Erzurum's strong winds and ever with the system's heavy, impenetrable halo of dark matter to leeward. Worse, even, than the system's shoals, that shell had made it so that Alexis' force, and any other ships, could only enter along the system's ecliptic plane. It would have been all those boat crews could manage to tack and tack, ever to windward, hoping to keep from having their fragile craft dashed upon that mass of dark matter and broken up, spilling men all unprotected to the mercies of the Dark.

"We could not speak," Kannstadt said, "his boat and mine. Even crowded as we were, we could spare no hands for signals, only to set the sail, hold the lines, then come inside for a rest and food before a man's next turn."

Deckard closed his eyes and turned his head away.

"He hears," Kannstadt said. "I am convinced he still hears and understands everything — it is the ... it becomes more difficult for him to make his thoughts known."

"I understand," Alexis said.

"Perhaps." Kannstadt shifted from squatting to sitting cross-legged on the farmhouse's floor. "Our boats were pushed from the others, farther and farther around the halo. We could see the other boats, but only just in the distance.

"For a time, it was as though our two boats, Ian's and mine, were all we had of the universe. We matched each other, tack for tack — I cannot say, even for myself — if this was to keep them in our sight or only the needs of the winds. I think it must have been to stay near, even if we did not think on it. To not feel so alone in the Dark as all the others spread out in clumps and alone.

"We saw the lights of some boats, blown off alone. Some onto the shoals, others found tricks of the winds to move away from Erzurum." Kannstadt shuddered. "In the Barbary, with so much distance between worlds, I think they must have been lost. But then, I wonder to myself, if we had tried harder to get our own boat past the winds, then perhaps I could have spared my men this world."

"There's been no word of any," Alexis said, understanding how the Hanoverese captain must have anguished, in his time on Erzurum, over whether he might have saved his crew by escaping with them, even in the face of weeks in the empty Dark. "Neither rescued by any ship, nor made planetfall."

Kannstadt sighed. He did not seem heartened, and Alexis understood that, too. He would always, she thought, wonder at what he might have done differently that would have spared one of his men.

"Perhaps," he said again. "We fought the winds, Ian's boat and mine, for days. Sometimes sighting the others, sometimes alone. The winds drove *die ruine* — the abandoned ships left behind — through the boats. Striking some, or only for us to watch them break up on the shoals. Men aboard those, I am certain. Some had a bit of power and stubs of sails where the crews left behind had tried to rig what they might.

"Then *die piraten* came.

"They set on us like sharks. We could see them, those gunboats, their sails bigger and brighter than our little craft, cutting through our fellows. If a crew resisted, the pirates simply fired. These little boats were not made for such guns as they had. One strike and the fusion plant ..." He grimaced. "Soon there is a stream of our boats and theirs, to where the pirates know where to enter Erzurum. A stream, then a river —" He closed his eyes. "All lit by the tiny suns of those who would not surrender."

KANNSTADT WAS silent for a long time, but Alexis waited with him.

"They came for us," he said finally. "Closer and closer. We worked the sails then, to keep them away, but ... one hit and we are all dead, we know. So, when they are close and signal for us to strike, we do.

"They put us in their gunboat's hold for the sail and this is where I first saw Ian —" Kannstadt smiled at the New London lieutenant who still looked away with eyes closed. "— my friend in *die Dunkelheit*.

"We are the only officers, *hein*? So we must talk. And all his men, from his boat, are French, so many do not speak English to him."

That brought Alexis' mind to Delaine and her search for him here on Erzurum. Deckard had been New London's liaison to Delaine's ship.

"It is easy to put the war aside with him," Kannstadt said. "Ian is a good man and knows the pirates are our enemy now, not each other, but not so easy for the crews. Hanover and these *Beerenfrucht* have history, so there is fighting, even in the crowded hold. Ian and I try to stop this, but *die Beerenfrucht* do not look to him and my men must defend themselves, *hein*?

"The pirates see this with other crews already and have their markets for each. Off the boat, *die Beerenfrucht* are taken from us to another place, but where we land has few of your New London, so the pirates do not know what to do with Ian. It is too much trouble to move one man, so they leave him with Hanover.

"By this time, we have talked, Ian and I, very much. I think, still, that he would have gone with *die Beerenfrucht,* he saw the captain of his ship among them, but —" Kannstadt took a deep breath and the knuckles of his hand on Deckard's arm whitened. "I am glad that he did not, but must wish he had, *hein?*"

Alexis nodded. More regrets and more questioning of the past she understood quite well. If Lieutenant Deckard had gone with Delaine's group of French, then he might never have been injured so severely — and he would not have been with Kannstadt in the cave for Alexis to learn that he'd seen Delaine alive and on Erzurum, but it seemed unkind to be glad of that in light of how badly the man had been hurt.

Deckard stirred for the first time and laid a hand over Kannstadt's.

"Do you see?" the Hanoverese captain asked with a soft smile. "He hears."

"CAPTAIN KANNSTADT," Alexis said, keeping her voice low. The reminder of Delaine had brought her back to their current situation and needs. "The farmer here, and how his family is to be treated —"

Kannstadt cleared his throat, cutting her off. "*Ja,* we must deal with the present, not the past." He sighed. "The past, though, prods us even now, *hein?*" He jerked his head toward the dining room where Isikli and the other men were still held. "Do you think there is no past with him? Do you think we put his ancestors on this world for no reason?" Kannstadt snorted. "You New Londoners think we of Hanover are hard and cruel, yet you have not fought as we have."

Deckard stirred again and his hand on Kannstadt's tightened more.

"*Ja,* Ian," Kannstadt said with a sigh. "As I said at the start,

Kapitän Carew, Ian was not always so. He studied philosophy, do you know? And we talked — hours and hours we have talked. There is so little to do else in the fields or *der Herr's* barns at night.

"We convinced each other, I think, that New London's softness is not so weak, and that Hanover's cruelty is not without reason — yet, there must be a middle, *hein*?" He sighed. "Still, there is too much of the past with Hanover and those like Isikli. Too much blood on both sides." He leaned back against the wall, as though settling in to wait for a long time. "You may try your softness with this farmer. For Ian's sake — perhaps for my own, if he is right."

TWENTY-TWO

ALEXIS LEFT KANNSTADT TO SIT WITH DECKARD AND RETURNED to the farm's dining room.

Kannstadt was correct in one thing, they had little time, and she was at a loss as to how she might convince Isikli to divulge the codes, if any, that would ensure the farm's comms system made no alert to his neighbors or the pirates.

If the farm were held by pirates, she might simply shoot one in order to convince others of their precarious situation, but doing so to these farmers, despite them also being slaveholders, seemed too close to what Kannstadt had been willing to do.

Where was that line? She wondered, and would she ever cross it if she, like Kannstadt, found herself facing a situation with the history of atrocities on both sides the Hanoverese captain suggested Hanover and Erzurum's settlers had. *Had she* crossed it already, with what she'd done to Daviel Coalson in tossing him off a ship into *darkspace* to float and perish there?

She sent the Hanoverese out of the room and left only Nabb at the doorway with a gun. Isikli and the rest were bound, so there was little for her to fear.

The men watched her with varying expressions of wariness or open hatred as she took a chair from the dining table and sat before them. She was quite close to Isikli this way, knees nearly touching, and wished for a moment that she'd had the lads scoot the table back against the far wall or even sat on its far side to provide some buffer of space.

"I thank you," Isikli said, "for my daughters."

Alexis nodded.

"I will not tell you the codes," Isikli went on.

Alexis sighed.

No, it couldn't be that easy, could it?

What did she have to bargain with the man? Really, only the threat of Kannstadt and his men taking over after they'd over-whelmed hers and then returning to their own way of forcing the information from him. It was a sad thing, but torture, despite its detractors, was quite effective at eliciting information. It might fail miserably at gaining confessions and such, a man being willing to admit to anything to make such torment stop, but to get information that could be verified?

Oh, yes, it would work.

"Mister Isikli," Alexis said, "we must have those codes to access the comms network without alerting your neighbors and the pirates. You must see that, don't you?"

Isikli shrugged, as though a return to Kannstadt's plan bothered him not at all.

Alexis wondered at the life he must have led here on Erzurum, to make him so stubborn and seemingly accepting of such a fate. Isikli had grown up with the pirates in control, seen how his father dealt with them — could he even imagine a life without them? Was he even able to respond to anything but threats and violence? What must it do to a man to scrape out his existence every day from Erzurum's mud?

"Nabb," she called, "send a man to the kitchen and bring me back a large knife, if you please."

"Aye, sir."

Isikli's eyes narrowed, but he said nothing. His hired hands and sons, Alexis wasn't certain how to tell them apart, dressed as they all still were in varying night-clothes, stared at her impassively.

In a moment, she heard Nabb set something on the table behind her and turned to find what must have been the largest knife available. The hilt filled Alexis hand as she took it up and turned back to the bound men.

Setting the blade of the knife against the rope binding Isikli to his chair, she found the knife was as sharp as it was large and parted the bonds with ease.

"Have someone put on a pot of tea, as well, will you, Nabb?"

There was silence for a moment. "Aye ... sir ..."

Alexis cut the rest of Isikli's bonds and motioned him to sit at the table. She moved herself to the table's end so that they were near each other, then remained silent, watching the man, until the tea was ready.

It came not in a pot, but in a large, brass samovar, and the cups Nabb had brought in were of metal and glass, not porcelain.

"Sorry there's no proper tea set, sir," Nabb said as he ushered the lads carrying the samovar from the room again. He glared at Isikli as though the farmer's lack of that were the gravest thing that had happened here.

"It's all right, Nabb," Alexis said. "Mister Isikli?" She gestured to the samovar and cups.

She was probably breaking any number of the man's customs regarding tea and guests, but despite freeing him from his bonds she did want it clear to him that she was now in control of his farm, family, and fate.

Isikli scowled for a moment, then took a cup, filled it with tea and a generous amount of sugar, then sipped. Alexis did the same. The tea had an odd taste — either the tea or the sugar, she couldn't be sure which.

Or possibly the water.

The Dark knew a spacer understood the ways in which poor water could change any number of things.

She sipped again, then set her cup down.

"Mister Isikli," Alexis began her pitch in earnest, "let me tell you about my home on Dalthus."

ALEXIS TALKED for nearly as long as she dared. Until Kannstadt appeared at the dining room's doorway to peek in and see what she was about, followed by Captain Ellender, his ear and neck red and raw from the removal of the slave accoutrements, though not so badly as Kannstadt and his men, as there was far better equipment at the farmhouse. She gestured for Nabb to keep others away after that and kept talking.

She described for Isikli her grandfather's homestead, with its house so very like the man's own, yet with no slaves. Yes, there were the indentures, but they had rights and were free to seek work elsewhere if they could find someone to buy their debt. Any number of them did so, though the flow was more toward her grandfather's employ than away.

She spoke of the thousands of hectares of golden wheat ripening under clear skies only here and there dotted with white clouds, and nary a swamp nor knee-deep mud in sight. Tilled, planted, and harvested by the great machines — though those fields were almost entirely for export. She could tell the idea of a field's crop being so in excess of what the farmer and his family needed to survive that it could be shipped off-world stunned the man.

The home fields, those worked to supply the farm or by individual tenants for their own use, lacked such machines, but still provided a bounty far in excess of what Isikli could easily imagine.

Beasts more than geese, as well. Chickens, goats, pigs — well, she saw him turn up his nose at that, but he seemed interested in the idea of vast herds of sheep and the mutton they supplied.

Finally, Isikli drained his cup and set it down harder than a man might wish to with something so prized as this tea set must be to a farm so poor.

"Enough," he said. "Enough of your brags. We know worlds like yours. Richer than ours, yes, but Erzurum makes one hard. And proud." He straightened his shoulders. "Tales of your nation's wealth and strength will not sway me."

"I don't wish to sway you with tales of my nation's wealth, Mister Isikli," Alexis said. "I wish to offer it to you."

Isikli stared at Alexis' tablet as though unsure the thing had translated properly, while behind her Nabb coughed, then sucked in air.

"I *will* leave Erzurum, Mister Isikli," Alexis said. "With my lads, and with or without these codes I need from you. If not from you, then from the next farm my forces take, you see? I will return to my home on that world I just described, and if you are the one to assist me, I will bring you along." She looked from Isikli to his sons and farmhands. "You, your family, these men who work for you —"

Isikli snorted. "As slaves to work your fields? A nice revenge."

"As freeholders, Mister Isikli, with no indenture. Land — good land — to work and profit from as you will."

She was making quite free with her grandfather's lands and goodwill with such a promise and could only be grateful that she knew him well and could promise he'd agree. Oh, she'd hear more about her bringing home more stray cats and broken birds — an odd phrase, given that as a child she'd only ever brought home a single puppy to care for, and that after the boys in town had abused it so horribly she'd set upon them with a stick and broken the nose of the farrier's son so that it never did look properly straight again.

A wild swing. I'd have thrashed the boy properly if I'd been more than three years old.

Alexis watched Isikli and the others carefully, seeing how they weighed her words.

She drained her own tea and set the cup down with far more care than Isikli had.

"You are caught up in these circumstances with me, Mister Isikli. What is there for you here after my men and I leave? Assuming I can convince Captain Kannstadt not to return to his own methods, I *will* take every slave from this farm. We'll have to destroy your comms, of course, so that you can't alert the pirates after we leave. Possibly we'll have to take you with us — a horrid trudge through these swamps to your neighbors?

"Then we will take that farm, and free more slaves, and make that farmer the same offer of a better life on Dalthus for his aid. Will all your neighbors tell me no, Mister Isikli? With you and your men here paraded before them to show the alternative?

"And when I've taken my men and one of your neighbors home with me, Mister Isikli —"

Alexis stood and picked up the knife, examining the blade for a moment before driving it down into Isikli's table and leaving it to quiver there.

"What will the pirates do with you?"

ALEXIS LEFT the farmer to stare at the still quivering blade and think about her offer, edging past Nabb to leave the farmhouse and move out into the yard under the ever-present drizzle. She wrapped her arms around herself and wandered through the knots of men idling about.

Within a few moments, Kannstadt was at her side.

"You heard, I suppose?" Alexis asked.

The Hanoverese captain nodded. "*Samt und stahl*," he said. "You have steel below your softness." He drew a deep breath. "Are all New Londoners so? As you and Ian?"

Alexis looked away. "I don't know that there was anything particularly soft about what I just did to that man," she said. "He has no choice. He knows it. If not Isikli himself, then his son, or son-in-law, or one of his hands must know the codes. He has no choice at all but to throw his lot in with complete strangers — worse, enemies, from his point of view, I suppose. No choice but to hope we win out against all the odds and then I make good on the promise."

She shivered, certainly from the rain creeping down from her vacsuit liner's collar.

"And what does he gain if he does? Travel light years to a world he doesn't know and doesn't understand, then try to make a new life where all those around him don't even speak his language. Would you welcome being forced into that, Captain Kannstadt?"

"You offer him better than he should receive," Kannstadt said, "and I fear you and your world will regret it one day."

"What do you mean?"

Kannstadt looked around Erzurum, as though taking in the whole world. "There are some things best to stamp out," he muttered.

Alexis suspected he was speaking again of that conflict between Hanover and Isikli's people, and how they'd come to be exiled to Erzurum in the first place.

"What do you —"

"Captain, sir!" Nabb called from the farmhouse door. "That fellow's asking for you!"

TWENTY-THREE

That Little Bit, that Bloody Bit,
She took what few she had,
And marched 'em 'cross the planet,
Just a handful of her lads.

"DAMN HIM!"

Alexis held back from throwing her tablet across the room, but only barely and only because it was so valuable to them.

"I should have slit his bloody throat when I had the chance!"

She'd entered the codes Isikli gave her — not without some trepidation — and expected to be able to contact Malcomson aboard his *Bachelor's Delight*, at least. Possibly even Villar and the rest of her crew, if one of the other ships would patch her through to wherever *Mongoose's* boats had landed.

Instead, the only signals she found on Erzurum's net were from the pirate ships — and those were, inexplicably, in orbit around the planet with no sign of Malcomson, the other privateers, or the crew of *Mongoose*.

In some final desperation, she tried to tune in on *Mongoose's* command channel, entering her own codes. It was a last-ditch move, for her former ship was dark and in some long orbit around Erzurum's star, so she nearly dropped the tablet with surprise when Villar's image and voice came on.

Villar's face was splotched with dirt and soot, and streaked with wet from his eyes. His voice cracked as he spoke, and he had to visibly square his shoulders and compose himself.

"Captain —" Villar cleared his throat and took a deep breath. "Captain, I'm sorry, but I don't see any other way." His throat worked convulsively. "They say — even Captain Malcomson says — that you must be dead or captured by the pirates and they won't admit it. I don't see how that could be — but ..."

He sighed.

"Captain Malcomson's agreed to drop one of *Delight's* satellites in orbit over where your boat went down. It's small enough the pirates might miss it in all the junk around the planet after the battle — and I've set it not to transmit except on *Mongoose's* command channel and only to your codes." He swallowed again. "I hope that was right — I hope you get this." Another sigh. "Or maybe not — perhaps it would be best if ...

"I don't know how much of what happened you're aware of, so I'll start from your boat's crash.

"We couldn't come for you, sir — the Dark knows we wanted to. There was nearly a mutiny against Hacking and his boat to try —" Villar's lips twitched. "— or maybe it was Boots they was after, sir. You know how some of them are. Nearly as bad as Creasy."

The slight smile broke to firm, thin lips as Villar clenched his jaw and his voice trembled. It nearly broke Alexis' heart to see her normally reserved first officer display such emotion.

"We were in a stalemate with the pirates, you see? I think we went after too many targets and spread ourselves too thin on the ground — they had more forces groundside, and more boats, than we expected. Not one of our boats could lift or they'd have three or four pirates after it. But neither could the pirates attack us — more boats than men, I suspect. From what I heard from the natives, it's more the ships in orbit and the boats that keep the Erzurum population in line. The pirates aren't from here, you see, they're ... well, sir, it's a mixed lot, as they all are, but their leader is this bloke named Ness, and he's from New London.

"Should've just stayed home if we wanted to fight our own pirates, don't you think, sir?"

A voice called from off camera and Villar turned.

"What?" More words Alexis couldn't catch, then, "Right."

Villar turned back to the camera.

"Sorry, sir, but Captain Malcomson's reminded me we have little time. We're aboard *Delight*, you see — all of us, save you and your boat crew. So, here's what happened.

"It was a standoff, but not a peaceful one, sir. The ships kept firing on one another, and there were a few hits — you know how a normal-space battle goes, I suppose. Down here they'd fire their boat's guns at our positions once in a while — from too far away to do any real damage, but there were fires from it and some casualties. I've attached the Discharged Dead lists for *Mongoose*, sir, but —" He turned to the side. "Yes, yes, time, I know, Captain Malcomson, but she's a right to know who's fallen."

He turned back.

"A few days into the stalemate, this Ness contacted us — well, he contacted the ships in orbit, see? He's commanding that frigate up there. Seems he saw things much as we were already doing — neither side could break the stalemate without suffering heavy losses. Our ships couldn't break orbit without exposing themselves to the frigate's fire, the pirate forces couldn't take ours in orbit without more damage than they'd like, neither force on the ground could really attack the other — we were too spread out and the pirates didn't want their infrastructure damaged, nor really have enough forces to take us on the ground, most being aboard the ships."

Villar closed his eyes and inhaled deeply.

"So, Ness offered a deal. He'd let us go — withdraw his frigate and other ships from the Lagrangian points as ours left orbit, if we'd leave the system."

Alexis frowned, wondering at how this Ness would ever think — and then she realized, or remembered, that she wasn't with a Naval force this time. Those ships up there weren't commanded by Queen's officers going on about the Queen's work. They were privateers — but one step, if that, removed from piracy themselves, and with only a few words above the Royal Seal making the difference.

Neither the captains nor crews of those ships were in it for any sort of honor or duty, they were after coin — and one couldn't spend one's coin if one had fallen in a hopeless fight.

"They're not Navy men, sir," Villar said, echoing her thoughts. "Captain Spensley was all for it — he'd recovered enough to take *Oriana's* quarterdeck back from Wakeling, you see, and it was him who Ness treated with the most. Pennywell was reluctant, but I think *Gallion's* crew wanted out of this mess and he had little choice but to go along." Villar wiped at his cheeks, smearing soot and tears in equal measure. "Lawson was opposed — and Kingston with her, of course."

Of course — Captain Kingston and his little *Osprey* were wont to follow Captain Lawson's *Scorpion* like a lost puppy.

Villar glanced to the side and spoke lower. "Captain Malcomson had some words, sir, both for the other captains and, ah, for you. He —"

"*Shooda split tae hacket dobber frae bawbag tae drampipe, ya daft caileag!*"

The big Scot's bellowing voice echoed from her tablet's speakers and nearly shook dust from the farmhouse's ceiling.

Kannstadt looked at her uncomprehendingly.

Villar's image glanced to the side.

"He's, ah, grabbing at his throat and ..." He cleared his own throat. "Ah, lower parts, sir, and making a sort of ... I think he means you should've gutted that bastard Spensley when you had a chance, sir."

"*Frae bawbag tae drampipe!*"

"From, ah, throat to ... ah, his *personals*, sir, if I have it right."

Alexis couldn't but agree. Perhaps there was something to the observation Nabb and Isom had made that she tended to not be sure a fallen enemy was dead before she left him behind. Would things have truly been different if she'd finished Spensley in their duel? Perhaps, or perhaps not — she couldn't be sure another of the private ship captains wouldn't have taken the lead in accepting Ness' deal. She sighed — it was one thing to kill a man in a fight, quite another to do it when he was helpless and injured — at least to no other purpose. Which, she had to admit, she'd done before with throwing a bound Daviel Coalson off to drift and die alone in *darkspace*.

"Well, yes, time, Captain Malcomson," Villar was saying, "but I did have to translate what you — very well, sir, I'll get to it!"

Villar rubbed at his forehead.

"In any case, sir, Ness would not allow us time to search for you and refused to admit his men had you captive, if they do — and, to be frank, Captain Spensley did not spend too very much effort in the asking, and him being the lead in talking to Ness, you see?"

Villar paused and clenched his eyes shut. A tear leaked out and cleared a path down the smeared soot on his cheek.

"I thought that we should stay, sir, me and the lads to look for you, but ... I couldn't think of how we'd get free of Erzurum if we did. Not after the others leave and it's all back in the pirates' hands again. Even Captain Malcomson can't stay and fight with the *Delight* alone, so I don't see how *Mongoose's* crew could do so with no ship at all. And I thought that ... what you would want of me was to get the lads free and away from ..."

Villar was silent for a long moment, more tears streaking his face.

"We found no sign of the missing spacers, sir. There were some slaves at the installations we took, but they were all from Barbary planets — no navy men, at all, from any fleet. A few from merchant-men, it seemed, but that's the risk of the Barbary. I'm sorry this was all for naught, sir, and there's little hope any expedition will be sent in return. I — I still must think you would want me to get the lads home."

Alexis' own throat tightened at the sight, knowing what the decision must cost and wishing she could have been there to ease it from him. Just one moment to tell him he was doing the right thing to get so many of Mongoose's crew safe and away from Erzurum, no matter it meant abandoning her and her boat crew.

"I'll find a way to come back for you, sir," Villar whispered. "I will — I swear it. I'll tell the Navy and ... sir, none of the other captains hold out much hope for a Naval expedition to come of this. They say this is Hanoverese space and Admiralty won't risk it, not without proof of our lads held captive there, and we found none while we were on the surface. They say the Hanoverese don't care about the Barbary, so there'll be no force from them either. I'll ... I'll turn pirate myself and take a bloody ship if I must! I'll speak to your grandfather and all Dalthus to raise the funds and put together a force — I'll — Oh, God, I don't even know if you're ... how will I tell your grandfather ... and Marie ..."

A large hand covered in red hair landed on Villar's shoulder and eased him from in front of the camera, then the image was filled with Captain Malcomson's bearded face.

"If yoo're alive, lass — an' the lad has some hope when he's nae pinin' — we'll dae what we can." The big Scot grimaced. "It'll nae be much, I think — New London will nae send ships, the Hannies dinnae care, an' we'll nae see anither boorichie ay private ships in th' Barbary after this." He shook his head. "A wonder ye managed these." Malcomson grinned. "But it was a graind plan ye hud, lass, 'til it went all tittes up an' sideways."

TWENTY-FOUR

"So," Kannstadt asked, "your ships have gone?"

Alexis nodded, staring at her tablet, body and mind numb from what she'd just heard.

Kannstadt snorted. He looked around the dining room, as though appraising things, and met Ellender's eye before turning back to her.

"You have killed us all," Ellender said. His ear and neck were red and shiny with wound sealant where the rings and explosive implant had been removed.

Alexis looked up to meet their eyes. There was anger there, as well as despair. She supposed she deserved that, but didn't understand what he meant.

"What do you mean? We've still taken this farm — we have more supplies, more men, more weapons. We can —"

"Will you teach me to suck eggs, *leutnant*?" Kannstadt said, sharing another look with Ellender. "I have commanded a ship and its men, *Kapitän* Ellender commanded a ship and men, other officers held on Erzurum commanded ships and men. Are you some savior come to tell us what we cannot see with our own eyes? Do you think when we first came here we did not think to make our escape to more than just the swamps? Do you think my men eat *schlange* because they like it?"

"I don't understand —"

"Some men escape to the swamps, yes, and we raid some farms for food, yes, but did you think this was the first one taken?" Kannstadt snorted. "Only your promise of ships, here now, made me take this risk — now, the pirates will make their reprisals. We were tolerated in the swamps and raiding the fields some — too much effort to root us out. But they will not tolerate this, as they have not in the past."

"No, they won't," Ellender said with a sigh. "As soon as they learn of this, the deaths will start. First, they'll order one in ten slaves on all the farms killed outright as a warning to the others and to those who've escaped. Then, I imagine, they'll turn their attention to this farm." He nodded to the farmer and his family. "Isikli and his family will be killed for not keeping better guard — the better to encourage the other natives to be alert." He smiled. "Some small bit of justice in that, I suppose."

"We will have to find another cave, far from here," Kannstadt said, receiving a nod from Ellender.

"How will they know that cave?" Alexis asked. "I thought it was safe."

"Until now," Kannstadt said.

"They don't need to know where it is," Ellender said. "They'll turn their ships' guns on the swamps and forest for ten kilometers around this farm in hopes of wiping out Kannstadt's band ... our band, I suppose, now. We've little choice but to come with you."

"Their ships' guns?" Alexis asked. "But that would violate the Abbentheren Accords."

That she'd once skirted the letter of those Accords herself, taking her ship deep into a planet's atmosphere to fire on the ground from a height just barely below that prohibited by the Accords, wasn't in it — she doubted the pirates would risk that with their ships, for the friction and damage had left the crew of *Belial* spending hours of every orbit repairing the hull before she took it in again.

Kannstadt and Ellender shared another look before the New London captain cocked his head at her.

"In your experience, Lieutenant Carew, are pirates *known* for following the law?"

ALEXIS FELT herself being shuffled to the back of the decision-making process as Kannstadt and Ellender discussed their next steps. She supposed it made sense — they were both senior officers and had more experience, both aboard ships and on Erzurum. Not to mention that she'd done such a fine job bolloxing up the whole thing already.

She'd rushed to Erzurum after convincing the Marchant Company "commodore," Skanes, to bring her ship here, only to see that ship, *Hind*, lost to the pirates. Then she'd convinced the private ship captains to do the same, only to see that force outnumbered, outgunned, and, in the end, outmaneuvered by this Ness and his pirate band. Then she'd convinced Kannstadt to take this farm with the promise of rescue by those ships, only to find them gone and discover that she'd doomed Kannstadt and his men, the farm's slaves, her own crew, and even the farm's owner and his family to being hunted to extinction by those pirates.

As well, if Kannstadt and Ellender have the right of it, one in ten captives on the entire planet.

The toll of death and suffering to be laid at her feet from this endeavor was staggering to think on.

And to no good end — the men held captive here will remain so, the pirates still hold Erzurum, and I've not found Delaine. Even finding that so many of our lads are here does no good if I can't get word back to New London about it.

No, she'd not found Delaine, but she did know he could be on Erzurum — and the thought that he might be one of those one-in-ten captives the pirates ordered killed in retribution for her taking this farm sent her even deeper into despair.

Or some of his men captured with him — how could he ever forgive me causing that?

So she sat in a chair to the side of the dining room while Kannstadt and Ellender made their plans. They discussed whether to move as one group or split into two, with Kannstadt and Ellender each taking one — there was no mention of Alexis, though she caught them casting looks at her from time to time. She supposed they were wishing she would leave so they might discuss her men — or, more probably, the weapons her lads still held and how to get them.

The farm had only a half-dozen rifles, all chemical-propellant and no lasers, while Alexis' crew had a weapon of some sort for every man, and some with two as there'd been enough pistols for all along with the few rifles. That did give her and her lads an advantage in any negotiations, but unless she was willing to set them to some sort of battle with Kannstadt's men — assuming they'd be willing to follow her — she still had little power. Kannstadt's numbers and both captains' greater knowledge of Erzurum left them with the upper hand.

Better, perhaps, too, to simply follow the more experienced captains so that she'd not get any more killed.

That did irk her, though, for the other captains had no hope of escaping Erzurum and returning home — they talked only of survival. Of defense and not of attack, at which she thought they still must have some chance of success. It couldn't be that their only choice was to slink off into Erzurum's swamps and eke out what existence there they might.

The pirates didn't know yet that they'd taken this farm — couldn't be certain that Alexis and her crew were still alive, even, much less met up with a large band of escaped slaves and retained modern arms.

She pulled out her tablet and began going through the data transmitted by Malcomson's satellite again. She'd not transmitted since the first which activated the satellite, but Villar and Malcomson had planned for that. Once activated, the satellite kept its own encrypted transmission active — replaying Villar's message, but also sending Alexis what information it could detect about the state of affairs in orbit and on the rest of Erzurum.

Despite Kannstadt's and Ellender's prophecies of doom, Alexis was somewhat heartened by what she saw.

The bulk of the pirate fleet, including Ness' frigate, did not appear to be in Erzurum at the moment — perhaps sailed in search of new prey to offset the cost of their battle with the private ships.

There were still seven ships in orbit around the planet, but only four of them belonged to the pirates.

The other three appeared to be merchantmen, come to trade at the pirates' market for stolen goods. They were well-armed, from what Malcomson's satellite could detect, but with no more guns than any merchant would be wise to carry in the Barbary, and Alexis would expect them to run at the first sign of trouble.

Four pirate ships were a goodly number, though, when paired with however many of their band were left on Erzurum's surface and the large number of ships' boats they had, even if they were converted merchantmen themselves and not the pirated frigate.

Alexis started reviewing what data there was, all images taken by the satellite from its lower orbit and recorded transmissions from those ships.

There was a brig with eight light guns, another with sixteen — more than she should bear, but the pirates had pierced her sides with more ports. It appeared they'd managed to put a hulk of some sort put to a bit of rights, though the damage she'd taken in a previous battle was still raw and unrepaired. The image of the fourth ship came up and Alexis' breath caught in her throat, making Kannstadt and Ellender look her way.

How?

The satellite's image of the ship was blurry, and there were many ships of similar type, but Alexis had the eye of all spacers when it came to such things. There were little things of note — the rake of a mast, the marks of dust and debris against the hull that, no matter the repair, one always remembered and could always see. The patchwork at her stern where shot had made it through to the fusion plant and shut that down.

They must have tracked her all the way, to have got aboard and repaired the damage so quickly.

And why wouldn't they, she wondered. Pirates only got their ships from taking others, and this one was far more valuable than the typical merchantmen they'd have as a prize.

Alexis set her face in stone and watched Kannstadt and Ellender warily. They'd neither care nor see the opportunity, only worry that Alexis would go haring off in the attempt of something other than skulking back into the swamps to hide and survive on Erzurum's meager offerings.

Which was exactly what she'd do, because if she could set her feet on *Mongoose's* quarterdeck once more, could wrap that beautiful ship around her with even half a crew, then bugger all Erzurum's pirates with this planet's bloody *schlange*.

TWENTY-FIVE

First found a captured Hannie
And tamed him with look.
"You come along with me," she said,
"And get off of this rock."

ALEXIS TURNED HER TABLET OFF AND ROSE. KANNSTADT AND
Ellender looked at her, Kannstadt's eyes narrowed.

"I believe you gentlemen have things well in hand, sirs," she said,
letting her gaze and head hang a bit. "I'll just see to my crew, if you
don't mind."

"Your crew, yes," Ellender said. "We should speak about that."

Here it comes — the demand for Mongoose's *weapons.*

"Of course, Captain Ellender, when you're ready, and you and
Captain Kannstadt have finished these more pressing matters, I'll be
available at your convenience."

She ducked out of the dining room quickly and then out the
farmhouse door before either captain could say another word.

Outside, the slaves from the farmstead milled around near the
doorway, waiting their turn to go upstairs where Kannstadt's man

was removing the explosives from their necks and the devices from their ears — such as that removal was, with the crude equipment available to them. It was better, though, than the rougher and more dangerous methods performed by Kannstadt's men in the swamps. At least here they had some medical treatment available and the risk of infection was less.

Kannstadt's men had built several fires along the dikes from the farm's outbuildings and slave barracks, and got the wood to catch even in Erzurum's ever-present drizzle. The warmth gave a welcome respite from the chill air and men crowded around each blaze holding out their hands or presenting their backsides to be warmed in turn. The farm's buildings would have sheltered them from the rains, but none of those who'd spent time on Erzurum would enter the farm's slave barracks willingly — better to be out and wet than in that place and dry.

There were several cookpots going, as well, and, Alexis noted, an entire absence of geese.

Her lads were all around one fire — a bit crowded, but they made a lane for Alexis as she approached.

The mood around the fire was low, but not despondent, and she heard more than one murmur of, "Captain's here, now we'll know what's what," or the like.

That surprised her. Word of their situation had clearly got out and amongst the men, so they must realize that they'd been abandoned on Erzurum and it was all her fault. She'd led them into this mess and could only hope they'd give her one last chance to get them out.

Waiting, as Kannstadt and Ellender seemed content to do, simply wasn't an option. Even with the private ships bearing word of Ness and his pirate band back to Enclave or elsewhere, what would be done about it? It was only word of the captive fleet members that would rouse New London or Hanover to take action, and no one aboard the private ships had any evidence the captives were really here — only Alexis' band had actually seen them. The rest had the word of one Barbary merchant captain that had brought them to Erzurum in the first place.

As well, they'd likely take that word through Enclave and Wheeley's casino, and who knew what that man might do? He was in league with the pirates and slavers, with such utter control over Enclave's New London compound, that it was almost certain he had measures in place to intercept and stop any message back to Admiralty.

No, they were on their own, with little hope of rescue from anyone else.

Dockett handed her a bowl of stew from the cookpot and the scent of cooked goose struck her — along with what she assumed was native *susomun* and more than a bit of cattail root to make up the balance. Either the *susomun* or cattail was less appealing than the goose — in fact, it reminded her of the geese when they were alive, or at least the ground under them.

All the men crowded around her as she sat to eat, including the outermost who turned toward the fire.

"Eyes out," Dockett hissed. "Surrounded by Hannies and you lot turn your backs?"

"Losin' track o' who we're fightin'," someone muttered back.

"The captain'll see to keeping that straight," Dockett said. "You just watch our backs."

"Dint sign up for this," another muttered.

Dockett rose and peered into the shadows for the speaker. "You signed up, though, and this is what we've got — trust the captain and —"

"And what?" another voice asked. "No ship, no captain, is there?"

"Why, you —"

"Mister Dockett," Alexis said quietly. "Enough."

"Sir, I —"

"Enough, Mister Dockett, they've a right to question what I've got them into."

There were more murmurs at that, but Dockett kept quiet and sat down. Alexis handed him her bowl — only a few bites eaten, not nearly enough to fill her — and stared at the fire for a moment. She needed these men, but would they follow her still?

"You've heard some rumors, I'm sure, so here's the truth of it. If you heard the other private ships we came with are sailed off and left us — that's true." She held up her palm to still their words, but kept her eyes on the fire. "They thought us likely dead, I suppose. And if you heard the pirates are back in orbit, well, that's true as well. And that they've a history of reprisals against escaped slaves to make the Hanoverese themselves blush?" She nodded. "True enough."

The murmurs grew, so Alexis lowered her voice, forcing those who wished to listen to silence their fellows and draw closer to hear.

"And if you've heard, or suspected, that there's little help coming? Well, that's certainly true as well. The one thing to have brought help would be word of the fleet spacers, and the private ships left with no evidence of that."

"So, we're bloody dead," someone muttered.

"You are if you give up," Alexis said. "You can join Captain Kannstadt or Captain Ellender and chew their *schlange* for your next dinner instead of this fine goose." She paused for the few, strained laughs that brought. "They plan to run off back to the swamps and hide for as long as they can."

She caught Nabb's eye across the fire and her coxswain almost grinned. He glanced around at the others then loudly asked, "What else're we to do, sir? If thing're so dire as you say?"

"Fight," Alexis said. "Take the fight to these bloody pirates and get ourselves, and these others free. Most of you were Navy lads, before your ships paid off and left you loose-ends, aye? Well, you know a fight and any one of you's the better of a dozen pirates, I say."

"Fight with what? There's only the few of us —"

"Hush," someone else said. "Hear her out or go swallow some *schlange*."

"Aye, we're few," Alexis said as the few chuckles died, "but is any man here worth less than a dozen pirates like I said?" No one seemed willing to admit that. "And there's Kannstadt's men, and Ellender's, and thousands more on this miserable world."

"You said they was runnin'."

Alexis nodded and heaved a heavy sigh. "They've forgotten, lads, what it's like to be a crew. Had it beat out of them by days trapped in the Dark, by the pirates, and by this world. Had their ears notched and their will broken until they just don't remember. It might be you, a proper crew, could help them find that again. Put some steel in their spines and some pepper up their arses, eh?"

There were outright laughs at that, but then someone asked. "How're we to get away, though? It's one thing to take a farm or some settlement, but we've no way off this ball of mud."

"With a ship, lads," Alexis said. "The pirates can't keep their whole fleet in orbit — have to go off raiding, don't they? Take most of their fleet and nearly all their men, but there're always a few left behind to hold this world from the poor natives. A few ships up there right now, and those of you who've heard of *Hermione* know it'll not be the first time I've taken one from a grounded start."

Alexis felt a bit of melancholy at so using the tales of *Hermione* and her escape from Giron with that crew, but if she was to have any hope of getting her lads home this time then they needed the confidence of hearing that she'd done it before and would do it for them. They needed the tales as they'd grown through the Fleet's rumor mill to make them believe. They needed the myth that had grown around that, not the truth of what had been a desperate midshipman, merely trying to get her too few lads home and herself along with them.

I pray to the dark I'm not reduced to invoking the Creature and Creasy's nonsense, but I will if I must.

"What ship? Some broken down —"

"With *Mongoose*, lads," she said, feeling the time was right to tell them that, "your very home. She's in orbit right now, just above your heads." Alexis grinned as half the crew looked up as though they could see the ship so far away and through the clouds. "The bloody pirates took our home, patched her up, and put her to guarding us, but they don't know her lads, not like we do. They got a lucky shot up her skirts that once, is all, but she's set to rights now and we know better. Put that ship around us and we'll never bare her knickers like that again, will we?"

The mutters that such a thing would never be allowed again heartened her.

"Not all of us was Navy."

Alexis looked through the fire to meet eyes of the spacer, Davies, who'd said that. One of the women who'd come aboard *Mongoose*, and the only one to crash with Alexis. This must be hard on her, come from a merchantman as she had. Alexis had known nothing but the dangers of the Navy since she went a'space, but Davies had had relatively safe berths, as some of the others who'd come from merchants to *Mongoose* had. Add to that the tales circulating about how the pirates would treat her if she were caught and, well, if there was anyone who should run off into the swamps and hide it was Davies.

"No, but you wanted to honor what the Navy'd done for you, didn't you say?"

"I thought —"

"All you who came from merchantmen, did a Navy ship ever save your hides? Take shot from a pirate to keep your course clear? No rubbish about the Revenue Service, now, you know what I mean." She tried to single out those in the crowd who she remembered came from such ships, then returned her eyes to Davies. "Those lads stood up for you more than once, I'll wager, and they'd do it again if they weren't so beat down by this world and what's happened to them here. Will you stand and remind them who they are?"

TWENTY-SIX

Alexis picked up her bowl of stew, cold now, despite being set near the fire, and left the crew to think or mutter amongst themselves as they would. She'd had her say and suspected those who wanted no part of it would drift away overnight. She thought of collecting their weapons, but sighed.

Let them go armed, at least. We have enough for every man who stays.

She was nearly finished with the stew when one of the farm's former slaves approached. He was still clad only in a scaled loincloth, as there were few other supplies on the farm. Even the farmer himself only had a handful of clothes, and most of those were as worn as the ragged, torn jumpsuits and liners Alexis and her lads still clung to.

"Lieutenant Carew?"

Alexis nodded.

"I'm Lieutenant Culliver, Captain Ellender would like a word with you."

"Of course." Alexis stood, she'd been expecting this.

She followed Culliver back to the farmhouse where Ellender and

Kannstadt still held the dining room. Isikli's family and hired hands were no longer there and she shot Kannstadt a narrow look.

"They are upstairs," Kannstadt said, reading her question, "and unharmed." He glanced toward a corner, where Deckard was seemingly engaged in an examination of the two walls meeting. "I must think upon some things."

"For now, they're unharmed," Ellender said. "We've yet to decide what to do with them, and damned if I'll let the treatment I've received here go unpunished. Sit down, Carew."

Alexis did and Ellender rose at the same time. He nodded to Culliver who got Alexis a glass of something from Isikli's cabinets — Ellender and Kannstadt had glasses as well. It was a foul-smelling brew, but she wet her lips with it.

"This is a proper mess you've left us in, Carew," Ellender said.

"With respect, sir, I'd think you and your men here are in a somewhat better position. At least you're free."

"Free to run off into Erzurum's forsaken swamps? Free to be hunted down by the pirates? This was a sorry place, but at least I kept my men alive!"

"As you say, sir." Alexis had been thinking about this meeting and rather suspected how it would play out — still, she must try. "I believe, though, that there's still a way for us to pull ourselves out of this. *Mongoose*, my ship, is still in orbit, you see."

"I thought you said you had to abandon your ship," Kannstadt said.

"We did. The fusion plant was struck through some previous damage to her stern and it shut down. With the shot we were taking, and being unable to fire back or maneuver, she'd have remained a target if we stayed aboard. The pirates, though, must have tracked her and brought her back after some repairs. She's one of only four ships they have in orbit at this time — the gunboats, I assume, are off in *darkspace* patrolling amongst the shoals as they do."

"Only four," Ellender said, scoffing, but Kannstadt looked thoughtful.

"She's the most powerful of the ships the pirates left behind — we destroyed both the hulk of a frigate they had in orbit and the Marchant ship, *Hind*, on our initial attack," Alexis went on. "If we were to take *Mongoose*, she'd have no trouble with the others in orbit — being there herself — and she has a decent mapping of the shoals in her systems from our attempts to get in. Getting *out* would be much easier."

Ellender snorted. "Ah, yes, we shall, naked and with small arms, take a ship in orbit, shall we?"

"*Mongoose's* systems are … a bit different than normal, sir," Alexis said. "She was outfitted by a … well, he's a bloody rogue and smuggler and probably a pirate himself at times, and he gave me all manner of codes before we sailed — some so bizarre I'd thought them useless. Now, though, if we can get a boat close I believe there's a signal which will get us back aboard, no matter the pirates."

"'Get close' — to the ship in orbit, while we are …" Ellender waved a hand at the rough farmhouse. "Here."

"We could take a boat, sir, and —"

"And then *what*, lieutenant? A slim chance for this motley group to reach a place of any real size without being pounded into the mud by those orbiting ships. A slimmer chance to take a boat from the pirates — *without*, I imagine, alerting those in orbit, as that would almost have to be part of any plan, yes? Slimmer still to approach your ship and get aboard. More slim yet for you to fight your ship against those other pirates in orbit — and then *what*? For as likely as your plan is to succeed, one might as well wish that the Queen herself shall appear from *darkspace* with a combined bloody fleet!" Ellender shook his head.

"Better than doing nothing!" Alexis said. "And I do have a plan for —"

"I've heard enough of your plans, now you'll listen to what we're going to *do*. Captain Kannstadt and I have been discussing this, as well as the division of resources."

Alexis set her jaw. She'd expected this — it was inevitable, really.

The Navy seemed to be divided between officers who'd listen to reason and see the right of it, and those whose thoughts were so narrow it was a wonder they could see at all. More of the latter, in her experience, and she longed for a superior officer who thought more of the larger picture than he did of his own skin. Unfortunately, she'd not found that in Ellender, but it was none the less frustrating that her lads out there, miserable and scared in the rain, would listen to her after she'd brought them to these ends, while this ... this puffed up, sorry excuse for a captain would not even give her that courtesy after she'd freed him from captivity.

She shot a look at Kannstadt, who, despite their earlier conflict, she thought might support her. He looked from her, then to Deckard in the corner and his eyes did not return.

"Of course, sir," Alexis said, "anything useful or portable must be taken from the farm when you leave for the swamps." She phrased it carefully, as she had no intention of following him. She hoped she might convince Kannstadt, at least, to join her in an attempt to escape, but she saw no outcome of following Ellender that would get her lads home — nor to any better end than years of being eaten away at by Erzurum's swamps.

"The farm's, yes, and the weapons," Ellender said.

Alexis nodded. Here it was, then. "Yes, the farm's weapons."

Ellender narrowed his eyes. "*All* the weapons, Carew, including those currently held by your crew. I'll want to see those in the hands of men I know can handle them."

Kannstadt cleared his throat, not taking his eyes from Deckard.

"Men *we* know can handle them — do excuse me, Captain Kannstadt."

Alexis took a deep breath. "No, sir."

"I beg your pardon, lieutenant?"

"You have it, sir, but there's no need, I assure you." That was probably a bit much, but Ellender was annoying her and it was rather satisfying to see his eyes widen. "Still, my lads won't be giving up

THE QUEEN'S PARDON 173

their arms, sir. Those are *Mongoose's* weapons and her crew, as their captain I'm bound to —"

"*Lieutenant* Carew, may I remind you that I am your superior?"

Alexis noted that Kannstadt was now glancing back and forth between her and Ellender with barely suppressed mirth. She had a feeling the New London officer had not endeared himself to the Hanoverese in their short acquaintance. Either that or he was simply delighted to see two of his former enemies fight amongst themselves.

"In a sort of Naval rank way, sir, I suppose you are. However —"

"*What did you say?*"

Alexis frowned. What had she — oh, yes, she supposed one could take that an entirely different way. She hadn't really meant it that way, but now Ellender was well and truly angered.

"What I meant, sir, is that I'm not here with the Royal Navy. I'm on half-pay and making my own way. In fact, sir, as captain of a private ship, and outside of New London space, I don't believe I'm bound by Naval—"

"You've lost your ship, Carew!"

"Well ... so did you, sir, if that's a thing we must note, so we're on rather equal footing there, don't you think?"

That she had meant, and if it sent the bloody fool into an apoplectic fit, then so be it. She was tired, utterly done, with men like Ellender assuming her obedience. It would be one thing if she were encountering him as a Naval officer — *that* was a matter of duty. But here, on Erzurum, she need answer to no one but herself and for Ellender to assume she must set her teeth on edge.

Still, it was a dire shot to send across a captain's bow, even if he'd done the same to her.

Kannstadt nearly laughed out loud, and it must be all the more amusing to him, being Hanoverese, to see two who were only recently his enemies squabbling so. He rose, still chuckling, and made his way to the corner where Deckard sat.

Ellender's jaw clenched so tight Alexis fancied she could hear his teeth cracking from the strain.

"You will turn over your weapons to Lieutenant Culliver, *Lieutenant* Carew, so he may see to their proper distribution."

"It is *Captain* Carew at the moment, Captain Ellender, and I will do no such thing." She glanced at Kannstadt to see where he stood on the question of those weapons, despite his amusement at her sparring with Ellender, but couldn't read what he thought. "You may try to take them, of course, but my men will resist and that will cause unnecessary hurt to both our forces."

"This is mutiny!"

"Captain Ellender, I am not currently under Admiralty orders nor under your command."

"I'll see you face a Court, Carew — I'll see you hang!"

Alexis sighed.

Well, it wouldn't be the first time.

"I suppose you might try, Captain Ellender," Alexis said, "but if you stay on Erzurum to rot away, I'm not at all certain I should have any worry about it."

While Ellender sputtered, Kannstadt laughed out loud.

"I don't see how her insubordination is at all funny, Captain Kannstadt," Ellender said, glaring at the Hanoverese.

"No, you do not," Kannstadt said. He laughed again and shook his head, then patted Deckard's arm and stood. "Do you know the story of God and the flood, Captain Ellender?"

"What? That Noah chap? What does that have to do with anything — though this bloody planet does bring arks to mind."

"No," Kannstadt said, "it is a later story, *hein?* The rains come again, you see, and the rivers begin to rise. There is an old man who sits at the front of his house and does nothing while all his neighbors prepare. Finally, one of these neighbors takes a farm truck to the man's home and calls out to him.

"'The waters are rising, old man,' the neighbor says, 'and we are all moving to town where it is drier — come! I will drive you!'

"The old man shakes his head and says, 'No. I will stay here. I have been a faithful man and God has promised He will not send the flood again, so I will put my faith in Him to keep me safe.'

"So, the neighbor drives away and still the waters rise. The old man does work to put sandbags at his door, but the water comes over them and he must flee to upstairs. Then, again, a neighbor comes, this time in a boat and calls out to him where he sits at his window.

"'Old man! The waters are rising and there is no end in sight. Come into my boat and I will take you to town where it is dry!'

"Again, the old man shakes his head and says, 'No. I will not leave my home. I have been a good man all my life and God will see me safe through this trial!'

"The man with the boat shrugs and goes away, and still the waters rise until the old man's house is nearly covered. He flees up to his roof and huddles there in the rain with a sodden blanket about his shoulders. Then a neighbor comes *again*, this time in an aircar, and hovers over the roof.

"'Old man!' the neighbor shouts. 'The water is at your feet and there is nowhere left to flee. Get into my aircar and come to safety!'

"But once more, the old man says, 'No! I have my faith and God will not let me be harmed!'

"So, the neighbor flies away, and the waters rise to cover the old man's roof, and the old man drowns."

Kannstadt shrugged.

"The old man finds himself at Heaven's gate and rushes past, angry as only an old man full of his own surety can be. He bursts into God's throne room, casting the heavy doors aside as though they weigh nothing, such is the force of his anger, and he yells at God Himself,

"'My Lord! Why did you forsake me? I was a good and faithful man, but you left me to die!'

"But God frowns for a moment, His mighty brow furrows, and He asks,

"'What do you mean, old man? I sent you a truck, a boat, and an aircar.'"

Kannstadt laughed again.

"We have been on Erzurum many months, *Kapitän* Ellender, and yet neither of our fleets have come to rescue us. I fear we may demand the waters stop and ignore the way to safety, *hein?* We are on the roof of our house with nowhere else to go." He glanced down at Deckard. "And for some, a return to the swamps is much the same as any fate we may meet in this attempt."

He turned to Alexis.

"I will get into your aircar a second time, *Leutnant* Carew, only this time please do not crash it."

TWENTY-SEVEN

The pirates came to stop her.
The pirates came to see.
But Little Bloody Bit, the girl,
Did make them bend the knee.

ALEXIS, KANNSTADT, AND ELLENDER ARGUED ABOUT THE
details of the plan for some time — well, Alexis and Ellender argued
while Kannstadt sat beside Deckard looked back and forth between
them as though watching a most amusing tennis match. Faced with
the prospect of losing Kannstadt's support, men, and knowledge of
the swamps, Ellender had come about to a new tack, now overriding
Alexis' thin plans for an escape and retaking of *Mongoose* with his
own much more elaborate thoughts.

"In the end, *Kapitän* Ellender," Kannstadt said, seeming to agree
with Alexis on one last point, at least, "surprise is our best asset."

"We need more men," Ellender protested.

"Certainly," Alexis agreed, "but not right away. Captain
Kannstadt has sent runners to other nearby groups of escaped slaves
and they will, hopefully, make their way here, but that may take

several days, perhaps a week or more, to accomplish. In the meantime, every day here is another where some neighbor of the Isiklis
may discover what's happened."

"Then we should take those neighboring farms now," Ellender
said, "and add the enslaved crews there to our own forces."

"We shall, Captain Ellender," Alexis said, "but each of those
battles will be yet another chance for us to be discovered, and brings
us closer to Téneto, which we do not have the forces to take outright."

Kannstadt nodded. "If the pirates discover us, *Kapitän* Ellender,
before we have retaken *Kapitän* Carew's ship, and the other ships in
orbit, then all is lost."

"If *Lieutenant* Carew's ship is so bloody important — and I
suppose I must agree it is — then we must have more men to take it!
And more than a single boat to carry them! Not rely on this bloody,
dishonorable trickery from some man she's as much as admitted is a
pirate himself!"

"One boat," Alexis said firmly. She was tired — weary in both
body and mind after the trek through the swamp, the battle for the
farm, and, now, the interminable discussion with Ellender, who
seemed to have no tactical sense other than to acquire and apply overwhelming force. The very thought of stealth and guile being useful
seemed to bewilder him — or, perhaps, anger him, as the current plan
did. The man's insistence on calling her lieutenant, instead of
captain, which, even were *Mongoose* a Royal Navy ship, she'd be
entitled to as having command, was yet one more barb under her
skin. "We've been round and round about how to acquire more than
one, Captain Ellender, and there's simply no way that doesn't carry
too much risk of tipping our hand. More than that, what are we to do
with the dozen boats you wish us to acquire? Do you not think those
ships' crews will find it odd that so many boats lift from Erzurum and
make for orbit?" She grasped her legs to keep her hands still instead
of waving them about as she wished. "One boat might make an
excuse to approach — a dozen, never."

"My men and I will be on the boat, then," Ellender said, renewing an old demand.

"No, sir, they will not," Alexis said.

"Damn you, Carew, I'm your —"

"We've been over that, sir — and I grant you that title as a courtesy only. The Navy saw fit to set me on my own bottom, and that's where we are for the moment." Alexis squared her shoulders, drawing herself up in her chair — which, she supposed, only served to emphasize her short stature, given where the farm's dining table still fell on her. Standing would do no better, though, for she'd find herself barely above the two seated men. There were times she thought she might have Nabb carry a little folding platform about with them for when she wanted to address a crowd or speak to a man's face instead of his elbow. "*Mongoose* is my ship, sir, and I'll have no man aboard during this who's not sworn to my command. Moreover, my men know her well and yours do not. What space is left will be filled by Captain Kannstadt's men, as he's agreed to put them under my command for this."

She shared a look with Kannstadt, who nodded. It was very odd to find herself allied with the Hanoverese, who'd readily agreed to instruct his men who'd be filling out Alexis' in the boat they hoped to capture that they were under Alexis' command for the duration. Odder still that she now trusted the Hanoverese captain's word on that more than Ellender's and hoped the New Londoner would not reverse himself and offer those men, for she couldn't bring herself to trust his word.

Ellender ground his jaw together and glared at Alexis, who met his gaze blandly.

"Very well," he said finally. "My men and I will be in the second trip, then."

Alexis looked to Kannstadt. Whoever made the second trip would be taking one of the other pirate vessels in orbit. Kannstadt shrugged, despite what Alexis was certain was a desire to put a ship around him again with no delay, after his months in Erzurum's muck and slave pits.

"As you wish," Kannstadt said. "You will need some of my men to fill your crew, as *Kapitän* Carew will have. They will be sworn to obey your orders, I assure you." Kannstadt frowned. "You do speak some German, *hein?*"

Alexis fought the grin that sprang to her face as Ellender realized he couldn't very well fight his captured ship if half or more of the crew couldn't understand him, and he had no tablet to translate as Alexis did, nor even the poor command of the language she had. There were the tablets of Isikli and his family, but they weren't even in German and there didn't seem to be a setting to change the language.

"Bloody foreigners," Ellender muttered.

ALEXIS, Nabb, and Dockett stood on one of the farm's dikes, hands bound behind them, though not securely. She kept her hands still, not fiddling with the rough ropes to ensure they'd fall away quickly, for fear they'd do so before she wished.

Isikli stood beside her, one of the farm's rifles — unloaded — over his shoulder and grasping her upper arm.

"I be good," Isikli said to her. Very nearly the only English he'd admit to knowing, learned from the pirates visiting his farm. His fearful, obsequious tone set Alexis' stomach to churning.

"Sons be good," he said, nodding to his two sons holding Nabb's and Dockett's arms as well.

"It will be all right, sir," Alexis said, hoping to reassure him.

Isikli didn't seem to understand — or if he did, he said nothing more. He only looked back to his farmhouse, where Alexis' man, Warth, dressed as one of Isikli's farmhands, held the cupola atop the roof with his rifle trained on them. Then Isikli looked forward to the wide part of the dike where the pirate boat would land, carefully keeping his eyes away from the water-filled fields to either side.

"I be good. Sons be good," the farmer repeated.

Alexis felt sorry for the farmer, slave-owner though he might be. Ellender couldn't say that he and the others had been particularly ill-treated by Isikli or his family — roughly, perhaps, but no more than they should expect as prisoners, he admitted under Alexis' questioning. Not that she forgave him and the other inhabitants of Erzurum for their slave-keeping, only that she now knew it was a way of life forced on them by the pirate band.

For Isikli now, he was between the fire and the pan.

Alexis only trusted him to do his part because she believed the pirates would kill all of the farm's inhabitants for allowing it to be taken by the slaves. The man had no choice but to cooperate in the hopes that Alexis' crew and the escaped slaves would prevail and be more merciful — that Alexis would be true to her word and take him and his family with her back to Dalthus.

That the rest of the farmer's family was still in the house under the guard of Kannstadt and his men, while Warth had made it clear his rifle would be trained on Isikli's head the entire time, only made the farmer more cooperative.

He'd certainly said nothing untoward when contacting the pirates. Alexis, Kannstadt, and Ellender had stayed near the farm's comms unit, out of sight, and Alexis' tablet quietly translating, as Isikli called the pirates in Téneto and informed them that he'd captured a small band of slaves raiding his fields. He would normally keep such a valuable find to work his own fields, but these slaves were different, he told the pirates. They were clearly new to Erzurum and wore, though much worn by the rains and mud, ships' jumpsuits and good boots, which were always taken from new slaves by the pirates, in Isikli's experience.

Was this of interest to the pirates?

Oh, yes, the pirates were interested and would come to pick up Isikli's captives, but it surprised Alexis that they first asked if one of the captured slaves might be a particular man of, perhaps, fifty years with dark hair and a square jaw?

The pirates seemed disappointed when Isikli told them, no, it is only an older man, squat and with a fat face — Dockett bristled at that — and a young man and girl.

Now they were just waiting for the pirate's boat to arrive and land.

Rain settled on Alexis' face and hair, running down her neck in an annoying rivulet she couldn't wipe away with her ostensibly bound hands. She was almost to the point where she thought she might ask Isikli to do it when the pirate boat appeared, circling down out of the overcast.

Then, behind the first, came a second, and Alexis felt a chill from more than just the rains.

Their plan was for one boat, not two.

THE FIRST PIRATE boat came lower and circled the farm, perhaps examining the swampy forest surrounding it. The second stayed higher, keeping watch. It was a caution Alexis wouldn't often attribute to pirates and it made her heart sink. If that second boat stayed in the sky above the farm, then they had no chance at all — even if they took the one that landed, the second would have them at its mercy.

Isikli turned her to face him and she saw real fear in his eyes.

He knew the plan and could tell the implications of that second boat staying aloft as well as she.

"I'm sorry," Alexis said.

Whatever happened to her and her lads now, killed or simply taken by the pirates and sold as workers onto some other farm, Isikli and his family were almost certainly doomed.

The farmer's eyes shot from her face to the circling boat, then to the higher one. He took a deep breath.

"Trust?" he asked. He touched his chest. "*Güvenmek? Vertrauen?* Trust?"

Alexis stared into the farmer's eyes for a moment, then glanced at the sky. Both boats were behind her and couldn't see her face. So much of her time on Erzurum did seem to have come down to that. Trust Kannstadt, despite his being Hanoverese and his despicable attempt to coerce Isikli through the man's wife and daughters? Trust Ellender — her countryman and from the same service? Trust Isikli — a poor man trying to get by as best he might, or slaveholding ally to pirates?

She made a decision. Isikli would do as he saw best for his family, and, for the moment, she thought that course was with her.

"*Warth, stand down!*" she yelled. "*Let him do as he will!*" She met Isikli's eyes again. "Yes, *ja.* Trust."

The farmer nodded and rattled off a string of instructions. One of his sons, the one holding Dockett, said something, perhaps to argue, but Isikli cut him off. The son bowed his head and released Dockett, handing his rifle to Isikli, and dashed toward the farmhouse.

"Trust," Isikli said. "Please?"

"We're all doomed if I don't, Mister Isikli," Alexis said.

"What's he up to, sir?" Dockett said.

"I've no idea," she admitted. "I can only hope he sees the situation as clearly as we do and knows the pirates well enough to have some plan."

Isikli's plan became clear enough in a moment as his son came back out of the farmhouse, along with Isikli's wife, daughters, and the son's wife. The women moved hesitantly at first, but Isikli shouted something to them, waving his hands, and they were soon moving along the dike, looking up at the pirate boats, smiling, and waving.

The circling boat seemed to shiver in the air, then turned in toward the dike, while the higher boat swooped down behind it.

"Well, that's clear enough, then," Dockett muttered.

Alexis nodded. She shouldn't be surprised that the Erzurum farmers and their families might sell more than crops to the pirates.

She could tell from the set of Isikli's jaw as he returned that it wasn't something his family normally engaged in, but it must be frequent enough at other farms that the pirates recognized the waving women as some sign of their availability.

There was barely enough room on the wider portion of the dike for both boats to set down. The second had its aft third hanging over a field, so couldn't lower its rear ramp. Not that either bothered. They both lowered fore ramps on the starboard side, and only three men exited each.

The three from the second boat stayed around the ramp, while the first, the nearer one to Alexis and her group, left one man at the ramp while two approached.

Isikli grasped Alexis' arm again and stepped forward to meet them, but the lead pirate waved him off.

"Yeah, yeah, Old Blackbourne'll get to you in a minute," he said, then, "*Inno minuteo*, you wog bastard." He nodded toward the farm's women who'd stopped midway down the dike when the boats landed. "Your whores'll get their coin too, but first —" He approached Dockett. "You're off that ship what crashed a boat, eh? Where's your captain? He weren't with those who left, we searched every boat in orbit a'fore they left."

Dockett frowned and Alexis answered for him.

"If you're searching for *Mongoose's* captain, you've found her."

"*Mongoose*, Old Blackbourne's wrinkled arse," the pirate said, turning to her. "That's the bloody *Elizabeth*, so now where's that sneaky bastard Avrel Dansby?"

TWENTY-EIGHT

"I don't know what you're talking about," Alexis said. "*Mongoose* is mine."

"That's shite," the pirate said. He stepped close to Alexis, his chest in her face and forcing her to look up at him. "Old Blackbourne served on *Elizabeth* near three years under that black-hearted bastard — there's no way in the Dark Dansby'd let another command her in the Barbary, not knowing we was still here. Now, Captain Ness, he thinks different — thinks the old bastard's got himself another, bigger ship out there somewhere. That'd be why he's off shadowing them flouncy privateers before taking more prizes. But Old Blackbourne? Well he says to hisself, he says, 'Tristian Blackbourne, that bastard Dansby's not a man to hang back, so if he weren't on the hulk of *Elizabeth* and he weren't on the boats that come up then he must be on the boat that crashed.' Y'wouldn't wish to call old Tristian Blackbourne a liar, now would you, girl?"

The pirate's, Blackbourne's she presumed, breath was rank as he leaned closer to Alexis to ask that last and she drew back from him.

Whatever is the matter with pirates and brushing their bloody teeth?

Blackbourne straightened to look down on her from his full height.

"Are y'not likin' Old Blackbourne, now?" He turned his head over his shoulder to call to his fellows. "She's not likin' Old Blackbourne, lads! Not like them farmgirls just waiting for your coin!" He gave a nod toward the farmer's wife and daughters still midway between the farmhouse and the boats, then returned his attention to Alexis.

"Oh, you'll like Old Blackbourne soon enough, lass," he said, grasping himself with one hand and thrusting his hips at her. "An' you'll whisper all o' that Dark-hearted Dansby's secrets to him, you will." His grin widened. "In a'tween the screams, an you'll —"

"Now," Alexis said.

"What?" Blackbourne asked. "No, not *now*, Old Blackbourne prefers a bit o' privacy an' —"

Alexis stepped back from him, let the ropes fall from her hands, and drew her flechette pistol from its pocket at the back of her vacsuit liner.

"What're y'pointin' at, girl?" Blackbourne asked, looking down.

I really should purchase a larger pistol, so a man will understand when I'm about to shoot him instead of thinking I'm bloody pointing.

Nabb and Dockett dropped their own bonds as well, pulling hidden pistols and dodging to the side.

Blackbourne started to move as they did, reacting more to the men than to Alexis, but before he could so much as twitch his hand, she fired. Not for his head or body, for he seemed to be the pirate's leader and she wanted that one alive.

Alexis shot Blackbourne in the hand, pinning it with needle-sharp flechettes to what it grasped.

THAT WAS THE SIGNAL.

Or, at least, a sufficient one.

The sharp *crack* of ionizing air split Blackbourne's screams as Warth fired from the farmhouse's cupola. The former poacher's shot took one of the pirates at the second boat's ramp in the eye, dropping him to the ground.

Dockett and Nabb sprinted for the near boat, firing as they went.

Isikli and his son dove off the dike, landing in their muddy fields in twin sprays of dark water, followed closely by his other son and the women farther down the dike. Alexis didn't blame them, they were unarmed and no further use in this fight.

Kannstadt's and Ellender's men, those not with Alexis' and armed with the extra weapons from *Mongoose's* boat, streamed out of the farmhouse. They'd be of little use, without guns and starting far away from the boats, but would at least feel part of the action and provide a bit of a distraction to the pirates.

The rest of Alexis' men were closer, heads and faces covered in Erzurum's thick mud, and ducked down amongst the cattail reeds of the farm's fields all along the dikes.

They emerged now and raised their own weapons — the guns' workings were made for keeping the vacuum of *darkspace* out, so just as effective with Erzurum's water and mud. Those with rifles fired immediately while those with pistols dashed for the boats — dashed as well as one could through the knee-deep muck, until they reached the dikes and could run faster.

The pirates were quite taken by surprise. They were armed, but not prepared, perhaps lulled into a further sense of security by the unexpected offer of the farm's women. Of the six pirates who'd exited the boats, four had rifles of one sort or another — but those were kept slung over their shoulders and not readied. The rest had pistols at their hips, but only those at the farther boat were able to draw.

Those at the closer boat fell to shots either from her lads in the fields or Dockett and Nabb, who raced past the bodies and up the boat's ramp.

Warth fired again from the cupola, this time taking a pirate at the second boat in the leg.

Alexis stayed with Blackbourne, reaching down to pull the man's own pistol, while keeping her own trained on him in warning.

"Tell your men to stand down!" Alexis ordered.

The pirate leader rolled on the ground, clutching himself with both hands now, and crying out.

"Oh, sweet Dark, y've done for Old Blackbourne!"

"Quit your whinging, man, and surrender," Alexis said.

"Oh, it burns!"

"Shut up." Damn him, but the pirate leader would be no use. She glanced away for a moment, trying to keep track of the fight and Blackbourne at the same time. She needed the pirate leader alive, at least for a time, for her full plan to work, but that meant guarding him and not engaging the others. It galled her to stand still while her lads ran into the fight.

Nabb and Dockett were in the nearer boat, while several others of her crew dashed up the ramp. They'd likely have that one well in hand, if the pirates hadn't left many men aboard — and she didn't think they would. Possibly only the pilot, or not even that.

The second boat, though, was another matter.

The two pirates at the ramp, one favoring his leg where Warth shot him, were ducked behind the ramp's struts, thin cover as they were, and firing at her lads, who'd ducked to the edges of the dike for cover and were firing back. That no more than fifteen meters separated the groups, while so many lasers and projectiles struck the boat's hull and the dirt and water of the fields without striking any man told Alexis that she should work her lads more on their small guns. The boarding actions they were used to were more of a jam-the-barrel-in-a-man's-belly-and-pull sort of thing than needing any particular skill at aiming — and that was if they didn't just rely on their heavy cutlasses to lop through the enemy's vacsuit.

Warth fired again, showing his worth, and the uninjured pirate at the ramp fell limp, a bit of his skull and hair disappearing in a haze of vapor.

"Oh, lord, it hurts!" Blackbourne moaned.

Alexis was tempted to shoot the pirate again to make him shut up.

"*Aargh!* It burns! Put it out, y'Dark-tainted witch! What'd y'do t'Old Blackbourne?"

"What did you call me?"

"*Witch!* Y'bloody, Dark-lovin' *witch!* Shootin' fire from yer finger at poor Old Blackbourne's tackle!"

Alexis was caught between amusement at Blackbourne's plight — she'd not shot him that much, after all, only a dozen or so flechettes, certainly — and irritation that she'd traveled all the way to the Barbary and shot a pirate in his "tackle," only to find the best he could call her was only one letter removed from what she otherwise heard so often.

"Is it a lack of creativity or —" she started to ask, then, "Never mind. Shut up or I'll burn the bloody thing right off."

"No, don't take Old Blackbourne's johnson from 'im, witch-woman!"

The one pirate remaining at the second boat's ramp was crawling up it, wounded leg useless. Alexis' men broke cover on the dike and rushed forward. She had a moment's hope, then the boat began to lift — its pilot likely wanting no part of those rushing to board.

Warth fired two rapid shots, faster than Alexis would think he could reload, but they splashed harmlessly off the boat's nose, not powerful enough to penetrate to the cockpit.

"Make it stop, witch-woman! *Make it stop!*"

"The only way to stop the pain is to cut it off all entire," Alexis said. "Would you like that?"

"*No!*"

The second boat was lifting and Alexis could see that her lads wouldn't make it to the ramp in time.

"*Gutis!*" she yelled. The only hope was for them to get the pilot into the first boat, lift, and shoot down the other — all before the pirate pilot was able to get a message of any sort off to the other pirates. With luck, he'd be so focused on clearing the farm and attackers that he'd wait on that. "Passing the word for the pilot, and he's to take down that bloody boat!"

Out of the mass of mud-covered men running for the second boat on the dike, a smaller form dashed forward.

It was Aiden, the New Londoner who'd joined her group from Kannstadt's men in the cave.

How he'd snuck in with her men in the fields without anyone noticing — or telling her if they did — she didn't know. Last she'd seen of him, he was back at the farmhouse guarding the inhabitants.

But he did have speed, and he made the pirate boat with just enough time to leap and catch the very edge of the lowered ramp.

"Witch-woman, say what you want! How's Old Blackbourne t'save his bishop?"

"Quiet!" Alexis kicked Blackbourne in the head. She could understand the man being in a bit of pain, but this degree of whinging was beyond tiresome. "*Gutis!* Where's the bloody pilot?"

The rest of Alexis' men reached the second boat with just enough time that their leaps barely brushed Aiden's feet, then the boat and boy were both out of reach and rising.

Alexis watched helplessly as their plan all went wrong. The pirate pilot would certainly calm himself in a moment — he was rising slowly enough and not maneuvering, perhaps concentrating on letting his fellow climb the ramp and get aboard. Once that was done, though, he'd surely be on the comms to his fellows and their surprise would be lost.

Fifty meters up, she could still see Aiden swinging from the ramp's edge. The boy gathered momentum then got a leg over the edge and crawled up.

Then, for a heart-stopping moment, Alexis thought it was Aiden falling as a body came off the ramp, arms and legs flailing. But she saw this body was too large and wore different clothes before it hit the fields, crushing cattails beneath it and sending up a plume of muddy water.

Gutis rushed up to her, chest heaving to get air. He'd been part of the group assaulting the second boat and took time to rush to her at her call.

"Get aboard and take that other boat down," Alexis ordered.

"Aye, sir, but —"

"No matter the boy," Alexis said, though her chest ached at the need. Still, the pirates had enough of a force on Erzurum that any alert would doom their plan. "If that boat gets away or even sends a message off, then we're all done for. We can hope Aiden's keeping the pilot too busy for a message, but ..."

"Aye, sir." Gutis gasped a lungful of air and rushed for the still grounded boat.

TWENTY-NINE

She shot one in the eye, she did.
She dumped one out the lock.
Then to make their bloody fate more clear,
She shot one in the ... Oooohhhh...

BEFORE GUTIS COULD EVEN MAKE THE RAMP, THOUGH, THE fleeing boat began to behave strangely, first making a sharp turn to port, then diving for the ground before leveling off and rising again, straight up on its antigrav, but with no forward motion. It rolled side to side several times, very nearly going the whole way around, but then stopped and hung in the air nearly three hundred meters up, twisted and canted, as though no one were at the controls.

Gutis paused at the ramp and looked back to Alexis. She held up a hand, palm out, to stop him.

All movement on the farm ceased, with everyone staring up at the hovering boat and waiting for it to do something.

All save Blackbourne, that is, who still rolled from side to side, moaning. He looked up at Alexis and from his perspective it must have appeared that Alexis had her outstretched palm pointed directly at the still, hovering boat.

"*Witch-woman,*" he moaned.

THE FROZEN TABLEAU of watchers broke when a figure appeared at the open hatch of the hovering boat.

Small and covered in the distinct grey mud of Erzurum's fields, it was clearly Aiden, and a cheer went up from the watchers.

Aiden grasped one of the ramp's struts and looked over the edge at the farm two hundred meters below. He seemed to draw himself up and cupped his hands to his mouth, but whatever he yelled was impossible to pick out over the cheers of his fellows on the ground.

"Quiet!" Alexis yelled, but only those nearest her could hear. "*Belay that!* Quiet now!"

Dockett sent two men into the grounded boat, likely to keep watch over that boat's pilot in whatever condition he and Nabb had left the pirate, and added his bellow to hers. Eventually word traveled through the group and the cheering stopped.

"... *down!*" Aiden's voice came from above, barely audible even with the men being still.

"*Say again, lad?*" Dockett bellowed back.

"*How ... do ... I ... get ... down?*"

IT TOOK several minutes of Gutis putting the grounded boat's comm laser on the hovering boat and then quite a lot of shouted instructions before Aiden got the right control to press in response to the incoming signal. Minutes that were a bit breathless for the watchers as there was more than one wrong control pressed as well — which sent the boat to twitching and turning in the sky.

Once communication was established, though, it was a nearly simple matter talk Aiden through the landing process.

"There ya go, lad, easy now — we'll have ya down in a jiffy," Gutis said, craning his head to see the descending boat from where he sat in the landed one's cockpit.

"Aye, sir, thank you, sir," came Aiden's shaking voice from the comms.

Gutis muted his own comms for a moment and turned to Alexis.

"The safeties are off for it to lift with the ramp down like that, an' I'd not want to talk him through raising it, as well," he said quietly. "Straight down's best, but he's not over a dike."

"Just get him down safely," Alexis said. "We'll worry about what's next after that."

"Aye, sir."

Back to his comms, Gutis leaned forward again so he could see the other boat.

"Alright, lad, now, ya see that stick in front of ya with all them buttons?"

"Yes, sir."

The hovering boat suddenly tilted forward, rolled to starboard, and fired its forward guns. Gouts of water, steam, and cattails exploded from one of the farm's farther fields.

"*Don't touch it!*" Gutis yelled.

He took a deep breath and closed his eyes as the boat stopped its twisting and righted itself.

"Sorry, lad, should have said that bit first, I guess." He cleared his throat. "So, the *don't* touches, lad — that stick, for a one, and none of the buttons on it, right?"

"Yes, sir — I mean, no, sir."

"Nor that sort of slidie thing to your left — that'll send you off an we'll never get you back, then." Gutis took a look around his own cockpit. "Fact is, lad, don't touch nothing — not a thing, mind you, save one. By your left side, there's a big lever. See it?"

"Aye, sir."

"All right, now, you give that lever a bit of a press down, just a bit, mind you an' —"

"*Oomph!*"

The hovering boat tilted forward, almost standing on its nose.

"*Lad!* What'd ya —" Gutis glanced down at his own seat. "All right, lad, there're *two* levers by your seat there. That one's your seat-back an threw y'into the stick — ease that up and you'll —"

The boat righted itself to level once more.

"There ya go, lad." Gutis muted the comms and turned to Alexis. "Bloody boat builders never met a proper pilot, I'll tell you, sir, puttin' the —"

"Might we get the lad down first, Gutis?" Alexis asked.

"Oh, aye, sir." He turned back to his comms. "So, lad, t'*other* lever there — the bigger one — see it?"

"Aye, sir."

"All right, lad, you grasp that, easy, now, mind you, and you push it down just a bit, see?"

The hovering boat descended a few meters.

"That's it, lad, you've got it. Press it a bit and hold it there — don't press more."

"Aye, sir."

Slowly, the second pirate boat descended and Gutis continued to offer Aiden encouragement, as well as warnings not to bloody rush it.

The boat's maneuvers had placed it over one of the fields and cattails waved and water rippled as the boat neared, then the landing struts parted the crop, bending and breaking those that weren't pushed out of the way.

"Aye, slow and easy. Just a bit more, lad, a bit — ya've got to sort of *feel* it when to let that lever go, see? I can't see where the ground's at for you."

The boat settled further, its open ramp's edge disappearing under the water.

One of the landing struts moved, and Alex could see its hydraulic cylinders compress a bit.

"There's one," Gutis said. "Ground's uneven in that field, lad, from the mud, I reckon." He shrugged. "Let go of that stick now and ya see that button under a cover in the middle of the controls? That'll cut the anti all entire and you'll be down. Safe as houses, lad."

"Aye, sir."

"Well, you flick that cover open and press it now."

The boat lurched, tilting and settling lower in the muddy field before its landing struts compensated and leveled it out.

A startled yelp came from the comms.

"No worries, lad," Gutis said. He looked forward from his own boat's cockpit, perhaps picturing the massive bole of a tree just ahead. "No worse than my last landing, sure."

THIRTY

O', pull me hearties, pull me mates,
And later raise a glass,
For our Queen and Little Bloody Bit,
Who'll kick pirates in the arse!

WITH BOTH BOATS DOWN AND NO INDICATION THAT EITHER
pilot had made use of his comms during the sudden and unexpected
attack, Nabb and Gutis took Aiden aside with some few of Alexis'
boat crew and a bottle liberated from somewhere in the boats' stores.
The lad had just seen the stuff of a hand-to-hand battle for the first
time, and the aftermath of the second boat's pilot being well and truly
dead, and there were certain proprieties and priorities the men felt
necessary.

"Do see that any other spirits aboard those boats are locked up,
will you, Mister Dockett?" Alexis asked.

"Aye, sir. See to it —" The bosun's voice trailed off as he eyed the
group huddled around Aiden.

It was a group that was growing, with even some of Kannstadt's

Hanoverese joining the New Londoners now they saw there were spirits about.

"Though I'd have you be sure there's enough for everyone to toast the lad," Alexis allowed with a sigh. "His saving the day and all."

"Aye, sir!" Dockett brightened. "Splice the mainbrace, is it?"

"So much as you're able, but not so much as they're *unable*, if you take my meaning? We'll be lifting soon and I'll not want the men fortified to the point they're bloody walls."

"No, sir — I'll see to it. It's only the lad —"

"I understand."

Alexis did. Beside his first ground battle, which he'd been in the thick off, laying amongst the reeds to wait and along the dike while the pirates' shots struck around him, Aiden had also just killed for the first time, and twice. Throwing one pirate from the ramp and ... well, the battle for the boat would be a tale the lad told when he was able. The scratches and bruises on both his face and the boat's pilot told of a close, hard-fought struggle that ended with Aiden's hands clamped around the pilot's throat and one of the lad's eyes so swollen it might have been gouged out if things had gone a bit longer.

The men clustered around him were clapping him on the back in thanks and congratulations or leaning close and offering a whispered word, depending on their own views of such things.

"Would you have Blackbourne here taken to the house first?" Alexis asked.

"Aye, sir."

Dockett moved off, shouting for two men to come and carry the moaning pirate, who they deposited, none too gently, on the farm's dining room table, it being the best place on the lower floor to put him for treatment. Two of the other pirates — the pilot from the first boat, who Nabb and Dockett had subdued, and one of those at the ramp who'd been shot through the shoulder and leg but might survive — were tied to chairs along the room's wall.

Alexis' own injured from the crash, brought up on their stretchers after the farm was taken, were along the other walls. One of

Kannstadt's men had been using the farm's medical supplies to treat them and, save for Morgan, they were all looking the better for it.

Alexis wondered if Isikli and his family would ever view this room the same after their own captivity there and its turning into a medical ward for their captors.

"*Aarrgh!*" Blackbourne moaned as he was set down.

Kannstadt and Ellender looked at the pirate. Blackbourne was on his back with one hand pinned to his —

"Oh, lads, *the gherkin* — save Old Blackbourne from the witch-woman, won't you?"

— his other hovering over as though to either protect himself from further harm or afraid to touch the dozen or so flechettes protruding from him.

The two captains shared a look, then glanced at Alexis and shared another.

"What?" Alexis demanded, perhaps a bit more crossly than she should.

"*Nein.* Nothing," Kannstadt said quickly.

"It is only ... did you have to ..." Ellender's voice trailed off.

Alexis snorted with disgust. "The two of you were quite prepared to visit bloody torture and worse on Mister Isikli and his family, yet you'll balk at a shot pirate?"

"It's not the shooting," Ellender said, "it's the —"

"Some things are not done," Kannstadt added.

"Yes, well, I'm bringing all manner of changes to Erzurum, it seems." Alexis pointed to Blackbourne's injury. "Now will you have your man remove those so we can get on with things?"

"*No! Don't let the witch take his majesty for her Dark-driven rites!*"

"Oh, shut up, you bloody whinger — I meant the flechettes, for ..." A sudden thought struck her. "Are the Blackbournes and Creasys related by any chance?"

"Old Blackbourne'll give you no more names for your spells, witch-woman!"

Kannstadt's man leaned over and examined the pirate before rattling off a string of German.

"Renke says, this will hurt," Kannstadt said with far more sympathy than Alexis thought the pirate warranted. Another exchange of words. "He also says that you should show more care in your use of this, as you have an infection and this is why it burns so from the cuts."

Both captains and, Alexis noted, nearly everyone in the room who was conscious, had their hands cupped protectively in front of them.

"Bloody men," she muttered.

The effect of having shot the pirate in that particular place might have some benefit, however, as they did need information on the pirate forces in the ships orbiting Erzurum, as well as those on the planet itself — and if he was thinking she was some sort of evil witch, well, then he might believe she was more prone to harming him than she actually was.

She knelt down at the end of the table near Blackbourne's head so that he had to either watch her or crab his eyes far to the side.

"Before Captain Kannstadt's man repairs the damage I've done to you, Mister Blackbourne, I do have a few questions."

"Old Blackbourne'll tell you nothing, witch-woman! He'll not betray his fellows to your foul arts! You'll get nothing! He'll —"

Alexis' only warning was an angry chittering she knew too well and the scrabble of claws on the floor before those claws dug into her shoulder. It was only the briefest impact, though, as the bloody Creature launched itself to her other shoulder and from there onto the dining table, likely thinking dinner was in progress and wanting some share of leftovers as it got aboard ship when her officers ignored her objections and fed the damned thing.

It was only Blackbourne's bad luck, she was sure, that the Creature's leap landed it squarely on the pirate's pinned hand, knocking and twisting flechettes all about and burying no small number of them deeper under its weight, as well as more than a bit of twist and gouge.

Blackbourne screamed — a sound of mixed pain and terror as he looked down his body at the brown furred thing landing atop him.

Alexis could have told the pirate that the Creature paid no mind to screams — not her own of outrage and anger over finding its leavings in her boots, nor, apparently, to terrified pirates. The thing simply spun about, planting each foot firmly on Blackbourne's hand as it did so, and bared its tiny but needle-sharp teeth at the man.

"*Demon familiar! Oh, sweet Dark, Old Blackbourne'll talk witch-woman! Ask yer questions — just don't let yer demon eat his Doubting Thomas!*"

THIRTY-ONE

MONGOOSE HUNG IN ORBIT IN RADIANT SPLENDOR, REFLECTING the light from Erzurum's star like a beacon.

Alexis recognized her even with her masts still struck down and with more than one new patch on her hull — ill-fitting and scandalously aligned, so that Alexis was certain Dockett would have to be restrained from taking out his anger over such shoddy work on any of the pirate crew they captured. She might herself, as her heart filled at the sight of the ship and she cataloged the indignities done to her by the pirates' attack and then their slapdash repair work.

She'd held herself a bit in reserve from her ships since losing *Belial* at Giron — neither *Nightingale* nor, she thought, *Mongoose* had meant as much to her as that ship and she'd not felt *Mongoose's* loss here nearly so hard, she thought.

Now the sight of the ship, and the idea of getting her back, of walking her quarterdeck once more and allowing the vessel some bit of revenge against the pirates who'd so scandalized her, set her blood racing and her knees weak.

The pirate boat's cockpit was crowded with the pilot at the helm,

Blackbourne in the copilot's seat so as to work the comms, and Alexis and Nabb behind the pirate to keep him in line.

That Nabb held the bloody Creature so as to keep it in Blackbourne's sight yet out of the comm's pickup only added to the crowd, and Alexis' mind was full of what might happen if Nabb dropped the thing. Those skittering paws dancing over the boat's control board would do their ruse no good — but there was no doubt the Creature had Blackbourne cowed in some way.

The pirate shied away as Nabb pointedly shook the Creature, causing it to bare its needle-sharp teeth.

"Aye, no one said we was comin'!" Blackbourne said to the comm and his fellow aboard *Mongoose*. "But them fellows the farmer picked up gave out a bit o' info, see? There's some'at o' value aboard an' Old Blackbourne aims to collect!"

"We tore this ship apart, we did," the pirate aboard *Mongoose* said. "Ain't nothin' still hid."

"An' Old Blackbourne says there is!"

"Ain't."

"Tinkham, yer a bloody fool an' the best part o' ya slid down yer mama's leg the one time she met yer da! Now, Old Blackbourne's comin' aboard an' lookin' fer treasure!"

"Old Blackbourne can go bugger himself with that scrawny worm he's so bloody fond of talkin' about!"

"Don't ya go malignin' Old Blackbourne's Little Billy, ya buggering bloody bugger!"

Nabb suppressed a laugh, which shook the Creature, which bared its teeth, which set Blackbourne's eyes to widening and his own mouth to set in a grimace of fright.

Alexis had to admit that when they'd finally collected the Creature off the pirate back at the farm and set it safely with Isom to allow Kannstadt's man to work on Blackbourne's injuries — well, both Kannstadt and Ellender had felt compelled to comment on Alexis' marksmanship, in being able to strike such a difficult target so very many times.

"Your scary looks don't frighten me, Blackbourne," Tinkham said. "Ness gave me this ship and I'll let aboard who I say!"

"An' it's Old Blackbourne in charge when Ness' off, so you'll be lettin' him aboard!"

"In charge of that mudball, not my bloody ship!"

"Am!"

"Ain't!"

"Is!"

Alexis sighed. The piratical hierarchy on Erzurum, once this Ness fellow was out of the picture, at least, seemed to be quite murky at best — possibly as obscure as their skill at arguing. It was quite a good thing that she didn't need Blackbourne's help to actually get aboard *Mongoose*, only to distract the pirates there until the boat was close enough.

Assuming, of course, that the codes Avrel Dansby'd given her still worked. He'd said the rechristening of his *Elizabeth*, as *Mongoose* had originally been named, wouldn't affect them, nor anything else short of a full system wipe — and even then, he'd smiled at some secret, he'd had the codes buried so deeply in *Elizabeth's* systems. Given many of those codes, and the sheer variety of them, Alexis could only conclude that Dansby's earlier life had been far more interesting than she'd previously suspected.

It was also clear that Avrel Dansby was not a trusting man.

And now they were close enough to the ship to find out if he was also skilled enough, or had hired someone who was, to embed his distrust in the ship's systems.

"*Elizabeth*, are you there?" Alexis said, speaking distinctly.

A chime sounded over the comms from *Mongoose's* quarterdeck.

"What were that?" Tinkham asked. "What're you up to, Blackbourne?"

"The witch-woman's demon-familiar made Old Blackbourne do it, Tinkham! Don't you blame Old Blackbourne!"

Alexis sighed. Blackbourne's histrionics aside, the chime in response to the ship's name and the code phrase over a comm channel gave her some hope the tricks Dansby claimed were buried so deeply in her systems that no rechristening or capture could ever hope to winkle them out, no matter how little sense the phrase itself might mean to Alexis, might work.

"*Elizabeth*, Kaycie's home and someone's in the house."

FOR A MOMENT, Alexis thought that Dansby's code had failed, as the comms screen went blank, shutting off Tinkham's next question in mid-word.

"*Mongoose* ain't broadcasting, sir," the pilot said. "Nothing — not a peep."

In fact, the ship had gone dark as well as silent, with all of her hull lights shutting off, leaving her illuminated only by Erzurum's star and what reflected off the planet's heavy cloud cover.

That was as Dansby'd said, yet it was still an eerie thing to see.

Eerier still to see the ship move, knowing that her quarterdeck must be as still and dark as the ship's exterior had just gone.

Mongoose — *Elizabeth*, rather, as Alexis felt like there was some long-hidden *other* awakening now, one she'd never quite know as well as Avrel Dansby did, that had just taken control of the ship she knew as *Mongoose* — twisted and turned in space, aligning the hatch along her port side with the approaching boat so as to facilitate docking.

The pilot sent the boat spurting forward and spun it to come alongside with the soft thump of their meeting.

"Two men from the boat crew to keep an eye on Blackbourne here, Nabb," Alexis ordered as she ducked through the cockpit's hatch to the crowded passenger compartment. "If he misbehaves, they may feed his toes to the Creature."

"Aye, sir."

"Old Blackbourne'll be good, witch-woman!"

"I'm not a bloody witch, but I'll not hesitate to shoot you again."

Blackbourne scowled at her. "Shot or hexed, it's all the same to Old Blackbourne's magic flute, ain't it?"

They'd stripped the boat of all its seats, so as to crowd in more men — all of Alexis' and nearly that many of Kannstadt's. It was so crowded that Alexis didn't bother to yell for the broad backs facing her to make a lane, as they had nowhere to go but out the hatch and into *Mongoose*. Her own lads were at the fore, their vacsuits, carried at such great effort from her crashed boat, would offer some protection against the pirates, while the force from Erzurum still wore their scaled skins or next to nothing.

Nevertheless, those fellows to either side of the hatch did hold back, allowing those in front of Alexis through first and her after.

Mongoose had a very different feel as Alexis launched herself through the docking tube and through the now open airlock hatch. Or, perhaps, it was *Elizabeth* that felt differently, while *Mongoose* had only been a facade for a time.

The ship now felt ... older, and angry — if such a thing were possible.

She'd loved every ship she'd ever served on, even the ill-fated *Hermione* and especially the doomed *Belial*, but she'd never, not truly, attributed to them the sort of awareness some spacers did. They were things — and while each might take on a certain character, that was more the combination of her captain and crew, along with some of the few mechanical or systems quirks such a complex bit of machinery and technology must necessarily acquire.

They weren't alive, they weren't aware, they didn't — Alexis shivered as she crossed the docking hatch threshold and the companionway ahead, dark until she arrived, lit up. The ship inside was as dark as out until she entered, and with the anti-gravity off so that her lads floated up and down the companionway to the other decks.

They did not, she assured herself, feel a sense of violation and demand vengeance.

"All the hatches're locked, sir," Dockett said, pushing off the wall to float her way. "There's power, but they won't open — nor the manuals, neither."

Alexis wondered at how Dansby'd managed to override the safety mechanisms to seal the hatches even against manual opening — but this was what he'd told her would happen. All the hatches sealed, the gravity off, and all the lights with it, so that the ship's inhabitants, whoever they might be, were trapped floating in darkness. All save those who entered with whomever spoke the proper codes.

She floated over to the hatch that would lead through *Mongoose's* officers' quarters, what would be the wardroom on a Navy ship, to the quarterdeck. The rest of her force crowded into the companionway, spreading out between decks to the other hatches and readying their weapons.

The hatch to the wardroom seemed to vibrate under Alexis' palm, but that must be her imagination, as that had never been the case before. Ships *did not* growl with anticipation, like some hound straining at the leash.

It's Dansby's silly, bloody codes, speaking to the ship as though she can hear — next he'll have me sitting with Creasy and asking to be ordained into some spiritual order of the Dark. And who's this bloody "Kaycie" all his codes mention?

Some past conquest, if she knew the man at all, and he'd not got around to changing things to impress the next one yet. She could imagine him playing the card, "Here, lass, see? I've made you the key to my ship, you're so much in my mind — now drop the knickers and between the sheets, right?"

"All set, sir!" Dockett called.

Alexis shivered again, it seemed the hatch's thrumming had grown stronger at the bosun's words and she would definitely need a drink to settle her nerves when this was done — and a good fortnight without Creasy's mutterings or Blackbourne's calling her a witch.

"All right — *Elizabeth*," she said firmly, "Kaycie says to open the doors."

THIRTY-TWO

THE HATCH BEFORE ALEXIS SLID OPEN, AS DID ALL THOSE leading off the companionway. The lights came on in the rooms beyond, as well, blinding the pirates after their time in the dark and giving Alexis and her crew a vital second or two to fire or slip into the compartments.

Alexis slid through while the hatch was still opening, her slight form making it through before any others could follow.

She dodged to port once through, a shot from one of the pirates narrowly missing her — blinded by the change from darkness to light or not, they knew the ship was under attack and were prepared. The missed shot struck the opening hatch but was soon followed by others.

More shots sounded from outside, up through the companionway, while the rest of her crew assaulted the other opening compartments.

At least the pirates had had no time to organize or mount a proper defense as the hatches had closed, trapping them wherever they were in the ship.

There were only two pirates in the wardroom, crouched behind the cover of the officers' dining table and chairs — simply the same thermoplastic as the ship's hull, decks, and bulkheads, molded into shape. As such it did offer more in the way of protection than a typical table and chairs might — though not as thick as the hull or bulkheads, it would stop a bullet or even a bolt from the laser pistol Alexis now carried.

Her lads fired back from the hatchway, while Alexis opened the first compartment to port and ducked inside. She leaned out, trying to take aim on whatever part of the pirates might be exposed, but a bullet *thunked* into the bulkhead beside her exposed face and she was forced to dart back.

A chant started from the companionway and Alexis readied herself.

"Oi! Oi! *Oi! Mongoose!*"

First one, then another, then more, vacsuited figures flung themselves through the hatch, some going high, some low, taking advantage of the lack of gravity to carom off the bulkheads and overhead. They forced the two pirates to fire at multiple targets, firing back themselves.

There was a cry of pain, but Alexis had no time to wonder if it was one of hers or one of the enemy.

She grasped the edge of the compartment's hatch and pulled herself into the common space, pushing off against the hatch's opposite edge with as much force as her legs could muster.

Her flight stayed low, scraping the deck, and she tucked and rolled midway so that her feet faced the pirates when she arrived.

Her memories of skylarking around *HMS Merlin's* hull with Philip Easely, her first friend in the Navy, as a midshipman, served her well. It might have looked a game, but playing tag and knock-about in zero gravity did prepare one well for fights like this.

She cleared both the tabletop and pedestal, her feet striking firmly at the chair one of the pirates hid behind. Slight though her mass was, forty-five kilos —fifty with her vacsuit — striking at speed was enough to knock the man back. Chair and pirate left the deck despite the magnetic set of the chair's legs. Neither pirate had been prepared for zero gravity, so didn't have their vacsuits on with their own heavy magnetic boots.

The pirate sailed up and back, clearing a shot for Alexis' men, while she twisted to bring her laser to bear on his fellow. She had just a glimpse of his startled face as she sailed by and shot him.

There was no time for her to waste on either pirate. Leaving it to the others to make sure they were down, Alexis tucked and rolled again, slapping off the deck to face the next hatch. She kicked off hard, flying headfirst toward the closed hatch, but trusting to Dansby's word.

"*Elizabeth*, Kaycie says open the quarterdeck ... now!"

The hatch before her slid open revealing the companionway and the quarterdeck hatch across the way. Alexis' shoulders barely cleared the opening hatch — in fact, her left grazed it as it slid open — and she dropped her spent laser to pull out her flechette pistol. There was no time to load a new capacitor, as those behind her were.

The quarterdeck hatch slid open and Alexis' eyes widened in surprise as she flew toward it headfirst.

She'd expected the quarterdeck crew, whatever semblance of one the pirates kept on watch, to be spread out anticipating an attack. She'd not expected the pirate captain, Tinkham, to be floating right there in the hatchway yelling at it.

"— *open!* Dark damn yer eyes, ya bloody, Dark-buggered, Dansby-cursed hunk o' rotting — *umph!*"

ALEXIS STRUCK Tinkham in his gut head-first, barely having time to tuck her left arm around her face. Her momentum sent them both back into the quarterdeck space, despite the pirate's larger mass absorbing some of it. She wrapped her right arm around his back to keep her grip.

The pirate wasn't wearing magnetic boots or a vacsuit, just some soft slippers and, disturbingly loose shorts, as though he'd been wakened by their boat's approach and come straight to the quarterdeck from his bed.

Tinkham folded over Alexis as her momentum carried them away from the hatch and farther into the quarterdeck. They had a slight, upward angle from Alexis' flight through the companionway, so cleared the circular navigation plot at the compartment's center.

The pirate captain's surprise gave way to his experience midway and he tried to twist so that Alexis struck the far bulkhead first, but she'd played that game before as a midshipman, and drilled more at boarding tactics with each of her crews. Whichever way Tinkham twisted, she threw her hips and legs the opposite, offsetting his larger mass with her own momentum and leverage.

She heard shouts behind her as the others crowded into the quarterdeck, but could spare no thought for them. There'd been, she thought, no more than two other pirates in the compartment when she entered. Perhaps three, as Tinkham's midsection had blocked a bit of it from her vision. Her lads should be able to handle those with no problem, armed as they were.

A glance down from her place with her head in Tinkham's gut, and between his tucked and twisting legs, gave her a glimpse of the navigation plot's far edge and she knew the quarterdeck's forward bulkhead was close on that. She tensed her neck and shoulders for the impact and got an elbow pointed forward just as they struck.

The elbow was low, not quite in Tinkham's solar plexus, but enough that the impact drove the man's breath from his body, stopping him in mid-curse, as he'd been letting off a stream of them through their entire flight across the compartment.

They rebounded from the bulkhead and Alexis took advantage of the pirate's momentary limpness to grasp an arm and swing him around in midair. His arm behind his back with one hand and her other on Tinkham's shoulder, she could just reach the upper bulkhead with her feet to impart a bit of force and get them out of midair.

Tinkham smashed into the navigation plot's surface with Alexis' full mass atop him, her knees tucked up so that the full force of the impact was focused on his upper body.

What little air Tinkham had been able to recover whooshed from his lungs and he went limp.

Alexis kept her grip on his arm, twisted well up between his shoulder blades, while she scanned the quarterdeck.

Nabb had stayed with her, and he had one of the pirates face-first against a bulkhead, his pistol at the man's head. Two others, Benny, of her boat crew, and the lad, Aiden, had the other in a similar position. There appeared to be only the two pirates, then, and Tinkham in the quarterdeck. Likely their middle watch for the crew, with Tinkham abed and only station-keepers on the quarterdeck. The few others of the boarding party who'd followed her here were clustered at the hatch.

"You lot find Mister Dockett and help clear the ship," Alexis ordered, and the men scattered down the companionway. She nodded to the others. "Benny, take this bastard, will you, so that I might get my feet on the deck?"

"Aye, sir."

Benny was an older man, topman turned gunner when his back would no longer take the strain of all the pulley-hauley outside on a ship's hull. He adjusted the younger Aiden's grip on the pirate a bit, passing on his own experience at keeping a man still and compliant.

"Watch the squirmy bastard," Benny said, "an' if'n he moves wrong, you pull on this —" The pirate screamed. "—see?"

"Aye," Aiden said.

Benny then pushed off the deck to meet Alexis in midair and take her grasp on Tinkham.

Alexis pushed off the pair and stretched out her feet to contact the deck with a satisfying click from her boots' magnets. That done, she reached up and grasped Tinkham's leg to pull those two down beside her.

"Thankee, sir," Benny said.

His own boots firmly on the deck he was better able to pin the still gasping Tinkham to the bulkhead with a thick forearm.

Alexis took a deep breath herself.

Mongoose's quarterdeck was well in-hand. Given the ship's time when they'd struck — quite late if Tinkham's dress was any indication — most of the pirate crew would have been on the berthing deck, with only watch-keepers and a few night owls awake. Dockett and the rest of the men should have no trouble overpowering those, assuming Blackbourne's estimate of the number of pirates aboard was accurate, something she'd taken with more than a grain of salt in her planning.

She nodded. "Right, then."

It was time to bring *Mongoose's* systems back to life and —

"Mister Dockett's compliments, sir, and the pirates in the engineering spaces are threatening to blow the fusion plant!"

The spacer hovering in the hatchway was out of breath from his race up and forward from the bosun, and white-faced, no doubt from fear the pirates would make good on their threat.

Alexis sighed. "Of course they are."

THIRTY-THREE

"YOU STAY AWAY!"

Alexis peered around the hatch coaming into *Mongoose's* engineering space.

The squat mass of the fusion plant took up most of the compartment's center, with a ring of control panels and monitoring stations around the bulkheads.

Past it, along the far, aft bulkhead, two pirates sat on the deck, hands atop their heads in surrender.

It was the third pirate, the one whose foot she could just make out where it extended from behind the fusion plant itself, who was the worry.

"He's got the bloody patch off the plant housing and his pistol right up in it," one of the surrendered pirates called out.

Alexis could see the patch made to the aft bulkhead, where it had been breached in *Mongoose's* approach to Erzurum. It lined up with where the threatening pirate sat, so that must be where the fusion plant's wall had been damaged, causing the SCRAM that shut *Mongoose* down in her attack on the planet.

"Would he have been able to get the patch off?" Alexis asked in a low voice.

Dockett shrugged at her from his position on the hatch's other edge.

"No telling what half-arsed work they made of it," he said. "Or if a pistol shot'll breach what's left. If they'd done a proper job, filled in the whole of it, we'd not be here."

Alexis shuddered. A breach of the plant's containment vessel would end it for all of them, her lads and the pirates both, as Erzurum came to have a brief, very small second sun in orbit around it.

It would not do the threatening pirate much good either, which made Alexis wonder what he hoped to get out of this.

"What's your name?" she called out.

"Pullink — and you stay away!"

"All right, Pullink, so what is it you want?"

"Off the ship and get away!" Pullink yelled.

"That was the plan, Pullink," Alexis said. It was. She'd have to do something with the pirates she took off *Mongoose* and, if she could ever get this settled and bring their second boat up, the other ships in orbit. Dumping them in Erzurum's swamps seemed to be the best option for keeping them out of the way. "You and your mates back down to Erzurum, safe as houses, right?"

"Not us, you lot!" Pullink yelled back.

"Oh." Alexis shrugged. "Well, that's not going to happen, Pullink, so what's your second choice?"

"Blow us all to hell!"

Alexis sighed. Well, at least they had the bargaining positions well-established.

"Look, Pullink, we're in a bit of a fix here, aren't we? All your mates have surrendered, even those two in there with you, see?"

The pair of pirates on the floor along the aft bulkhead nodded vigorously, their eyes never leaving Pullink.

"Give it up, mate," one of them said.

"Is that devil, Dansby, out there?" Pullink called. "Let me hear his voice again before I send us all to hell!"

"Who's Dansby?" Dockett asked.

"That fellow we got *Mongoose* from," Nabb said.

"What, the sort of ..." Dockett frowned. "Odd I can't recall what he looked like, but —." He shivered.

Nabb shook his head. "No, that'd be the Foreign Office man what makes your bollocks crawl up inside. Dansby's the one you'd like to have a pint with and hear a tale or two ... providing your purse was never out of a hand." Nabb pursed his lips. "Better your purse were left hidden elsewhere with him, come to that."

"Oh ... well, he seemed a decent sort — for all that."

"Gave the captain Boots, he did."

"Well, then, a fine gentleman, ain't he? What's he got to do with this lot?"

"Gentlemen?" Alexis interrupted. "If you don't mind?"

"Aye, sir, sorry."

"Pullink," Alexis called. "Wouldn't you rather just go down to the planet than blow up?"

"*Ha!*" Pullink yelled. "'Just give up,' he says. 'We'll drop you on a nice planet,' he says. *You tell Dansby I'll not fall for such again!*"

"He's been going on like this since we come aboard," one of the surrendered pirates said. "Recognized the ship as some old *Elizabeth* and ain't shut up since about how we're all doomed to be aboard her."

"I told you!" Pullink yelled. "I told you Dansby filled his ships with trickeries and treacheries and what'd we just get, eh? *Trickeries!* Now that devil's aboard and we're all doomed anyways!"

"Avrel Bloody Dansby is not here, Pullink!" Alexis yelled.

"*I'll not turn myself over to that devil Dansby!*" Pullink yelled. "See you all in hell, first!"

Alexis opened her mouth to respond, then frowned and shook her head. "What in the Dark did Avrel Dansby *do* to these people?"

Alexis knew Dansby to be a rogue and smuggler, with little regard for the law and likely only helping her these two times for the profit and some hold the Foreign Office man, Eades, had over him, but the very real fear in Pullink's voice, Blackbourne's demand that Dansby must be here, and even Tinkham's cursing spoke to a deeper, darker past than even Alexis had considered. Why, even Wheeley, at his casino, had been on guard when Alexis invoked his name.

"When he said he'd not return to the Barbary," Alexis muttered, "I'd thought it was for his own safety, not that the whole bloody sector would pack up and flee for *Hso-hsi* at his approach."

"It does seem he left an impression, sir," Dockett agreed.

That particular serpent's past, however, was something to winkle out of him another day. For now, she had the problem of a desperate, probably deranged, pirate with his laser pistol's barrel pressed against an ill-patched fusion plant.

"Bring down Blackbourne and Tinkham, Mister Dockett — we'll see if the man's leaders can do anything with him."

"SHE'LL SHOOT ya in yer man axe, if y'don't come out, Pullink!"

"Mister Blackbourne, I don't think that's helping."

"Did it t'Old Blackbourne, lad, and he'll say y'won't like it a bit! Blackbourne's word on that!"

"Belay that, and be silent!"

Alexis rubbed her temples in frustration. Of the two pirate leaders, Blackbourne, at least, would try talking to Pullink, while Tinkham sullenly refused, but neither did his words seem to have any hope of easing the tensions.

"Talk t'the man, don't talk t'the man — make up yer mind, bitchwoman."

Blackbourne had finally accepted that Alexis wasn't some witch.

The pirate now seemed even more unhappy that Alexis had "duped" him into believing she was a witch than when he'd thought she shot fiery bolts from her fingers and was about to set her demon familiar to eating him, and Alexis wasn't at all certain his current term for her was an improvement.

Neither anger at what he saw as being duped, though, nor any lingering loyalty to the band of pirates, seemed to deter him from cooperating with Alexis so long as she gave her word not to either shoot him again or hang him, should she succeed in retaking her ship and escaping.

Blackbourne's true loyalties appeared to lie with whichever path might keep him alive and unharmed at the current moment, rather than to anything larger.

Dockett gave the back of the pirate's head a knock.

"Watch yer tongue!"

"Our goal, Mister Blackbourne, is to get Pullink to surrender, understanding that he will not be further harmed if he cooperates."

"Didn't give Old Blackbourne the chance."

"And you'll have none again if *you* don't cooperate — I've a goodly number of flechettes left, you should know."

"See, Pullink?" Blackbourne called out. "She has it in for the old faithful, lad, guard yerself an' do as the bitch-woman says!"

"Get these two out of here before they do us more harm," Alexis said, stepping away from the hatchway.

"Aye, sir."

Dockett detailed two men to take the pirates away and joined Alexis and Nabb a few meters from the hatch.

"This's eatin' at our time, sir," Dockett said.

Alexis knew it was. "Yes, I know."

They had control of *Mongoose*, and all the pirates save those three in the engineering space safely locked in the hold — in a compartment Dansby's notes assured her had no secret panels or locks for them to escape by. There were the three other pirate ships in orbit with her, though, and some merchantmen — plus however many pirates on Erzurum's surface.

No one had tried to contact the ship or Blackbourne's boat yet, as the pirates were an independent lot, with each crew and captain making his own rules, but one certainly would sometime — and when that happened, the whole pirate force would join to recapture *Mongoose*.

She needed to execute the next steps of their plan with some element of surprise, but couldn't very well proceed with her one ship held hostage by the manic pirate intent on ending them all.

"We could shut down the plant from the quarterdeck, sir," Dockett suggested.

"It's four hours' time to restart it —" Alexis shook her head. They were merely going over options they'd already discussed while waiting for Tinkham and Blackbourne. "— and we'd be helpless all the while."

"Storm in and grab him?"

"He'd certainly hear even the most speedy rush, I think, and we've those two others staring right at the hatch."

She'd tried to get those two surrendered pirates out, but Pullink would have none of it, despite his mates being quite willing, even eager, to go and get away from him.

"They'd certainly react somehow, and a mere twitch of his finger's all that's needed to send us up. He's already objected to us telling them move away."

A stealthy approach had been ruled out as well. With the fusion plant in the center of the compartment as it was, there was no real way to get to Pullink on its far side without crossing some sort of open space and being spotted by either him or the other two pirates. While Pullink's mates might not be any more interested in becoming a new sun than Alexis and her lads, they'd almost certainly react in some way and give Pullink a warning, whether intended or not.

Nor was there any secret way into the compartment that didn't carry the same difficulty. There *was* such a way detailed in Dansby's notes about the ship, but it let out beneath one of the consoles in full view of Pullink.

"It may be we must try Warth's suggestion," Alexis said.

The poacher'd been brought up to gauge his chances of sneaking up the side of the fusion plant and slitting Pullink's throat or shooting from hiding around the corner, but they'd all agreed any approach silent enough to make no noise to alert the pirate would present far too much opportunity for the other pirates to give the game away with furtive glances or widened eyes.

Warth had mentioned a possibility, though.

"It's daft, sir," Nabb said.

"Daft and dangerous," Alexis agreed. "We'll try again to talk some sense to the man and then —"

Alexis' tablet pinged for her attention. It was one of the spacers she'd left on the quarterdeck — not a one of them qualified to stand a watch, nor, really, to man the stations, as she had no available officers, but the best she had at the moment. One of Kannstadt's men had a passing knowledge of the signals console, at least — though she couldn't risk having him use it.

"Yes?"

"The Hannie lad pressed a button on the signals console — couldn't understand a word he said, me, but he played the message. One of the other ships is signaling for Tinkham and now wondering why we don't answer, sir."

"Nabb, get Warth about his daft-business instanter! Mister Dockett, have Tinkham and Blackbourne brought to the quarterdeck and you stay here with your best men to deal with the aftermath!"

THIRTY-FOUR

ALEXIS HADN'T HAD TIME TO NOTICE IN THE FIGHT TO RETAKE the ship and then the rush down to the engineering spaces to confront Pullink, but *Mongoose's* quarterdeck was a mess, with bits of food and trash on the floor and more than one empty wine bottle about. She took that in with a glance as she returned there with Dockett and the two pirates.

Pirates and merchantmen — they've no idea how to keep a proper ship.

The men she'd left manning the stations had done some work to at least push the bits of trash away from the more critical systems, but they'd been too busy to clean and there weren't enough crew to devote anyone to it. If the quarterdeck was this bad, though, she wondered what the state of the berthing areas and gundeck were.

"Are we cleared for action, Mister Dockett?" she asked.

"Best we're able, sir." The bosun led Tinkham and Blackbourne to the navigation plot, keeping a wary eye on both despite their hands being well bound behind them. "Guns are loaded, but not run out. We've cleared the decks of the worst debris and cleaning up the rest as we wait. I shudder at how this lot goes to vacuum with so much trash about."

"Very well." Alexis made her way to the signals station, making sure she was out of sight. "Mister Tinkham, you're already dressed for having just gotten out of bed, so please make your excuses to this other ship's call and then Mister Blackbourne will have a say."

"It's Captain Tinkham and I'll not dance to your tune."

"She'll shoot you in yer peppito," Blackbourne whispered, "if you don't do as she says."

"Shut up, you traitorous bastard. It's your fault I let them aboard."

Alexis motioned for Dockett to move Blackbourne away. The man wasn't doing them any good. "You're no captain aboard my ship, Tinkham, and I can make this work without you." She wasn't quite sure of that. "You, however, cannot avoid the noose without helping me."

Tinkham snorted. "I think it's you needs me more. You've this one ship, undermanned, while we've three in orbit, gunboats blocking the Lagrange points in *darkspace*, and a fair, fine force below on the surface. You'll not escape and if *you* want to live, you'll turn my ship back to me, I think."

Alexis stepped closer to him and looked up into his face.

"I have no intention of escaping, Mister Tinkham, I intend to take Erzurum all entire." She ignored Tinkham's second snort of derision. "Now, I may fail in that, but whether you're alive or dead at the time depends entirely on this decision."

"Guard yerself, Tinkham!" Blackbourne yelled, cupping his hands before him. "Old Blackbourne's seen that glint in her eye before!"

"Stop yer gob," Dockett said with a shove.

Tinkham bent down to Alexis' ear and whispered, "You don't scare me, little girl."

"I see. Mister Dockett? Would you be so kind as to send someone to the hold and bring up Mister Tinkham's former first mate?" She paused, then, "No, first and second, if you please."

"Aye, sir. Aiden, you go and get them, lad, but tell them down on the gundeck to send two stout fellows back with you."

"Aye, aye."

The youngster hurried off and Alexis took a step back from Tinkham.

"My men are loyal," Tinkham said, "you'll get no joy from Armfield or Hallows, neither."

Alexis ignored him and turned to the signals console.

"What's your name again, lad?" she asked of the Hanoverese there. She wracked her brain for the German before keying her tablet to translate. "Name?"

"*Name*," the tablet said, prompting Alexis to sigh.

The man smiled and nodded. "Reginhard Schwalheimer, *hauptgefreiter*."

Her tablet told her the man's rank was likely the equivalent of able spacer, but Alexis despaired of having to pronounce his name. Fighting *Mongoose* with this mixed crew was going to be a chore, but she had no choice. Her thirty-odd men wouldn't be able to do so alone. In fact, the sixty she had now wouldn't truly be enough — she'd like another boatload before they went into action and couldn't bring them up until they'd established some reason with the other pirate ships in orbit to do so.

Even then, half the men aboard would speak no, or little, English and her lads had no German past what would tell them the reckoning for a pint, poke, or fight in some Hanoverese port — neither of which would do them much good in dealing with the Hannie spacers. What conversation New London and Hanoverese spacers *did* engage in when in the same ports during peacetime didn't exactly lend itself to cooperative actions.

Knowing the German for "I buggered your mother, you fatherless bastard," is unlikely to be helpful.

The signals console pinged again, indicating an incoming

message and Schwalheimer held a finger over the controls, glancing the question at her.

"Yes," she nodded, "ignore it again."

Schwalheimer tapped the key.

Alexis moved back to the navigation plot and brought up views of *Mongoose's* hull. Warth's suited figure was visible, making his way aft from the airlock along with another spacer. They'd know soon enough if the poacher's plan would work — the failing would, at least, mean she didn't have to find a way to convince Tinkham or one of his officers to play along in her ruse with the other pirate ships. She'd use one of her own lads to respond to the other ship, but it seemed likely these crews would know each other and become wary of a stranger. Moreover, a known officer would be better.

Blackbourne might work as a last resort, but he was known for being on Erzurum's surface, so why would he be speaking for *Mongoose?*

No, Tinkham or one of his officers was required for this, and the pirate captain showed little sign of being persuadable. She could threaten him, even shoot him in the ... whatever Blackbourne's next euphemism might be ... but would that convince him to do as she bid? The only real inducement she could offer would be to not hang him for his piracy, and that would work only if he became convinced Alexis could win this fight in the first place.

The quarterdeck hatch slid open and Aiden returned, followed by two pirates, hands bound behind them, and then two burly spacers — one of Alexis' lads and one a large Hanoverese.

"Neither of you help this bitch," Tinkham said. "Our lads on those other ships'll have us loose in a —"

She had a lunatic at the fusion plant, an enemy ship off her port quarter, and less than half the crew she'd like to fight with. Though she might hate the coldness of it, she had no time for bravado and reticence from a pirate and slaver liable to be hung for his crimes in any case. Whether she herself had that authority at the moment as a privateer might be in some question, but she *was* authorized to take what action she felt necessary in an action against pirates herself — if *Mongoose*, and those other ships out there, were not fully taken, then any of the pirates in opposition to her were still part of that action.

"Mister Tinkham!" Alexis called.

Tinkham turned to face her. "What, you —"

Alexis raised her pistol and sent a flight of flechettes into the pirate's left eye.

The quarterdeck became a silent, still tableau, save for the fall and thump of Tinkham's body. It remained so for several seconds, until Blackbourne nodded and muttered, "Warned him not to trifle with the bitch-woman, Old Blackbourne did."

Alexis turned to the newcomers, who were staring at Tinkham's crumpled form with open mouths.

"Now, which of you gentlemen would like to assist me with a thing?"

THIRTY-FIVE

"Cap'n Tinkham's busy —"

    "Very busy —"

    "— down in the hold —"

    "— lookin' at what Blackbourne told —"

    "— seein' to the split of some —"

    "— us was hid there. All the lads, really —"

    "— juicy bits, and we'd like to get —"

    "— as you know we want to see a fair —"

    "— back ourselves, so as to be —"

    "— split and no doubts —"

    "— certain of our share —"

In retrospect, Alexis considered it might have been a mistake to allow both of Tinkham's officers near the signals console at the same time. She'd thought two of them might add some believability to the story that Tinkham was busy in the hold looking at whatever secret trove Blackbourne had supposedly brought word of, but the two men were speaking over themselves in an effort to convince the other pirate ship and Alexis couldn't follow it even knowing what the story was supposed to be.

She could only hope that those on the other ship thought the two men's nervousness and constant glancing in her direction could be attributed to their desire to get back below and see that some treasure was properly accounted for and divided.

"Mister Blackbourne," Alexis whispered, not quite believing her sudden conviction that the man might do a better job. She nodded to the signals console. "Do you suppose you might ..."

"Aye, bitch-woman, no need to threaten Old Blackbourne's quivering member with more and worse."

Blackbourne stepped around the console to stand behind the two men and clap a hand on each of their shoulders, cutting them off. None of the three's hands were bound now, but the console's camera couldn't see the armed spacers aiming weapons at the pirates, nor Alexis herself keeping her little pistol trained on them.

"You two lads go on back to Captain Tinkham, will you?" Blackbourne said with a nod to the console. "Old Blackbourne has a thing or two to discuss with Captain Hampson there."

The two stopped talking over themselves and glanced at Tinkham's corpse before cutting their eyes to Alexis, who nodded and jerked her head at the quarterdeck hatch.

"Ah, right," one of the pirate officers said. Alexis hadn't bothered to find out which was Armfield and which Hallows.

"We're going to go help Captain Tinkham now," the other said, with nary a glance at his captain's corpse.

"Down in the hold, where he's at," added the other.

"With Dansby's hidden treasure."

They stepped away from the console.

"And the crew."

"In the hold."

Once out of sight of the camera, both turned and offered their hands to Aiden and Dockett to be bound again without so much as a gesture of command.

"So, talk to Blackbourne!" one called to the console.

"He's got the right of it!" the other added.

Alexis motioned with her pistol, causing both men to flinch, and the two were taken back to the hold.

"So, Dansby weren't aboard?" the other ship's captain, Hampson, asked as Blackbourne settled himself before the console.

Blackbourne shook his head. "Don't appear so."

Hampson grunted. "Never knew the man, but don't see how he could be the bogey Ness and you oldsters make him out to be."

Blackbourne shrugged. "Think as y'will, but your *Fang's* one Dansby near gutted way back when."

Hampson grunted. "Not with me in command, and not with that tube of junk you're in. So, there was treasure aboard that shoddy hulk, there?"

Alexis shot Dockett a glare as the bosun growled to hear his ship described so.

"Some," Blackbourne said. "Operating funds, as Dansby was always wont to store."

"Tinkham's good luck to be put in command, then. That'll not be shared with the rest of us."

"Oh, aye," Blackbourne said with a glance at where the body lay. "Tinkham has his luck — of a sort."

"And you for bringing the word, I suppose."

Blackbourne smiled, showing teeth, but placing a hand protectively in his lap. "Aye, Old Blackbourne got a piece, sure." Alexis jerked her head at him, prompting him to get on with it. "There's more'n the treasure, Captain Hampson, though not so fine — if you've a mind, that is."

"What's that?"

"Turns out the farm those folks from the crashed boat was caught at had more to hide than them privateering lads. Had a fine still, an' kept it to themselves, all unwilling to sell to our lads for the fair prices we offered."

Hampson laughed at that.

"And more," Blackbourne went on. "Had a fair parcel of girls the old man hid from us."

"Oh?"

"Brought two to the lads here." Blackbourne grinned widely and Alexis thought it was an honest look that showed the man's true nature. "Their shares o' the treasure'll not sit in their purses long."

"Always after a profit, eh, Blackbourne?"

"Old Blackbourne gets nervous w'out the clink o' coins — little enough chance, him stayin' behind on that mudball so much."

"Shouldn't have pissed down Ness' back and told him it were raining, then," Hampson said.

Blackbourne shrugged. "Always bloody raining on Erzurum these days, who'd a'thought he'd notice?"

Alexis filed that bit of information away. If Blackbourne and this Ness, who seemed to be the pirates' leader, were on the outs, then all the more reason for Blackbourne to cooperate — and she might be able to get even more from the man.

"So, these girls?" Hampson asked.

"Oh, aye," Blackbourne said. "Three more, and half the old man's stock from his still, back there with my other boat. Just waitin' for the best offer."

"And you're thinking what? That my lads'll make it?"

Blackbourne shrugged. "Fresh an' brought up to 'em, or take some other crew's leavings when they finally get down to the surface. Either way, Old Blackbourne'll get their coin, eh?"

"Greedy bastard."

Blackbourne grinned at him.

"All right," Hampson said. "The lads did well in that dustup with the privateers, and it's been an age since they saw fresh mutton — they're fresh, you say?"

"Old Blackbourne's word on it. Your lads'll nary see the like again."

Blackbourne and Hampson haggled a bit over the price his ship would pay for the ostensible girls and liquor, then settled it and Blackbourne promised his boat would lift from the farm instanter.

It would, indeed, Alexis thought, but not with farmgirls and spirits — instead, pirate Captain Hampson's ... Alexis checked the navigation plot for that ship's name ... *Fang*, would receive a boat full of Captain Kannstadt and the rest of the Hanoverese. Captain Ellender was none too pleased to be left behind again, but Kannstadt had enough men left to him to man and fight a ship, while Ellender's were fewer in number and a haphazard mix of New Londoners, Hanoverese, and French from the Berry March.

"Oh," Blackbourne said, "and there's a new man at the boat's helm — Gutis, is his name."

"New?" Hampson asked.

"New to the boat. Held back that he could pilot so's to be in the thick of an action, but when he got stuck on Erzurum he let it loose he could fly the things."

Hampson nodded.

Alexis had left Gutis back on the farm to pilot the second boat, so as to have a reliable hand, and a New Londoner's voice, at the helm when they tried to take a second ship.

The two pirates finished up their business and ended the call.

"Old Blackbourne'll expect fair dealings from you," Blackbourne said, looking away from the console. "Turnin' on his mates like this."

"You're a pirate and a slaver, Blackbourne," Alexis said, "but cooperate and I'll not hang you when this is through."

Blackbourne stood and nudged Tinkham's body with a toe, eyes cutting to the flechettes protruding from the other pirate's eye. "That's terrific specific o'you in regard to times an' methods. Old Blackbourne's not comforted, bitch-woman. Not nearly."

MATTERS with the other pirate ships settled for the moment, Alexis turned her attention to the navigation plot and its images of Warth out on *Mongoose's* hull.

There was little she could do to monitor or assist, as it was all in Warth's hands — and his assistant's, for the poacher had another man with him, carrying a pair of laser rifles Warth had selected from those aboard.

The pair made their way aft, then down *Mongoose's* stern and between the massive plane and rudder the ship needed to maneuver in *darkspace*. Those were folded tight against the stern, as they weren't needed in normal-space, but there were gaps and hollows the men could fit through without her having to extend the devices.

They found the shoddy, hastily-applied patch the pirates had placed over the shot-hole there, and Alexis heard Dockett grunt at his first sight of the state of the work.

It wasn't even a proper hull patch, just a bit of thermoplastic laid over the hole and sealed. A ridge of more material surrounded the patch, a ragged, raised weld that hadn't been smoothed at all.

"Buggerin', slip-shod, cunny-thumbed, cack-handed —"

"It's all right, Mister Dockett," Alexis said, despite her own feelings being much the same. *Mongoose* was a fine ship and deserved better in the way of care than she'd received from the pirates. "You'll have time to see her set to proper rights."

"But look, sir," Dockett said, as Warth and his assistant cut away the patch and pulled it from its place. "They've not even plugged the bloody hull — just slapped the patches on either side."

"That *is* what we hoped for, you know," Alexis said. Their glimpse of the repairs in the engineering space had led to Warth's idea. It appeared the pirates had simply slapped the emergency, usually temporary, patches in place and left them, without properly plugging the full hole in the hull's stern that lay between.

The patches were intended to close a hull breach until full repairs could be made. The thin, no more than a few millimeters, patches would do next to nothing to stop an incoming shot — in fact, they were worse than useless, for they'd not diminish the shot to any appreciable extent, while adding a bit of molten thermoplastic to be sprayed about.

It was Warth's belief, proved out by a test in the hold with a similar patch from the carpenter's space, that the one patch on the inner hull would do nothing to diminish or deflect even his rifle's beam.

"Ain't a proper way to treat a ship," Dockett insisted.

Warth took one of the rifles from his assistant and extended the barrel into the hole in the hull, putting the muzzle almost against the inner patch. He rested it against the outer edge to steady himself and seemed to sit still for quite a long moment, though Alexis suspected he was minutely aligning the rifle with some mental picture he kept of the engineering space and the pirate, Pullink, next to the fusion plant.

Pullink was sitting cross-legged on the deck, facing forward, with one arm extended to place his own laser pistol's barrel against the weakened armor of the fusion plant.

"There's still time to shut the plant down, sir," Dockett said. "Shut her down, rush Pullink, then start her back up again."

"Hours to restart," Alexis said. She'd considered that. It would be safer in the sense that Pullink could still do damage shooting a plant that was already shut down, but it would be short of destroying the ship. The time to repair what damage he did and restart the plant would leave them vulnerable, though. "Hours of being here helpless with no power — and explaining to the other pirates in orbit why we'd not like them to come alongside and run a cable aboard to turn those hours into minutes."

"I don't entirely disagree, sir, but Warth ... well, let's say he didn't leave home and go a'spacing for his talent at judging risks."

"And myself, Mister Dockett?"

Dockett cleared his throat.

Alexis watched the images unfold from aft. The timing would be entirely on Warth, when he felt he had the shot lined up properly with his mental picture of where Pullink sat. The man had a poacher's patience for sitting in the dark, evading watchers, and taking his prey.

Warth pulled the trigger.

His shot burned a hole in the inner patch and took Pullink in the back of the head before *Mongoose's* sensors could even react to this new hull breach.

Alexis had the quarterdeck alarms turned off, but there was a klaxon in the engineering space. The hatches in the aft companionway sealed as air rushed out. Nabb and a few others had the hatch to the space locked open, four of them in vacsuits, but well away from the view of the two surrendered pirates there. Nabb and two others stood in full view without their helmets on so as not to alert those pirates and give the game away to Pullink.

They all rushed in, prepared to grasp Pullink and pull him away if he'd survived the shot and made to further damage the plant, but that proved to be unnecessary even before Warth grasped the second rifle from his assistant and took a more hurried shot to be sure the job was finished.

That one took Pullink in the back, as Warth aimed lower, thinking the pirate might duck down if he survived the first.

He hadn't, though, merely slumping a bit forward to rest his head against his arm where it held the laser pistol.

"I wouldn't say you're averse to risk, sir," Dockett said. "And damn me if I'll ever make a book against you."

THIRTY-SIX

ALEXIS HAD A COMMS LASER LAID FROM *MONGOOSE* TO THE boat remaining on Erzurum's surface.

It was one of the few things she preferred about operating in normal-space as opposed to *darkspace,* where she'd have been reduced to flashing the lights on the ship's hull and masts to produce signals. The accumulation of dark matter in *darkspace* affected comms lasers much as it did those of the ship's guns, condensing them and warping their path so as to make them an ineffective means of communication.

Regular light was affected as well, but not so much — something to do with a laser's coherence, as well as the density and phase of the photons involved. She didn't fully understand it, but, then, there was a great deal about the Dark she didn't understand.

Kannstadt responded quickly, he had the second boat already loaded with his men and ready to lift.

"I had thought you had these codes to retake your ship quickly," he said. "*Schnell, schnell!*"

"There was a bit more to it," Alexis allowed, "and to convincing someone aboard to play along."

"But it has worked?"

Alexis nodded. "The first and second officers were quite cooperative."

Kannstadt cocked his head. "But not the captain? Was he injured in taking the ship?"

"Captain Tinkham served a purpose," Alexis said.

Kannstadt grinned causing Alexis to wonder at herself. It seemed the Hanoverese understood her quite well, and that bothered her. He made no more mention of it other than to ask, "The next ship is expecting us?"

Alexis nodded again. "With a new man, Gutis, at the helm." She spared a glance her pilot, changed, as Kannstadt was, from the clothing they'd worn through the swamps into those taken from one of the boat's pirate occupants. "Just talk to them like a pirate, Gutis, and they'll let you come alongside."

"Aye, sir —" He frowned, then narrowed his eyes. "*Aarrr.*"

Alexis frowned.

"Sorry, sir," Gutis said, looking back to his console.

ALEXIS THOUGHT they were less ready than they should be when Gutis lifted Kannstadt's boat from Erzurum's surface.

She'd have preferred a fuller crew aboard *Mongoose*, and that of men who'd understand her commands without the elaborate coaching. On the other hand, those on the quarterdeck with her spoke English well enough — save Schwalheimer on the signals console, though he was the best she had for the job. Layland was at the helm, having come to her boat when they abandoned the ship on their approach to Erzurum, which gave her an experienced man there, and one she knew well. Tite was on the tactical console, an older man from her boat crew and one who had been a gun captain before Erzurum. The Hanoverese she had filling the crews' ranks knew how to load a gun well enough and in normal-space that tactical console was more important than the aiming of a single gun.

They had time, yet, to work up the crew on the sails, for they'd not be transitioning to *darkspace* just yet, if she could help it. There were enough ships in orbit around Erzurum for her to deal with.

She watched Kannstadt's boat enter orbit and shape its path for *Fang*.

"*Gewehrdeckel* ready, *kapitän*," Schwalheimer said.

Alexis assumed that was the gundeck, as that's what she'd asked the man to notify her of its readiness.

"Drop us down, Layland," she ordered when she thought it time.

"Aye, sir."

Mongoose was in a high orbit, near *Fang's*, the better to defend against any incoming attack. The other pirates were lower, along with the merchantmen here for the market in pirated goods.

While she might prefer to stay where she was and support Kannstadt's attack with *Mongoose's* guns, the Hanoverese captain had no way to shut down his target's communications as she had *Mongoose's*. As soon as his men burst from the docking boat, *Fang* would squawk a warning like one of the Isikli farm's geese, and Alexis planned to both prevent the other ships from responding, while also, she hoped, distract the crew of *Fang* at some crucial moment.

Mongoose accelerated and dropped toward the planet. Alexis planned for a lower, faster orbit that would take her around the planet quickly enough to bring her guns to bear on those other ships. There were no gunboats in the system's normal-space, so far as she could tell. They were all in *darkspace*, keeping watch for an intruder coming from there. She didn't want a single one of these ships in orbit being able to make it to a Lagrangian point for transition to *darkspace* to give them a warning.

Kannstadt would be on his own to take *Fang*, and then, if he was able, assist her.

The merchantmen would be no problem, they'd be hesitant and wary of the pirates surrounding them as they took on cargo, but wouldn't question Erzurum's masters for fear of having their own ships taken. The two other pirates, and *Fang* until Kannstadt gave them something else to worry at, were a different story. Armfield and Hallows, Tinkham's two mates, had told her, and Blackbourne confirmed, that there was no particular hierarchy to the ships in orbit, pirates being an egalitarian lot, and so each captain might do as he wished with regard to orbits or working his ship — but that didn't mean the others might not become suspicious of her maneuvers and question them.

"Zignal, *kapitän*," Schwalheimer said.

"This is your moment, Armfield," Alexis told the pirate first-mate. She'd decided not to repeat the farce of having both mates at the console, choosing Armfield as the marginally more intelligent and compliant.

The pirate glanced at the spot on the deck where his captain had fallen. There was surprisingly little blood from a burst of flechettes to the eye, but a few drops still stained the decking there.

Armfield swallowed and nodded, then hunched over Schwalheimer's shoulder and the console.

"What is it, Kerry?" he asked as Schwalheimer accepted the incoming signal.

Alexis couldn't see the other captain's image, staying out of sight as she was, but his voice boomed over the speakers.

"Where's Tinkham?"

"Captain's busy, you fat bugger, and no time for someone worthy, much less your ugly self," Armfield yelled back, making Alexis jump.

She narrowed her eyes at him and gestured with the hand that held her flechette pistol, as well as giving a pointed nod to where Nabb stood with pistol and rifle.

"*Busy?* Why's he not on the quarterdeck with you sending that ill-made, tube of shite all about our orbits? What are you about, you shitting excuse for a man?"

"Tinkham don't answer to you and I don't neither!" Armfield yelled.

Alexis relaxed a bit and nodded to Nabb. It seemed this was simply what was expected with the captain of the other ship and not some ruse to warn him there was something amiss on *Mongoose*.

"You'll answer to my boot if I have to alter my orbit for your foolishness!"

"You keep that bloody tub of yours out our way!" Armfield yelled back. "We'll go where Tinkham says!"

With that, he reached forward and cut the connection.

"Things are not so very cordial between this Captain Kerry and your Tinkham?" Alexis asked.

"Could say that," Armfield allowed.

"I see." Alexis thought for a moment. "Layland, I'd admire it did you make this Kerry squawk a bit more in our course — laying us well for Captain Kerry's ship —" She checked the navigation plot. "— *Talon*, to be our first target."

The helmsman grinned. "Aye, sir."

Layland touched the helm controls and *Mongoose's* course altered so that it would intersect that of *Talon*, before continuing on around Erzurum to catch up with the last of the pirate ships — Alexis read the plot — *Claw*.

I detect a singular lack of thought in their ships' names.

Layland kept their course after that so *Mongoose* would then close on the cluster of merchant ships, which were staying together in Erzurum's orbit as though that offered them some protection. It wouldn't, Alexis knew, not from the pirates and not from *Mongoose*.

"Zignal, *kapitän*," Schwalheimer said.

"Ignore it."

"*Jawohl.*"

The two ships' courses continued to converge, *Mongoose* dropping down on *Talon* like a stooping eagle, while the pirate ship obstinately maintained its own course.

"Zignal, *kapitän*," Schwalheimer said. "From *Talon* still."

Alexis eyed the plot, watching the ever-adjusting curves of their orbit and the other ships as Layland made minute adjustments. Their path was not such that they'd be in the way of any other than *Talon*, so she imagined the other ships were simply watching the game of chicken with some amusement — assuming it to be a show of bravado between two captains who did not like each other very much.

She could, if she wished, fire upon *Talon* at any time — every ship not behind Erzurum's bulk was well within range of her guns in normal-space — but patience, and the distracting game she played with *Talon*, were more to allow Kannstadt's boat time to reach *Fang*. That and to leave less time for the other ships in orbit to realize what was happening and react.

"Boat's near *Fang*," Tite, on the tactical console, informed her.

"Thank you, Tite. Schwalheimer, keep a close watch on general signals, if you please. I wish to know the moment *Fang* cries an alert."

"*Jawohl.*"

It would take time for Kannstadt's boat to dock and the hatch to open. Afterward, she hoped, even a few moments for the pirates, expecting drink and women, to realize that the scale-skin clothed Hanoverese were neither of those things. Every moment brought her closer to her own targets.

"They scream, *kapitän*," Schwalheimer said.

"Now, Layland! Take us close astern!" *Mongoose* had closed enough on *Talon*, and the other ship was accelerating enough, that she could take *Mongoose* behind the enemy and rake her.

"Aye, sir!"

Mongoose spun on her axis and Layland fed more power to the engines, not stopping her motion, as that would be impossible in so short a time, but altering it so that she curved even more toward Erzurum and *Talon*. It took but a moment for *Talon's* continued acceleration to pull the pirate ship ahead of *Mongoose's* course and expose her stern.

"*Fire!*" Alexis yelled.

THIRTY-SEVEN

MONGOOSE'S GUNPORTS FLEW OPEN AND LASERS LASHED FROM her sides.

They were not quite astern of *Talon*, still a bit off her starboard quarter and above, but the other ship's stern was in view and in range. *Mongoose's* first broadside, aimed and controlled by Tite at the tactical console, rather than the individual gunners, was on target and struck the pirate ship a massive blow to her conventional drive.

Talon skewed and swerved as the thrust from her drive became unequal for a moment, her helmsman trying to adjust to the damage done to the drive outputs even as *Mongoose* rolled and turned to bring her port broadside to bear for another shot.

"Zignal from *Talon*," Schwalheimer called.

"I imagine so," Alexis said, nodding to Blackbourne.

The bearded pirate sighed. He hadn't liked this bit of her plan, less so than her actually attacking his fellows, to Alexis' surprise.

Schwalheimer opened the general radio circuit around Erzurum, where all the ships in orbit could broadcast in the open, rather than a ship-to-ship laser.

The channel was already abuzz with broadcasts as Hampson on

Fang called for help against Kannstadt and his boarders. Kerry, on *Talon*, called for assistance against *Mongoose's* attack while simultaneously berating the memory, though he didn't know it, of Tinkham. The remaining pirate ship, *Claw*, demanded to know what everyone was about, and the merchantmen in orbit squawked and cawed in alarm, like a farmyard's geese.

"*Belay that, y'scurvy addle-pated, vat-starved curs!*" Blackbourne yelled into one of the few gaps between those transmissions. "An' y'listen to Old Blackbourne or face our Captain Ness' wrath when he returns, y'will! Kerry an' Hampson, y'stand down, hear? Yer perfidy's been discovered an' Ness's sent word of it! Trumper!" Blackbourne named the captain of the as-yet unengaged *Claw*. "You stay quiet or name yerself in their treachery and get dealt the same hand!"

Reluctant or not, Alexis had to admit that Blackbourne played his part well. She hoped that this ruse, pretending that the pirate leader had sent some word back to his second that *Talon's* and *Fang's* captains were involved in some treachery might sow enough confusion. It was unlikely that either of those being now attacked would surrender in the face of the accusation — she assumed this pirate leader, Ness, was not known for clemency in the justice he meted out — but it might cause *Claw's* captain to hang back and see where the winds blew things.

"You merchants keep t'yer orbits an' shut yer gobs!" Blackbourne yelled, keying to transmit again. "Y'let us sort this out, y'hear!"

Those ships, at least, Alexis saw, were doing as Blackbourne ordered, ceasing their transmissions and doing their very best now to draw no attention from the pirates fighting it out above.

That had been her greatest worry —

Well, after the bits about successfully taking Mongoose, *getting Kannstadt's boat close enough to* Fang *for a boarding, and then fighting this* Talon, *and, hopefully, distracting* Claw *from joining in the fight.*

In truth, she had a great many worries right now, more than she could successfully number, it seemed, but the merchantmen were certainly one of them. The appearance of a single gunboat in system, whether from happenstance or should one of the merchantmen make its way to a transition point and signal what was happening in Erzurum's orbit, would drastically skew the odds, already well against her force. Those gunboats, small though they might be, were numerous and could fire on her from a Lagrangian point and be gone before she even knew they were there.

By this time, Kerry and his *Talon* had time to react and were veering away from *Mongoose*, trying to gain a bit of room to maneuver and get Alexis off her stern. *Mongoose's* port broadside lashed out, damaging more of the other ship's engines and thrusters and making control even more difficult.

Mongoose rolled again. She was nearly astern of *Talon*, or astern of the pirate ship's course, no matter which part faced her, and the starboard broadside was ready again. Her rate of fire was greatly enhanced with nothing for the guncrews to do but load shot, not having to worry about laying the guns for the vagaries of their shot in *darkspace*.

"Blackbourne, what're you about? Where's Tinkham? Damn your eyes and bloody red ender, stop firing on my ship!"

"Tinkham's busy fightin' his ship an' left Old Blackbourne t'jaw with the likes o'you!"

More fire from *Mongoose* struck *Talon*, many of the guns had no angle on the enemy's stern, so spent themselves along the hull, sending great gouts of vaporized thermoplastic off into space, the effect of these adding to the woes of *Talon's* helmsman as each was a tiny, random thruster.

No matter the surprise, though, Captain Kerry had his men somewhat trained and *Talon's* gunports opened to reveal the crystalline tubes of her guns' barrels.

Mongoose rolled to present a fresh broadside, and *Talon* fired at the same time.

Lasers flashed across the intervening space, showing only the sparkles of what matter there might be between the two ships.

Mongoose shuddered as coherent light lashed her sides and there was a scream, abruptly cut off, over the open comms channel to the gundeck where one or more of *Talon's* guns found an open port.

"Number four's set over, sir," Tite said.

"Come about — pass under her stern again and give her another," Alexis ordered.

Talon was twisting and rolling herself, her helmsman attempting to bring her other broadside to bear while keeping *Mongoose* from raking her stern again, but Alexis' largely undamaged ship had the advantage.

Tite swapped ends, decelerating relative to their target, and cut across the stern before *Talon* could react.

"Hold fast and ready to give her both sides, Tite," Alexis ordered, eyeing the skewing stern of the other ship. *Talon* was whirling about like some sort of dervish — with vapor spewing from her port quarter where her hull must have been breached and remained unsealed. "*Fire!*"

Mongoose herself spun like a top to bring both broadsides to bear in a surprisingly short time. All of *Mongoose's* guns fired — save her chasers and the overset number four — sending twenty-three streams of coherent light into *Talon's* stern.

The other ship disappeared behind a cloud of vaporized thermoplastic, before reappearing as *Mongoose* passed.

Talon had power, as evidenced by her hull lights, but no propulsion and little in the way of maneuvering power. The ship tumbled and twisted along her last course, her helmsman seeming to make no effort now to regain control, or merely unable with so much damage to the drive and thrusters.

Blackbourne was still throwing as much confusion into the pirates' communications as he could — which, Alexis had to admit, was quite a lot, for it would take any listener some time to pick out the gist from within the shell of profane curses the pirate spewed forth.

Captains Hampson and Trumper, of the boarded *Fang* and

oncoming *Claw*, were involved in a heated exchange, with Hampson demanding Trumper come to his aid in fighting off the boarders and Trumper alternately demanding Blackbourne, Hampson, and Kerry all stand down, as though he were the voice of reason in some internal piratical dispute.

"Bloody hell, there ain't no call t'be shootin' up ourn own ships!" Trumper broadcast. "Ness'll be back in a fortnight or two and clear it all up, damn you! Blackbourne — stop Tinkham from shooting and call your bloody men off *Fang*, you scabrous dolt!"

That exchange gave Alexis a bit of valuable knowledge, as she'd trust Trumper's excited outburst far more than any questioning of the pirates she might do. If this Ness were expected back so soon as a fortnight, perhaps ten or twenty days, allowing for the vagaries of *darkspace* winds, then that told her how long they had to secure those kept captive on Erzurum and flee the system.

"Damn you, Blackbourne, you traitorous scum!" Captain Hampson's voice cut across the channel, the sound of pistols, lasers, and screams of men from behind him. "Trumper, they're not our men, they're bloody Hannies!"

"*Claw's* accelerating and coming up to our orbit, sir," Tite called from the tactical console.

It appeared Captain Trumper of that ship had decided on both whose side he came down on and the action to take, leaving Hampson to fight off the boarders himself and coming after *Mongoose* and, Alexis presumed, Blackbourne.

"Steady on, Layland," Alexis ordered. "We'll get around Erzurum and take on *Claw* once we're in view of those merchantmen."

It would be better, all told, to fight the last pirate vessel away from those merchant ships, so that one of their captains wouldn't take it into his head to ingratiate himself with the pirates by assisting, but she had the further duty of preventing those very merchants from escaping. Just one of them transitioning to *darkspace* would alert the gunboats and set those on their newly captured ships like bold rats.

The merchants had clustered together in their orbits, as though there might be some strength in numbers from the chaos surrounding them, but just as *Mongoose* rounded the planet's curve to bring them into sight one was seen to break off and make away from orbit — probably to head for the L4 point, if Alexis judged his course correctly. L1 was closer, but would have meant staying in the vicinity of the planet, something she suspected that the captain would prefer not to do.

"Get yer scurrilous arse back in orbit, y'running dog!" Blackbourne transmitted. "Or ye'll never take a cargo here again and ye'll forever be a target fer Ness!"

It was a brief, but noticeable, lag for Blackbourne's words to reach the other ship, and more for the response to return.

"It's not my fight, Blackbourne!" the merchant captain yelled. "We came for a bloody cargo, not to get caught up in whatever you and Ness and whoever else have going on! And if I know Ness, he'll not care a whit that I chose not to stay under your bloody guns, so long as I bring enough coin for those cargoes!"

"Old Blackbourne has to admit the man's the right of it, bitch-woman," Blackbourne said to Alexis.

Alexis sighed. "Do you suppose you might stop calling me that?"

Blackbourne shrugged. "Yer a hard girl, bitch-woman, and Old Blackbourne's thinking a word or two'll not change how you treat him in the end."

Alexis might have insisted, but she did still need the man, even though his presence didn't seem to have influenced the merchantmen. If anything, the merchant captain's response might have convinced another it was time to leave, for a second ship was making to break Erzurum's orbit.

Well, then, if threats of pirates wouldn't cow them, she'd take a different tack.

She edged Blackbourne away from the signals console and made to transmit herself.

"To all merchant shipping in orbit around Erzurum, this is Lieutenant Alexis Carew of Her Majesty's Royal Navy and commanding the private ship *Mongoose*. Heave-to and prepare for inspection, on suspicion of complicity in piracy and slavery. I also speak for Captain Kannstadt of the Republic of Hanover, in whose space we lie." She paused. "Gentlemen, I assure you we have neither the time nor patience for the niceties of shots across your bows nor chasing down rabble." She paused another moment, watching the navigation plot and then, as there appeared to be no immediate change in the fleeing ship's course, opened the channel again. "Very well. Tite, put both broadsides into that fleeing bastard and keep it on until he returns to orbit."

"Aye, sir."

Mongoose was twisting and spinning to bring her guns to bear even as the merchant captain's voice sounded over the quarterdeck speakers.

"*What?* Who are you? Blackbourne, what are you about now?"

The guns lashed out, sparkling across the distance between the two ships and striking the merchantman all along her starboard side. Gouts of vapor, thermoplastic, and air all spewed from the ship as her hull was shot through, then then *Mongoose's* second broadside flashed across the intervening space, wrecking more havoc and damage on the fleeing ship.

The merchant's hull was thinner than a warship's — thinner, even, than *Mongoose's* or the pirates', which had both been strengthened to take some enemy fire, though even they weren't up to a true warship's. *Mongoose's* shot had holed the merchantman in more than one place, exposing the inner compartments to vacuum and dumping what air there was before inner hatches slammed shut.

Alexis had a moment's qualms for the merchant spacers aboard, but they'd sailed with a captain willing to carry goods pirated from his fellows and they'd have to take what fates awaited them for it.

"Come about, Captain —" Alexis checked the navigation plot for the information. "— Yavuz, and return to orbit. I don't think your ship will stand another broadside and I've time for one or two more before dealing with your fellows."

Alexis gave him a few seconds and was relieved to see the ship turn and begin decelerating for a return to Erzurum's orbit. Part of that was not wanting to have to fire into the ship again and kill more of the crew, though they'd all likely hang when this was done anyway, but another part was that she needed every ship in orbit.

If Ness and the rest of the pirates were returning in a fortnight, then she'd need as many ships as she could take to get the freed New London spacers away or meet him if there were too many to flee.

"Damn your eyes, whoever you are!" Yavuz said. "There's good men dead here for no good reason!"

Alexis ignored him, there were good men dead with Captain Kannstadt in the taking of *Fang*, too, for all they were Hanoverese and often enough her enemy. Good men dead by the pirates taking their prey. Good men dead in Erzurum's swamps and on its farms. There were enough good men dead in this mess that she'd not spare too much of a thought for those who'd profit by it.

Satisfied that Yavuz was returning *Gabya* to orbit, Alexis could turn her attention to the last oncoming pirate.

"Come about, Layland, and set us on this *Claw*."

THE PIRATES on Erzurum's surface were in it now, having heard Alexis' broadcast to the merchantmen, and calling for Blackbourne to explain himself. As well, those merchant spacers still on the surface with their ships' boats, some feeling abandoned by the ship which attempted to flee, wondering at its state and if they were to be abandoned on the pirate planet, and others wishing nothing more than to get to their own ships so as to steer clear of further conflict.

Kannstadt had gained control of *Fang's* quarterdeck, if not the entirety of the ship, and put a man on the signals console who, for some inexplicable reason, added German to the babble of voices. What he hoped to accomplish by that, with so many of the ships in orbit speaking English or, in the case of most of the merchants, the Barbary patois, Alexis couldn't imagine.

Nevertheless, Schwalheimer was able to pass along enough of Kannstadt's status for Alexis to understand that he might have the quarterdeck, but did not yet have control of *Fang's* guns and would be no help against the oncoming *Claw*.

THIRTY-EIGHT

THERE WAS LITTLE NEED FOR LAYLAND TO BRING THE SHIP around, for *Claw* was well on her own way to engaging *Mongoose*. The last pirate ship was accelerating and dropping toward their orbit in order to better catch up with them.

"Steady on, then, Layland," Alexis said. She went to the helm and laid a hand on his shoulder. "Let's draw her in."

"Aye, sir."

They kept on, both Alexis and Layland with a wary eye for the plots and any movement from *Claw*, looking for the start of the twist and roll that would present her broadside and send the shot from her guns streaking to bury itself in *Mongoose*.

"Gunners ready, sir," Tite announced from the tactical console.

Alexis merely nodded, nearly all her attention on the other ship. She'd assumed her own would be ready when the time came, something which might have been a mistake with so many new-come aboard and after they'd spent so long on Erzurum — but she'd had a word with each man as the boat loaded to lift them, and, if they hadn't understood the word itself, they'd understood the tone of a captain taking their measure and reacted as she wished.

The way a man nodded, the set of his jaw, a narrowness of an eye, the matter of fact "Aye, sir" or "*Jawohl*" — all told her they were steady enough for what was coming.

Mongoose had her stern toward *Claw* — an open invitation, or taunt, for the pirate captain, if he knew or suspected the slap-shoddy way of his fellows' repairs.

The distance closed. *Claw* drew nearer.

Ahead of their course, lower now for both ships and among the orbits of the merchants who'd wanted less travel in their cramped boats, those merchants scattered out of the way, much like a flock of birds all hoping they'll not be the stooping eagle's target this time.

The angle of *Claw's* bow to *Mongoose's* stern reached a certain point, not one calculated by the navigation plot or announced by Tite from his tactical analysis, but something felt. Alexis' hand tightened its grip and Layland's hands danced over the controls — neither could swear to which came first or if either reacted to the others, only that they felt it.

Alexis cut off the order, seeing that Layland was already moving, setting *Mongoose* to twist in her course even as the shot from *Claw's* bowchasers arrived to splash harmlessly against the ship's port flank.

They waited, steady on, twice more for *Claw* to fire chasers, twice more for Layland and Alexis to react to either their feel of the battle's rhythm or some twitch of the pirate's bow as it prepared to fire. Twice more *Mongoose* swerved to present her flank, Layland's hands dancing over the controls to correct for the push of vaporizing thermoplastic from her hull.

Even as they settled back to their course, Alexis knew the distance was right.

Still she waited, keeping *Mongoose* on course, as though wanting to lead her pursuer right around Erzurum and back to Kannstadt's taken *Fang*.

It was the right thing to do, to lead the pirate a merry chase and then turn to strike when her enemy was under the guns of two ships.

Claw's captain would know that too, and would want to finish his foes in detail, not have to maneuver against two.

The pirate's bow twitched — once, twice, as though undecided or wishing *Mongoose* to react and commit to a roll in response, perhaps allowing him to twist and send his whole broadside at her still exposed stern.

Claw's bow edged to starboard.

"*Now!*" Alexis yelled, feeling the feints were done and this was the other captain's true move. "Hard a'port! Roll and put our keel to her! Gunners ready!"

"Aye, sir!"

Mongoose twisted to put her stern away from the gunports being exposed along *Claw's* port side. It was too late for the other captain to change his maneuver — doing so would bring his bow back around to face *Mongoose's* broadside and give Alexis the opportunity to rake his full length with her largest guns.

Committed, *Claw* turned faster.

Mongoose turned and rolled, presenting her heavy keel, the full length of it retracted as unnecessary in normal-space and laid like armor to face the oncoming assault.

Claw fired.

Shot after shot struck home, the pirate's computer being able to lay the ship for each in normal-space, and more accurately than a man ever could. Pock marks of vanished thermoplastic appeared on *Mongoose's* keel.

Claw continued her roll, bringing first her own keel and then her other broadside to bear.

Alexis thought that would end the worst of it, unless *Claw* had far more pirates aboard than either *Mongoose* or the others. They'd not have enough, as she didn't, to reload and fight both sides of the ship past these initial broadsides.

"Roll to port!" Alexis ordered, even as the first of the new shot struck *Mongoose*.

She'd seen *Claw's* best, she thought, a heavy, ponderous roll for such a small ship — enough to cow a merchant, but not nearly enough to face her *Mongoose*. *Claw's* captain would not reverse his ship's roll, wanting to keep what momentum he had.

Claw made to put her own keel forward to take the fire her captain must know was coming and give his crew time to reload at least one side, but *Mongoose* was, indeed, faster, and her own broadside was coming to bear on the disappearing side of the other ship, rather than oncoming keel.

Alexis gripped the sides of the navigation plot, casting her gaze from the computer's plot of both ships' courses to the images of *Claw*. "Port broadside, fire as you bear!"

MONGOOSE LASHED OUT, finally freed to respond to her adversary's pinpricks.

Gun after gun fired, crossing the intervening space in an instant and nearly invisible in normal-space. Only the occasional flash in the vacuum as it vaporized some bit of dust or gas left behind by those pinpricks *Mongoose* had felt against her keel.

Mongoose's guns sought out *Claw's* open gunports at increasingly difficult angles as the other ship rolled to hide them, but not quickly enough.

Some hit the edges of the ports, pocking the other ship's side or carving crescents from her hull as they spent themselves against the tough thermoplastic.

Others struck true.

Through the ports without even the thin gallenium nets that would have protected them in *darkspace*.

One struck a gun captain, already crouched to load a fresh canister of shot into the breach. The full force of *Mongoose's* shot took him in the helmet, the energy of a nine-pound capacitor vaporized the pirate's head, and the helmet before continuing on to strike the shot rack running down the middle of *Claw's* gundeck.

The gallenium shot canisters, scratched and dinged from heavy use, provided enough reflection to splinter what energy was left into a dozen beams, each enough to cut a man down.

A gun carriage overturned, struck in the side and its parts not able to absorb the energy of the shot, it released that energy by sending bits of itself into its crew.

Men dove for the decks, throwing themselves prostate to avoid the oncoming fire, even though they knew they couldn't possibly be fast enough — if they were able to reach the deck, then the fire was already done.

At least for the moment — until their enemies' next turn in this deadly game.

With that realization, and with the sight of dead comrades, wrecked guns, and bits of molten thermoplastic still liquid about their gundeck, came the knowledge that, for all they'd fired first and more, their enemy was still whole.

"STARBOARD GUNS, AS YOU BEAR! FIRE!"

Alexis knew her next broadside would be largely wasted against *Claw's* keel, and she might have saved those guns for later, but wished to put the other captain under the psychological impact of steady fire.

If this battle with *Claw* went on too long, another of those merchant captains might take it into his head that escaping while she was occupied would be fine idea. One word to the gunboats in *darkspace* and they were finished.

"Put our keel to her and reload!"

"Aye, sir!"

Claw was continuing her own roll, so as to bring freshly loaded guns to bear.

"Give us a bit of thrust, Layland," Alexis said, tracing possibilities on the plot. "Make him maneuver a bit."

"Aye, sir."

A rolling battle of broadsides would take too long, she thought, better to force the other captain to judge her intentions and react — perhaps some mistake and opening would —

Fire lashed out, sparkling as it destroyed what bits of matter remained in the void and thermoplastic spewed from a hull — but not *Mongoose's* as Alexis had expected. This shot came from a distance, mostly bracketing *Claw*, but one or two striking home on the part of her hull facing away from Erzurum.

"Ah, Captain Kannstadt's in range with *Fang*, sir," Tite announced.

"Indeed?" Alexis would have to have a talk with the man about keeping his eye on more than the battle at hand from his tactical console — or, perhaps not, as she saw him flush and hunch over his screen. There were times a single word was quite enough. It seemed that Kannstadt had managed to fully take his own target and bring *Fang* within range to assist Alexis with taking *Claw*.

Fang was, indeed, in range, though still distant, but closing and Alexis could well imagine the chaos and uncertainty aboard the only ship the pirates still held. *Claw* was already damaged and with little to show for their first exchange with *Mongoose*, they were now facing two foes, with one high enough in orbit to fire on their exposed flanks no matter how they rolled.

"Signal to *Claw*, Schwal —"

Bloody hell, but I'll mangle the man's name if I try —

"Signal to *Claw* — Strike your colors, instanter."

THIRTY-NINE

THE PIRATES OF ERZURUM'S GUNBOATS AND THEIR ROUTINES were, Alexis thought, quite the most satisfying thing she'd seen in some time.

Going by Blackbourne's word and some schedules left in *Mongoose's* systems by the unlamented Tinkham, Alexis, Kannstadt, and Ellender determined that their timing in taking the orbiting ships could not have been better, as the crews of the gunboats were due to rotate back to the planet's surface in only a day's time. Just long enough to work up *Mongoose*, *Fang*, and *Claw* with their small crews, leave a few men aboard the more heavily damaged *Talon* to keep watch over the captured merchantmen, and sail for Erzurum's planetary-lunar L1 point.

Their crews were more to each captain's liking, as well, with Kannstadt's more numerous Hanoverese manning his *Fang* and the damaged *Talon*, while Ellender had *Claw* and Alexis' boat crew, augmented with the New Londoners and a few Hanoverese from Kannstadt's group, had *Mongoose* at nearly half her full complement.

"Transition," Alexis ordered, then before the screens in *Mongoose's* quarterdeck could even register their return to *darkspace*,

"Sail crews to the hull, drop main and fore — Layland, put us on the starboard tack. *Ready on the gundeck!*"

Mongoose's optics caught up with her change and displayed the surrounding space, dozens of gunboats hove-to around the Lagrangian point, some come together for their crews to come and go, and all waiting for a ship from Erzurum's normal space to appear loaded with replacement crews.

Though what those pirate crews were expecting — fresh men to take their place while they returned planetside for their own fortnight of revels after the tedium of sailing about Erzurum's shoals — was quite a bit different from what they got from *Mongoose, Fang,* and *Claw.*

"As you bear!" Alexis ordered. "*Fire!*"

COHERENT LIGHT LASHED from *Mongoose's* sides, followed quickly, but still beating them, Alexis noted, the same from *Claw* and *Fang.*

Even at the half-charge she'd ordered, noting Blackbourne's description of just how close the gunboats would heave-to around the transition point, the damage done was stunning.

Shot burst through the thin hulls of the gunboats, sending vapor, clouds of thermoplastic mixed with air, from the holed boats, spewing away in great gouts.

The gunboats' bare masts were shot through where some shot missed the hulls, cut cleanly or notched so that they'd not hold a sail.

Where two boats were set together, some shot ran clean through both, *Mongoose* was so close and their hulls so thin.

"I've bite to the rudder, sir," Layland said from the helm. "We've a way on. Starboard tack, aye."

"Fall off a point," Alexis said, eyeing the crowded space around the Lagrangian point. Ellender and Kannstadt were maneuvering as well, taking their ships toward other clusters of gunboats.

Mongoose was the fastest and most maneuverable of the three, so her purpose, truly, was to make it free of the boats and ensure none escaped the other two. Still, one path to that was as good as another, and falling just a point off the wind and a bit down would take her directly between those ...

"And down twenty, Layland, make for that space between those four there." She highlighted her targets for the helmsman to see.

"Aye, sir."

"A guinea for every man aboard," Alexis said, "if the guncrews can reload both sides and fire as we pass."

It was a hard challenge, undermanned as they were. With only two men per gun, and that fighting only one side, there'd be empty shot canisters rolling about the deck as they dumped them from the breeches in their hurry. Cleanup could come later, though, once they'd assured not even a single gunboat could escape them.

"Aye, sir!" Creasy called as he passed the signal on. "Bless Boots, and they'll see it done."

Alexis' elation at catching the gunboats so unawares fell a bit and she wondered if Kannstadt might trade her a signalsman — Schwalheimer's English was not *so* bad, after all, and at least he didn't seem the sort to set up some kind of religion around the Vile Creature.

"Port guns ready!" Creasy announced a moment later.

Alexis watched the plot as *Mongoose* slid between the two pairs of gunboats.

"As you bear! *Fire!*"

She'd have preferred to fire in broadside, wanting the satisfaction of seeing those boats crushed in one blow, but the ship had too few men aboard for that, not when asking them to load and fire both sides, at least.

One gun lashed out, holing the nearest gunboat. Then another, then a third, all on target and well-laid.

"As you bear to starboard!" Alexis called out. "*Fire!*"

And the corresponding guns on *Mongoose's* starboard side began firing, as their crews rushed from the just fired port guns to lay and fire to starboard.

These shots were a bit rushed as the ship slid past the still stationary gunboats, but any hit did devastating damage.

One boat was stern on to *Mongoose*, and a shot struck the gunboat, splintered on some reflective surface inside, and fully three of the splinters made it through to exit the boat's hull further on, one even striking, but not holing, a second boat.

Alexis felt her cheeks pull back in a predatory grin and pushed down all thoughts about the devastation inside those boats. In all likelihood the pirate crews had not even been suited, thinking the ships coming from Erzurum's normal-space were friends and anticipating their fortnight's pleasures on the planet's surface before returning to their cramped patrols.

These boats were not only fragile in their hulls, but small, without the interior bulkheads and compartments to seal off a holed space and retain what air they might. Any hole would dump all their air into the surrounding vacuum and there'd be only seconds for the crew to don vacsuits or seal helmets if they were wearing them already.

Moreover, she knew from Blackbourne that the pirates over-crewed these gunboats, in order to cow the arriving merchantmen and protect the system.

The carnage aboard each boat as her shot struck them must be horrible.

To starboard, a boat's stern was breached, cracking its fusion plant and turning it, for a few moments, into a miniature sun — perhaps the only one in *darkspace* at that particular time.

Alexis watched in fascinated horror. She'd never been this close to such a thing before and without the distortions of more distance in *darkspace*, she could see that what she'd always taken for a single, vast explosion when a plant went up was more of a progression.

The light of the reaction expanded in a ball from the boat's stern, its brightness overcoming *Mongoose's* optics to flash the image white before the ship's systems compensated.

Then, from the stern, the ball of plasma made its way toward the bow, taking only a second or two. She could make out its movement as it ate away at the gunboat's hull, consuming all before it until there was nothing left and the raging ball of fire began to slowly dim and dissipate.

Alexis shuddered, wondering at the fate of those aboard and whether they'd had a lungful of air or were suited. Had they been aware when it came? Had they seen, even for a fraction of a second, that wall of blinding fire coming for them, devouring all within its path, and known it came for them?

She pushed that thought down as she did so many others.

No matter the horror of their fate, those men had chosen their path and known it could end here or at the gallows. They'd taken ships, murdered crews, sold others into slavery, and untold other acts just as vile.

Other images on her plot were of greater importance at the moment, and she could wonder at how many had just met their fate at her hands another time, likely in the dark of night.

For now, there was a suited figure on the hull of a gunboat to port, just one, but laboring to swing the boat's yard about on its fore-and-aft rig in order to get under way.

They'd strike soon, she thought, once the surprise wore off and the extent of their foe sank in, but for now they were the enemy and she was determined to leave them in horrified, shaken awe when they finally did so. There were few enough of the freed slaves crewing her ships for the moment and she wanted every pirate so trembling with fear that they'd not think to raise a hand.

"Gunners to port!" Alexis ordered. "And I'd admire it did that bloody boat not gain a scrap of sail!"

FORTY

Kannstadt and Ellender looked around at Alexis' cabin on *Mongoose* and she couldn't help but flush with embarrassment. The pirate captain, Tinkham, had not been the tidiest of men, but she suspected their own quarters, now aboard *Fang* and *Claw* respectively, were still no better. It was the first time they'd all met together since leaving Erzurum's surface, there being no time if they wanted to take the gunboats by surprise, and there'd not been time to fully clean the ship either.

Isom had set about some tidying, but with *Mongoose* so undermanned, Kannstadt having retrieved most of the Hanoverese for his own new ship, cleaning simply wasn't a priority.

"Sit, gentlemen, please," she said, indicating her dining table, which was, thankfully clear of Tinkham's detritus.

Kannstadt, attended still, oddly, by Lieutenant Deckard, for all the junior officer was from New London, was dressed in a ship's jumpsuit now, as was Deckard, rather than the snakipede skins he'd worn on Erzurum. Ellender had changed from his ragged slave-garb, as well, but his jumpsuit was shabbier, perhaps there being less to choose from aboard *Claw*. Ellender, too, had an officer with him, but Alexis couldn't recall his name.

The man had also brought along a full boat crew, rather than only a pilot and one or two others as Kannstadt had, which must have left his newly taken ship even more severely undermanned.

Isom brought bowls of nuts to the table, part of what few provisions she'd had aboard that might have survived the depredations of the pirates taking *Mongoose*, and a rough beer that seemed to be all the spirits left aboard.

Blackbourne had a seat at the table too, and both Kannstadt and Ellender eyed the pirate with thinly disguised disgust. Blackbourne simply smiled back at them from his seat and nodded.

Alexis raised her mug, sniffed, then set it back. She pushed her bowl of nuts to the side as well — they'd only make her thirsty and increase the risk she'd drink the poor beer.

"Well, gentlemen," she said, "standoffs seem to be the order of the day for Erzurum, do they not?"

They found themselves in much the same situation as her own private ships had when they first arrived, though with no force to windward in *darkspace*.

They held Erzurum's orbit, with all the pirates' ships plus merchantmen, and all of the gunboats taken from *darkspace* — all horribly undermanned — with their small force of rescued spacers, while the pirates on the surface had more boats and men, making any assault to free more slaves to man the ships impractical.

And all with Ness' return, with more men and ships than we have, including his thrice-bedamned frigate, more and more imminent.

"A bloody mess," Ellender huffed, sipping, then spitting back a bit of the beer in his mug. "Is there no proper drink?"

"If there were, I'd have it served," Alexis said. "It appears the pirates went through *Mongoose's* store of spirits right off and we're left with this local brew."

"My new ship is the same," Kannstadt said.

"Well," Ellender said, "we'll have proper drink once we're back in civilization. I presume that's why you've called us here, Carew? To decide where we sail for?"

"Sail?" Alexis frowned.

"Yes," Ellender said "I've been reviewing the charts and prevailing winds, and, while I'm no fan of Hanoverese, you understand, it does appear we can reach a proper Hannie system quickest." He shot a glance at Kannstadt. "With the cease-fire on and never having been properly captured you understand, I expect we'll be allowed to resupply and be on our way."

Alexis stared at him with shock. True, she didn't like the man, but she'd not have expected this from him. There were thousands of spacers still enslaved on Erzurum and, small though their forces were right now, she, Ellender, and Kannstadt were only just above them, wanting only a plan to free them. What sort of man's first thought was to sail away?

"I had thought, Captain Ellender, to discuss how we might rescue those still in captivity on the planet. We have the ships to carry away some large number of them, perhaps all."

There was considerable debate about how many spacers were enslaved on Erzurum, the practice having been ongoing for some years, perhaps even decades. It was even unclear how many were naval men, captured from broken ships as the Hanoverese and New London fleets fought their way through nearby *darkspace*. Both Ellender and Kannstadt agreed there'd been hundreds of ships lost from the fleets, but how many spacers Ness might have taken up was unknown.

Ellender snorted. "As you said at the start, a standoff. Though we hold the orbital space and the ships, we have few enough boats and the pirates have more. More men, as well. Any assault on the planet is doomed to failure even if we concentrate our forces — they'll simply concentrate their own and bring far more force to bear than we can." He popped a handful of nuts into his mouth and chewed. "Those men's best chance, Carew, comes from us passing word to Hanover and New London about what's happened here."

"Sir," Alexis said, "this Ness fellow's due to return in, perhaps, ten days' time — thirty at the outside."

"The more reason for us to be well away beforehand," Ellender said.

"Yes, but we'll not have a chance to bring word to even the closer Hanoverese systems, assemble a force, and return before then. Mister Blackbourne here tells me that this Ness is not the sort to —"

"Your Mister Blackbourne, of course," Ellender said.

Alexis grimaced at the necessity of defending the pirate, but there was no doubt he'd been helpful. "Mister Blackbourne proved himself quite useful, I think, in the retaking of *Mongoose*, and the taking of the rest. I think —"

"Trying to save his own skin at the expense of his fellows," Ellender said.

Alexis nodded. There was no doubt of that, but the man's desire to keep his skin intact, and his neck unstretched, was exactly what they needed at this time. "His motives are clear, yes. If I might finish, Captain Ellender —"

"What is there to finish, Carew? We haven't the men to crew what ships we've taken, much less fight the pirates on the surface — certainly not to fight some unknown number of fully-manned pirate vessels when they return — with a frigate, mind you. Your own force — though private ships and not proper Naval fellows — saw the right of it themselves, which is why you're in this mess with us. The only sense of it is to sail now!"

Alexis looked to Kannstadt for some sense of support, but the Hanoverese captain simply sat and looked back and forth between her and Ellender, managing, somehow, to appear both amused and thoughtful at the same time.

"This situation is different," Alexis explained, "in that the pirate forces have no ships pinning us to Erzurum's orbit. We have only one front, that of the planet, and I believe Mister Blackbourne has given us the means to free our fellows there." And find Delaine, though she didn't say so — and did try to ensure, for her own comfort, that her desire to find and free him wasn't coloring her thoughts on what they must do. "But this does require your assistance, Captain Ellender — and you, Captain Kannstadt — as senior naval officers in the system. Now that you have a ship again and are no longer held captive."

"I don't see how things are different — your fellow private ship captains were offered an escape from their predicament and took it. The pirates are in no such state. They need merely wait until their fellows return."

"A few minutes' time, Captain Ellender?" Alexis asked. "To hear Mister Blackbourne out, please? A small return for his assistance in putting a ship around you again, don't you think?"

Kannstadt stretched and cracked his neck, holding his cup out to Isom for a refill, then sipping. He shared a look with Deckard, who nodded.

"I will hear this," Kannstadt said.

Ellender sighed as though long-suffering. "Oh, very well. Let the pirate have his say."

Blackbourne grinned. "Thankee, cap'n," he said, bobbing his head. "Old Blackbourne appreciates that, he does, and —"

"Before he's hung," Ellender said.

Blackbourne's grin never wavered. "Aye, and it's that very thing Old Blackbourne'd speak to, sir." He drained his mug and held it out to Isom for his own refill. "How much are y'knowing about pirates, captain?"

"That they wave about quite handsomely when strung up to the mainmast," Ellender said.

"Aye, sir, we do aim to go out with a bit o' style, when we can." Blackbourne held up two fingers. "There're two types o' pirates, sir, if you'll pardon Old Blackbourne actin' like a schooler for a time." He changed to holding up a single finger. "The first — oh, pardon, sir —" He corrected the single finger he held up to one less offensive. "— first are those come by it natural-like. Now, Old Blackbourne's one o' them, he'll tell you true, and come to his first ship with nary a scale o' doubt nor fantasy o'er his eyes, see? Knew what it were and what it were about, for a certainty.

"Second, though, are them come to it ... well, let's say it bein' a bit better than the alternatives, y'understand?

"A merchantman's taken and the pirate band's had luck — good or ill — what sees 'em a bit short-handed at the time, well, they might call for volunteers, like. An' a spacerman — decent, honest, all law-abidin' a'tother times ... well, a man looks at a time in a boat all adrift, or some time on a rock somewheres, both waitin' fer rescue that there's nary a guarantee'll come ..." Blackbourne trailed off and shrugged. "Well, such a man might see that pirate ship and a band o' murderous, deceitful cutthroats an' say to hisself, he says, 'Well, least it ain't the navy.'"

Blackbourne grinned widely and looked around, then cleared his throat as none of the watchers grinned with him.

Alexis rubbed the bridge of her nose and shook her head. "*Without* attempts at humor, Mister Blackbourne? Is that at all possible?"

Blackbourne cleared his throat again. "Old Blackbourne's point, captains, would be to the nature o' those men. Them as took to the Brotherhood as more o' what you might call a lesser evil than a voca-tional calling, as it were. Some o' those men'd have homes an' families — ain't seen fer years, as any spacer won't, but no word neither, there bein' no, what y'might call, scheduled delivery of such t'our ships. An' no word sent back, neither, it not being strictly advisable to tell yer mum what merchantman y'took last."

The bearded pirate's face split to show teeth that were, compared to his black beard, quite white, and he leaned back in his chair cupping his hands behind his head.

"Them men, captains, might jump at o' chance t'see their homes ag'in — without, y'understand, the bits o' ropes an' yardarms an' twitchin' about the like o' which yer so disturbingly fond, Captain Ellender, sir. Them men, took to the life o' the Brotherhood through no real fault o' their own as they were an', fer that, not so mightily trusted by a certain pirate captain o' Old Blackbourne's acquaintance, might make up a fair bit o' a force left planetside when that acquaintance be off somewheres about his business. More'n that —" He took a hand from behind his head and held up three fingers. "— there'd be the third sort o' pirate —"

"You said there were two sorts," Ellender said, narrowing his eyes.

Blackbourne snorted. "Ain't never just two sorts o' folks — a man's more complicated than that." Blackbourne looked at his upraised fingers and appeared to mentally count them. "So ... third sort o' pirate, aye? That'd be a man like Old Blackbourne hisself, captains. Come t'the Brethren natural-like, loved his time, but gettin' on in years an' slowin' down an' thinkin' t'hisself, 'Old Blackbourne, lad, yer gettin' on in years an' slowin' down. Could be it's time t' think on yer declinin' times.'" He shrugged. "Well, captains, it ain't like t'Brotherhood's got what y'd call a pensioning plan, see? Might could take a bit o' land here on Erzurum an' set up — but what damn fool'd want t' be about that? All that damp? Bad fer Old Blackbourne's joints, t'be certain."

"What is your bloody point?" Ellender demanded, then turned to Kannstadt. "In fact, I don't believe this man has one at all. He's merely attempting to delay us further, and Carew has foolishly convinced us to allow it."

Kannstadt shook his head. "Oh, no, *Herr* Blackbourne's point is quite clear, I am thinking — him finding himself in a unique position amongst his kind."

"Being liable for a hanging is the natural state for his kind, so I hardly see how it is unique."

Kannstadt shook his head again, then raised a questioning eyebrow to Alexis. Much as it galled her, she nodded. Ellender would likely look more kindly on the suggestion from him than her.

"*Herr* Blackbourne is saying that he and those, like him, getting older," Kannstadt said, "in addition to his fellows who became pirates only to avoid what they saw as a worse fate would be willing to give up the pirating life."

"Aye," Blackbourne said. "Yon Hannie's the right o' it. Eager, even, y'might say."

Ellender nodded. "Then they should do so, and Erzurum seems a fine place for them to go about their business."

"That, they're less than willing to do, y'see?" Blackbourne said, his grin widening to its largest stretch yet. "Which'd be where you fine fellows come in, o'course."

"How's that?" Ellender asked.

Blackbourne spread his arms wide. "Your pardon, sir."

"I said, 'How's that?' man, are you deaf?"

Blackbourne glanced at Alexis, who cleared her throat.

"We do seem to have here, gentlemen," she said, "a rather unique situation." She looked to Kannstadt for confirmation. "The Barbary is Hanoverese territory, but much left to its own devices, while a great deal of New London shipping traverses the corridor when our two nations are not actively at war."

Kannstadt nodded, but Ellender still looked confused.

"And here in Erzurum," she went on, "we have these pirates who hold something we want, our captured spacers, and, now, captains from both those nations. Senior captains —" She looked pointedly at the two. "— in-system, possibly, likely even, senior in the region, given the state of our most recent conflict and the withdrawal of both Hanoverese and New London forces during the ceasefire."

Kannstadt was nodding, but Ellender frowned and looked at Alexis quizzically. "I'm not at all certain I'm senior, for what good it does. There could be any number of men senior to me still in captivity on Erzurum."

Alexis nodded. "'In captivity,' would be the important bit there, Captain Ellender, as they are out of the chain of command while captive. You are the senior, *free* New London captain in the Barbary." She looked at him intently. "The senior representative of Her Majesty's government with regard to these matters."

"*What* matters?" Ellender asked. "All I've heard so far is some nattering about these foul pirates regretting their decisions and wanting to run home to their wives and, likely of dubious parentage, children."

"Your pardon, sir," Blackbourne put in.

"You've already —"

"A royal pardon, Captain Ellender," Alexis added, before Blackbourne, already staring at Ellender as though the man were a fool, could speak again.

Blackbourne nodded. "Aye, that'll do it for most, and those who won't agree'll be knocked about and y'can do what y'will w'em after."

"A pardon?" Ellender asked, eyes narrowed. "For piracy? These murderous, rapacious scum, taken untold ships, sold the crews into slavery, no telling what else, and you'd suggest we pardon them? Even if it were within my power, it's an absurd idea!"

"In return for their assistance in taking Erzurum from those pirates who don't accept a pardon, and the freeing of all captives, slaves, there," Alexis said. "We'd likely have enough of a force to fully man all these ships we've taken — with *Mongoose, Talon, Fang, Claw*, and the merchantmen and gunboats fully manned we could present a rather nasty surprise for Ness' force when it returns, or simply sail away if we've space enough to clear Erzurum space with all our lads."

Ellender looked to Kannstadt. "You can't really be considering this farce —"

Kannstadt shrugged. "This band of pirates appears to be nearly all of New London." He pursed his lips. "Do they agree to leave the Barbary, and all of Hanover space, and never return, on pain of losing it, I will give this pardon." He shrugged again. "It may be that my superiors will not uphold it, but if these men do not return, this does not matter, *hein?*"

Blackbourne leaned forward and nodded. "It's the thought what counts, sir, truly. Most o' the lads'd be just as happy t'never see a Hannie in life again, if y'don't mind Old Blackbourne sayin' it."

"It's preposterous," Ellender said.

"Pardons have been issued in the past, sir," Alexis said. "It's not unheard of."

Ellender was silent for a long moment, eyes narrowed and lips pursed. Alexis had just enough time to hope, before he shook his head.

"No." He shook his head more. "No, I'll not do it. I'll not be known as the man who pardoned untold numbers of thieves and murderers. Sweet Dark, the Crown would have my head, and the press, the Mob ... well, I'd never be able to walk the streets of any New London system again."

"Sir," Alexis prompted. "You'd be the man who brought back our captured spacers. You'd —"

"My career would be over, Carew, as would be your own," Ellender snorted and jerked his head at Blackbourne. "Oh, he'd have his pardon, and the rest, they'd certainly be upheld by the Crown, if for no other reason than to reinforce the absolute authority of Her Majesty's captains, but privately? Admiralty would never stand for it and I'd never stand on a ship's quarterdeck again, save to sign in some hulk at the worst Fringe-world station they could find for me. And that if I wasn't hung, myself."

"Sir, I —"

"No, Carew, it's out of the question, though I am heartened to hear that you do acknowledge me to be senior officer on station. That does simplify things, you see."

Alexis felt a chill. Ellender was just the sort of officer she most despised — too political, too obsessed with thoughts for his own skin and career, too lacking in any sort of obligation to the men under his command, or others.

"Simplify, sir?"

"Yes, I'd been concerned you might object and make some space-lawyerly argument to my authority, and it's good to see that won't be the case." Ellender cocked his head to one side. "In fact, I think it's time we had a little chat. I've been reviewing the Naval regulations, you see — part of the data packet I requested from your *Mongoose* when I went aboard *Claw*, you see? And *as I'm senior officer on station*, which you've graciously acknowledged here, I've decided what we must do, which is to notify New London's forces of the situation here as quickly as possible."

He nodded to Kannstadt. "I would hope, Captain Kannstadt, that you would do the same with the Hanoverese forces."

Kannstadt smiled. "I will do as I think best, of course."

"That being the case," Ellender said, "and this ship being the fastest of the lot we took, I shall be transferring my command to *Mongoose*. You may consider yourself recalled to Her Majesty's service, *Lieutenant* Carew, and this ship commandeered to the needs of the Royal Navy."

———

ALEXIS WAS STILL FOR A MOMENT, her thoughts running furiously.

She'd thought it possible that Ellender would refuse the pardon for the pirates and likely sail off — escaping Erzurum was nearly all the man talked of, save his thinly veiled disdain for Alexis and the Hanoverese, no matter his brittle politeness toward Kannstadt. What she'd do then, she hadn't really planned out — possibly attempt to free some other New London captain, if she could determine where one might be held, and attempt the same with him. Or simply wait, in standoff with the pirates, for either Ness' return or the thin hope that Ellender would return with a rescue force. Perhaps she'd be able to put Ness in the same sort of stalemate the private ships had, then hold off until Ellender returned with whatever force he could assemble.

In either event, she wouldn't, couldn't, simply sail away and abandon hundreds, or even thousands, of spacers to their lot on Erzurum, especially given what they knew, or suspected, of the pirate Ness' plans for them if he were forced to abandon his stronghold.

What she hadn't considered was the possibility Ellender might recall her to service and demand her ship.

Did he have that authority? She wondered.

Probably. She'd been the one to just acknowledge him as senior in the Barbary, after all, and recalling a half-pay officer to service, even requisitioning her ship, were small things compared to the pardon she'd just suggested.

Ellender was looking at her both expectantly and impatiently.

Beside Kannstadt, Deckard stirred for the first time in the meeting. "What? Leave all our lads behind?" He frowned. "Not right, is it? No."

Ellender glanced at him irritably.

"Captain Ellender," Alexis said, choosing her words carefully. "*Mongoose* sails under a letter of marque — the ship and crew are not subject to impressment."

That was true enough. There was also, if she needed it, a further letter from Eades and the Foreign Office, exempting *Mongoose* from the needs of the Service, should such a thing arrive, but Alexis was reluctant to pull that from her bag, as Kannstadt didn't know of her involvement with the New London spymaster and she'd rather that weren't bandied about Hanover too very much.

Nor even New London — the stench of some associations is difficult to lose in the wash.

"Is that right?" Deckard asked. "To leave them all in the muck? No, I don't think so. Not at all."

"Will you shut your pet idiot up, Captain Kannstadt?" Ellender asked, then to Alexis, "Come now, Carew, these are clearly exigent circumstances. I'm certain Admiralty will back my decision to commandeer this ship — and, if not —" He shrugged. "— well, I'll apologize to her owners. Though, with the alternative of leaving her behind for the pirates to strip, they'll likely reward me, don't you think?"

"Not right," Deckard muttered.

"Oh, do shut up."

"Captain Ellender," Kannstadt said, jaw tight and eyes narrow while he laid a hand on Deckard's forearm, "you are being uncivil. And, perhaps, not thinking enough on Captain Carew's suggestion. *Herr* Blackbourne, what is it you fear this Ness will do when he returns?"

Blackbourne sat forward from where he'd been leaning back in his chair, watching the events with a wide grin. "And Old Blackbourne thought the bloody Brotherhood were a backstabbin', untrustworthy lot." He shook his head and chuckled. "What'll Ness do? Well, this hidey-hole o'Erzurum's been found out a time or two before by private ships or wayward merchants, so it's generally no never-mind." He nodded to Kannstadt. "Yon Hannies never were ones t'do a thing about it, see? Always suspected they looked on us an' t'others in the Barbary as a sort o' irregular sort o' force, snipin' away at New London's merchant traffic to *Hso-his* as we do."

The pirate drained his mug and held it out for Isom to refill, which the clerk did, though with wrinkled nose.

"This be different, though. Least to Old Blackbourne's eye, an' likely our Ness, as well. See, never were the navy folk captive when we was found out afore. Ness laughed off your private ships, as he knew they'd not seen a thing more than those that come before, but now? With all these navy lads in orbit and off t'holler at New London an' Hanover about it?"

Blackbourne sighed.

"Well, Old Blackbourne won't say his thoughts on what was t'become o'Erzurum didn't factor into his own decisions with regard to assisting you, eh, bitch-woman?" He shook his head. "No, Old Blackbourne figures Erzurum's over if word gets back to the navies, sure. Figure our Ness is smart enough to see the same.

"Sad, though, our Ness — he's a saltin' o' the earth, sort of fellow, Ness is. Y've heard o' cuttin' the nose t'spite the face, have you? Yes? Well, Ness's more like t' cut t'other fella's nose — an' an eye or two, come t'that. Old Blackbourne expects he'll load up his ships with what men he can, then strike every bit o' that mudball from orbit. 'Til he's bored with it or thinks he's no more time."

"*Das ist verboten*," Kannstadt whispered.

Blackbourne snorted. "Are y'like t'hang him twice, sir? Or him t'care if y'do?"

Ellender waved a hand, dismissing Blackbourne. "The pirates will do as they will. Those men's best chance, and our own, lies with us informing our forces and leaving their rescue to our respective governments and a proper force."

Kannstadt snorted nearly as loudly as Blackbourne, then frowned and creased his brow, as though disturbed to be found in agreement with the pirate.

"They'll be dead before we've even reported to Admiralty, sir," Alexis said. "Before we've even cleared the Barbary, if this Ness returns in only ten days' time."

"You've had your say, *lieutenant*," Ellender said. He stood, his officer with him.

"Lieutenant Culliver?" Alexis asked, hoping for some support.

Culliver looked down at the deck. "I wish to get home," he whispered. "All our men do."

"Do you suppose those still on Erzurum do not?"

"A hopeless stand won't free them," Culliver said, not looking up.

Deckard made to get out of his chair, but Kannstadt laid a hand on his arm. Still, he fixed his eyes on Ellender. "Is it a cowardly, cringing thing?" He nodded. "Oh, yes."

"Control your pet madman, Kannstadt, or I'll take him back with me, locked in the hold as he deserves." Ellender gestured for Alexis to stand. "On your feet, lieutenant, and let us to the quarterdeck for you to turn over this ship to me."

Alexis remained seated, thinking furiously.

"Now, Carew!"

"Sir," she said, choosing her words carefully. She'd already acknowledged Ellender as senior in-system, if she were to outright refuse him, then that could be viewed as mutiny unless she resigned her commission, ending her career. She'd do it if she must, but perhaps the knowledge that she would might dissuade Ellender from this course. "If I were recalled to service and ordered to abandon the men on Erzurum, I'm afraid I should have to refuse the recall and resign my commission." She swallowed. "I implore you, Captain Ellender, there must be some other way. If you insist on sailing, take some other ship and leave *Mongoose* here to defend those men. She's the best armed."

"And the fastest, which would get us to safety all the quicker. Stay and fight? A useless gesture, which would only —"

"Yer a bloody pegger," Blackbourne muttered.

"Is he?" Deckard asked, then nodded. "Seems true enough. Yes. Bloody pegger, him."

Ellender's jaw clenched. "I've had enough from the pets — and *that one* —" He pointed at Blackbourne. "— I'll see hung as soon as we're in *darkspace* and clear of this place. Lieutenant?"

Alexis hesitated.

"I expected as much," Ellender muttered. He tapped his tablet, which he must have got from aboard *Claw* and drew his pistol, Culliver doing the same, but slower and with some reluctance.

"Captain Ellender?" Alexis asked, startled.

"Stay where you are." Ellender tracked his pistol from Alexis to Blackbourne and on to Kannstadt. "All of you. My men and I are taking this ship and sailing for New London."

Alexis' own tablet pinged for her attention. Ellender jerked his head at it.

"Take the call, Carew, and let's avoid any unpleasantness."

Alexis tapped the device and Dockett's voice sounded. The bosun spoke slowly and carefully, as though trying not to spook an angry dog. "Ah, sir, we've a bit of a kerfuffle with Captain Ellender's boat crew ..."

"TELL your crew to stand down, Lieutenant Carew."

Captain Ellender kept his pistol trained on her, as though he thought Alexis might come over the expanse of her own dining table and grasp at his throat.

Which, when one thought about it, showed the other captain had a rather good understanding of Alexis at the moment.

"Captain Ellender," she said, keeping her words as slow and calm as her bosun had a moment before. "This isn't necessary."

"I've seen your sort before, Carew. Convinced of your own rightness and judging others — and I know the sorts of extremes you'll go to. My men want to go home, and I do too — we've had enough of the Barbary, enough of enslavement, and enough of the bloody Hannies."

Kannstadt snorted at that.

"This ship," Ellender went on, ignoring the Hanoverese captain, "is far faster than those others, and better armed. We're going to take it and go home, then let a proper fleet worry about the pirates and bloody Erzurum."

"You heard what Blackbourne told us this Ness will do," Alexis said. "Captain Kannstadt's seen the sorts of repercussions the pirates took on Erzurum for simply attacking a farmstead. Do you not think they'll do that and worse for our escape? You're dooming those men left behind to death. All the men from our fleets and the civilians of Erzurum as well."

"Perhaps," Ellender said. "It's a risk we all took when we first sailed. But, as you pointed out, I'm senior in-system, and I think their best chance lies with notifying the Fleet and Admiralty." He jerked his head at Kannstadt. "If you're so concerned, Captain Kannstadt, then you should sail for Hanover as well, as your own fleet is closer."

Kannstadt was watching Ellender with lips curled in disdain. He slowly reached out and grasped his mug of poor beer, then took a sip. "I believe I will follow Captain Carew's plan." He chuckled. "The water is rising yet again, and I do not wish to be caught on my roof."

"Enough of your bloody platitudes." Ellender jerked the pistol he still pointed at Alexis. "My men have spread out through the ship and drawn their weapons when I signaled them. Tell yours to stand down." He nodded to her tablet. "There's no need for bloodshed."

"What is the state of the ship, Mister Dockett?" Alexis asked to her tablet.

"All that prissy so-and-so Ellender's men've gone and drawn on us, sir. The lads haven't drawn back, them being our own, and all, but it's a bit, what you might call, tense, sir." Alexis could almost hear Dockett swallow. "They've men in engineering and on the quarter-deck." He paused again. "Sorry, sir, but with all to do putting things to rights still the hatches were open. We didn't —"

"It's quite all right, Mister Dockett." Alexis gave Ellender a hard look. "One doesn't expect family to come bearing a serpent."

"Ah, well, sir, you've not met Mistress Dockett's —"

"Another time, Mister Dockett."

"Aye, sir."

"For now, please pass the word for all to stand easy while I discuss things further with Captain Ellender."

"Aye, sir."

Alexis disconnected and stared at Ellender while she wracked her thoughts for some solution.

She could, indeed, resign her commission. It was entirely possible that she was recalled to active duty even now, simply by Ellender's stating his intent to do so. Admiralty was not known for demanding its captains follow the niceties of formal, written communications in the midst of action, and it could well be argued that all of Erzurum was an ongoing action against the pirates.

So, she could resign, and throw her career away, which she'd readily do if there were no other way to keep *Mongoose* in-system to try and stop the pirate Ness when he returned, but would it? *Mongoose* was, indeed, exempt from Ellender commandeering it, both by her letter of marque and Eades' more shadowy declarations. Neither of those would leave her in command, though.

Ellender would almost certainly take her resignation and refusal to give him *Mongoose* poorly and she couldn't see where he wouldn't have her put in chains aboard whichever ship he did take. He might even hang her alongside Blackbourne, leaving it to Admiralty to decide whether he'd had cause and authority to do so — and those worthies would almost always back their captains, as to do otherwise invited chaos and loss of authority. He'd certainly still take *Mongoose*, letters and declarations aside, leaving it to Admiralty to work out.

The worst of it was that he'd likely see no consequences from it — his actions were reasonable on their face, to save what he could and bring back word, rather than face the overwhelming force when the pirate Ness returned.

Alexis caught Isom's eye where he stood in the pantry doorway and shook her head slightly. Her clerk had a weapon or two in there, but he was a poor shot and that wasn't the way to handle this situation anyway, not with Ellender's men armed and spread throughout *Mongoose*.

Ellender's officer, Culliver, despite his own weapon never wavering, did have the grace to look a bit embarrassed by the whole thing, and Deckard, the New London officer who'd so oddly attached himself to Kannstadt, was watching her intently. She thought she might even detect a hint of sympathy behind whatever madness stretched the poor man's eyes so wide and unblinking.

It might be, that without Ellender's cooperation, she had no choice but to give him *Mongoose*. Even if he took her in chains, she *could* give the ship to Kannstadt, though she'd likely be hung for that by Admiralty, even if Ellender didn't — giving the fastest, best-armed ship in-system to the Hanoverese would not be looked upon fondly, ceasefire or no. All that would accomplish, though, would be to get Kannstadt and his men killed when Ness returned. With no New London captain to offer pardon, there'd be no deal with the pirates, no more men to crew the ship, and he'd be outnumbered in both ships and men when the pirates returned.

Giving Ellender the fastest ship, no matter how it galled, might well be the best option left to her.

Deckard caught Alexis' eyes and raised an eyebrow.

"I —" Alexis started to say, not sure what unasked question she was about to answer, when Deckard sighed and his shoulders slumped.

"No ideas, right?" the man said. "Of course not. None to be had. Not a one? No good ones, certainly."

"Captain Kannstadt," Ellender said, turning slightly toward him and Deckard. "You and that bloody madman will leave my ship immediately. Do as you will with him after, but I've had —"

Deckard launched himself to his feet, surprising everyone, and with enough force to tip his chair despite the magnets in the legs to hold it fast to *Mongoose's* deck in a *darkspace* storm.

His legs drove him upward and his right fist struck Ellender in the gut, doubling the captain over. He wrapped his left arm around Ellender's gun arm near the elbow and twisted his body away, using all his mass to bend the elbow the wrong way.

A sickening crunch echoed through the stunned silence and Deckard plucked Ellender's pistol from the captain's nerveless fingers before holding it to Ellender's head.

"Is that enough?" Deckard asked, spinning Ellender around to put him between himself and Culliver.

"Ian!" Kannstadt shouted over Ellender's cry of pain.

"Stay back!" Deckard yelled, though to whom Alexis couldn't tell.

The tableau around Alexis' dining table resettled in quite an unexpected way, with Kannstadt half-risen, Deckard with an arm about Ellender's throat and the captain's former pistol pressed tightly to its owner's temple. Ellender's officer had backed up a step, his aim wavering from Alexis to Deckard, despite the latter being sheltered by his grip on Ellender.

"You mad fool," Ellender hissed. "You'll hang for this."

"Should someone hang?" Deckard asked. "Oh, aye, they should. Who, though? Me? No, you? Oh, yes. Abandon all those lads?"

"Ian," Kannstadt said gently, holding out his hand. "Give the pistol to me, *hein*? We will talk."

Deckard shook his head.

"Listen to him, Lieutenant Deckard," Alexis said. "This isn't the way. No good will come of this for you. Give Captain Kannstadt the gun and we'll talk this through with Captain Ellender."

"Talked before, heard everything. Heard his words. Were they good? No, they weren't. Bad words to say, and he'll only say more." He jerked his head at Alexis. "Were her words good? They were. Balanced the bad ones. Scales are balanced now. Stay that way? Have to. Another word, another breath — too much." He clenched his eyes shut and knocked his forehead against the back of Ellender's head. "Bloody narrow beam to walk, this."

Deckard took a deep breath, closed his eyes to wrinkled slits, and grimaced as though in pain or going through a great effort.

"Captain Ellender," he said, his voice not holding a trace of the madness it had a moment before. "Tell your men to put up their weapons and return to your boat. I will escort you to your ship and you may sail. If I'm attacked or shot, I've nearly more pressure on this trigger than it will take as it is, sir."

ELLENDER DID AS DECKARD DEMANDED, though every step of acquiescence was punctuated with threats.

He didn't seem to know quite who to lay the blame on, so alternated between cursing the treachery of Kannstadt and the Hanoverese, assuring him that this plot he'd hatched with Deckard would end in the war being resumed and the other captain's nation destroyed; insulting Deckard with the very worst of curses Alexis had ever heard from a host of bosuns, all of which the poor lieutenant ignored as though he didn't hear; and accusing Alexis of being complicit in Deckard's act, assuring her that she'd hang along with him as soon as Admiralty heard about it.

Deckard let the man rant, though any time Ellender's words trailed toward what could be considered an order instead of recriminations, Deckard would smoothly and calmly return from whatever place he went to in his silence. He held the barrel of his pistol to Ellender's ear with enough force that a trickle of blood ran down the captain's neck.

"Don't think this is done, Carew," Ellender said as they made their way to his boat. Deckard kept him walking sideways, so as to keep himself sandwiched between the captain and a bulkhead, with no one ever at his back. "I demand you —"

"*Ah!*" Deckard jammed the barrel of his pistol so far into Ellender's ear that Alexis thought he might do damage with that alone. "Been enough bad words, haven't there? Oh, yes. No more, or I'll have to stop them all. Would that be right? Not at all. Don't want that. Get them aboard your boat, sir, will you? You will, if you like your brains as they are — all of a piece and sheltered, yes? Best for them to work that way? So I've heard. Would you prove the rule? Maybe, but let's not find out."

They'd reached the hatch where Ellender's boat was docked. His men milled about the hatchway, weapons lowered, but not put away. A group of Alexis' lads, led by Dockett and Nabb had positions some bit farther along, their own weapons out now and at their own sides, though they seemed perplexed at the turn of events.

"You'll all hang!" Ellender shouted at them. "This is mutiny!"

"Is it?" Deckard asked. "Whose then? Everybody says, 'Give me the gun, Deckard,' and I don't, then who's to blame, eh? Heard those words? Didn't you?" He tightened his grip on Ellender's throat. "*Didn't you?*"

"Did I *what*, you barking fool?" Ellender asked.

His face was red, though from rage or Deckard's grip around his throat Alexis couldn't tell.

"Hear them say give them the gun. Did you?"

"I —"

Deckard blinked again. "Does it matter? Doesn't. No, not at all. Log was running, yes? Is this hard? Too hard — no time. Too hard.

Get on the bloody boat, you lot!" He ground the barrel of his pistol into
Ellender's ear. *"Tell them!"*

"Board the boat," Ellender ordered, trying to pull his head away
from the pistol's barrel, but blocked by Deckard's arm about his
throat. He grimaced and grunted as Deckard pressed it harder. "We'll
deal with these later — or Admiralty will."

Ellender's men filed into the boat, sending dark looks in their
wake. When they were all aboard, Deckard nudged Ellender toward
the hatch and pushed him through, keeping a tight grip.

"Let him go, Ian," Kannstadt said. "We'll seal the hatch and he'll
be gone. No more to worry on, *hein*? Please, *mausebär*? You need
not go."

"Can he be trusted?" Deckard asked. "No. He'll talk — more
words. More bad words. Tip the scales." He grimaced again, as
though pushing a mighty weight up a hill and his eyes seemed to clear
for a moment. He looked first to Alexis.

"Listen to the words, Captain Carew," he said. "Your log from
our meeting. Listen to it carefully once we're on our way and you'll
see what I see. Where the balance lies." He grinned. "You'll not need
to be mad to find the key, I assure you."

"You're not mad, Ian," Kannstadt said, hand outstretched, "only
troubled. Please, leave the *fickfehler* to his boat and come here to me."

Deckard shook his head and his eyes filled. "I am mad,
Wendale. I can feel it pressing in, like the Dark itself and I'm
without a ship. Every day it's stronger and I lose more of myself."
He sniffed. "What would there be for us after Erzurum, in any
case?" He chuckled. "Should I come with you back to Hanover? An
inselaffe among the *boche*? Or would you come home with me?
Either way I'm —" He grimaced with effort. "— *bloody* useless,
aren't I? Yes."

Kannstadt took a step toward them, but stopped as Deckard
shook his head. "You're not useless, Ian," he said. "Not to me."

"No, not useless yet, I suppose," Deckard said. "I've strength yet
... enough? It must be. Has to be." He shook his head hard. "Let me

do this thing, Wendale. I must. You'll see why." He smiled. "Trust the madman, will you."

Kannstadt's shoulders slumped.

"I've one other thing to ask you, Wendale," Deckard said, he tightened his grip on Ellender. "Once we leave, once *Claw's* transitioned, don't let this bastard return, will you? You mustn't — it'd ruin everything. He must be well away, you see?" He shrugged. "If he comes back, it'll mean I'm dead, after all."

Kannstadt turned his wet eyes to Ellender.

"Do not come back, *Kapitän* Ellender," he said in a voice that sent chills down Alexis' back. "When next we meet, here or where I find you one day, we shall have a reckoning. By ship or sabre or my bare hands to still your heart, you will face me."

ELLENDER'S BOAT returned to *Claw*, which immediately broke orbit for the transition at L1, the closest of the Lagrangian points offering access to *darkspace*.

Alexis and Kannstadt went to *Mongoose's* quarterdeck where Kannstadt took over the signals console from Creasy and opened a channel to *Claw*.

The other ship's quarterdeck was sparsely manned, Deckard ordering all but essential personnel off and enforcing it with the pistol he still held to Ellender's head. He put himself with his back to the bulkhead, Ellender in front of him, and in sight of *Claw's* signals console, so that Kannstadt could see him, but kept his attention on the quarterdeck.

He stood such, unwavering save for the occasional grimace or wince, for the four hours it took *Claw* to reach the Lagrangian point.

Kannstadt simply spoke.

He no longer attempted to dissuade Deckard from his course, apparently accepting that this was something the other man felt he had to do.

Instead, Kannstadt talked of his home and family, his career, his aspirations for the future. As though trying to fill the last hours he had to speak to Deckard with a lifetime of words.

Ellender had stopped objecting to this or interrupting when a larger trickle of blood appeared from underneath the barrel of the pistol Deckard held to his head.

"No words from you," Deckard told him. "Are any of them good? No, they're all bad."

Then Deckard simply listened while keeping his eyes ever moving to watch those on *Claw's* quarterdeck.

"You would like *Dübenstal, mausebär,*" Kannstadt said, seemingly as oblivious to the presence of any others on *Mongoose's* quarterdeck as he was to the tears staining his cheeks. Isom set a fresh mug of beer on the console, as he had from the first time the Hanoverese captain's voice had grown hoarse and strained from his words. "I think that with enough prize money I will retire to that world." He raised his mug and wet his lips. "There is a place where the mountains rise from the sea and one can go from sunning on the beach to skiing in no more than an hour." He smiled. "A place for those who wish all things, and not to decide too much, *hein?*"

"*Claw's* in the transition zone, sir," Tite said from the tactical console, his voice low, as everyone on the quarterdeck kept theirs, giving Kannstadt as much privacy as they could and still work the ship.

Kannstadt's body tensed as the same was announced on *Claw's* quarterdeck.

Alexis moved to offer him what strength she could, placing a hand on his shoulder and squeezing tightly. She could feel the other captain tremble with the effort to not beg Deckard to stop his mad plan and return to him. What she might do in his position, if it were Delaine aboard that other ship and about to transition to *darkspace* where he'd almost certainly be killed by Ellender as soon as his guard dropped, she couldn't bear to wonder.

Deckard turned to look at *Claw's* signals console for the first time since boarding.

"Thank you, Wendale," he said. "For everything." He jerked his head at Ellender. "Transition."

"*Ian! Ich liebe dich, mausebär.*" Kannstadt reached out to touch Deckard's image on the screen, though with the time lag *Claw* was already gone. "*Lebewohl.*"

ALEXIS HAD NABB, Dockett, and Isom about her table this time, along with Blackbourne and Kannstadt.

The Hanoverese captain was red-eyed and looked weary beyond words, but refused to return to his ship or even the offer of Alexis' bunk for a few hours' rest.

"No," he said. "I wish to see what we will do now. What Ian saw — if it was not his ... his madness that made this. I do not wish his sacrifice to have been ..." Kannstadt trailed off.

"He may not be —" Alexis broke off, knowing the truth.

"Ian is dead," Kannstadt said bluntly. "If not this moment, then so soon as he is unable to hold his weapon. Ellender will not return here, even after ..." He closed his eyes. "This chance is bought dearly and I can only hope his vision was not clouded.

Alexis nodded.

She'd wracked her memory of their conference for some clue and thought there was something there, but couldn't be sure. She'd not replayed the log while on the quarterdeck as *Claw* made its way to the transition point, for fear Ellender might hear and come to understand whatever it was Deckard had seen so clearly. Nor had she wished to leave the quarterdeck to review the log in her quarters until Ellender and *Claw* were truly gone.

Now that they'd transitioned, she felt certain they'd not return. She was certain Deckard wouldn't allow it while he lived and had no doubt that Kannstadt, knowing that as well, would make good on his promise to Ellender, no matter the cost to himself, his own ship, or those still on Erzurum.

There were some things, she thought, that transcended duty — some sacrifices that were too much to ask — and she prayed she'd never face a similar choice.

Isom shifted uneasily in his chair.

"Should I bring fresh beer, sir?" he asked, half rising. "Perhaps a bit of cheese? I think there's a bit at the back of the pantry the pirates didn't take."

"Sit, please," Alexis said. "You've the legal training and I wish your mind at work on this."

Isom settled back into this chair, but grumbled, "Ain't natural."

"Lieutenant Deckard saw ... something in our previous meeting," Alexis said. "I wish all of you to watch the log with me and tell me if you see it." She turned to Kannstadt. "Are you certain you wish to be here for this, Captain Kannstadt?"

He nodded. "I must try to help in this."

"Very well."

Alexis brought up the log of their meeting and played it from the start. Kannstadt winced at Deckard's image, but watched nonetheless. She did stop it before Deckard attacked Ellender, though, thinking that whatever it was must have been before that and there was no need for them to see that bit again.

At the end, Alexis sighed. She saw nothing there — Ellender had been quite clear in his intent and reasoning, reprehensible as she might find it. There was even something to his argument, if one weren't actually here and were instead listening to it from the safe, far away confines of Admiralty — the chance of getting more and official forces to Erzurum, though Alexis still thought it not possible, would seem a perfectly reasonable choice.

"I'm afraid I don't see it. I suppose our original plan could hold — if we were to somehow free another New London officer from Erzurum, he could offer the pirates a pardon — though we have the problem of getting there and back to do so," she said, turning to Kannstadt. "Do you see anything else, Captain Kannstadt?"

The Hanoverese shook his head. "I do not, but it must be there — Ian was so certain."

Alexis looked to the others. Nabb and Dockett shrugged, but Isom was frowning in thought.

"Something?" she asked her clerk.

Isom's face twisted in a grimace. "There's a bit —" He reached for the tabletop where the log played. "If I may, sir?"

Alexis nodded agreement and Isom tapped the controls. Ellender's voice echoed from the speakers.

"That being the case, and this ship being the fastest of the lot we took, I shall be transferring my command to *Mongoose*. You may consider yourself recalled to Her Majesty's service, *Lieutenant* Carew, and this ship commandeered to the needs of the Royal Navy."

Isom paused it and ran forward a bit before resuming at Alexis' words.

"Sir, I beg you to reconsider, if I were recalled to service and ordered to abandon the men on Erzurum, I'm afraid I should have to refuse the recall and resign my commission. I implore you, Captain Ellender, there must be some other way. If you insist on sailing, take some other ship and leave *Mongoose* here to defend those men."

Isom sat back, his brow creased.

"Isom?" Alexis asked.

"It's a twisty-turny bit of business, sir," Isom said, hanging his head and flushing. "The sort as gives a solicitor a certain reputation."

"My reputation's unlikely to be further tarnishable once Ellender speaks to Admiralty," Alexis said. "A bit of space-lawyering will do me no further harm, I think."

Isom shrugged. "Well, sir, it's that you didn't so much as refuse Captain Ellender as, well, say you might, imploring him to reconsider, as you were."

Alexis nodded. "My intent was clear, though. Should he have

continued in his attempt to take *Mongoose,* I would have resigned my commission and resisted him."

Isom cleared his throat and flushed, as though embarrassed by what he was about to speak. "But you *didn't,* sir, and he didn't have time to change his own intentions — orders, more — clearly stated for the log, sir, that you should consider yourself recalled."

Blackbourne was, apparently, the first to see Isom's point, for he grinned widely, leaning forward and clapping the slight-framed clerk on the back with a heavy hand. "Aye, yer a clever one — worthy o' the Brotherhood, y'are." He turned to Alexis while jerking his head back to Isom. "Old Blackbourne'll be wantin' this one t'draw up them pardons when yer ready, bitch-woman. The man's a good eye fer a snakey-phrase."

"We're a bit ahead of ourselves with that, I think," Alexis said. "We'll need to free a senior officer and convince him of this course, and the pirates still have nearly as many boats as we do to counter any rescue attempt. Without that we ..."

Alexis trailed off as she noted everyone around the table was looking at her expectantly. Isom embarrassed, Blackbourne with amusement, Dockett and Nabb thoughtful, while Kannstadt had a predatory gleam to his eye.

"Ian was a clever man," Kannstadt said, his voice sad.

Alexis thought about what Isom had said, then Ellender's words and her own again. She closed her eyes and sighed. "Oh, Isom, I'd see a man's backbone at the gratings for such a space-lawyerly bit of gibberish."

Isom shrugged. "It *is* an interpretation of the events, sir. Captain Ellender recalled you to service, clearly, and while you tried to dissuade him he did not respond. Didn't have time to respond, see? Thanks to Lieutenant Deckard. It could be said his order stands, without those conditions you said would force you to resign, and while he's now sailed and circumstances have changed, leaving you recalled to Service and senior in Erzurum — in the Barbary, as well, for Ellender's stated he intends to make way for New London."

Alexis did see it. It *was* an interpretation. Whether it would be *Admiralty's* interpretation was quite another thing.

Their Lordships would back the decisions of a commander on the scene to the hilt and beyond, ensuring that everyone knew the commander of a Queen's Ship, months from any higher authority, spoke with the Queen's Voice and Authority. There were rules, of course — both written and unwritten — but those rules were often, perhaps even frequently, broken and ignored by captains and admirals on remote stations. Some of that rule-breaking was censured, privately, by Admiralty and a captain's career might even end over it — but his actions were nearly always upheld. The authority of the Crown, conferred on the Queen's Officers, must never be in question.

It could even be argued, she supposed, that she might be considered in a state of mutiny if she *didn't* now either return to active service or resign her commission, one. Ellender's words were clear.

"Captain Ellender stated his intent," Alexis argued, "but sent nothing official. No recall, no commission, nothing."

"Exigencies of the circumstances and needs of the Service, sir," Isom said. He had the Naval Regulations open on her tabletop now and was searching and scanning as he spoke. "Not unknown to tidy up the paperwork when there's a bit of a breather."

Alexis was starting to accept the idea, mad though it might be — and, she reminded herself, first seen by Deckard who was clearly mad.

Or not so mad at all.

"Captain Kannstadt?" Alexis asked. "Your thoughts?"

Kannstadt chuckled. "I would be a poor man to argue against Ian's sacrifice. *Ja, Kapitän* Carew — Hanover recognizes you as senior New London officer in Erzurum." He sobered, perhaps thinking about the risk she was taking with her career and even life. "And may *die Dunkelheit* show you mercy."

"The Dark is unlikely to take notice, captain." Alexis turned to Blackbourne. "Will the pirates — will you — accept my authority to issue a pardon? It hardly seems worth it to write one if I'll merely be laughed out of the system."

Blackbourne shrugged. "Yer betters'll hang you or not, as they will, but they'll honor what you do. We know how that works, we do — though it's usually the summary hangin' without trial what comes our way from it."

Alexis winced. She'd not always been above that herself and, despite her better consideration, she actually found herself liking Blackbourne a bit and —

"The lads'll need a day or two t'ponder on it," Blackbourne continued, "but Old Blackbourne'll vouch fer ye, bitch-woman."

— or, perhaps not.

"Isom?" Alexis asked, wondering if she was signing her own death warrant. "Is there any chance of a proper uniform yet remaining aboard Her Majesty's Ship *Mongoose*?"

BY ALEXIS ARLEEN CAREW, Lieutenant, Commanding HMS Mongoose, Senior, to her knowledge, Officer of Admiralty in the Barbary, and in the Queen's Name and that of Her Naval Forces and Admiralty,

Annalise R
(Alexis Arleen Carew, Lieutenant RN)

A PROCLAMATION for Suppressing of Pirates

WHEREAS WE HAVE RECEIVED INFORMATION, that several Persons, Subjects of New London, have, for some years, committed diverse Piracies and Robberies within and about the Systems of the

Barbary, or adjoining to such Places, which hath and may Occasion great Damage to the Merchants of New London, and others trading into those Parts; and tho' we have appointed such a Force as we judge sufficient for suppressing the said Piracies, yet the more effectually to put an End to the same, we have thought fit, by and with the Advice of Diverse Council, to Issue this Proclamation and Offer of Amnesty;

And we do hereby promise, and declare, that in Case any of the said Pirates, shall on, or within five days of, the date of this Proclamation, surrender him or themselves, to one of our Officers of New London, or to any Officer or Man of the Naval forces of New London, Hanover, the French Republic, or the Berry March, be He Commissioned, Ordinary, In Service, or in State of Captivity; every such Pirate and Pirates so surrendering him, or themselves, as aforesaid, shall have the Queen's gracious Pardon, of, and for such, his or their Piracy, or Piracies, by him or them committed, before this Proclamation's date.

And we do hereby strictly charge and command all New London Admirals, Captains, and other Officers a-space, and all our Governors and Commanders of any Forts, Stations, or other Places in our Realm, and all other our Officers Civil and Military, to seize and take such of the Pirates, who shall refuse or neglect to surrender themselves accordingly.

And we do hereby further declare, that in Case any Person or Persons, on, or after, the date of this Proclamation, shall discover or seize, or cause or procure to be discovered or seized, any one or more of the said Pirates, so refusing or neglecting to surrender themselves as aforesaid, so as they may be brought to Justice, and convicted of the said Offence, such Person or Persons, so making such Discovery or Seizure, or causing or procuring such Discovery or Seizure to be made, shall have and receive as a Reward for the same, viz. for every Commander of any private Ship or Vessel, the Sum of 100 pounds, for every Lieutenant, Master, Boatswain, Carpenter, and Gunner, the Sum of 40 pounds, for every inferior Officer, the Sum of 30 pounds, and for every private Man, the Sum of 20 pounds.

Further, that in Case any Person or Persons, on or after the Day of *this Proclamation, shall discover and cause to be released to Freedom, any Officer or Man of the New London Royal Navy, or the navies of the Republic of Hanover, the Berry March, or the French Republic, held in bondage or servitude within the confines of the system of Erzurum, such Person or Persons, so causing the Release and Freedom of such to be made, shall have and receive as a Reward for the same, viz. for every Commander of any Vessel, the Sum of 100 pounds, for every Lieutenant, Master, Boatswain, Carpenter, and Gunner, the Sum of 40 pounds, for every inferior Officer, the Sum of 30 pounds, and for every private Man, the Sum of 20 pounds.*

And if any Person or Persons, belonging to, and being Part of the Crew, of any such Pirate Ship and Vessel, shall, on or after the date of this Proclamation, seize and deliver, or cause to be seized or delivered, any Commander or Commanders, of such Pirate Ship or Vessel, so as that he or they be brought to Justice, and convicted of the said Offense, such Person or Persons, as a Reward for the same, shall receive for every such Commander, the Sum of 200 pounds, which said Sums, the Lord Treasurer, or the Commissioners of Treasury, or the Admiralty, or such ship of the Royal Navy, being able and taking possession of such captured Pirates, for the Time being, are hereby required, and desired to pay accordingly.

Given at Erzurum, the Barbary,
God save the QUEEN.

"IT DO HAVE A CERTAIN SOMETHING," Blackbourne said, rereading the document for a last time before he was to broadcast it to all of Erzurum.

Isom grinned broadly and nodded, worries of space-lawyering forgotten in his pride at the wording or a particular turn of phrase he thought quite the thing. "It is, I think."

"I thought the offer of a reward for those who don't surrender was very good," Kannstadt said, causing Isom to flush, as it was him who'd had the thought the pirates might not wish to fight their more resistant fellows for only the pardon. He and Blackbourne, along with Isom, had collaborated well into the night in negotiating the appropriate amounts. There'd been a bit more haggling about the rewards for freeing fleet spacers, and no little grumbling from *Mongoose's* crew when it was found that their fellows would be valued at the same number of pounds as captured pirates, but, in the end, Alexis did agree it was a fine incentive.

What Admiralty and the Exchequer would think of it, she couldn't bear pondering.

Alexis closed her eyes and leaned against the navigation plot.

"They're going to bloody hang me."

FORTY-ONE

ALEXIS DIDN'T SO MUCH TUG AT HER UNIFORM AS PULL IT tightly around herself in defense, then glanced about the quarterdeck to see who might have seen. It wouldn't do for the crew, newly informed they were called back into Naval service at Alexis' order — and, curiously, mostly not averse to the news — to see their captain hugging herself.

It was only that it felt rather good to be wearing it again, even if it were old, a bit worn, and somewhat musty from having been stuffed in the bottom of one of her chests and stored in the hold since she'd come aboard. It was still a proper uniform, if scuffed and stained in places, and she hadn't quite realized how much she'd missed that since taking command of *Mongoose*. The costumes of the private ships, her own included, were well enough for the play acting of those captains — taking merchantmen and reveling in the captured wealth and prize money — but that wasn't for her. She'd been a bit ... lost, she thought, during that time. Cast loose from some mooring she hadn't truly understood.

Perhaps she didn't understand it now, even, but she did feel relief at the snug fit of her uniform jacket, the clasp of a proper beret atop her head, even if the gold band of command was a bit of frippery from some pirate's vest sewn on by Isom, and even if the beret did have a tendency to rise up and fall to the wrong side, it being a part of her old midshipman's kit.

Even the boots felt better — proper shipboard boots, and not the high-topped, higher-heeled boots she'd worn as a privateer. Though these boots were the most worn and ragged of the whole bit, being a pair she'd cast off and Isom had kept for the use of the Creat —

Alexis broke off that thought and forced herself to stop wiggling her toes. Isom assured her he'd thoroughly cleaned the things, and she'd have to accept that, there being no alternative. She turned her attention to her crew.

She had those who'd crashed with her on Erzurum aboard and those few New Londoners amongst Kannstadt's men. The Hanoverese who'd fleshed out her force in the retaking of *Mongoose* were returned to Kannstadt, there being only so far she felt they could properly stretch the regulations. They were already certainly at the point of snapping, what with her returning to active duty on the excited utterance of a captain who was then taken captive and forced out of the system, effectively Impressing her own lads back to service (there being no other way for them to get home), and commandeering her own ship, *Mongoose*, against her own letter of marque's immunity to such, into service.

Manning the newly sworn in HMS *Mongoose* with Hanoverese would surely cause all of Erzurum and its surrounding space to swirl into a maelstrom of a farce.

Isom had helped her with the wording of *Mongoose*'s commissioning, so as to assure that she needn't worry about Avrel Dansby hanging what Admiralty left of her a second time for giving over his ship.

Though the bit about "such commission to expire with her commander, Lieutenant Alexis Arleen Carew" did give her pause, despite Isom's assurance that it meant her own command of the ship and not her bodily expiration, and was only meant to ensure

Avrel Dansby got his ship back once they returned to New London space.

Still, the wording made her neck itch, nooses being much on her mind of late.

She glanced around the quarterdeck again.

She had Layland on the helm, Tite on the tactical console, and a good master's mate, Puryear, standing ready to assist her in lieu of a first officer, freeing Dockett to set *Mongoose* to rights, now she was a proper ship again.

First lieutenant, *us being a proper Navy ship now.*

The young man, Aiden, stood ready at the hatch to run messages for her, should that prove necessary — which it should not, since they were not going into an action. Nabb was on the gundeck, the ship and crew, such as they were, called to quarters. More to impress upon them that they were returned to Naval discipline — or experiencing it for the first time in the case of those merchant spacers such as the woman Davies — than any expectation of a fight from the pirates.

Creasy was back at the signals console, Blackbourne beside him and ready to read out the text of her proclamation at her order.

A proclamation ... in the Queen's name ... by me.

Alexis took a deep breath, then nodded to him.

The ships they'd taken were spread out in orbit around Erzurum, repeating the broadcast in the absence of those satellites Alexis and the other private ships had destroyed in their first attack. Most of Erzurum's settlements were enough below *Mongoose* to receive the transmission, but there were a few more remote.

Creasy opened a general broadcast on all channels and Blackbourne — after a moment's indulgence to shout, "Oi! Shut yer gobs an' listen to Old Blackbourne, mates!" — stated with remarkable sobriety that there was a Royal Navy ship with a Royal Navy captain overhead and then faithfully read her proclamation without a single interjection of his own.

"Make o' that what y'will, lads," he finished, "but Old Blackbourne's puttin' his name down an' goin' home with a full purse an' the bloody Queen's kiss o' forgiveness on his cheek. You all do as y'will, but be warned — there's a bloody bitch-woman here in orbit who'll see your shriveled sacks tacked to her wall as trophies afore she hangs you, an' don't doubt that!"

He then turned to Alexis and said, with the transmission still open, "All right, bitch-woman, Old Blackbourne's makin' his rescue o' your lot, that bugger Ellender's, an' some sundry fellows with the Hannie t'be —" He frowned. "— five-thousand three hundred ten pounds. 'T'will be coin in hand, aye?"

WHETHER BLACKBOURNE'S DEMAND OF over five thousand pounds over an open transmission was a purposeful thing on the pirate's part or not, Alexis couldn't ask — of course the pirate would say simply that Old Blackbourne was just the clever sort to do such a thing a'purpose.

Whatever his intent, the thought of Old Blackbourne collecting both a pardon and such a large sum of bounty on rescued spacers seemed to galvanize many of the pirates.

They'd not even bothered to wait for Kannstadt to start his own transmission following Blackbourne's, an offer of the same general pardon from Hanover for those few among the pirates who were citizens of that nation, before taking to the airwaves to accept.

To the airwaves and to the air, as those boats which had so recently been put to use in patrolling to thwart Alexis' attempts to land on Erzurum's farms and far-flung settlements to rescue enslaved spacers, were now put to use in collecting as many of those men as the boats' crews could manage.

So exuberant were some of the pirates in liberating the captives that Alexis had to have Blackbourne make a further broadcast insisting that the people of Erzurum not be harmed, then a further by Kannstadt, urging Erzurum's natives to not resist the freeing of their slaves, and, finally, another, by Alexis, offering recompense, again in the Queen's name, for their taking.

Alexis retired to her quarters after that, leaving it to Kannstadt to organize the details occurring on the planet below, as the Hanoverese captain seemed like he could use the distraction from his own sorrows. Erzurum's main spaceport was entirely under the control of those pirates accepting the pardon, most of their fellows having fled to other parts of the planet, and both she and Kannstadt would be taking boats there soon. They needed to quickly gather as many freed spacers as they could, before the pardoned pirates realized just how scant the "Navy" presence in-system was.

Alexis shut her cabin's hatch, loosened her collar, and hung her beret on the wall before running fingers through her hair.

"Let's see ... I've returned to service under dubious authority, Impressed my own crew, commandeered my own ship, issued a proclamation in the Queen's name as a lowly lieutenant, granted amnesty and pardon to, at last count, nearly seven hundred pirates, indebted the kingdom, to pirates and bloody Hannies no less, to the tune of ... what's the total now, Isom?"

The slight-framed clerk barely glanced up from Alexis' dining table where he had an impressive number of documents open on its surface as he coordinated with Kannstadt.

"One hundred thirty-two thousand six hundred eighty pounds, sir," he said. "There's a bit in dispute due to the conflicts of those pirates as want the pardon with those who don't, and us not specifying the, ah, *state* of a body in which it's been seized, so to speak."

"What?"

"There's some question, sir, as to if a pardoned pirate shoots an unpardoned pirate in the head, as to whether the bounty's still good, sir." He frowned. "As well, which *parts* might represent the body. There may be some as are trying to, ah, double or even triple their takes."

"With bodies? But —"

"Well, a man's got two hands of fingerprints and a pair of retinal scans to identify him, don't he?" Isom said. He looked back to the table's surface. "Don't you worry, sir. It's only a few early ones to settle, as Mister Blackbourne told them — the pardoned pirates, I mean — then to only wound their fellows if they could help it. There's no more than ten percent of the total in dispute, sir."

Alexis walked slowly to her pantry, drew a mug of beer — cursing the pirates who'd held *Mongoose* for draining her store of bourbon — and took a long pull.

"A hundred thousand pounds," she muttered.

"Plus ten percent, sir," Isom called. "Probably best to just pay on all the parts — goodwill and all."

"Plus ten percent, then," she muttered, "in Admiralty notes of hand under my name."

"Don't forget the recompense, sir," Isom called, and Alexis almost told him to mind his bloody table and leave her be.

"Oh, yes," she said. "I mustn't forget the bit where I buy a few thousand slaves in Admiralty's name. That will endear me to the Crown all entire, I'm sure."

"Wouldn't be so bad, sir, if so many of the farmers weren't demanding receipts."

Yes, the receipts ... all with her name on them. At least there was no sliding scale of rank for those, only a straight-forward ten pounds per slave paid to the slave-owner, those who weren't also pirates, and be done with it. Isom was paying even on those slaves who'd formerly been merchant spacers, regardless of nation, and from other Barbary systems the pirates had raided — for goodwill, Alexis reasoned.

There was a chime from her hatch.

"Come through," Alexis called.

Nabb slid the hatch open and poked his head in.

"Boat's ready, sir."

FORTY-TWO

O', listen hearties, hear me mates,
For this'll touch your hearts.
It wasn't to the officers
Our Alexis went to first.

THE LANDING FIELD NEAR ERZURUM'S LARGEST CITY WAS NOT
so very big to begin with. Neither was Erzurum's largest city, come to
that — more of a town, smaller than Port Arthur back on Alexis'
home of Dalthus. The field was bare earth, but, thankfully, Erzurum's
first settlers had chosen to put their primary settlement in an area *not*
under the perpetual gloom and cloud cover Alexis had come to
associate with the planet in her brief time there.

Here the sky was clear and bright, with Erzurum's slightly orange
tinted star only rarely passing behind the occasional white cloud,
which made it all the easier to see how crowded the field was. Not
with boats, though there were many, but with men.

The pirates, those who'd accepted the pardons, had turned the
field into a sort of clearing ground for themselves while they waited
for Alexis and Kannstadt to come down and claim their goods —

whether those goods be captured pirates unwilling to accept the pardons, surrendering pirates awaiting confirmation of their pardons, or newly freed spacers, grouped by whatever pirate band had garnered their release and awaiting a final count and confirmation of their bounty before being grouped by nationality on the bare, open space.

The field teemed with bodies, cordoned off into groups of varying sizes, and Alexis thought it must be nearly as uncomfortable for them all to be standing in the bright sunlight as it would have been if there'd been rain. At least there wasn't the cold of the rain and perpetual mud for them to be milling about in.

It was, in fact, quite dry and warm here, which made for a dusty field and billows of the stuff rolled away from *Mongoose's* boat as Gutis, returned from his assistance to Kannstadt, put the boat down at the very edge, some hundred meters from the masses of men. They waited until Kannstadt's own boat grounded nearby before letting down the ramp and then Alexis strode down to meet the other captain.

Alexis kept her back straight and shoulders back, head at just the proper angle to display her beret and its gold-rim denoting her command. This was a touchy time, their first meeting in person with the pirates on the surface, and she wanted to give the impression of a Royal Navy officer, fully confident in her ability to reduce these pirates, their boats and ships, and anything else offending her, to much the state of the dust puffing up from each of her footsteps.

Should they discover or suspect just how slight and under-manned her forces truly were, they might well think their chances better with their former captain, Ness, and all this would fall apart.

Kannstadt met her between the two boats. Some one of his men must have been a fair tailor, for he wore a reasonable approximation of a Hanoverese captain's uniform. A darker color, not quite black, than her own blue, and with far more gilt than all but the most osten-tatious Royal Navy captains would think proper, but certainly better for this meeting than the scaled snakipede skins she'd first seen him in.

Closer, she could see that the material was not quite right, nor the color, but it looked as though it would do well enough.

"*Kapitän* Carew," Kannstadt said with a nod as she reached him.

"Captain Kannstadt."

A firming of his lips told her that he was, perhaps, as nervous as she was herself.

They waited while their respective boat crews disembarked and assembled near the ramps. Kannstadt had brought more men, having more available, while Alexis had a bare score and few enough left aboard *Mongoose* with that.

"No one comes to greet us," Kannstadt observed.

Indeed, though everyone on the field was flashing looks their way, no one approached.

Kannstadt removed his brimmed cap with its odd folds of fabric and wiped at his forehead before settling it back on his head. "Your pirate says the leaders, what there are of them, will meet us in a tavern — the ..." He trailed off.

"The *Randy Whistler*," Alexis supplied. "Our own officers, those released so far, will be there as well."

They'd brought Blackbourne down with them, him being the former, or perhaps still, despite his capture, leader of the pirate force on Erzurum's surface. Kannstadt glanced back at their force, which consisted of Alexis' twenty-man boat crew, his own of not quite forty, and, perhaps, another hundred, all told, in orbit and split between all their captured ships. Alexis followed his gaze, then looked to the mass of men across the field.

They must only get through this meeting without quashing what the pirates had already accepted, then all those spacers would begin being transported up to those ships, and they'd have more than they'd ever need.

Enough to meet this Ness when he returns and grind him to dust for what he's done here? Perhaps, if I've any say in it.

She looked to Kannstadt who raised his own eyes from where they watched Alexis' foot twist her boot into the dry earth of Erzurum's field. She flushed and cleared her throat, but Kannstadt gave her a predatory grin as though he understood exactly what she'd been thinking.

"*Ja, Kapitän* Carew." He gestured across the field. "After you?"

TO GET to the town's buildings, and their meeting place, they had to first cross the empty space between their boats and the waiting men, then walk through those men themselves.

The crowd quieted as they approached, but there were still sounds, and Alexis could see that the groups of men were segregated in some way. The pirate groups were clearly identifiable, for they all had proper ships' jumpsuits or other clothing, rather than the loin cloths or skins of the former captives.

Alexis paused for a moment to take in the scene. There must be thousands of men on the field already. "So many," she muttered.

Kannstadt stopped beside her. "They are not yet done," he said, nodding to a pirate boat setting down at the outskirts and another coming in behind it.

She realized the Hanoverese was right. The masses of men assembled on the dusty field were not the whole of it, and the pirates were still bringing in former slaves from outlying farms and plantations. Despite her shock at the running total Isom kept of both men and pounds owed, those numbers would not nearly be the end of it.

"We need more ships," she whispered.

They resumed walking and as they got closer and she could make out the occasional voice, she could tell that the former captives were also segregated, with some groups speaking English, some German, and others French. Apparently, the pirates, or the released crews themselves, were put together in groups by their former fleets.

A boat's ramp lowered and a group of three-dozen half-naked, more-than-half-starved, captives was ushered out of the boat to stand on the field. They weren't bound, but might as well have been, edging away from their captors, the pirates still being armed with both pistols and some sort of stunstick to keep order.

Alexis supposed she couldn't blame them for that — it would be as foolish for the pirates to trust their former captives not to take some sort of revenge as it would be for those captives to accept the pirates' word that they should just stand easy and everything would be all right in a bit.

There were armed pirates, these with rifles, all around the groups of spacers, as well, and some of these had boxes similar to what the farmer, Isikli, had used to control the slaves on his farm. So the pirates had not yet removed or deactivated the explosives implanted in these former slaves either.

The men off the new boat were pointed toward larger groups which they approached tentatively. Those at the edges of the group smiled and waved them forward, patting backs, wrapping an arm around shoulders, and explaining, Alexis supposed, what was going on to the new arrivals — whether they explained the truth or whatever rumor was most prevalent at the moment, she couldn't say.

There were grins as their new situation, perhaps not perfect or perfectly understood yet, but certainly better than what they'd expected sank in, and then came the calls — ship name after ship name.

"*Onslaught?*"

"*Comète?*"

"*Mölders?*"

"*Pompee?* Hey, lads, any off *Pompee?*"

Then from farther inside the group — from the middle, its edges, wherever the fellows from that ship had found each other and formed their tight knot of shipmates thought lost forever.

"*Oy! Onslaught* here!" With an upraised arm. "That you, Osburn? Bloody Dark, man, thought you were a dead 'un! Make a lane for Osburn, lads!"

"Ici! Ici! Comète! Ici!"

"Hier! Mölders, hier!"

Heartbreaking were those who received no answer. To have seen their ship beaten and wrecked, they and their mates left behind the fleets to fend for themselves, the arrival of the pirates, and then to be sold off into servitude on Erzurum — only to have this glint of rescue, but without their fellows.

"Pompee, lads! Any off *Pompee?"*

Left to idle at the edges, wondering at the fate of their mates, and smile half-heartedly at the back pats and assurances of those around them that, "Easy, lad, there's more boats comin' every minute — no tellin' where a man got to on this Dark-forsaken ball o' mud. You'll see."

Alexis squared her shoulders and walked on.

There was a group of pirates outside a building with a hanging sign, all watching her group as they came on. She couldn't read the sign yet, but she assumed this was the *Randy Whistler* pub, confirmed by Blackbourne who nodded in that direction.

"Them's the lads," the old pirate said, "an' yer officers'll be inside."

The way led between a block of New London spacers and a smaller mass of unsurrendered pirates. The former, perhaps three hundred strong in this group, were rising from where they sat in the dust to watch her approach. The latter watched her as well, but were fewer and didn't rise.

Alexis kept her eyes front, intent on the coming meeting, and watching the pirates outside the pub. What she longed to do is break from her path to the block of French forces on the other side of the New Londoners and call out for Delaine or any word of him. That wouldn't do, though. She was the senior Royal Navy officer in-system, here to treat with these pirates, and finalize the pardon and turnover of the prisoners and their fellows, not some lovestruck girl who couldn't control herself.

She strode between the two groups, walking faster to take the lead from Kannstadt and Blackbourne.

The captive pirates to her left cat-called and offered up other insults, but it was the words from her right, from the New London spacers, that caught her ear.

"Look, that a proper captain?"

"Uniform's not ragged, what's this about?"

"Did the fleet come back fer us?"

"What's t'happen now?"

"Thought we was bein' led to slaughter, me."

Sweet Dark, did their own commanders not tell them what we were about?

Alexis could well imagine the pirates not doing so for the common spacers, while the officers, better housed in the surrounding pubs and buildings, would have got the story, but did none of them tell their men? She looked around — no, there were no officers, not captains nor lieutenants nor even midshipmen amongst the masses of men. Not to keep order in the ranks or to tell the lads what to expect or would become of them. What must they have thought, herded from farms and plantations back to the spaceport? That question, what they must have thought, was answered by further comments.

"Thought we was t'be sold off-planet. What's a proper officer doin' here?"

"Cap'n — what's the word, eh? We rescued or sold or they set to blow our bloody heads off?"

"Why's t'Hannie here? We t'be prisoners?"

"Damn sight better'n here, a Hannie prison."

Alexis slowed, Kannstadt and Blackbourne caught up to her and passed, then looked back. Alexis slowed more.

"Old Blackbourne's lads're waitin', bitch-woman," Blackbourne said. "They're pumped up an' full o' themselves w' pardons an' bein' treated with, so y'don' want t'be takin' 'em down."

"*Kapitän* Carew?"

"What's t'happen to us, sir?" the spacer closest to her asked, in a voice so devoid of hope that it froze her in her tracks. "We prisoners of the Hannies now?"

Alexis turned to him, she couldn't just pass them by, leaving them wondering at their fate. Properly, she should finish treating with the pirates, then report to the other New London officers, where she'd no longer be senior in-system, them being now freed. It should be to them to organize their crews and pass on what information they would.

She eyed the mass of men before her, ragged, dirty, and skinny from their time on Erzurum, all wide-eyed and fairly quivering with uncertainty, then stepped toward the last who'd spoken.

"Carew?" Kannstadt asked.

"Bitch-woman?" Blackbourne asked at the same time.

Alexis glanced their way, then at the waiting group of pirate leaders. Those were clearly irritated with the delay, crossing their arms and glaring at her. She narrowed her own eyes.

"You may tell your fellows, Mister Blackbourne, that a Queen's Officer will attend them when she is bloody ready, and they may await my pleasure with respect or take their insolence there —" She jerked her head to the huddled groups of unsurrendered pirates. "— and turn in their bloody pardons, for I'll not brook it, I tell you."

Blackbourne opened his mouth to speak.

"And if you call me 'bitch-woman' just once more, Mister Blackbourne, I swear by the Dark I'll leave you bleeding your life out in the Erzurum's mud while you watch the last of your fellows lift to their new, pardoned lives." She locked her eyes with him. "Are we clear, sir?"

Blackbourne closed his mouth and nodded.

"Very well." Alexis turned back to the New London spacers. She took a breath to speak, but realized that she was facing a wall of chests, her own bare meter and a half not quite being up to the task of addressing such a crowd from the same ground.

"What's your name?" she asked the last man who'd spoken.

"Tinner," he said weakly, then straightened when Alexis

narrowed her eyes and cocked her head at him. They might be down, but damn them, these men were Navy and needed stiffening. He cleared his throat. "Tinner, sir. Estcot Tinner — quarter-gunner off'n *Ghurka*, forty guns, out'n Strathmore."

Alexis laid a hand on his shoulder and squeezed. She could feel the bones through less flesh and muscle than a quarter-gunner should have to heave the carriages about against their mass and the magnets holding them to the deck.

He was no worse off, really, than Kannstadt, Ellender, or their men had been when Alexis first encountered them, but his state affected her more. Perhaps it was that he was at the front of a group that stretched back behind him to number three times those with Kannstadt and Ellender. Perhaps it was the knowledge of further groups, the Hanoverese, the French, then more of each, off behind them. The sheer scope — the number of men abandoned to the mercies of the Dark, then the pirates, then the farms of Erzurum — astounded her. How could Chipley's hatred of the Hanoverese drive him to this? Force him to follow his foe and leave those who couldn't behind to whatever fate came without even a single ship to attempt rescue?

Her eyes burned and she narrowed them to keep back tears.

"All right, Tinner, I'll tell you what this is about." She scanned her eyes over the men around him. "You lot pass the word, right, as my voice won't pass your chests and I've no platform to speak of here." She gave them a look of caution as they nodded. "Handsomely, now, mind. So the meaning's not changed."

"Aye, sir."

"Right, Tinner, so here's the state of things." She paused while those far enough back to just hear her repeated what she said, and those back from them did the same, her words rippling through the crowd of spacers as from a pebble tossed in a quiet pond.

"First, the war's over — or paused, at least, with a cease-fire. There's a force in orbit, Royal Navy and Hanover —" She gave a nod to Kannstadt who stood nearby. "— holding all the ships in-system.

You're here on this field, lads, because you've not been forgotten. We're here to get you up to those ships, as many of you as will fit, and then blast the remnants of this bloody pirate force to atoms when they return. There'll not be a spacer-man left on Erzurum against his will when we're done. I've just to finalize things with the pirates and tell your officers, then we'll be about it and you'll, some of you, have a proper deck under your feet and a proper bulkhead overhead, and no more of Erzurum's bloody dry, wet, or whatever else this planet has in store for folk."

Alexis was a little surprised she'd made it through all that without any interruptions, neither from those near her nor from those who couldn't see and were listening to their fellows. Not a murmur went through the crowd save for her words — nor the cheers she'd have expected at the news of the war's end or the chance for revenge against the pirates or the prospect of being inside a proper ship once more.

She cleared her throat. "So that's it, lads. You've just to be patient a bit more and you'll be on your way home."

More silence greeted that, then a man behind Tinner spoke.

"What fleet did they send, sir, t'bring us home? Who's commanding?"

Alexis cleared her throat again. Perhaps engaging the men had been a mistake — they'd want to know, of course, what size force, what ships had come to their rescue.

"Captain Kannstadt and I are senior in-system," she said. "Until we've met with your own officers and freed them, of course."

The spacer glanced at Kannstadt and then at Alexis' sleeves, which showed her rank clearly, no matter the gold band of command around her beret.

"But yer a lieutenant and he's a ..." The man broke off and fingered the rings in his ear, clearly meaning the ragged edge of Kannstadt's, denoting his status of former slave.

"It's no matter," Alexis said. "Just wait a bit and you'll —"

"Ain't no fleet, is there?" the man said. He glared at Kannstadt over Alexis' head. "Stupid Hannie went an' took a ship or two some-hows." He fingered his neck. "Now we'll alls get our heads blowed off." He glanced down at Alexis and shrugged. "Don't know who you are, but we're dead men now, lads."

"Belay that!" Alexis hissed at him. Damn her for a fool, but she should have gone and spoken to the officers first. They'd understand the precariousness of the situation and want to believe, just as the pirates who'd accepted a pardon did, that there was a way out. That belief was half, perhaps more, of what Alexis needed to pull this off — the desire for a plan with so many spindly legs to be possible.

If the common spacers became restless, talked too much, came up with rumors, as they would, then the pirates might become suspicious and the whole thing might fall apart.

Alexis took a deep breath. "There are risks, lads, but we'll get you out of this. I swear it."

"An' we're t'believe you? Some whiff of a lieutenant an' a girl? We fought at Giron, lass, an' followed Chipley on his mad dash t' Hell. Ye'll not blind us so."

Alexis bristled at that. "I was at Giron as well, so watch your tongue, man."

Alexis noted that those repeating the words for their fellows had trailed off, paying more attention to the action, and there were mutters growing from further back in the crowd as those who couldn't hear demanded answers.

"It's Clarance Patience, *lieutenant*, sir," he said with some scorn. "An' what ship brought *you* there? One of Cammack's fresh out of the Core? Spent the action polishin' yer captain's brass?"

"I saw enough of the action, Patience," Alexis said, jaw tight and resisting the urge to call Dockett over to shut the man up. Even her bosun wouldn't be able to keep order as Patience's doubts spread through the men.

"What ship?" Patience insisted.

Alexis turned her gaze toward the waiting pirates at the door of the *Randy Whistler*. She hoped the guise of a haughty officer, impatient to be about her business, would hide the pain she knew covered her face at the need to think about that action. She also thrust down her own anger that Chipley's fleet, the ships these men had served on, had been so fixated on the Hanoverese that they'd not bothered to see Alexis and her ship's state — noticing that desperate action against an enemy frigate to protect the fleeing transports only when it was done and her ship had been pounded to a hulk and all but a handful of the crew dead.

"*Belial*," she said, "commanding."

Patience made a rude noise. "My arse."

"Belay that, Patience," Tinner said. "There's no Core Fleet fop'd try to steal *that*."

Alexis turned back to find him looking at her oddly and she flushed. There was too much of that action that seemed to attach itself to her, and not nearly enough to her ship or the crew who'd manned her.

"Ain't no fleet come, is there, sir?" Tinner asked.

Alexis flushed again and wished, not for the first time, that she could control that particular reaction as well as, say, her expression.

"We have ships," she said, "and you to man them once the pirates release you to it. My word on it, Tinner. We need just a bit of ..." She glanced at his fellow who was still glaring at her and quirked her mouth. "Patience."

Tinner frowned. "Why'd the pirates do this? They've a big enough force."

"A pardon," Alexis said. "The Queen's Pardon, offered from a Royal Navy officer, senior in-system."

Tinner stared at her a moment, and she could very nearly see his mind working on her words as he put together the whole of it. Finally, he raised his eyes and looked around the field, taking in the sheer number of pirates not captive and working on retrieving their fellows. Alexis herself was no little appalled at the number of pardons Isom had drawn up in the Queen's name for Alexis signature.

"Pardoned all them? On your word?"

Alexis nodded. "Aye."

"They'll hang you," he whispered.

"Thank you, Tinner," Alexis said with a wry grin. "I'd rather been afraid I might forget that outcome. So good of you to point it out."

"But —"

"The hangman must have me in hand to do it, Tinner, and that means I'll have got you home — so no need to worry yourself on it, is there?"

Tinner frowned and shook his head. "No, sir — I imagine we've no need to worry ourselves now." He took a deep breath. "I'd know your name, sir, if I might."

"Carew."

"Thank you, Captain Carew."

Patience snorted in disgust. "If you —"

"Belay that, Patience," Tinner said, "or I'll bloody gag you." He fingered his ratty, dirty loincloth — the only thing he possessed to do such a thing. "An' you'll not want that, I promise." He nodded to Alexis. "You be about yer business, sir. I'll handle this lot. I were master's mate and had a good bosun to learn from, may his soul rest in the Dark where he fell."

Alexis started to ask how he meant to do that, but he'd already turned.

"Make a place for me to stand, lads," Tinner said, then nodded at Patience. "He'll do."

"What —"

Patience broke off as those to either side of him grasped his arms and drove him to hands and knees so that Tinner could climb up to stand on his back and face the crowd of spacers.

"Y'hear this, lads!" Tinner yelled, his voice surprisingly strong for his emaciated frame. "The Queen herself's sent for us!"

"That's not —" Alexis protested, but Tinner was already going on.

"Pardoned all these rotting, scurvy bastards t'get us back safe, lads! Forgivin' all their crimes t'get us home, so y'see our worth to her!" Tinner yelled. "An' sent the captain o'bloody *Belial* t'bring us, so y'know there'll be no givin' up, no matter what these bloody pirates think!"

Tinner looked down at Alexis and made a shooing gesture toward the pub before resuming his call.

"Three cheers for Queen Annalise, lads, who'd not leave Her loyal spacers behind!"

Alexis sighed and rejoined Kannstadt and Blackbourne as Tinner's first call of "*Hip-hip!*" rang out.

Kannstadt said something, but Alexis lost it in the resounding "*Hooray!*" that followed.

"What?"

"Your officers will not like this, I think," Kannstadt said.

They continued their walk towards the pub as the second cheer filled the air above Erzurum's field, growing to include the groups of Hanoverese and French who, perhaps, didn't even know what they were cheering about. Even the pirates, those who'd accepted pardons, at least, joined in, while their sullen fellows sat in the dust and hunched over even more.

Alexis shrugged. "It's not as though they were going to like how I've got them free to begin with." Ellender was a fine example of some officers and Alexis had no delusion that more than a handful of those awaiting her in the pub would agree with her methods. "A bit more will hardly change that."

Behind them, Tinner had finished his cheers and called out again.

"And three cheers for Captain Carew, lads! Her *Belial* saw those sloggers safe at Giron and she's on to do the same for us! *Hip-hip!*"

Alexis flushed and winced as the spacers bellowed a "*Hooray!*" that nearly drowned out the engines of an incoming boat loaded with more of their freed fellows. Tinner seemed to take that as a challenge and waved his hands upward. "*Hip-hip!*"

She caught Blackbourne staring at her and glared until he looked away.

"What?" she asked when the next cheer subsided.

"Nothing," the pardoned pirate muttered, looking from her back to the mass of men on the landing field. He shook his head, slid his eyes quickly over her again, then looked back to the pub with a muttered, "Witch-woman."

FORTY-THREE

Now, Alexis, Annalise did send
To fetch her errant spacers.
Little did she think they'd end up
In the Randy Whistler.

THE RANDY WHISTLER BORE A HANGING SIGN WITH WHAT looked like the image of a woman playing a tune. As they grew closer, Alexis looked away quickly.

That is not a whistle, she thought. She glanced back, then away again. *Nor a flute.*

Well, that explained the pub's name, and likely its primary offering under the pirates' management.

The pirates waiting outside the entryway were grinning now, where they'd seemed annoyed when Alexis first stopped to speak to Tinner — perhaps the spacers' cheers were infectious.

There were more men at the pub's windows, looking out at the commotion. These she assumed were captive officers, for they bore the same signs of deprivation as the men and were equally dressed in rags, though some still clung to their berets or the strangely folded

caps of the Hanoverese service — Alexis supposed as some remnant
of their command or authority. At first glance that might have seemed
odd, but Alexis thought it might have provided some comfort and
familiarity to the men wherever those had been held captive.

That thought struck another in her head and she paused to
glance around the field once more. Blocks of spacers, milling about
and not so sullenly still, now that Tinner's announcement had made
its way through them all, sparser blocks of captive pirates, and
amongst them all, the pardoned pirates — the *surrendered* pirates, she
thought — standing as some sort of armed guard. The only ones
armed on the field, save her own and Kannstadt's boat crews.

No, that will never do.

She eyed the waiting pirate leaders, who were grinning even
wider. No, it would not do to have these pirates think they held the
upper hand as these negotiations began — and, while the pardon had
been proclaimed and many things settled, the devil was always in the
details, as Isom was so fond of pointing out.

The mistake, she thought, was in terming this a negotiation at all.
That was done — pardons accepted and back under the authority of
Queen and country. No, she might now meet with the pirates, but
there'd be no negotiating, only orders that any lawful Queen's subject
must follow, and they'd best understand that. The pirates, armed
though they might be, were no longer in charge of Erzurum — the
bloody Navy was.

Alexis squared her shoulders and strode forward, Kannstadt and
Blackbourne following, until she neared the pub.

One of the pirates waiting outside let his face split in a wide,
tooth-baring ... well, somewhat toothy — and did pirates never ...

Alexis shook her head to recenter her thoughts and walked
straight past the pirates to the pub's door and through it.

Inside, the pub was much as she'd expected it. Dirty and somewhat in disarray. The group of officers at the window, perhaps ten of
them, turned to stare as she entered. A number of tables had been
pushed together in the center of the room and more officers sat there,

also staring. All, no doubt, wondering at the commotion with the men outside and, as well, wondering at Alexis herself, walking in with Blackbourne, who they must know, and Kannstadt. Alexis could fairly see the question of what were a New London lieutenant, a Hanoverese captain, and the somewhat leader of the planetside pirates doing together work its way through their minds.

The pub's main room opened up to a balcony above where she could see doorways and hallways to further rooms — perhaps where the whistling must occur when the place was in full swing. The balcony's rail was lined with more disheveled and ragged men, these younger than those on the ground floor, and clearly junior officers.

"I've need of lieutenants! Outside with me, all — lively now!" Alexis bellowed in her best voice and cutting across the querulous murmurs which rose at her entrance. "*Lieutenants, à l'extérieur! Vite!*" she added for the Berry March fleet, though she suspected she hadn't got it quite right. It had been ... far too long since she'd practiced her French with Delaine, and she'd forgotten some.

She forced down her disappointment that he wasn't part of the group of waiting captains in the room — there wasn't time to think about that at all, nor where he might be, if not here. Nor that he might not be left alive on Erzurum at all.

"Captain Kannstadt, gather your countrymen's lieutenants, if you please," Alexis said, then spun on her heel and walked out of the pub, leaving three approaching captains to deal with later. They'd likely not love her for the snub, but she was certain setting the proper tone with the pirates was far more important.

She could almost feel Kannstadt's confusion behind her, but he did call out, "*Leutnants von Hanover, komm nach draußen — schnell! Schnell!*"

Alexis strode past the waiting pirate leaders again, ignoring the, "And yer bein' —" one of them said her way. She paused a dozen paces from the pub and was quickly joined by Kannstadt and Blackbourne.

"I know a countryman inside," Kannstadt said, giving her an

amused look. "One of the captains. He has a look of not being pleased just now."

"I'm certain few are pleased with me," Alexis said, "but I'll not leave these scum armed around our spacers another moment." She glanced at Blackbourne. "No offense."

"It's fair enough for Old Blackbourne," he said with a wave of dismissal.

"Now, look, you —" the pirate leader said, fairly stomping his feet as he approached, which was all Alexis could ask for, thinking that if he came to where she was then she was halfway to getting her way regardless of how angry a show he might put on.

Alexis held up her hand, index finger up in the fairly universal "a moment, please, I'm quite busy with any number of things far more important than your words" gesture and he fell silent.

Lieutenants, or she assumed they were such, began pouring out of the pub and assembling before her. About forty in all, she estimated.

"Who's senior of New London?" she asked.

"I am," one of those in the front row answered immediately, which she'd expected, since one couldn't put a gaggle of junior officers together for a full minute without they'd determined each other's seniority. "Mountjoy, off *Perseus*, forty-four. And you are?"

"Captain Alexis Carew, commanding *Mongoose*," she answered. "Senior officer free and with a ship, for the moment, Mountjoy, and I've work for you and your fellows."

Alexis held the man's gaze, wondering what sort he was and knowing all depended on it. Some men were so bloody touchy that they'd argue a point no matter the cost — whether to fire port or starboard first when there were enemies close alongside to either.

Mountjoy glanced at her sleeves, where her own lieutenant's insignia wrapped the cuffs, then to the bold band of her beret.

"I'm unfamiliar with *Mongoose* ... sir," Mountjoy said.

"She's new," Alexis told him flatly, "but here to bring you home."

If you don't set it all arse over bollox, she added only to herself.

"Blackbourne, who's this —"

Alexis raised her you-are-unimportant finger again, and the pirate cut off, face going red. She kept her gaze fixed on Mountjoy, hoping her expression was somewhat like the sense of stern confidence she was trying for.

Mountjoy took in the red-faced pirate, met Alexis' eyes for another moment, then nodded. "Aye, sir — what do you need of us?"

Alexis nearly sighed with relief that she'd got a lieutenant with a brain for senior here — a minor miracle of odds fair to set Dockett's book on end, given her experience with most other officers.

The lieutenant to Mountjoy's left nudged his senior's shoulder.

"I say, Mountjoy, should we not consult our captains inside?"

Ah — so he balances it out, I suppose.

The other fellow looked around the field. "This entire business has an ill feel to it — and she's only a —"

"Shut up, Poncy," Mountjoy said, keeping his eyes on Alexis. "Do as Captain Carew says."

"Thank you, Lieutenant Mountjoy." Alexis turned to the red-faced pirate. "And you are, sir?"

The pirate narrowed his eyes at Alexis, but addressed Blackbourne. "Blackbourne?"

"I have a Blackbourne already," Alexis said, interrupting him. "You'll need another name, sir — shall you give it to me, or would you rather I pick it?"

"What?" the pirate asked. "Pick it?"

"Very well — Shufflebottom." Alexis pulled out her tablet. "You shall be Mister Shufflebottom. That's the name I'll put on your pardon — the pardon I've yet to sign, mind you — but I'm uncertain how well that will work out in the long run. Would you not prefer to tell me?"

Shufflebottom's face showed a great deal of confusion now, but a couple of his fellows were hiding snickers, and that was what Alexis was after. She could not allow any of these pirates, nor even those spacers she was to rescue, to question her authority. Once questioned, the whole bloody deal might fall apart.

"I'm no bloody Shufflebottom," Shufflebottom said.

"Then a name, sir," Alexis said. She advanced on him in his confusion and he backed up into the group of following pirates exactly as she wished him to. "A name for your pardon over my signature — for I assure you, Shufflebottom, I have a rather large list of them yet to sign and I'm quite willing for yours to be lost right off the stack. I'm sure whoever thinks he's after you as leader of this motley band would appreciate the bounty on your unpardoned head."

Alexis scanned the group of pirate leaders then returned her eyes to Shufflebottom.

"I am Captain Alexis Carew of *Mongoose*," she said, loudly enough for them all to hear, but staring at Shufflebottom. "I'm the senior New London officer in-system and the holder of your pardons, so you'll bloody well do as I order, or you may join your fellows there —" She pointed to the group of pirates who'd refused pardon. "— and have some few pounds' value to who's next in charge of your little band. *Starting with your bloody name, sir* — your legal one and not some nonsense!"

Shufflebottom's shoulders seemed to slump as he looked for support and found none. Perhaps his fellows were thinking of how many pounds he was worth in bounty if Alexis did choose to lose his pardon from the stack.

Shufflebottom mumbled something.

"What was that, Shufflebottom?" Alexis asked. "I didn't quite catch it."

"Legal name's Glasscock," he muttered.

"Oh," Alexis said, barely audible over the snickers from the other pirates. "That is ... unfortunate." She shrugged. "In any case, Mister Glasscock, you will turn over your sidearm to Lieutenant Mountjoy."

Glasscock looked to his fellows, but found no support, only calculating looks as though they were each wondering if they could put hands on him first and claim some bounty.

"But ... I told yer my name!"

"You did, and you'll get your pardon under it," Alexis said, "but neither you, nor Mister Blackbourne, nor any of you others —" Alexis scanned the group around Glasscock. "— are in charge of Erzurum or even this town any longer. Your sidearm to Lieutenant Mountjoy, if you please, sir. Lively now!"

Glasscock grumbled, and looked worried, but with no support from his fellows he pulled his weapon, an older propellant pistol, but well-cared for, from his belt and held it out to Mountjoy. For the lieutenant's part, he half reached for it, then raised a hand to his neck and glanced around the landing field.

"We'll have that out soon, Lieutenant Mountjoy," Alexis said. "In the meantime, should a single one of those vile devices be set off, there's not a pirate on Erzurum who'll live to see tomorrow. My lads in *Mongoose* and the other ships will see to that."

Her words were more to cow the pirates listening and possibly encourage Mountjoy after his time of having to be so careful of his actions than any real threat. The only way *Mongoose* or the other ships would truly be able to harm the pirates would be to fire from orbit, which, even with the pirates' own violations of the Abentheren Accords, they would not do. She doubted, more, that her current crew had the skill or fortitude to make the sorts of attacks into a planet's atmosphere that she'd done with *Belial* at Giron — too few and too weakened by their time here on Erzurum to meet the grueling pace of repairs necessary between dives below the mesosphere.

"Small comfort," Mountjoy muttered, but reached out with a wary glance at the group of pirates and took Glasscock's pistol from him.

"Now the rest of you," Alexis said, running her gaze over the other pirates. They'd been grinning, all but a couple who seemed to sense what she'd order next, at Glasscock's plight, but their faces fell now. "Hand over your weapons and device controllers to who Mountjoy points out. You three —" She gestured at three closest to the edge of the pirate group. "Give yours to who Captain Kannstadt indicates.

Will you be so kind as to find the senior amongst the Hanoverese lieutenants, Captain?"

"*Jawohl, Kapitän* Carew," Kannstadt said.

He made a come-along gesture to the three she'd indicated and Alexis nearly sighed with relief as they hung their heads and followed him.

"Next," Alexis said to Glasscock, "you'll take these lieutenants around the field to your men guarding the spacers and have them turn over their own weapons and controllers. There's not to be an armed pirate in this town when we're done here, Mister Glasscock, and I'll hold you and your fellows here responsible if I find differently."

"But —" Glasscock broke off and looked at the others. He seemed to see enough support for a question, at least, for he continued. "There's the negotiating t'be done still."

"What negotiating?" Alexis asked. "A pardon was offered, and you've all accepted. A bounty was offered, and it will be paid."

"Well, paid how's in question, ain't it?" Glasscock asked. "There's lads wish coin and none o' that —"

"You'll receive notes on Admiralty, Mister Glasscock," Alexis said, "as my own spacers do for their prize money."

Glasscock shook his head. "That won't do a'tall. Have t'go find Admiralty offices or give over half t'some agent? We want coin."

"Do you think, sir, that Admiralty sent me out here with a ship or three full of gold coin?" Alexis asked, leaving off that Admiralty hadn't sent her at all. "Do you suppose Queen Annalise herself helped load them, then shared a wet with the rest of the crew? Perhaps the First Space Lord dug into his own purse to top it off?" Alexis snorted. "You've a fine offer before you, Mister Glasscock. A Queen's pardon and wealth from the bounty on those who wouldn't take it and these rescued spacers, you'll take a note in hand for that or nothing."

Glasscock squared his shoulders and some few of his fellows did as well. "It's still you who's outnumbered here, girl, no matter the ships y'have in orbit or out in the Dark. We refuse t'help an' you'll be delayed 'til Ness returns." He squinted at her. "I'm thinkin' y'don't have enough to take him, quite, an' want to get away clean." He shrugged. "May be no chests o'gold, but we'll take what coin y'have, an' one o' them merchants y'took — that'll get us away an' —"

"Mister Glasscock, in order to bargain, you must have something to do so with, and your threat of this Ness is, I'm afraid, more on my side of the scales than your own." Alexis gave him a thin-lipped smile. "You accepted a pardon, sir, which my clerk has drawn up — as have all of you. And cheerfully sent him lists of those of your fellows you'd captured and those of my spacers you'd freed in order to receive the bounty. Should my *Mongoose* still be here when your Ness arrives, Mister Glasscock, do you not suppose I should transmit those documents to him?"

Alexis waited for those bright enough to understand their position to pale. Glasscock did not appear to be in their number, making her wonder how he'd got to be second after Blackbourne.

"Should you delay me now, Mister Glasscock," Alexis said for the slower of them, "there shall be no possible winner of the fight for Erzurum you won't have crossed. It's notes in hand from the Queen's Admiralty, or throw yourself on the mercies of your pirate king."

FORTY-FOUR

The Whistler was a tawdry place,
With pirates run amok.
They'd split their blood-stained takings,
Then trade them for a ... Oooohhh...

ALEXIS WAITED UNTIL THE PIRATE LEADERS WERE GROUPED with Mountjoy, the Hanoverese lieutenants Kannstadt had found who spoke some English, and the senior French lieutenants who had the same, then sent them all off onto the landing field to relieve those pirates guarding their respective groups. She thought the spacers, no matter the earlier cheering, would feel a bit more secure with their own armed officers about instead of pirates.

Mountjoy sent Poncy, who must have been next after him in seniority of the New London lieutenants, and some few others off onto the field, while he and Glasscock stayed behind. Mountjoy motioned for Glasscock to stay where he was for a moment, then came to Alexis a few steps away.

"That could have gone worse, sir," Mountjoy said to her quietly.

Alexis let her shoulders relax a bit as she saw the first of the pirate guards turn his rifle over to Poncy with only the slightest hesitation.

"Yes, it did go rather well," she agreed.

"No, sir," Mountjoy said, "I meant that it could easily have gone worse, much worse. I think I've worked out what you're about, though not how you've managed to start it, but —" He shook his head. "— you've a narrow passage to navigate here, haven't you?"

Alexis took a deep breath. "The wind shifts half a point and it'll be all snapped masts, tattered sails, and crushed hulls."

She watched as another pirate sentry handed his rifle off to a Hanoverese lieutenant with only a few words exchanged with the pirate leader accompanying them. With each, as the remaining pirates saw their fellows handing over arms, the rest would come easier, and she relaxed more — enough to hazard a small grin to Mountjoy.

"But it is quite satisfying when one's out the other side," she said.

"Safer to get such satisfaction at the card table, I'd think," Mountjoy said, "than hazard it all on this. I'm surprised Admiralty sent only a lieutenant, commanding or not, to attempt this."

Alexis cleared her throat and looked away. It wasn't time, quite, to admit that Admiralty hadn't sent her — that would bring up the question of her own return to service and status. Better to save that for her discussion with the waiting captains, and only the most senior ones, at that.

Let them work out the complicated bits. I expect they'll wait until we're safe in New London space to hang me, in any case.

"I've noticed my luck runs a bit more to this sort of thing than cards," Alexis admitted. That brought to mind Wheeley and his casino on Enclave, as well as the man's involvement in the pirates' dealings and slavery. "I do imagine, though, that my next visit to a casino shall be ... eminently satisfying."

She turned her attention back to the *Randy Whistler* where some few of the captains were back at the windows, with a group of three at the doorway. They were some hundred meters away from the pub and she supposed it was time to meet those worthies ... the handover on the field from pirates to naval forces seemed to be going well.

Alexis nodded to Kannstadt and Blackbourne, indicating they should return to the pub.

"What do you know of those waiting captains?" Alexis asked.

It was a bit of a risk, not knowing Mountjoy well, or at all, really, but she thought he seemed a solid sort.

"The three seniors, there in the doorway, are a bit hidebound," Mountjoy said, confirming Alexis' opinion of him, "as you'd expect them to be, but they're anxious to understand what's going on — won't be too fond of you grabbing all their lieutenants out the door in such a rush."

"I expected as much," Alexis said.

"I know most about our own Service, you understand, with only the day or two we've been gathered here to see the Hanoverese and French officers — I didn't liase much with the French while we all still had ships around us." Mountjoy lowered his voice a bit, as they were approaching. "So that's Mattingly, Gotthart, and Neault there on the porch, seniors of the three fleets — and hasn't it been interesting to watch them sort each other out in the face of these pirates, instead of firing into each other's ships? Makes one wonder if we shouldn't turn all the politicians over together to be made slaves to rogues and scoundrels before they're allowed to start a bloody war in the first place. A bit of time in Erzurum's fields with a Hannie at your side does wonders to clear the animosity, I must say." He through a glance at Kannstadt. "Meaning no offense with the term, Captain Kannstadt."

Kannstadt merely smiled. "Of course, Herr 'Bloody'."

Mountjoy chuckled. "See what I mean, sir?"

Alexis nodded. "So those three are senior, but a bit hidebound?"

Mountjoy nodded. "Senior for the moment — until another boat lands with someone higher on the lists. That causes no end of shuffling and sorting. And I don't mean to say they're at all hesitant to be getting off Erzurum, sir, only that ... well, your own rank. Mattingly, especially, would like nothing more than to have a ship around him again. Offer him that and he'd forgive the devil himself a liberty or two."

"I expect as much and have a few ships to offer, at least. All right, anyone else of note?"

"The younger captains took to the back room at once, much as we lieutenants took to the upper floor — the better to stay out of our betters' sight. Stuffed the snotties all in some back rooms upstairs and told them to keep quiet on pain of garnering a post-captain's wrath. So I've met few of those. There's a frigate captain, Esworthy, who's hot to take on the pirates, and a Hannie ... Hanoverese, named Wendt, who seems a good sort."

"I know *Kapitän* Wendt," Kannstadt said. "He is a good man."

Mountjoy nodded.

"Of the French, it's hard to say, they keep to themselves, the Hannies viewing them as traitors, you see, and being treated a bit second-class by us." Mountjoy shrugged. "They're good fellows, to my mind, but I'm no captain. If you're looking for allies to speak to for convincing the French, though, then Theibaud is well-respected amongst them, it seems, and —"

"Theibaud?" Alexis asked, barely daring to hope. She hadn't seen him in her brief time in the pub to collect the lieutenants, and it was a common name. "*Delaine* Theibaud?"

"I think so, yes, he —"

Alexis left Mountjoy and his words behind her.

She didn't run, quite — at least for the first few steps — only hurried her pace. Then a bit more, and a slightly longer stride.

Then ... well, running was certainly excusable, them being in quite a hurry to finish things up before this Ness and the rest of the pirate forces returned, so the senior captains in the doorway would certainly forgive her rush, wouldn't they?

"What —"

"*Ooof!*"

An elbow was, perhaps, not quite so forgivable, but it was delivered to the Hanoverese captain who didn't have the courtesy to get out of her way as she arrived at the doorway, and they'd so recently been in a proper shooting war with one another, that one *could* consider it only a slight and forgivable incident ... she hoped.

"*Delaine!*" Alexis called as she entered the *Randy Whistler* again.

It took a moment for her eyes to adjust, but she distinctly heard a surprised, "*Alexis?*" with the distinct French enunciation she'd thought she might never hear again. It came from over where the bar stood and she rushed in that direction.

A few steps were all it took to spot him, behind the bar, pouring wine into a glass, and staring at her with wide, astonished eyes, and something deep inside her broke apart. The hard shell she'd built up around the certain knowledge that Delaine must be dead and she would never — despite sailing for the Barbary, despite Deckard's word that he was here on Erzurum, despite any hope — see him again.

"*Delaine!*"

"*Alexis — ooof!*"

Leaping atop a stool, launching oneself over a pirate pub's bar, and wrapping arms and legs about him was not, strictly speaking, how the Royal Navy advised its officers greet those of a foreign service, but Alexis didn't care.

The kiss — well, kisses, as one couldn't rightly call it just the one — was likely right out as well.

All her fears for him through so much time since Chipley's fleet had sailed off after the Hanoverese at Giron fell from her, and she'd realized she'd not truly understood their weight.

Tears of relief and happiness stained her cheeks and touched both their mouths where they joined in the kiss she refused to break just yet.

He was here, and he was real, with a solid body pressed to hers and strong arms around her. So unlike the phantom sensations from her dreams these far too many months and she could barely trust he wouldn't dissolve to nothing as she woke, as he had so many times before.

It was not so much the throat-clearing as the applause and cat-calls that got her attention and led her to pull back from that kiss, reluctantly, and look around the pub.

Quite nearly everyone was staring at her, save those few, mostly of New London and Hanover, who were pointedly looking away with discomfort at her display.

Mattingly, the senior New London captain, had approached the bar and was scowling at her with displeasure, while Neault, the senior French captain, was openly grinning. At least he was not applauding and, she noted, what could only be described as hooting, as so many of the French were. The Hanoverese merely looked amused, so there was that.

Mattingly cleared his throat. "And you are?" His frown, though she would have sworn it not possible, deepened. "Lieutenant?"

"Ah ... Lieutenant Alexis Carew, sir, commanding *Mongoose*." She took a breath, well-needed after Delaine's kiss, which, she thought, he'd thrown himself into admirably despite the audience. "Senior officer in-system, sir, at least until we've put a ship around you again."

She hoped the reminder of that prospect might distract Mattingly from her lack of decorum.

"Indeed." Mattingly made an expansive gesture to the tables put together on the pub's main floor. "Well, lieutenant, please, do, brief us on the situation." He raised an eyebrow. "If you can find your way clear to climbing down off Captain Theibaud, that is."

Alexis realized that her face was on a level with Delaine's, instead of mid-chest where her height ought to have placed it, because her legs were wrapped around his hips and locked tightly behind him.

She flushed even while thinking, *Must I?*

FORTY-FIVE

There captains waited for her word,
But to them, she didn't go.
Instead Alexis offered comfort first
To a spacer-man laid low.

"How many?" Alexis asked in shock.

Captain Mattingly exchanged a glance with his counterparts, Gotthart and Neault, the Hanoverese and French seniors. "Did I misspeak?"

Both the other captains shook their heads.

"As near as we can tell," Mattingly repeated, "we three having discussed the action around this mudball, nearly three hundred ships were lost in Erzurum space by our fleets before the rest sailed on. Some were destroyed outright, but the bloody pirates pulled us out of our boats in job lots and set us down here."

"We will need more ships," Kannstadt said, echoing Alexis' words from the landing field.

She could only nod. When she'd said it, she'd thought they'd need dozens of ships to evacuate Erzurum — but the number of wrecks Mattingly claimed —

If even half their crews survived to be taken prisoner —

Her mind worked at it — mostly frigates, supported by pinnaces and sloops, perhaps a few third-rates thrown into the fray as heavy support.

"Sweet Dark," she breathed.

Thousands, tens of thousands, ten times more than the thousands on the field right now.

She caught Isom's eye where her clerk had bent over his tablet, busily tapping away at some new estimates. He looked from her to his tablet then back again.

"Some numbers best not thought on, sir," he said.

"What?" Mattingly asked.

Alexis hesitated. She'd told the senior captain about the pardons, and he'd taken that well enough, though distancing himself from it as all the rest seemed to.

"There was a bounty, sir," Alexis said, "in addition to the pardon. On both the pirates who'd not surrender and on, well, yourselves." She gestured around the room full of captains and lieutenants. "And the men. Scattered as you were to all the farms on Erzurum, it seemed the most expeditious way to convince the pirates to retrieve you and keep you safe."

Mattingly raised his eyebrows and the Hanoverese pursed his lips.

"Bounty?" the French captain, Neault, asked. His own brows went up. "For every of the spacers?"

"How much?" Mattingly asked.

"A hundred pounds for a captain, sir," Alexis said. "Twenty for a common man."

The listening officers muttered amongst themselves while the three seniors eased their chairs from the table as though Alexis carried some contagion they'd as like not get too close to.

"And the recompense, sir," Isom said.

All eyes returned to Alexis.

"Recompense?" Mattingly asked.

"Well, sir," Alexis said, wishing Isom hadn't felt the need to bandy that bit about. "The farmers were loath to lose their ..." She glanced around at the watching faces. "... workers? It seemed ... easiest to compensate them ..."

"Compensate?" Mattingly asked.

"You *bought us?*" one of the watching captains demanded.

"I — well, for the Queen, yes, I suppose —"

"How much?" Mattingly asked again.

"Ah, ten pounds each, sir, seemed to be what the farmers thought fair ..."

The mutters and dark looks grew until Mattingly's hearty laughter cut across it.

"Oh, leave off, you lot!" he yelled. "Queen Annalise got us all for a shilling each at the start, just be glad your bloody stock's risen so high!"

"SO THAT'S the gist of it, sirs," Alexis finished. "The pirates are nearly all unarmed, only those still out and about collecting more of our spacers have weapons, and Lieutenant Mountjoy is seeing to taking those as they arrive. I've no idea how long it will take to retrieve all our men from the outlying farms — I had no idea there'd be so many, you see."

She sighed.

"We hold the planet, well and truly, with so many men, of course, and the orbit, but Ness' return with his own ships, and a frigate, make that a fragile thing."

"And all because your boat crashed," Mattingly mused. "If you'd set down as intended, you'd have had no proof at all we were here and likely had to leave with your fellow privateers. With no proof, there'd be no rescue." He shook his head in wonderment. "The thinnest of threads to get us here."

"And slimmer to get us all out," Alexis said.

"Providence," another captain put in.

Alexis looked around to ensure none of her own lads were about the *Randy Whistler* and heaved a sigh of relief that they were all outside seeing to other tasks. The last thing she needed was word of that thin thread leaking back to Creasy and him convincing a dozen or so New London captains to worship the Vile Creature in thanks for their rescue.

"I'll settle for Providence, indeed," Mattingly said. He rubbed at his face where pink skin shown, as it did on so many of the captains, now that they'd been freed and had a chance to shave. "You say this Ness's off on a cruise for more prizes? Even after having been discovered here?"

Alexis nodded. "We've little hope of assistance from anyone, you see, with no evidence that you're here."

"Our Captain Ness's a confidant sort," Blackbourne said with a wide grin. None of the naval captains were particularly welcoming of his presence, but he did offer the pirates' perspective on their situation. "Erzurum's been a pirate holding fer a long time, an' Ness' fief fer near as long. He knows yer fellows'll not come an' he's set a proper spanking on the only force o'private ships to assemble in all his time here."

THERE WAS a bit more talk and the senior captains detailed some others to go out on the landing field to join Mountjoy and the lieutenants in their work. More questions than Alexis felt comfortable answering, but she did so — even those about Ellender and how she'd come to be back in uniform though she'd arrived as captain of a private ship.

As the hour grew late, many captains sought rest, while others sought out the surgeons to have the marks of slavery removed from their ears and necks.

The crowd in the *Randy Whistler* gradually thinned and Alexis caught sight of a lone figure hunched over a table to the side. One not a captain or other officer in the naval fleets and one she'd not expected to see again at all.

When Mattingly seemed to have had all his questions answered, Alexis took her leave.

"Well, look on the bright side, Carew," Mattingly said as she stood from his table.

"What's that, sir?"

"New London's founders may have brought back the farthing, but drawing and quartering was right out, so you've no need to fear that from Admiralty, at least."

FORTY-SIX

"Take heart and tell your fellows,"
She said unto the man,
"For your Queen has not forgotten you
And together we've made a plan."

"Commodore Skanes," Alexis said, stopping beside the table.

Up close, the woman looked more ragged than Alexis had first thought. Her uniform was oddly intact, not at all ravaged by the conditions on Erzurum, but she herself was worn and haggard. Red-rimmed eyes, the lines on her face seeming to have deepened in the short time since Alexis had last seen her, and her shoulders slumped over the table, her face hanging above the glass she drank from.

Skanes was — had been — commander of the Marchant Company ship the *Hind*, a massive hull ostensibly the stores ship and command center for the fleet of private ships Alexis and *Mongoose* had joined in the Barbary. That the captains of private ships were, to be kind, less than amiable to the strictures of command, and less than partial to the prices of Marchant Company stores, had left Skanes and her ship with little to do but sit and wait for the occasional visit from those captains.

The merchant captain had styled herself an erstwhile commodore over her "fleet" and taken the title on, which Alexis used as a courtesy, despite the woman having no right to it — also because Alexis felt somewhat responsible for the loss of *Hind* to the pirates.

It was Alexis who'd convinced Skanes to take *Hind* along with *Mongoose* on Alexis' first assault of Erzurum, and the woman had to surrender the much larger ship when it became mired in the system's dark matter shoals and been surrounded by the pirate gunboats while *Mongoose's* rudder was damaged. She still thought Skanes could have held out, with the larger ship and far more guns than the pirates, but the "commodore" had surrendered without firing a shot.

Skanes looked up and narrowed her eyes at Alexis, who prepared herself for the merchant captain's rebuke for abandoning her. They'd not had proper signals for Alexis to spell out that *Mongoose* had been damaged and she must withdraw for a day or two of repairs, if only *Hind* could stave the pirates off until then.

"Carew," Skanes said, then looked back to her glass as if seeking something in its depths. "I'm sorry."

The words left Alexis dumbfounded — it was not at all what she'd expected of Skanes.

"Commodore?" Alexis said softly.

Skanes snorted. "Captain, if you please, no need to mock me. I suppose you're here to have your say — go on then?"

"My say?" Alexis asked.

Skanes looked up and peered at her closely. "You're in a Naval uniform — haven't you returned with some rescue force? Captured that Ness fellow?" She frowned. "You're not here to arrest me? I'd thought when I saw you enter that you must have asked for the pleasure of that job yourself."

"Arrest you? Comm — Captain Skanes, I honestly don't know what you're talking about."

This woman was nothing like the haughty commodore Alexis had last spoken to.

Skanes laughed but there was no humor in it. "So you don't know?" She gestured at the chair across from her. "Sit, then, if you will. It's fitting you're the one I surrender to, I suppose."

Alexis sat but remained silent. She felt Skanes was far enough in her cups to keep talking, but she didn't want to risk stopping her. This talk of arrest and whatever Skanes had supposedly done seemed important, but Alexis hadn't an inkling what it might be.

"Do you want the particulars?" Skanes asked. "Or only the charges you should level?"

"Tell it as you will, captain," Alexis said. "I'm listening."

Skanes looked around to see if anyone else was near, but the naval officers were all in their own groups — mostly by nation, but with a few odd friendships visible between former enemies after their shared ordeal on Erzurum.

"I'll start it as I found out, then," Skanes said, "after you sailed off and left us."

Alexis thought to argue that, to explain about the damage to *Mongoose* and not wanting to explain via signals the pirates could intercept and read, but stayed silent.

"Probably best," Skanes said. "So many of those damnable gunboats about." She drained half her glass and squared her shoulders.

"So," she said, "I surrendered *Hind* to them. Arranged the crew. The pirates boarded and were quite rough — knocking us about and searching for hidden weapons, I suppose — then one who must have been a sort of leader found me. I did what I thought I should ... told him who I was and that the Marchants would pay a reasonable ransom for the ship and crew. Didn't mention he'd be marked by every Marchant ship from then on — probably wouldn't do any good, him holed up on Erzurum as he was, but I thought to start with the promise of reward for my crew's safety, and not the certain retribution."

Skanes looked up at her, so Alexis nodded for her to continue.

"Next I knew, it had all changed. This fellow started bellowing for the others to leave off — stop the searching, stop the knocking about, all of it. Even recalled those searching the ship as though he had not a single care if there were some spacer holed up in a compartment with a pistol waiting to ambush the boarders."

She looked back to her glass.

"They didn't let us go, exactly, not that far, but they treated us quite well, thereafter. Put *Hind* in orbit and shipped us all down to the surface, then put us up in rooms in this town. It was all quite … unexpected."

Alexis thought so as well. She'd expected *Hind's* crew to be sold off as the pirates' other captives were. Could the pirates have feared the retribution of the Marchant Company more than that of the combined Hanoverese, French Republic, and New London navies?

She supposed they might, given those navies' reputation in the Barbary for doing next to nothing — and the next being on the far side of nothing, at that.

"It was bewildering," Skanes said. "Especially as I learned the fate of other crews and those captured naval forces. We were treated well — fed and housed well — and other than keeping us away from any boats that landed, the pirates avoided us. It was quite as though they hadn't the foggiest idea what to do with the lot of us. We weren't entirely free, but we weren't entirely prisoners, either — not guests and not captives. Then their leader, Ness, returned."

Skanes took a deep breath.

"He had me brought to him aboard his ship, that big frigate he repaired for his pirating. The working one, there was another, little more than a hulk, in orbit. He bade me sit, had one of his crew — a dirty pirate with one eye and who hadn't bathed since he'd come aboard, I think — served me wine as though I was just one captain visiting another and this filthy animal was a proper steward. Then he asked me and I knew — it all made sense."

Skanes was silent for what seemed like a long time, but Alexis waited patiently.

"He asked me why I'd come here — and if I had some message that couldn't go through normal channels."

Skanes drained her glass.

"And then he said, 'I've done everything the bloody Marchants have asked — if they want more it'll cost them.'"

FORTY-SEVEN

"She's pardoned all these pirates,
Save those bastards there who'll hang.
And bought with gold your freedom
From this misery and pain."

"I worked it out," Skanes said, filling her glass again. "Without telling him I didn't know what the bloody hell he was talking about. I was afraid if he found out I didn't know, then he might do something awful to me or what was left of my crew. So, I pieced together the gist of it from what he said and made him think some other things of me and *Hind.*"

Alexis merely listened. It seemed like Skanes had been waiting some time to tell this story to someone.

"There's some deal — has been for years, maybe decades — between this band of pirates and Marchant Company. The pirates leave our ships alone and the Marchants pay them a small sum, as well as other tasks. There have been Marchant ships that stopped here, I'm told, and carried goods on to *Hso-hsi.* Even our routes, which went through some bits of space with high pirate activity, though they cut our transport time, were arranged with this Ness fellow. Many of our captains thought it was because our ships were better armed and could handle the pirates — maybe even deal them a blow or scare them off." Skanes laughed, but it was a bitter sound. "Help the other merchants, you see? Ha! It was all because there were already agreements no Marchant ship would be attacked." She drank again. "Then there's me, the *Hind*, and what I must apologize to you for."

Skanes took a deep breath.

"It always bothered me, deeply, that you and the other private ships didn't report more often, didn't stay in your proper areas of operation, started working together. That was part of the payoff, you see, though I never knew it. That was part of the deal, you see? 'There are too many privateers,' he tells the Marchants, and, 'Don't worry,' they say, 'we'll take care of it.'"

Skanes hung her head and Alexis thought her red-rimmed eyes had grown wetter before she scrubbed at them angrily.

"Send a stores ship and gather reports — *my* ship. All those reports of yours and the other captains? Sent by courier to the Company?" She waved a hand. "Dropped off straight to the pirates on some Barbary world. The forces spread out with assigned hunting grounds so as to cover more space? Only a further guarantee that there'd be no privateer force with enough strength anywhere to take on Ness' frigate alone, much less with his other ships. A prize here and there? A merchantman carrying pirated goods? Not too great a loss — but nothing that could possibly hinder his main efforts. You know the way the private ship captains think — profit and ease, neither of which comes from a real fight. And any ships taken? A pittance in prize money paid, the hulls, cargoes, and crews delivered up the line and just like the courier's reports — turned loose and back to their business again. I suppose there'd be some Company report that the ships would be sold and the pirates hung, but those are just words." She stared into her cup. "Only words and numbers in someone's report. Once a thing's all words and numbers, does the reality ever matter?"

Alexis finally broke her silence. "And they had Wheeley, on Enclave, to take possession of those prizes and pirates we didn't bring to you."

"You know about him?"

Alexis nodded, fingering her ear. "I knew he had dealings of some kind — and know more now. The slaves he keeps there to work his casino."

"Cheaper than the local labor and afraid to do a thing with explosives in their necks. I realized that, as well, seeing some of the slaves the pirates keep here. Kept, I suppose, with all this going on." She looked around the pub. "Your work?"

Alexis nodded. "With a great deal of help."

"I'm sorry I couldn't be one to help you," Skanes said.

"But the Marchants? Really? You're certain?"

Alexis had had dealings with the Marchant Company before and found their captains, Skanes included, to be a haughty, arrogant sort. But she'd never have thought they'd have dealings with pirates — especially not to the degree Skanes was describing.

"No doubt. That pirate, Ness, didn't know what to make of me. He's waiting word back from the Company on what to do with me and my crew." Skanes looked close to tears. "I gave my life to the Company, thinking they were —" She broke off and scrubbed at her face again.

FORTY-EIGHT

"Annalise has sent me here for you,
And from here you'll be taken.
No crime or purse of coin is worth
A single subject left forsaken."

THE BARBARY COMBINED FLEET, ALEXIS THOUGHT, MUST BE
the oddest ever put together.

The senior captains of those held on Erzurum had been oddly
cooperative with Alexis and each other; and not at all in opposition,
though she wondered still what fate awaited her with Admiralty on
their return to New London space.

She was still in command of *Mongoose*, the largest, best-armed,
and fastest of their ships, making her, to a certain extent, the flagship
for Mattingly, who was acting as ostensible commodore of their
ragtag band.

"Well, Carew," he'd said with a smile when the other captains
agreed to it, "as senior in-system it only falls to you to confirm me."
He laughed. "Never thought I'd receive my first flag from a lieutenant, though, to tell the truth."

Mattingly might think it funny, but she could tell the other captains did not, to a large extent, share his amusement.

Some scowled at her whenever she passed, clearly thinking she'd taken too much on herself, while others, and perhaps worse, shook their heads with expressions of pity, clearly thinking of what would likely happen to her when Admiralty learned the full extent of what she'd done here.

At last count, it was seven-hundred forty-eight pardoned pirates, a number that astounded her still, and bounties to be paid on some eight-hundred ninety-nine who'd not accepted the pardon — and not been captured by Alexis and Kannstadt in taking the initial ships — in the bewildering sum of seventeen thousand nine-hundred eighty pounds. At least all those had been on the surface and not aboard ships, thus Isom had valued them at only the base twenty pounds per head. Or head, hand, and eye in some cases, but she'd not quibble over it.

And all that before the bounties paid on rescued spacers who were still being brought in to Erzurum's port town, despite there being nearly thirty thousand there already.

Never mind the notes in hand to Erzurum's farmers for those, which Kannstadt's agreed Hanover will see to collecting for them.

She did wish Isom had not looked it up to confirm that, for the few days pending her return to Erzurum's surface and officially "freeing" the captured spacers, Alexis, and through her, Queen Annalise of New London, now held the dubious distinction of personally owning the most slaves of anyone in recent history, if only for the time it took to get them off Erzurum.

"Not to worry, Carew," Mattingly said with a grin as the last of Alexis' gear came out of her cabin on *Mongoose*, that space now being Mattingly's for the time being and Alexis moving to the first officer's compartment. "It's not the worst thing Admiralty's forgiven a captain on foreign station for doing — assuming they see your recall by Ellender as valid, of course."

"Of course, sir." Alexis paused, then took the moment to ask something she'd been avoiding. "Will you, ah, be confirming my actions, sir? Now that you're free and senior in-system yourself?"

Mattingly's smile fell.

"Oh, look," he said, "there's the last of it." Without another look at Alexis, he strode into *Mongoose's* master's cabin where his gear, acquired on Erzurum after his release, was being stowed. "I'll see you on the quarterdeck once I've had a proper shower and a bit of a rest, Carew — ages since I've been near either, don't you know. Your man will see to what can be done about a proper uniform for me, yes?"

Alexis sighed and kicked Isom in the ankle as he muttered, barely under his breath, something which sounded suspiciously like, "Overbearing, arrogant, bastard."

"Of course, sir, yes," she said loudly over Isom. "It might be rough but we'll do our best."

Mattingly nodded, still not looking at her, and slid the hatch to her ... his cabin shut.

"Not another word on it," she said to Isom.

Her clerk snorted and went off, muttering something about sewing.

Alexis took herself to her new cabin. Most of her things, what remained after the pirates were done with them, at least, were struck down into the hold, there being so little space in the ship's officers' cabins.

If it wouldn't scandalize the crew and certainly put her in deeper trouble with Admiralty — as though that might be possible — she'd have the bulkhead between first and second officers' cabins removed and share the thing with her new first officer, who'd been displaced before he'd even moved into his cabin by Mattingly's taking hers.

Yet another oddity of this Barbary Combined Fleet — a rather ostentatious name for these few ships, she thought — being that Alexis was now likely the only lieutenant in Royal Navy history to both command a commodore's flagship and have a full captain as her first officer.

For she'd insisted on bringing Delaine aboard and he'd been elevated to captain during his time with Chipley's fleet.

Since he was aboard anyway and there being no one amongst the other officers she knew and trusted — and in the interest of the "combined" part of the Barbary Combined Fleet, she threw in for hope it might make a bit of sense — it only made sense for him to act as her first officer.

It was a transparent ploy, of course, and anyone who'd seen or heard of her display on first finding Delaine in the *Randy Whistler* — that being, she assumed, every officer and spacer, pirate or fleet, in the whole of Erzurum, tales being what they were for spacers — could see right through it.

Mattingly had simply pursed his lips for a moment, then shrugged. "It's not the worst thing Admiralty's seen, I'm sure," he'd said.

Captain, ostensible Commodore, Mattingly, Alexis found, was not the sort to say the most comforting things, and tended to overuse a phrase.

She left her quarters and made her way to the quarterdeck, feeling restless and ill at-ease. Delaine was there, having the watch, and she had to resist the urge to grab him up in her arms again, or at least to poke him to ensure he was real and not some phantom of her imagination. She settled for standing too close to him at the navigation plot, using the crowded conditions of the quarterdeck as her excuse.

All stations were manned for the first time since the ship had flashed past Erzurum in their attack as a private ship and they had been forced to abandon her. More than manned, for they had a full complement aboard and more. Each station was double-manned, as those familiar with *Mongoose's* systems passed on their knowledge to the new men, or, where she'd not had a man with her in the boat, two or three of the newcomers familiarized themselves with what of *Mongoose's* quirks they could find.

"An' here," Creasy was saying, "the port relay — you'll find you might wish to have those on the hull repeat a thing back to you. There's a kink in the fiber that ain't never been right."

The man beside him, Alexis didn't have his name yet, as so very many had crowded aboard *Mongoose* and the other ships that she'd not had time to see them all, much less put names to faces. *Mongoose*, and all the ships they held in their little fleet, were over-manned by double or treble, and still they'd not taken a quarter of the captured spacers up from Erzurum's surface, with still more being lifted in from farms and villages every day.

The dream of lifting all and sundry and sailing off was simply impossible. Would still have been even if they'd had Ellender's *Claw* still here, but the sheer number of men did give them another option.

"An' what's that?" the new spacer with Creasy asked.

"Oh, that's Boots," Creasy said.

Alexis glanced over, but saw no sign of the Creature. She'd ordered Isom to keep the thing crated and in her cabin, there being so many new hands aboard and so much work being done to put the ship to rights.

Creasy picked something up off his console and held it out to the new man, while Alexis tried to see what in the Dark he might be talking about without seeming to watch.

"Started carvin' that in the swamps, when Boots saved the captain from one o' them giant snakes," Creasy said, and Alexis caught a glimpse of a piece of wood, perhaps five centimeters tall, with tiny legs and a bushy tail opposite a pointed snout. "Sort of a ... representationing sort of thing, as he can't be everywhere at once, you see? He'll watch over me now, same as he does the captain, sure."

Alexis sighed, wondering at how events could be so distorted. *She'd* shot the bloody snakipede right through the eye — a fine shot, if she did say so herself — and likely saved the maddening Creature from its own impetuousness in attacking a thing it couldn't even fully get its bloody jaws around.

"Watches over?" the new spacer asked.

"Oh, aye," Creasy said. "Boots is like a ..."

The signalsman shot a glance her way and Alexis made a show of studying the navigation plot, so as not to have been caught listening. She did wonder, though, if she oughtn't to contact Admiralty when they returned to New London space and see if they might have one of those psychologists they'd been so keen to have her talk to see about Creasy. The man was —

"I'll explain later," Creasy said in a lower tone. "There's a group of us what meet to —"

"Transition!" Tite announced from the tactical console. "Transition L1!"

Alexis turned her full attention back to the tactical console, the images were in at the same time as the transition alert, along with the newcomer's automatic transmission of her identity — one of the surviving gunboats, repaired enough to still make her way in the Dark and set to keeping watch with a crew of released Hanoverese spacers instead of pirates.

They had the pirates' codebooks and recognition signals, decrypted thanks to Blackbourne and the other pardoned pirates, who wanted nothing more than for Alexis to make good on her promise to get them away from Erzurum with their pardons, purses, and persons intact — something they'd accepted wouldn't happen if Ness returned and triumphed over their little fleet.

The gunboat captain's transmission followed quickly along after the automated identification, but it was in excited, hurried German that the ship's translation system, much less Alexis' limits, despaired of making sense of, but one word was clear.

"*Raumschiff.*"

Ships.

FORTY-NINE

"Not Ness, then?" Mattingly asked.

"No, sir," Alexis said.

They were in conference aboard *Mongoose*, in Alexis' — Mattingly's — cabin. She, Delaine, and Mattingly in person, with Kannstadt aboard *Fang* with his officers and the captains of the other captured ships attending via their comms.

"Prizes, as Old Blackbourne told you," the pirate himself put in as he wandered about the cabin, examining what contents were left as though sizing up what he could pocket.

Mattingly scowled at the man as though he'd forgotten he was there, much as Alexis wished she might. Sadly, he was still their best source of information about the pirates.

Blackbourne opened a cabinet and began rooting around in it before Isom appeared to slap at his hand and close the cabinet with a steady *clack* and a sterner glare.

Blackbourne merely smiled and returned to the table to join the others, one hand sliding into a pocket as though he'd managed to palm something, though what it might be Alexis couldn't imagine — what few of her things remained had been moved to her new cabin and Mattingly had little enough. Perhaps the pirate was merely after tweaking Isom's nose, as her clerk hurried to open the cabinet again and peer inside.

Mattingly snorted. "Business as usual, then? The man's brazen as sin."

Blackbourne went to the sideboard, freshly stocked — as much as possible — from pirate stores on the planet's surface and took a glass. Isom hurried over and plucked it from his fingers, which only made Blackbourne take up an entire bottle. Isom made to take that from him as well, but Blackbourne took a long swig and held the remainder out to Isom with raised brows. Her clerk sighed and Alexis couldn't blame him — despite that being the only bottle of bourbon aboard, she'd not want a bit of it now.

"Not so much brazen, our Ness," Blackbourne said, taking a seat at the table and another long pull at the bottle, "as knowing. Yours is not the first time some private ship or even navy's set upon us here. A bit of a dustup then on to easier picking's the norm, do you see? So our Ness expects the same again." He grinned widely. "The man's not counted on Old Blackbourne thinkin' on his declining years, and how Erzurum's not so fine a place to contemplate the spending of those."

He looked around at those present and at the images of those shown on the table.

"You're welcome," he said into the silence.

Mattingly pointedly turned his gaze from Blackbourne to Alexis.

"Well," he said, "ill-manned prizes we can certainly handle — and the Dark knows we need the ships."

———

THE PRIZES WERE, indeed, something they could handle.

Utilizing the pirate's codes and signals, they directed the incoming ships to transition at L4, where the three captured merchantmen emerged to find not a few weeks' ease planetside to enjoy their gains, but *Mongoose*, along with three of her own captured ships, all waiting with guns run out and filled to bursting with freed spacers eager to get a bit of their own back after their time on Erzurum.

The pirates surrendered nearly as quickly as the next arriving ship, a merchant from the Barbary eager to purchase ill-gotten gains on the cheap, profiting from the ill-fortune of his fellows.

Nary a shot was fired in anger to take them, only a crisscross of chasers to show their intent and a signaled demand to stand down and strike.

The worst resistance came not from the now captured pirates or merchant crews, but from the newly freed captains and crews of the pirates' prizes.

"No, captain, I'm afraid you and your ship must remain," Alexis was forced to say over and over again to one captain or another, Mattingly handing the distasteful task over to her.

"But — but —" the merchant captain's sputtering would be almost comical if Alexis didn't have so much sympathy for him. Having been taken once by pirates and now rescued, she could well imagine how much he must wish to be back in *darkspace* and away, not set down in-atmosphere on the planet of those pirates' very base.

"We'll see you safely back to New London space when we can," Alexis said. "In the meantime, we've need of every ship here at Erzurum."

"But you've *taken* my ship!" the merchant captain fairly yelled over the comms and Alexis felt a bit ashamed at her relief she wasn't having to do this in person.

"The needs of Her Majesty and the Service, Captain Eddings," Alexis said. "When the full pirate force returns, we must have every ship we can to meet them."

"He'll destroy you! All of you! And we'll be marooned here! I'll file complaint with Admiralty, Captain — Carew, was it? I'll see you court martialed — you've no rights to take a New London vessel!"

"Your concerns will be duly noted, I'm sure, captain," Alexis said, noting with relief that Creasy, back on *Mongoose's* signals console now there were more freed spacers than were needed to man the ships, was trying to get her attention. "If you'll excuse me, Captain Eddings, I've another call."

"Signal from the gunboats, sir," Creasy said, no sooner had she disconnected. "Ships crossing the halo."

Alexis sighed and brought up the accompanying images of these incoming ships — more merchant crews for her to give hope to before dashing it.

"My respects to Commodore Mattingly, Creasy," she said at the sight of the first ship — no merchant, this, but a frigate, and one she could recognize even in the grainy image from the gunboat, "and tell him it's time."

Ness was back.

FIFTY

The waiting and not knowing and not *bloody* seeing were the worst, Alexis thought.

A crew still weak with so much time of hunger and deprivation on Erzurum, no matter their success against surprised merchantman and under-crewed prizes, was bad, as well, and, no doubt, the men from a dozen different ships thrown together aboard *Mongoose* to make up the crew, with no more than a few weeks to work themselves up, learn the habits, good and bad, of the man beside them, the proclivities of their captain or the near godlike bent of now-Commodore Mattingly, and pressed all close together as they were — well, that was bad too.

Knowing they were outnumbered — twenty-two ships, and one of them Ness' frigate, in the returning pirate fleet, to their seventeen — most of their numbers merchantmen, not fully converted to carry more guns nor their hulls nearly finished being reinforced — and a double-handful of gunboats. Not nearly what one might name good, that.

The crowding couldn't be comfortable for the men, for *Mongoose* and the others were crammed to the bulkheads with every able-bodied man they could lift from Erzurum. It was their one advantage, such as it was, but only if they could force a boarding. In a shooting fight, those men were only vulnerable targets, meaning nearly every shot which made it through a hull, every splinter of the lasers from any reflective surface, would surely find a home in a man's body.

Delaine was there now, walking the ship and seeing to those in the forward sail locker, waiting to go out onto the hull as soon as *Mongoose* returned to her element of *darkspace*. Those on the gundeck, waiting to fling open their ports and lay their barrels on a target. Those who, for a wonder aboard a fighting ship, had no task but to wait for the call of *Away boarders*.

Those men would likely agree with her. The waiting was the worst.

Alexis tapped her fingers against the smooth top of the navigation plot, the *thump, thump, thump* of each fingertip oddly comforting.

"Patience, lieutenant," Mattingly said.

Alexis looked up from the plot to find Mattingly watching her — a not-quite smile playing across his lips. The reference to her true rank and not the brevet thanks to her command served to remind her that Mattingly had far more experience in action than she. Alexis snatched her hand back from the plot and flushed.

"It's only the waiting, sir, and not being able to see what they're doing — they *should* follow the gunboat, we've the proper signals from Blackbourne and the others, but what if this Ness doesn't believe the channels have shifted so much?"

Mattingly nodded. "Patience."

The commodore was the very image of the word, standing straight, hands clasped behind him, looking nearly resplendent in the uniform Isom had run up for him — even if he had given Isom an odd look and scratched at a couple places when he first wore it. Alexis wondered if her clerk's comments about seams had been — but, no, Isom wouldn't do such a petty thing to the senior officer, no matter how put out he was at Mattingly taking Alexis' cabin. Still, no matter

Mattingly's own worries — or how much his new uniform might itch in certain places — the commodore stood straight and still.

"Aye, sir," Alexis said.

"You'll be a proper flag captain one day, Carew. Serving a proper commodore or admiral, and under circumstances just as nerve-wracking as this. They'll not want you tapping on their navigation plot as though it's an egg in its cup and you've yet to break your fast."

"Aye, sir," she said again, though she was thinking it likely she'd never see a quarterdeck again, much less be made post, and certainly never command a flagship. Not after word of what she'd done here got back to Admiralty ... along with the bill.

And the bloody receipts.

"Set your worries about that aside too," Mattingly said as though reading her thoughts. "The future can take care of itself well enough, and this fight is what's important. If we don't succeed here, you've no worries about what our superiors might think of your actions, right enough?"

"That is true, sir."

"And success here will cover over any number of things. A grand victory, Carew, is the finest plaster in Admiralty's eyes, and they are masters at applying it. There's many a pock-walled career made smooth and whole by a smashing win."

"Aye, sir."

There was little else for her to say, and it seemed to satisfy the commodore, for he took his eyes from her and returned them to his own maddeningly calm perusal of the navigation plot.

Alexis stepped away to review the stations, starting with Tite at the tactical console, so that she might make her way around the quarterdeck and not arrive at Creasy's signals console until last. She wished to put off seeing his little carved figure of the Creature again so long as she might. Things were bad enough without having to acknowledge that her crew was carving bloody pagan totems to the thing with such an unnatural affinity for her footwear.

Tite's console was in good order, and Tite himself in good spirits. She clapped a hand on his shoulder and nodded to him.

"Ready to set these bastards back a pace?" she asked quietly.

"Aye, sir."

"Good man."

As she turned to move on to the next console, she caught sight of Mattingly. She was behind the commodore, who still calmly peered down at the navigation plot, so that she could see his hands, clasped at the small of his back.

One of the commodore's fingers twitched. Then another. Then five rose and fell in an impatient sequence of tapping against his other hand, before he clasped them tightly together in a white-knuckled grip which relaxed only after several moments.

Alexis moved on to the next console, shooting Mattingly's back a glance as she did so. There was more than one thing that could be plastered over with a facade, and more than one reason to.

She clasped her own hands behind her back and squeezed, then relaxed her grip.

Yes, that would work admirably to keep the things out of trouble.

She moved on to speak a word to the next man.

"Transition, sir, gunboat!" Tite called out.

"They're in the channel, sir," Creasy said, receiving the signal the gunboat was transmitting as soon as it transitioned to normal-space.

"Signal all ships to transition, Creasy. Transition now, Layland," Alexis ordered.

THE STARS DISAPPEARED, replaced by the swirling, black and blacker masses of *darkspace*.

Most of the quarterdeck's consoles went dark as well, or the information from their sensors, unavailable here, replaced by whichever images from the ship's optics which might be somewhat useful.

Alexis, and Mattingly for the fleet, knew what to expect from those images.

They'd planned out the bluff and subsequent attack in detail with the men aboard the repaired gunboats.

Ness and his pirate fleet had sailed in, finding what they'd expected to — a system full of gunboats, all signaling properly that all was well, thanks to Blackbourne, the pardoned pirates, and those gunboats' own systems giving up any secret signals that existed. Those not being so very many at all.

The only hitch to Ness' return was a shifted channel through the shoals of dark matter that permeated the Erzurum system in *darkspace*.

This was not found suspicious. Those channels shifted frequently — part of the gunboats' job was to chart, rechart, and rechart again, in their never-ending tracks throughout the system.

Such shifts could be sudden, rather than gradual, as great masses of dark matter broke off from their trailing of some normal-space mass, like one of Erzurum's moons. Perhaps they were affected by the normal-space presence of the planet itself, or some other in the system, or perhaps they simply grew too massy themselves to bother following and simply went their own way, drifting until caught by something else to follow.

Or broken up by a storm, driven aside and scattered, only to be then driven to join some other stretch of dark matter by the dark energy storms which pummeled a system.

Regardless of what cause was given, Ness and his fleet accepted the signal that they should follow a gunboat down this other channel, not the one on their older charts, else they'd become mired in the stuff.

That gunboat's crew had the worst bit of the waiting, to Alexis' mind, being closest to Ness' fleet and surely their first target should they suspect a ruse.

They were game, though, and all volunteers — as were all those aboard the ships and gunboats, whether anxious for a chance to strike back against the pirates or simply feeling an urgent need to leave Erzurum's surface and have a proper hull about them again.

The channel that boat led the pirate fleet down was not, of course, the new way through to Erzurum's transition points and the other gunboats waiting there. It was just clear enough to be believable as that — for a time.

Until it narrowed and twisted to the point that the pirate fleet could barely come about, and the leading gunboat put on full sail and ran before the winds.

Another gunboat at the transition point disappeared to normal-space.

Seconds later, *Mongoose*, *Talon*, *Fang*, and all their makeshift fleet of taken merchantmen appeared in its place.

ALEXIS TOOK IN THE SCENE.

It was nearly as perfect a match to what they'd hoped for as could be.

The pirates weren't entirely trapped, but they were quite unable to maneuver as freely as they might like, and Alexis' ... Mattingly's, she supposed, though she had trouble not thinking of all the ships as hers ... fleet had the advantage in, at least, the freedom to maneuver.

It wasn't a telling advantage. They were still outnumbered in ships and guns, so laying off and pounding Ness' ships would get them only more damage in return. Nor could they wait, for once Ness worked those ships, especially his frigate, around and back through the shoals, Alexis' fleet would be pounded into submission in short order.

No, they had only one true advantage over the pirate fleet, come back with their prizes, and the men Ness'd sailed with come back to be captured piecemeal over time, and leaving the pirate leader with many ships, but few men aboard, while Alexis' little fleet was packed futtocks to mastheads with former slaves eager for a bit of payback against their captors.

"All sail on the fore and main!" Alexis ordered. "Put her on the port tack and down fifteen, Layland. Keep us to the channel, man, for the shoals will rip her hull open if we strike at speed."

"Aye, sir!"

"Four men to the bowsprit with leads, Creasy, and four to run capacitors for them. Open the ports and run out your guns! Port and starboard, both — we've men enough to fight two sides, the chasers, and more!"

"Aye, sir!"

It was merely confirming the order set before they'd transitioned, and Delaine would be in the bow sail locker himself to see to it. They had no shortage of men now, so could spare them for this. The leads, firing short, small bursts of lasers ahead so that she and Layland could see their fall and judge the shoals by how much each shot of coherent light was warped and twisted by the dark matter, would be a mapping of the channel Alexis trusted more than any chart.

"And helmets, all, even those waiting in the hold! We'll be in their range immediately, and I'll not have men die for not wanting to smell their own bloody farts, you tell them!"

"Aye, sir," Creasy said, repeating her order throughout the ship and sealing his own helmet in place.

Alexis sealed hers in place as well, then glanced to Mattingly, her ship taken care of and the other captains certainly doing the same, it was time for his orders to the fleet.

Mattingly gave her an odd smile and simply nodded. The order was already decided and by saying nothing he ceded the honor to her.

Alexis straightened, stepped to the signals console, and laid a hand on Creasy's shoulder. Despite everyone aboard all their ships, from the captains to the ordinary spacers, knowing what the plan was, there was a certain formality to such things, and she felt the pride of Mattingly's giving her the honor of voicing it first.

She keyed her helmet's comm so that not only Creasy would

hear, but all those aboard *Mongoose*. Even those on the gundeck, now with open ports and exposed to vacuum and the effects of *darkspace* — the gallenium netting over the ports would allow their radios to function, at least until those nets and the hull were shot through enough to let the radiations in.

"To all ships, Creasy, and keep it flying 'til the bitter end's in hand," Alexis said, her lips twitching in what was, most assuredly, *not* a smile as the signalsman reached out to lay a fingertip on the tiny wooden carving that sat atop his console.

"The signal is *Imperative — Engage the enemy more closely*."

FIFTY-ONE

O', pull me hearties, heave me mates,
Tale an' labor's almost done.
There was just a bit of cleanup
The last pirates set to run.

MONGOOSE SHUDDERED WITH BEING STRUCK BY FIRE FROM THE pirate frigate even before she'd made it to the shoals.

They were still out of range of some of the frigate's guns — the former *HMS Roebuck*, she saw, identified from her appearance by *Mongoose's* systems — but not the twenty eighteen-pounders of her upper gundeck. There were still the twenty nine-pounders of her lower gundeck to look forward to, and even a quartet of six-pounders on *Roebuck's* quarterdeck.

Alexis studied what information she had on *Roebuck*, for she'd not call the ship by whatever name the pirates had given her, even if she'd known it.

A complement of two hundred eighty, so room for that and more. No one of the pirates, from Blackbourne on down, seemed to know exactly how many men had sailed aboard each of Ness' ships.

Bookkeeping seemed to not be in it for the pirates as a whole, though each ship knew their shares and complement to the last man and farthing.

Nearly a thousand tons burthen, though — so I know she could have sailed with nearly five hundred aboard, if they were packed so tight as Mongoose *is right now.*

They'd not have, for certain — even pirates, or perhaps even more so pirates, wouldn't accept such cramped conditions for a lengthy cruise.

Mongoose shuddered again and Alexis checked the time.

Four minutes between broadsides — either an ill-trained crew or undermanned.

She tried to guess, again, how many might have sailed on each ship Ness'd left with, how many he'd put aboard his captures as prize-crews, and how many might be left aboard *Roebuck*, but it was an idle, wasted effort.

And won't change what we must do, regardless.

"Steady on, Layland," she said instead, then keyed her radio so that the crew could hear. "Steady on, lads — we're nearly to the channel, then a few twists and turns and we'll have our own chance to show them."

Mongoose had no guns to retaliate with yet, her having all nine-pounders, without enough force to reach *Roebuck* through the shoals. Even the frigate's eighteens were so distorted and torn asunder by the shoals that they were lasing off only the barest outer layer of *Mongoose's* hull when they hit.

That they were hitting at all at this distance, though, was worrisome.

Ness' guncrews might not be quick, but they were laying their shot with more accuracy than she'd credit to the motley pirates she'd seen on Erzurum. What that accuracy would mean for *Mongoose* once they were closer and *Roebuck* could bring her lower deck to bear as well, wasn't a pleasant thought.

Ten eighteens and ten nines per side, and I've my mere dozen nines to reply with — and that if we can bring the one in my, Matting-ly's, quarters to bear as well.

She eyed the navigation plot and its chart of the channel they were following.

"Let loose staysail and jib as we make the turn," she ordered.

They'd be coming onto the starboard tack, nearly straight on to *Roebuck* and the other pirates, who'd come about and were working their own way out of the dead-end channel. A bit more speed was in order.

She turned to meet Layland's eyes. The helmsman's face gleamed with sweat, but he kept an easy hand on his controls, not clenching or jerking the ship about. She was asking a great deal of him, as she increased sail and *Mongoose's* speed through the channel, barely twice the ship's width in some places. They'd scraped keel and mast against the shoals more than once already, causing *Mongoose* to shudder and groan even more than all of *Roebuck's* shot had managed.

Speaking of which, it's nearly time for —

Shot flashed out from *Roebuck's* side, condensing and flowing toward them while it was pulled this way and that by the shoals. This time three struck — two with no more damage to the hull than any before, but one in the rigging. Cut lines rebounded as the tension left them and flailed about as their stored energy dissipated. Men clambered up the masts and shrouds to set things right.

"You have the ship in hand, Layland?" Alexis asked, keeping her eyes on the helmsman.

"Aye, sir," he said, then glanced at his own copy of the plot and chart. "Fore topsail'd give us a knot or two, 'til we come about again."

Alexis glanced toward Mattingly, but the commodore kept his eyes on the plot, as though he'd not heard. She didn't believe that for a moment, but if he said nothing, it was for her to decide. She nodded. If Layland felt he could keep the ship on tack with a bit more speed, then she'd take him at his word.

"Hands to the foremast and let go the fore topsail, Creasy," she said. "Lively now, so we may get as much of it as possible before bringing it in again."

"Aye, sir."

They were already ahead of the other ships of their fleet, and adding more sail would increase that, but *Mongoose* had one task in this. She was the largest, fastest, and sturdiest of them, so must gain and hold the attention of Ness' frigate.

Delaine entered the quarterdeck from a turn about the ship and came to stand beside her. Alexis tucked her hands behind her back and clenched them to keep from reaching out to touch him and ensure he was still real.

"All is well, captain," he said.

Despite her having drafted him to serve aboard a New London ship, Delaine told her he found himself unable to apply the Royal Navy's *"fou"* convention of calling female officers "sir". To Alexis' ear the French *fou* summed up her own thoughts on the matter better than the English "bloody mad", even despite that she was so used to it after all these years.

"Thank you, Delaine."

Delaine eyed the navigation plot and raised an eyebrow. "We outpace the others," he said and grinned. "They will think you wish to keep all the pirates for yourself."

"Plenty for all, I think."

Mongoose was halfway down this channel on the starboard tack, nearing where she'd have to come about to the opposite tack in a space barely large enough to do so. Then she'd parallel, or nearly so, the pirates' channel for a time, before the two joined near the clearer, though not entirely clear, space away from this set of shoals.

That was where she must take *Roebuck*, where the two ships could come together, but before the pirates could gain open space where their superior numbers could be brought to bear with maneuvers.

"Our guns will bear on them after this next turn," Alexis said, not adding that if her own nines could make the range, then *Mongoose* herself would be vulnerable to all of *Roebuck's* guns.

Delaine nodded and said nothing, he could see that as well as her and his face grew somber.

Until then, the pirate frigate had the range.

FIFTY-TWO

Shot after shot struck Mongoose, not in broadside, but one after another, in a seemingly endless stream from the nearing Roebuck.

The pirates didn't strike with every shot, but even those that missed did damage to the crew's morale. Those that went through the rigging required men to climb the masts, to grasp and splice the flailing lines before the damage was so great that the dark energy winds could twist and pull her masts right out of the ship.

Those men were vulnerable there, and more than one was struck by further shot from Roebuck. Those who were lucky were killed in an instant, while those less fortunate might be injured and knocked off the masts — left to drift behind the ship and, if they had the fortitude to endure the oppressive effects of the dark matter shoals, hope their air would last until the battle was done and they might be rescued.

The shot which did strike Mongoose had no trouble penetrating the hull now, and the ship shook and groaned with each blow. The off gassing of vaporized thermoplastic was so great that it forced the ship off course, making her wallow like a punch-drunk spacer in the last bit of an evening's brawl. Layland worked the controls constantly, easing and correcting their course as he fought both the winds and blows. Alexis fancied she could tell merely by the sounds if it was an eighteen- or nine-pounder which had last run through her.

Stuck in the channel and laying on ever more sail so as to catch up the frigate before she could make use of the coming open space, there was little Alexis could do to alleviate the pounding her ship was taking. She couldn't even roll to present her tougher keel, for that would make the hold more vulnerable and there were hundreds of men crammed in there with barely room to move. Rolling to present her top would only expose more of her sails and rigging to damage, and the hull was full of spacers ready for the boarding as well.

That left her port side, and the guns there — ports all open to expose the deck to the frigate's shot. Not that closing the ports would make a difference at this point, as the space between them was a gap-toothed grin of holes through the thermoplastic hull.

At least those working the guns had a task to concentrate on. The never-ending feeding of new shot for the loaders. Pull the breech, yank out the spent canister and toss it back to some fellow — there were plenty enough idlers aboard to rush below, and grateful for the chance to spend a moment in the more heavily protected space around the fusion plant and magazine.

A new shot canister from the racks and into the breech, nearly taking a finger off the man cleaning the barrel if he weren't quick enough at his task or like to bash him in the head with it if he were peering too closely.

Wait, likely, for the two inspecting the barrel for flaws to step back and throw up an arm that they'd seen none — the wait gnawing at every man on the crew, but better that than to fire a barrel damaged from some previous shot and have it burst, splintering their own shot throughout the deck.

Then the gun captain laying his aim to account for the distance, the angle, the fall of shot through the dark matter between *Mongoose* and *Roebuck*, though there was little need of that now, with the ships growing closer and that bloody monster of a frigate being so buggering big, was there?

There was no careful laying of broadsides now, even by *Mongoose*, no hoping to demoralize an enemy into striking with the sudden arrival of so much massed shot. Now it was all fire as you will, fast as canisters could be loaded, and hope to kill as many of the bastards as you could before you and your fellows must give up the guns and join the others in what was to come.

On the quarterdeck, Alexis judged her moment as the two ships cleared their respective channels into a larger — by the standard of having nearly a full ship's length to sail through and turn — space where the channels joined.

Roebuck's captain seemed content to lay off and pound his smaller foe, which Alexis couldn't fault the pirate Ness for, even shying a bit to port and following the edge of the clear space, opening up some distance between her and *Mongoose*.

That wouldn't do, though.

This was no Giron, where she sought only to engage and delay the enemy. There were no fleeing transports for whom a few minutes, a few seconds, might mean the difference between reaching better winds and escaping or facing a frigate's guns themselves.

Nor was there any fleet coming to rescue them, for even if Captain Ellender might convince some captains or an admiral to enter the Hanoverese space of the Barbary, he and *Claw* would only just now be arriving at some New London station to tell them of what had happened on Erzurum.

Alexis glanced over to Mattingly, who'd said barely a word through the entire time. Isom was with him, though she hadn't seen him enter, assisting the commodore to attach a sword — a simple, thick-bladed spacer's cutlass, his own having been lost in his capture and enslavement — and a brace of pistols. Her clerk seemed to have forgiven the man for taking on both the commodore role and Alexis' cabin ...

Though perhaps not, she thought as she saw Isom jab a pistol into

Mattingly's vacsuit belt with a bit more force than was strictly necessary.

Isom had her own sword and a pair of pistols for her, as well, and came around the navigation plot to her side.

Mattingly caught her look and grinned. "The honor's yours, Carew, she's your ship to fight. I've always hated those flag officers who insist on mucking about with the ship — it is, after all, why there's a captain." He even chuckled. "Still, with so little room to maneuver and the plan all set, I do find my first flag remarkably free of the need for decisions."

"Aye, sir," Alexis said, then hazarded, "I'll try to arrange a more challenging action for you, when next we're all captured by pirates."

Mattingly laughed. "I'll leave that honor to some other, as well, if it's all the same to you. More than one admiral I think could do with a bit of digging in Erzurum's muck, to tell the truth."

"Indeed, sir," Alexis said. She might like Mattingly and agree with the sentiment, especially if it were that bloody Chipley, who was the cause of this mess when one got right down to it, but it wouldn't do for a lieutenant to agree too far with such sentiments — even if she was certain to hang regardless.

If I'm lucky, perhaps I'll catch a blade in the belly in this next bit, and save them all the trouble.

"Send the word, Creasy," Alexis ordered. The other ships of both fleets were nearing the end of their channels and at any moment Ness might think to put *Roebuck* about and bring those guns to bear on the far lighter hulled ships that followed. A single broadside from the frigate might send any of their merchantmen up in one shot. "More sail on the fore and main, let loose any bits of the staysail that might remain." She turned to the helmsman. "Increase the charge, Layland — to the bloody stops."

"Aye, sir."

On *Mongoose's* masts, more sail was let loose and seemed to burst with azure brightness as though struck by some new shot from *Roebuck*, but it was merely the particle projectors at full power.

White sparks and arcs of lightning flew across the surface of the sail's fine metal mesh, arcing to the masts and even to the men too near. Though it would do them no harm, Alexis knew from her own time as a midshipman on those yards that it was an eerie thing, both in sight and feel.

Mongoose leapt forward.

They were on the starboard tack, close-hauled to the winds, which gave her an advantage over the ship-rigged frigate which could not sail so close. She might even, in the space they had, pull up even a point or two closer to those winds and escape while *Roebuck* would have to fight tack upon tack to make up the ground. Only a point or two to starboard and *Mongoose* could run for that next channel and be gone from Erzurum — on her way home, free and safe with Delaine and her crew.

Alexis watched the plot carefully. Starboard for freedom, home, and safety.

"Hard a'port!" Alexis yelled. "Keep the sails taught! Layland, put us in her masts and twist the bloody things right out of the bitch!"

MONGOOSE TURNED TOWARD *ROEBUCK,* seeming to spin in place with both her rudder and falling off the wind.

As in every action, to Alexis, the long hours, then minutes, of approach, even with the exchange of fire, had been in slow motion, the ships lagging along. Now, so close, they leapt for each other, eager to come together like a pair of fighting dogs taking the last lunge to clamp jaws on their foes.

Men outside on both hulls scrambled to get clear of the impact and the two ships came together with a grinding, grating rumble that resonated through their hulls.

Layland spun his helm to put *Mongoose's* bowsprit and then her masts into a horrid tangle with *Roebuck's* mainmast.

Rigging snapped, along with the yards, and that debris sliced through both ships' sails, clawing great rents in the metal mesh and sending gouts of azure and white flashing out in vast displays.

Men on *Mongoose's* hull, those who'd successfully braced themselves for the impact, fired lines toward the other ship. Compressed air sending grapnels across the short space to further catch at masts, rigging, and sails, to tie the ships together.

Those lines were wrapped to winches, through pulleys, and even around *Mongoose's* masts and yards, pulled tight and made fast, then the men joined their fellows even as Alexis' next command was given, echoing through vacsuit helmets of those aboard whose radios still worked, flashing on the hull for those outside to see, and passed from man to man, helmet to helmet, on the open, battered gundeck where the radiations of *darkspace* had rendered the radios useless.

"*Away boarders!*"

FIFTY-THREE

But Little Bloody Bit would have
Not a gram of that.
She set upon their frigate
Like a cat upon a rat.

Alexis was first out of the quarterdeck, Mattingly close behind. The others were locking their consoles before following, and in a moment, *Mongoose's* quarterdeck was empty.

There was nothing more to do there, and nothing to defend — not even a bit of air, as the companionway was in vacuum, and what there was in the quarterdeck space rushed out with them.

The task of everyone aboard was simply to take *Roebuck* with nothing left for them if they failed.

Nabb was waiting in the companionway, along with some few others of her boat crew, including, she saw, the new lad, Aiden.

Alexis ran for the nearest lock, which gaped open, both its hatches wide to the vacuum beyond, the better to let *Mongoose's* crew pour out.

At the lock's edge, she found a gap of perhaps five meters

between *Mongoose* and *Roebuck*, the ships having come together at an angle.

Even as she leapt across, shoving off with as much force as she could muster to cross the space as quickly as possible, she saw that the two ships were not yet so tightly bound as she might like. They rocked apart and came together, each working against the other, driven by the winds in their sails and each ship's momentum.

While Layland had doused *Mongoose's* sails after the impact, cutting the particle projector and rendering them inert to the *dark-space* winds, *Roebuck's* were still charged. They were a tangled, scandalous mess, but still took the winds to some degree, pulling *Roebuck* away from *Mongoose* as the winds caught the scraps, then subsiding as they fluttered and spilled.

The lines between the two ships went alternatingly taught, then slack, as *Roebuck* pulled away, paused, and *Mongoose's* momentum from the tug brought them together again with a grinding crash.

A man misjudged his leap and landed on *Roebuck's* hull too far from an entry, be it a hatch blown open by those who'd preceded him or even a shot hole large enough for him to squeeze through.

Alexis winced, wondering who it might be, as the hulls came together and ground him, vacsuit and all, to nothing between their massive bulks.

She had other things to worry about, though. Just as time seemed to have raced as the two ships came together, it seemed to slow and crawl as she leapt between them. The journey of a few meters felt like it took forever, with her and those around her vulnerable and unable to change their paths.

Roebuck's crew took advantage of that.

Those with firearms drew them and took aim, picking off *Mongoose's* boarders one by one before they ever touched a finger to *Roebuck's* hull.

Others drew their swords and braced themselves to swing at the incoming men.

Something tugged at the sleeve of Alexis' vacsuit — bullet or flechette, she couldn't tell. A laser would have gone straight through without her noticing, as one did for a man ahead of her, whose body went limp in his suit and continued on to crash into *Roebuck's* hull.

Ahead of her, a pirate raised a boarding pike to intercept her path.

Alexis had her blade in hand and struck out at the pike. She didn't have the mass to shift it, so used the leverage to shift her own path instead. The pirate tried to move to intercept her again, but merely pushed her to the side as she kept her own blade in contact with the pike's shaft, sending a grating vibration through both weapons and forcing the pirate to drop the pike as her blade neared his hands.

She absorbed her impact on *Roebuck's* hull with bent knees and sprang up to drive her blade into the pirate's midsection. The point held, then punched through his vacsuit and he staggered back, lost to her in a moment in the swirling chaos of bodies on the ship's hull.

Another pirate rushed her and she turned the wild swing of his cutlass to the side, opening him up to her following slash.

Red-tinged air and sealant gushed from a long gash in the pirate's vacsuit and he backed away from her. She stomped forward, rear leg working to bring her fore back to contact with the hull, then using the force of that and her arm to bring her sword down in a heavy, overhand blow that skittered off the man's helmet to cut into his shoulder. Alexis pulled back from that and drove her blade forward, quicker than the injured man could react, and into his belly.

Her target swayed back to fall to *Roebuck's* deck, feet held in place by his boots and given momentum by the gust of escaping air and blood from his suit.

Alexis moved on, screaming into her helmet as she knew her crew was. No matter that they couldn't hear each other, they still knew.

"*Mongoose!*"

There was a gunport near her, so she made her way there, then grasped the edges and swung herself inboard. The gun itself was overset — barrel cracked and shattered into pieces — and there was a bit of space around its carriage for a wonder. The rest of *Roebuck's* gundeck was a teeming mass of men and blades, bullets and flechettes, all with the rare twinkling of a laser cutting through space and bodies, both. Others from *Mongoose* were along her side, coming in from hatches and ports to engage the pirates, who were being forced back from their ship's side by sheer force of numbers if nothing else.

No matter what number of pirate crew *Roebuck* had sailed with, Ness had sent enough off to prizes that *Mongoose's* overfull complement was enough to overwhelm her if they held.

The space of the gundeck, opened to vacuum when the action started, was no longer clear. Gobs of vacsuit sealant and globes of blood filled the space, floating about as *Roebuck's* gravity generators must have been hit in the action. Every cut through a suit's fabric added to the mess, with even the tiniest drop of blood finding some of its fellows to join with and form the rather horrifying blobs that floated about until splashing against some surface.

One of those struck Alexis' helmet, obscuring her vision until she wiped it away to leave a gory smear behind, and distracting her so that she didn't notice the oncoming pirate until his blade was through her left leg, adding her own blood to the mess.

She blocked his next thrust, turning it aside to grate against a gun's jagged barrel, even as she felt her vacsuit grow tight around her leg. The constriction of the suit itself and expanding sealant would, she hoped, stop any bleeding, but it also restricted her mobility.

She dodged to the side as her foe brought his heavy cutlass down with such force it surely would have cracked her helmet's faceplate. As it was, the man's blow brought his blade clear to *Roebuck's* deck.

Through the port she'd just cleared, another figure came. She recognized the markings on Nabb's vacsuit.

Her coxswain's boots landed on the pirate's sword, pinning it there. His own blade stabbed out, but it was an awkward blow, coming off-balance through the port, and only grazed the pirate's side, turned away by his vacsuit.

Alexis made to attack, but a second pirate pushed through the lines to stab at her, then a third.

Even as she parried these blows, she stepped atop a gun carriage to take in the full battle. She could see a suited figure deeper within *Roebuck's* gundeck, grasping pirates by the shoulders and directing them to attack, perhaps the captain, Ness, down from the quarterdeck to rally his men against the boarders, and that should be her target.

She stepped back toward the hull, and began assembling a force as men came through the gunports, grabbing them and holding them for a moment so they'd not simply bull their way into the mass of fighters.

Nabb touched helmets with her.

"Do you see that one there?" Alexis asked, pointing. "With the orange blaze on his helmet?"

"Aye."

"That's who we want! Form a wedge and go for him!"

"Aye, sir!"

Nabb quickly formed the men into a group, and they lunged forward as one.

They broke through the first few fighters, into the mass of pirates behind the line. Step by step, trudging forward to shove the foe aside, men moved to replace those at the edges as they fell, passing their fallen comrades back for what help might be offered.

Alexis rode the familiar rush of battle, every blow, every parry, like some sort of drug that made her vision sharper and her limbs tingle. She knew later would come the visions — memories of bodies, dead and ravaged — but in this moment the thrill of the contest was greater.

Blades struck at her. She parried, twisted, dodged, and, in no few cases, was spared by the blade of the man beside her deflecting the blow, just as her blade was there to save her fellows.

She knew Nabb was with her, and the new lad, Aiden, and one or two of the others from her boat crew, but others around her she didn't know — brought up from the rescued forces to make up *Mongoose's* complement, and she'd not had time to learn all their names.

In the battle it didn't matter, though.

They had *Mongoose's* colors on their sleeves now, making them all one and all hers.

They fought on in silence in the vacuum, helmets full only of their own raspy breath and the cry of their own voice carrying over the muted clangs and thuds of blades that could make it through into the aired suits.

Alexis lost sight of the pirate captain, Ness, in the swirling mass, but drove her lads on through. He'd be at the rear, and cutting the pirate force in half would do them well in any case.

A glance behind showed her own force filling in the space her wedge made, starting to encircle the remaining pirates fore and aft on the gundeck.

Nabb, at the wedge's fore, broke through to *Roebuck's* port bulkhead and the rest followed into the odd sort of empty space that sometimes develops in such battles.

Shoulders slumped and hands rested on knees as they bent to catch their breath. Alexis' own breath was harsh in her helmet and she adjusted her oxygen mix to give her a bit more and recover faster.

Nabb pressed his helmet to hers and pointed down to the gun they rested against. *Roebuck's* port guns were nearly pristine, compared to those to starboard where they'd boarded. Most of the action had placed the two ships closing *Mongoose's* port to *Roebuck's* starboard, with little chance to come about in the tight channels.

Nabb tapped the gun's breech.

"'At's loaded, sir!"

FIFTY-FOUR

"This is what you get," she said,
"When you dare Annalise's wrath.
For I'm her good right arm and
She set me on your path."

IT WAS BUT A MOMENT'S WORK FOR HER LITTLE BAND TO unclamp the big gun's wheels, pull it inboard, and swing its massive, crystal barrel about to face forward.

They'd split the pirate group in two with their charge and made a lane clear across *Roebuck's* deck from starboard to port. The larger group of pirates was still to forward.

Alexis took a place at the gun's breech, not wanting to put the act on another, while Nabb cleared their own lads from the barrel's path.

He didn't bother passing the word, simply took Aiden and two others with him to the fighting line. They picked a spot where the gun was laid and grasped two men, pulling them hard to either side, and never mind if an enemy's blow landed or their own was mislaid by the grappling. They pulled, shoved, touched helmets to scream instructions, and in a moment had cleared a space of six men from the fighting lines.

The pirates surged forward into the gap, thinking the tide had turned in the fight and they'd break through *Mongoose's* line to join again with their fellows aft.

It took them two steps see the gun's barrel, and that was enough for Alexis to bring her palm down on the gun's trigger.

SHIPS' guns were a wonder.

They were on *Roebuck's* lower gundeck, where the eighteen-pounders sat.

Time froze and the battle with it as the pirates at the fore tried to retreat.

Alexis recalled her first time aboard ship and being handed a nine-pound shot, asking how that could be, since the shot's casement was gallenium and with so much expensive metal must cost more than nine pounds.

The measurement was archaic, brought, with so much else, to New London with the kingdom's founders, a group her grandfather had once described as "not being cursed with a surfeit of sanity". Along with labeling their colonization company shares as a heredi-tary monarchy and reviving the bloody farthing, the Navy's founder had insisted on measuring their shot's weight in pounds instead of the eight kilos most other navies would call this. It measured the weight of the capacitor set in the base of the shot, its stored energy released in an instant as Alexis triggered the gun. That energy struck the lasing tubes, which interfaced to the gun's barrel. Then, even as the foremost pirates stopped, stared at the length of crystal barrel they faced, and were yet shoved forward by their fellows behind, the gun fired.

Though *Roebuck's* gundeck was open to *darkspace*, there was no, or little enough, dark matter to affect the shot. No foreshortening or compression as it flew, in fact it didn't become visible at all — only its effects.

The lead pirate was shot through, and the one behind him lost an arm, which spun and tumbled up into the space above the fighters' heads.

As though that were some sign, like the first cover to soar into the air at a graduation, more limbs and whole bodies quickly followed behind.

The shot began splintering midway up the deck, any reflective surface on an ill-maintained suit splitting it to kill and wound even more. The carnage fanned out from the shot's original path until it struck the fore bulkhead. A few places were shot through there, but by then the shot's force was mostly dissipated and dispersed amongst the mass of pirates.

Stillness followed, as both sides were shocked by the carnage. Only the spinning limbs and floating bodies moved, save for those injured who writhed in pain — either on the deck itself or floating above their mates' heads where all could see, propelled about by the gore and sealant spewing from rents in their vacsuits.

The forward group of pirates, seeing so many of their fellows cut down in an instant and now surrounded and outnumbered, dropped their weapons.

Those aft made to fight on, but wavered.

Behind them, near the aft bulkhead, Alexis saw the helmet with the orange blaze push and shove at the men, trying to get them to attack, but there were too many hesitating. In a moment they'd lay down their arms, and the pirate captain must have seen that too.

He hopped up, feet leaving the deck, and pulled a laser pistol from his belt.

Alexis shoved Nabb aside as the pistol's barrel came to bear, then made to dodge herself, but she was shoved aside too.

The shot came, striking Aiden, who'd taken her place.

The lad was taller than Alexis and the shot meant for her head had taken him low in the chest.

"Bloody fool," Alexis muttered. She grabbed Nabb's arm and dragged his helmet to hers. "Get him to the surgeon!"

She turned back to find the pirates aft laying down their arms, but the captain's orange helmet nowhere in sight.

Alexis rocked her boots free of the deck, then shoved off from the bulkhead, sailing over their heads toward the aft companionway. Whatever this Ness was about, it couldn't but mean ill for her and her lads.

Behind her, Nabb sent two of her boat crew sailing after her while he pulled Aiden's now still form to starboard for transfer to *Mongoose*.

The rest of her crew was busy at collecting pirate weapons and binding pirate hands. They'd taken enough ships to know the way of it without her giving the orders.

Alexis twisted in midair to strike the aft bulkhead with her feet and absorb her momentum before settling to the deck again. Two men were quickly with her, she couldn't tell which in their vacsuits, and she cycled the lock.

In a moment, they were out of the gundeck and through to the companionway.

Four pirates waited there, helmets off and looking more confused than anything else.

Alexis barely paused — she had her blade at the foremost's throat as soon as she was clear of the hatch and the man raised his hands hurriedly.

"Where's Ness?" Alexis demanded.

"Aft!" the man said. "Come like the devil hisself was after 'im an' tossed us'n out o' engineering!"

"See they're secured," Alexis ordered the two men with her, then hurried aft.

She transferred her blade to her left hand as she went and drew her flechette pistol. *Roebuck's* hull was whole here, so the little gun would work — she'd emptied her other pistols in the fight, though she couldn't have numbered each shot if asked.

The hatch to *Roebuck's* engineering spaces opened at her touch, but a bullet richocheted off the coaming as she went through, sending her to launch herself to the side and cover behind a console.

Alexis hunched down. She should wait, she thought, until some few of her lads made it through, but they were busy with the other pirates and she worried at what mischief the captain might be up to.

She keyed her vacsuit helmet to echo her voice over its external speakers.

"Your men have surrendered, Ness!" she called. "It's over!"

Another bullet answered her, leaving a streak of grey on the cream-colored thermoplastic of the bulkhead.

"Where is he?" a voice called from deeper in the compartment, past all of the consoles and machinery.

"Who?"

"Dansby! Where is he? I want to see his face one last time before we go!"

Alexis cursed under her breath and shook her head. She'd led a fleet of private ships to this man's threshold, taken his whole bloody planet while he was away, and now taken his own ship by boarding ... yet he was worried about Avrel Buggering Dansby?

"What in the Dark did Dansby *do* to you people?" she demanded. "And what must *I* do for you to worry about me, who's right bloody here with a full crew to pry you out! Now throw down your weapons and let's have no more of —"

The crack of Ness' pistol sounded again.

"You out there, Dansby?" Ness called. "Listening? I regret what happened with the girl, man, but I'd thought — never mind. I'll not go easy, you hear! Nor alone, neither!"

Alexis stuck her flechette pistol around the console and fired.

The thin, tiny darts of plastic stripped from a solid block and propelled down the barrel filled the compartment, clattering off bulk-heads and consoles without doing much damage beyond a scratch. A few struck solidly enough to penetrate, as they would with flesh, and stuck out of the opposite bulkhead like quills.

"That the best y'got, girl? Some little toothpicks? Come t'clean my teeth, have you?"

"Give it up, Ness!" she yelled.

"He sends a girl to do his work again?" Ness called back. "I'll see that end the same as last time, I swear it!"

Alexis cursed under her breath. Aside from the need to capture Ness, it was infuriating that the pirate cast everything in the light of that damned man Avrel Dansby. The bastard should be afraid of *her* for what she'd already done to his force — well, her and her lads, but it was no plan of Dansby's that had brought them this far.

The pirate captain was busy at something on the other side of the fusion plant. Alexis couldn't fire too near that — not because her flechettes would do the thing any real damage, but because her firing at such a solid shield would likely only result in raising Ness' spirits.

Still, the man hadn't fired back at her, nor had she seen him peek around the edges, which must mean his attention was elsewhere.

Alexis glanced at the hatchway she'd entered by, wondering at where the rest of her crew had got to. She'd set Nabb to a task before following Ness and there was the matter of disarming and securing all of the pirates, yet surely, they'd have someone to follow her soon ...

Unless they hadn't seen where she'd gone. She'd set Nabb on his task then flung herself away, and past the mass of pirates to follow Ness. It was possible they hadn't noted where she'd gone ... and she hadn't ordered them to secure the ship, which they might have started to the fore, thinking she'd gone to *Roebuck's* quarterdeck to start.

Damn me.

Alexis edged around the side of the console and peered across the space. There was no sign of Ness, but she could hear him moving about — the rasp of his vacsuit against itself and the slight tap of his boots as he moved — over the gentle hum of the machinery.

Damn me twice, she thought again as she darted from cover and rushed across the compartment.

NESS WAS HUNCHED OVER A CONSOLE, back to her, as she rounded the corner of the fusion plant.

Alexis raised her flechette pistol and fired, but his suit was better armored than most. The tiny darts stuck, but didn't penetrate to flesh, save in a few places, and those only shallowly.

The pirate's own reaction was swift.

He spun to her even as he grasped his blade from atop the console and swung it in a wide arc, forcing Alexis to jump back.

She fired again, holding the trigger down to send a steady stream of darts into the man's suit, but with little more effect.

She had to duck back again from the pirate's backswing and drop her pistol as useless.

Ness advanced on her, alternating stabbing and heavy chops with his short, wide blade, while she had barely time to interpose her own blade awkwardly with her left hand before taking the chance to switch to her right.

She'd barely got a grip on it before Ness swatted it aside, twisting her wrist painfully, and catching her in the side with his return. It was a glancing blow, with the flat of his blade and not the edge, else she feared it would have gone through her vacsuit to the flesh beneath.

His next blow caught her helmet, making her see stars even with the padding, and she dropped to the deck to roll away and gain some distance.

Though Alexis loved an action, and a boarding, and the task of pitting her skills against another with all on the line — she did despise a vacsuit. She lacked the mass to face most men in a brute exchange of blows, relying instead on her size and speed. The bulky suit slowed her, though it did her opponent as well, and reduced her advantage.

Ness advanced on her with slow, deliberate steps — blade held in guard, but ready to attack when near enough.

Alexis came to her feet more slowly than she had to, hiding her speed and feigning more effects from the blow to her head. She took a step back, then another, nearly to the console she'd ducked behind on entering. The ring of consoles faced the room's center, where the engineer of the watch would sit, so that he could face the man on each station. There was a bit of space between that console and the next, and a bit behind for the console's seat and for a man to walk, but it was a tight space.

Her hip hit the console's edge and she adjusted to go between it and the next, which was when Ness lunged.

He rushed straight for her, thinking her trapped between the consoles and seeking to overbear her with his weight and strength, but Alexis had counted on that. Even as he started forward, she was falling back and to the side, using all her speed now, recklessly, perhaps, in the bulky vacsuit, she scrambled back and to the side, flinging the console's seat into Ness' path to slow him.

She rushed around the console's far edge back into the compartment's center, faster than Ness could follow and he did exactly as she wished.

Foregoing an attempt to follow her, which would have been only a feint, he turned to return to the room's center through the gap between consoles, but his size betrayed him. It was a space meant to access the console's insides for repair when the ship was aired and at peace, not during an action with everyone in bulky vacsuits.

Ness could turn, but only in mincing steps, and, now committed, couldn't turn back without exposing his back to her for longer.

Alexis lunged, sinking the tip of her blade through his back, then again and again as he turned. None were lethal wounds, the tough fabric of his vacsuit slowed her blade even as it made Ness slower than a normal vacsuit would, and penetrated no more than a few centimeters. She couldn't even be certain that she'd got to the man's flesh beneath his thick, bulky suit.

She got her tip into his side next, as he turned, going in just above his hip and probing, hoping to disable him somehow.

Ness lashed out with his own blade, having turned enough to strike at her, and she had to duck back again. He was free now, and advancing, with no visible sign of weakness from any wounds, so that

Alexis had to wonder if her blade had made it through his vacsuit at all. Only a bit of blood mixed with the sealant that oozed from the cuts let her know the man must be hurt at least a little.

A heavy swing from Ness' sword forced her to back off farther and the pirate jerked at his vacsuit helmet to send it clanging along the deck towards the hatch.

He was an older man than she'd expected, or appeared so in any case. Long hair streaked with grey and tied back in a queue, with a sharp, craggy face and a beard that mirrored Avrel Dansby's goatee, if the trimming of that had been left to a barber both lazy and half-blind. All was damp with sweat from his exertions in the vacsuit, much as Alexis felt, and he gulped air.

Alexis took the chance to toss her own helmet aside, giving up its protections, as Ness had, for a breath of more and better air. Heat from her activity was drawing out some of the older odors from her vacsuit, as well as some new ones that seemed to have crept in from Erzurum's swamps, and the dry, cool air of *Roebuck's* engineering spaces was welcome.

"Who are ya, girl?" Ness asked, then darted his sword forward.

Alexis swatted the thick, heavy tip aside with her thinner blade and circled to the right, Ness turning to follow.

"Captain Alexis Carew, commanding *HMS Mongoose*," she said, probing his defenses.

Ness beat her attack aside, but made no counter.

The pirate snorted derision. "I *know* that ship —"

Their blades clanged together, then rasped as they closed. Alexis couldn't hope to overpower the larger man, not unless she could get him off balance, so disengaged.

"— an' it's not Royal Navy. Wouldn't ever be, that one." Ness shot a glance at the closed hatch. "He not here, though? Really?"

"No, damn you," Alexis said, "It's me you should be fearing."

"Disappointing, that." Ness laughed. "No, lass, it's you an' yours should fear — battle's lost an' you'll take me, but I'll take another o' Dansby's girls and one last ship with me."

Their blades met again, but she felt Ness was merely playing with her now and she considered his words until a chill ran through her.

Alexis disengaged again and looked to the console the pirate had been at when she'd entered. Controls for the fusion plant, which now displayed a countdown and gave off a steady beeping. A scuttling charge, leaving time, if they knew, for a crew to abandon the ship in their boats, but that time now half gone.

Ness laughed again. "Guessin' I'll have t' see the man himself in Hell."

Alexis launched herself at him, blade, elbows, knees, anything she could throw a blow with, all blocked by the pirate who displayed far more skill than she'd expected. He merely deflected her attacks and backed away laughing.

Even if she'd had her helmet on still, she couldn't have warned her crew, for the gundeck and much of the rest of the ship was so open to *darkspace* that no signal would get through. Her only chance was to take Ness down and then either stop the process, though she was certain he'd locked the console, or get her lads off *Roebuck* and far enough away.

His blade scraped her forehead and blood sheeted her vision. She had to shake her head to fling it away, but more returned.

Ness laughed again. "Come, lass, just wait it out. We'll go together, shall we? Y'can spend yer time in Hell with me."

Alexis bound his blade and was able to leverage it aside, then whip her own at his face on the return. It might have done for him, but the high collar of his vacsuit deflected it to slice along his ear and cheek instead of through.

"Take my ear!" Ness cried, laughing harder. "Like that mad dog o' his, Presgraves, sent me? Oh, you bring back memories, girl! Keep 'em in boxes t'talk to on lonely nights, you know —" He lunged, setting off a flurry of blows that drove Alexis back. "—*along with that crazy bint's head!*"

The pirate leader was clearly mad, Alexis determined, once

they'd both circled and backed off once more. Still she thought there was a long session of questions with, perhaps, several bottles of bourbon in Avrel Dansby's future.

And a pistol to his head if he proves reluctant, but I'll know about these ears and heads and whatnots..

"Almost time," Ness said with a glance at the fusion plant's console.

"There's no need for that, Ness," Alexis said. "Time enough to save yourself and your crew."

Ness snorted and stood, almost relaxed, waiting for her to move. "Bugger my crew — a more worthless bunch of whoresons I've never seen. Not like the old days, not like the start. No, girl, I'm old and don't care no more —"

Ness whipped his blade at her, unexpected after his casual, almost careless, stance. The heavy cutlass cut through her vacsuit above her left elbow and into the flesh beneath. He jerked it back, twisting so as open the tear in both suit and arm. Sealant and blood oozed out to fill gap, and her arm burned.

"Careless, girl."

Alexis attacked, knowing her opponent would take a moment to gloat over getting a blow in and expect her to take one to recover. She leapt toward him as he backed away, knocking her left elbow, despite the pain from her wound, and the slightly stronger suit material there into the side of his blade as he raised it. She grasped the back of his blade near the guard. That got her inside his reach and she swung hard, not at his exposed head, but at his left leg where he had his weight as he stepped back.

His vacsuit was strong, but not enough. Her blow cut through the suit, then sliced into the flesh beneath as she drew it back.

Ness pulled against her grip on his sword, but she went with it instead of resisting, sliding her own blade back along the cut, the sharp edge slicing deeper, like carving slices from a Christmas roast.

The pirate captain screamed and clubbed at her with his free hand, knocking her in the head again and again, but she kept her grip.

With every blow and every movement she sliced at Ness' leg until her blade grated against bone.

Ness grasped her face and no matter how she twisted he got his rough gloved thumb into her eye, forcing Alexis to back and twist away, but she sliced with her blade as she did, angling down so as to bite into new flesh in the pirate's leg, carving along the bone to separate a slab of flesh.

He staggered back, left leg weak and not bearing his weight.

"You rotting bitch," he muttered through a tight jaw, clenched at the pain.

Alexis backed further, trying to catch her breath and looking for another opening. A quick glance at the fusion plant's console showed time was running out and, though she knew it couldn't be the case, she felt it was growing hotter in the compartment. Sweat ran down her face and her left eye was puffing up from where Ness had dug his thumb in.

She took another step back and something rattled on the deck. A quick glance down showed that her boot had knocked against her discarded flechette pistol. It might have been useless against Ness at the start of this fight, but now he'd removed his helmet and no longer had the full protection of his armored vacsuit.

The pirate saw it at the same time and howled — that was the only word for it — raising his sword in both hands and rushing her with a lurching, knee-buckling gait as his injured leg gave way with every step.

Alexis reached down, transferred her blade to her left hand, and grasped the pistol. She rolled to the side, to Ness' right, forcing him to put more weight on his injured left leg to make the turn, and brought the pistol up as she came to her knees. The grip vibrated as she pulled the trigger, telling her there was little of the thermoplastic block the thing stripped its darts from left.

Those darts pattered against Ness' vacsuited chest, then up to pepper his neck and face as he reached her.

She barely had time to raise her own blade and that only

deflected his. The flats of both still came down on her head, making her vision blur.

Alexis rolled again, this time to her right, then again to get behind Ness and fire as he made his lumbering turn. Darts peppered the back of his skull, but none with enough force to fully penetrate the thick bone. They'd do well enough with thin bones of a foot or knee, but really needed to strike soft tissue to do damage to a person.

Soft tissue like that covering Ness' face, Alexis saw as the pirate turned.

He must have turned his head, for she'd missed his eye, but darts stood out on the side of his face and blood poured over his cheek and ear from those higher in his head.

Alexis raised the pistol to fire again and finish the man now that she could see his eye clearly, but the pistol was done with warning and demanded a fresh block of thermoplastic.

Ness, shuffling horror that he was, charged again before she could even think of the magazines tucked into her vacsuit pouches.

She holstered the pistol automatically and gripped her blade, timing his approach with it raised as though to block his heavy, over-handed swing again, then lunged upward from her knees. Under his blow, not so high as to strike his face, she put all of her forty-five kilos of mass into it, plus the five or so of her vacsuit, driving them with all the force her legs and arms could add.

The tip of her blade struck Ness in the belly, his own momentum added to it, and the point pierced his vacsuit to the flesh beneath, digging deep.

Pain screamed through her injured arm as she forced it to add to her lunge.

Alexis threw her weight into him offsetting his lunge and driving him back. She pushed him across the compartment, Ness' every other step staggering and jerking on his injured leg so that her blade sawed at his insides. The tip of her blade punched through the back of his vacsuit as they came up against a console. The lip of that took Ness in the hip, bending him backward over it and the force drove her blade through the console's glass top and into its insides.

Sparks flew, and some smoke billowed out, but not enough to shock either her or Ness, whatever she might wish.

Ness' hands clubbed at Alexis' head, weak and ineffectual blows. He'd dropped his own blade somewhere in that last shove across the compartment.

Alexis stepped back, panting. Her body felt weak, drained of all energy, as though it recognized her foe was done for and the fight over. Then she heard the continued beeping of the fusion plant's console, the very console she'd just driven Ness into, and new energy flooded her.

Ness smiled at her with red-stained teeth. He had to spit blood to clear his mouth.

"Yer too late," he laughed. "Can't stop it."

FIFTY-FIVE

Alexis rushed from the compartment.

She didn't bother with her blade or the console under Ness, the one wasn't worth the time and the other was clearly ruined, though the incessant beeping told her the last command entered was still in force.

She paused only to grasp her vacsuit helmet, sealing it in place as she left the engineering compartment.

There was no one in the companionway, they were still all on the gundeck in the process of disarming and restraining the surrendered pirates. Had her fight with Ness truly taken so little time? And how much time did she, they all, have left?

She tried to estimate with what she'd seen of the countdown and how long she'd fought with Ness, but, as usual, a fight seemed to have taken forever in her mind and she couldn't think why the fusion plant hadn't already blown, turning them all to a bit of light that would brighten *darkspace* for a few moments before fading to nothing.

She grasped the first man from *Mongoose* she found and touched her helmet to his.

"There y'are, sir — Nabb were lookin' fer —"

"*Belay that!*" Alexis yelled. "Pass the word — evacuate this ship and cut *Mongoose* loose! Their fusion plant's about to blow!"

It took no more than that. Every spacer knew what a blown fusion plant meant and the man passed the word to another, then two more, then four and eight and so on. Even to the captured pirates, though *Mongoose's* crew made sure to strip those of what weapons hadn't been tossed aside to float about the deck.

In a moment, the tide of men taking *Roebuck* reversed to stream out the ship's locks and through holes in her hull to make the leap to *Mongoose.*

"Pass the word!" Alexis said to another. "Cut the ship free — chop down the masts if you must, and prepare to pull her away!"

"Aye, sir!"

"Where's Nabb?" she asked. "Have you seen Dockett?"

"Quarterdeck, sir!" she was told in a voice she was certain quavered at the thought she might ask the man to accompany her.

Alexis headed aft again, but up instead of down in the companionway, meeting Nabb and Dockett on their own way down.

"Been lookin' for you, sir," Dockett began. "Thought you'd gone t'take the quarter —"

"There's no time," Alexis interrupted him. She passed on her orders and the situation.

"Aye, sir," Dockett said. "All our lads're on the main decks still, save those we took t'quarterdeck thinkin' you'd gone there first."

"See to clearing those off the main decks, Mister Dockett," Alexis said, "and set men to freeing *Mongoose* from this deathtrap."

"Aye, sir."

"Nabb, with me to the quarterdeck."

"Aye, sir — the lad's with the surgeon. He'll be all right."

Alexis had a moment's relief that the lad, Aiden, had not been too badly hurt by the shot he'd taken, but then hurried on — he'd have no chance to recover from his injury if they didn't get *Mongoose* away.

The quarterdeck was still aired, but there was little time wasted by its inhabitants in getting their vacsuit helmets on once Alexis passed the word of what was happening.

The two captive pirates and pair of *Mongoose's* crew left there, followed Nabb and Alexis up onto *Roebuck's* hull, then across to *Mongoose*.

The last of the lines holding the two ships together were already cut, and most of *Mongoose's* foremast as well, caught up as it was in *Roebuck's* rigging.

They passed the stub of it, a pair of spacers with their gas torches climbing down from the cut, even as Dockett was gesturing others to rig one topmast spar to it so they'd have a bit of sail to spread there for the task of working away from *Roebuck*, and a second to push against the frigate's hull and shove *Mongoose* away.

Alexis left him to it. The bosun knew what was needed. She caught sight of Delaine near the mainmast, setting men to angle what sail they could, and left him to his work as well, only grateful to know he was off *Roebuck* and safe ...

No, not safe yet.

Her vacsuit helmet came off as she entered her own quarterdeck and she thought she might be sweating more now than during the boarding or her fight with Ness — those had been mostly personal danger, while now her entire crew and ship could be destroyed at any instant.

"Charge the sails, Layland!" she called.

"Aye, sir!"

There were still crews on the mainmast, cutting away either *Roebuck's* rigging or their own where the two were tangled, but they could continue while they started to pull away.

Mongoose's particle projectors fired and sails, what there were of them, sparkled azure shot with white lightning.

Dockett had those on the foremast pull the makeshift yard and the bit of jib he'd rigged there was about to catch the winds right, while Delaine had crews of men to haul on lines and cut away those sails so hopelessly entangled with *Roebuck* still that they were doing more harm than good.

Mongoose's hull groaned and creaked, her mainmast strained.

"Off, Layland, then on — rock her away — get a bit of rhythm going."

"Aye, sir."

Glowing followed by dark, Layland worked the projectors, alternating between a charge which would let them catch the wind and darkness which left them attached to *Roebuck* where the two hulls had ground together.

Off and on, the men on the sails alternating as well, between hauling the full sails about to taking in their slack so that the next charge wouldn't snap lines or pull them from their grasp.

Slowly, too slowly for Alexis' comfort, the two ships parted. Men stretched out on the mainmast yards to cut what tangled lines remained, and then *Mongoose* was free.

Free, but not yet safe.

"Douse the main and let the fore — what there is of it — bring us around!" Alexis ordered.

Finally, *Mongoose* moved away from *Roebuck*. Slowly at first, her bow ponderously coming about with so little foremast and sail to work with, then enough of a roll to bring the main into play and she moved faster.

The other ships were still engaged, though *Fang* appeared to have taken her first target and moved on to assist one of their merchantmen with another.

"Roll ship, Layland," Alexis ordered. "Put her keel to *Roebuck*. Creasy — pass the word to those on the hull to come topside and not face that frigate! We're still too near for my liking!"

"Aye, sir!"

Mongoose rolled to place her thicker keel toward the other ship, and Alexis had a moment to wonder if Ness had truly set a timer, or if the damage to the console had turned it off, before *Roebuck* disappeared in a blast that made *Mongoose* buck and twist despite the distance.

Alexis closed her eyes. There were men from both the pirates and *Mongoose* still aboard that ship, most dead and fallen to the deck or floating free where the antigrav had failed, but some would be the injured — unconscious or too hurt to be differentiated from the dead. She'd condemned those to their fate and they were gone now, but to have waited even a moment more —

Mattingly rushed onto the quarterdeck, out of breath and his face red. Alexis had very nearly forgot about the senior captain and ostensible commodore. His hair was damp with sweat and his vacsuit was covered in a mix of blood and suit sealant, either his own or others'.

Wide eyes took in the navigation plot, then he relaxed, took a deep breath, and smoothed his hair, then joined her at the plot.

"One oughtn't look away for a moment when you're involved, eh, Carew? I was in the midst of that fight, jolly good fun, then seeing to the prisoners squared away, when next there's a full tide of men streaming back aboard and I'm jammed up the arse-end of your hold. Like a bloody box puzzle to get out — 'a step to your left, if you please, sir, and I'll move up,' eh?"

"I'm sorry, sir, I should have sent for you, but —"

"Any closer and we'd be a part of that," Mattingly said, pointing to the fading, shrinking ball of plasma that had once been *Roebuck*. "Fight your ship, Carew, always fight your ship. Leave those with a flag to worry about their fleets and such — speaking of which —"

Mattingly peered at the navigation plot, but it quickly became apparent that there'd be no ordering about of the fleet necessary. One after another, their other ships were signaling victory over the pirates as the light from the former *Roebuck* came to them and made it clear their flagship frigate and leader were no more.

"Well, that's that," Mattingly said.

FIFTY-SIX

"Let your fate be a lesson
To all who'd harm our lads.
Let your howls fill their ears,
And turn them from that path."

MATTINGLY GAVE THE PIRATES, THOSE WHO'D SURRENDERED AND accepted pardon, one of the merchant ships, stripped of guns, both ship's and personal, and packed to the gills with nearly four times the men she could comfortably hold. Each had nothing but the clothes on his back and a note in hand for whatever his share of the bounties Alexis had offered was ... that and their last memories of Erzurum.

They had instructions to sail for New London — trailing *Mongoose* and the other ships if they liked, but in no way a part of the returning fleet — and make their own way from there.

With the bounties, Alexis hoped most would see their way clear to living lives on the right side of the law, though she suspected many would not. While the bounties were, in most cases, enough to set the bloody pirates up for life, some would have theirs disappear in a burst of drink and depravity.

Given the amounts in hand and the toll of the sheer amount of drink and depravity they could buy, even some few of those would find themselves set for what short life they had left.

Old Blackbourne was, for once and a marvel, somber as he prepared to board the last boat for that waiting merchantman, and the only boat Mattingly allowed the pirates to take with them. The rest, those that wouldn't go with the freed spacers, being given to the people of Erzurum.

The very last of the nearly twelve hundred pirates hung over the previous days and nights were being cut down from the gallows, and Blackbourne and the others who'd accepted pardon had been there to witness each and every one. At Mattingly's insistence they'd been put on the field and forced to watch "Your very own fates, save for the grace of Queen Annalise through her emissary!" Mattingly barked at them.

"Some won't listen or learn," he'd whispered to Alexis, standing ramrod straight and staring at the ten gallows as the first pirates were made ready to drop. "Hard men, born to it and with a taste — but others will and might come, someday, to make amends for whatever it is they did while running with Ness."

Alexis kept her own face impassive as the first sentences were read out and the pirates danced at the ends of ropes. There was a gunshot from across the field where those awaiting their fate were held — not the first and not the last — as one or more tried to break from the group and run for Erzurum's wilderness.

Kannstadt stood to her other side, face as still as hers and Mattingly's. He had a brief discussion with the Hanoverese senior captain, then turned to them.

"We will watch five, I think, *Kapitän* Mattingly?" the Hanoverese officer asked. "And then retire?"

"Yes," Mattingly nodded. "Turn the supervision over to some junior for the rest."

There were plenty of volunteers from among Erzurum's former slaves to oversee the hanging of the pirates.

The trials had been ... concise and *en masse*, but Alexis had no doubt about their fairness, at least. There were no innocents on Erzurum or with Ness' fleet to be caught up in the mess by mistake. They'd freed and pardoned any of the crews of the newly taken ships from the pirates' last cruise, but all others who'd not accepted the pardon were complicit in their fellows' acts.

The more senior captains from New London, the French, and Hanover had formed the tribunals and quickly passed sentence on the lot, which announcement filled the tiny port town with Erzurum's natives, come to watch their former overlords hang. Which had then presented them with the problem of keeping those former slave-owning natives from being slaughtered themselves by the freed spacers of the three navies.

Only Mattingly's announcement, echoed by the French and Hanoverese commanders, that the punishment for any spacer taking action against the natives of Erzurum would be exile on Erzurum when the fleet left, kept the peace. There was not a spacer of the fleets who hated his former captives more than he wished to see the back of this world and get home.

Those crowds of natives had dispersed back to their other towns and farms after the first day, though — even a well-deserved hanging can only entertain for so long.

She wasn't quite certain why she'd come to see this last boat of pirates, and Blackbourne, off — he was a rogue, and a scoundrel, and had been with Ness' group so long that he'd certainly done a host of despicable things, the total of which could never be redeemed, but, oddly, she found she liked the man.

"Well, witch-woman, Old Blackbourne's away," Blackbourne said.

"If ever you return to piracy, Blackbourne, I'll see you hang as your fellows did," Alexis said.

Blackbourne grimaced. "Ah, why'd y'put a geas like that on Old Blackbourne?"

"I mean it, man. You've a black heart, but you'd best spend the rest of your days scrubbing it clean."

The pardoned pirate took a little hop off Erzurum's field to land on the boat's ramp, as though he didn't wish to have himself touching both at once.

"Away, away, lass," he said, smiling now, "for Old Blackbourne's a touch of the Sight more than yer own witchy-ways, so geas for geas, lass." He met Alexis' eyes. "You'll be busier with more'n how Old Blackbourne spends his days all the rest o' yourn."

"Fair enough," Alexis said.

Blackbourne took a deep breath, then, quite unexpectedly, extended his hand. "It were fair dealin' y'gave Old Blackbourne," he said.

Alexis took the offered hand, torn a bit between liking the rogue and wondering at how much blood had stained that hand over the years — still, she'd not have taken Erzurum without his aid. "And you in turn."

Blackbourne smiled and skipped up the boat's ramp, keying it to close as he entered the boat, but not before his voice drifted down to her.

"Watch yerself, witch-woman!"

THERE WERE MORE FREED spacers than would fit aboard their ships, even for the relatively short sail to Enclave, where they'd decided to go first, it having representatives from the French Republic, Hanover, and New London all in one place, though Alexis hoped there was a proper consul from New London arrived, for Wheeley wouldn't do at all now that she knew he was involved with Ness and the pirates.

Mattingly determined to remain on Erzurum with those left behind, both to maintain order and reassure them they'd not be forgotten again.

"Send word to New London that we're here and request trans-port, but little else," Mattingly told her. "Save the full report for when we all sail into Penduli." He glanced around the landing field where those who'd been unlucky in the draw and would remain for the next ships gathered to see their more fortunate fellows off. "You'll want all these voices heard before there's a board of inquiry empaneled on this."

"Aye, sir," Alexis said. "Thank you."

"Even success should be presented in the best of lights, Carew, especially when you've bent the rules to get there."

FIFTY-SEVEN

Their arrival at Enclave was rather like a planetary assault.

Though the French and Hanoverese had no real quarrel with Wheeley, nor desire to create an incident in the ostensibly shared system, those captains nevertheless made transition with *Mongoose* at the L1 point and made for orbits over their respective territories. They broadcast very nearly the same message *Mongoose* did, that all ships in-system were to heave-to for inspection and not interfere with the New London force arriving. It was made easier by the fact that there were no naval ships from any nation in-system, only merchants who wanted nothing more than to go unnoticed.

The other New London captains deferred to Alexis as well, despite any misgivings or irritation that might have caused, on Mattingly's order — that she intended to assault the New London port and take New London's acting and de facto consul up for hanging might have made it easier for them to swallow. They could simply say they were following orders. For Alexis' part, she felt she was already so far into a rather foul-smelling pool that a bit more couldn't matter, and she dearly wished to see Wheeley get what he deserved.

Mongoose's boats put down, full to groaning with her original boat crew and freed spacers from Erzurum, fitter now for a fortnight and more's feeding on the ship's stores enroute.

The ramp lowered and Alexis was first off, uniform coat tight against the cold wind that shrieked across the ice-covered field.

The men on guard at the hatch were Wheeley's, she had no doubt, as he'd taken over so much of Enclave from his lair deep in the casino. She strode up to the hatch, Delaine, Nabb, and Dockett at her side.

"Open in the Queen's name!" she demanded.

"Bugger off!" came over the speakers. "Who're you, then?"

"Captain Alexis Carew, HMS *Mongoose*, commanding — now open the bloody hatch!"

"Ain't no such thing! I 'member you — yer that skinny bint off a privateer. Yer writ ain't got no —"

Alexis stood aside from the hatch, the others with her hurriedly did the same and she nodded back toward the boat where a ship's gun had been rolled down the ramp immediately after she'd exited.

"Bloody —" was all the speaker had time to say before the gun fired.

The bits of the hatch that weren't vaporized or blown inward by the shot creaked and swayed against what was left of their supports.

Alexis pulled a pistol from her belt and rushed through, splashing through the ankle-deep water melted from the ice walls of the corridor by the shot.

Following, like a great wave crashing through that water, came three cramped boatloads of spacers anxious to get a bit more of their own.

"*Mongoose!*"

A CASINO, Alexis found, was not greatly difficult to assault, yet was, somehow, immensely satisfying.

The common folk of Enclave, much like anywhere else, had the sense to take to their homes and hunker down at the first sign of trouble, clearing the corridors leading to Wheeley's casino.

Likewise, her lads had orders to harm none who didn't stand in their way and — though they didn't really need to be told, bearing the scars of Erzurum themselves — to treat any of the casino staff with the earrings marking them as slaves gently. Those would be sent out to a makeshift surgical center where the explosives could be removed from their necks.

Wheeley's security forces, on the other hand, were simply overwhelmed. Those who drew weapons received the same in kind, with greater numbers and power, while those who tried to block the first wave were knocked aside or down. The wisest simply widened their eyes at the approaching horde of spacers, some again wearing their Erzurum lizard skins as a sort of symbol, and ran.

Once through the casino's hatches, her lads spread out and Alexis slowed to watch.

She'd expected them to make for the cages and the coin stored there, but many seemed more interested in tables and machines. Blades came down to shatter gambling table tops, machines were overturned, kicked, and knocked to pieces. It was as though the spacers were taking out their frustration at every bad bit of luck they'd had in a game of chance on the casino itself.

Still, she was gratified to see that the lads were heeding her words that the staff not be harmed. The merchant spacers who'd been gambling when the chaos started quickly joined in, though most of those would find their tactic of looting the tables where actual checks were used not so profitable as they might have wished. Alexis doubted the next owner of any gambling establishment on Enclave would honor Wheeley's checks.

Satisfied that the chaos and destruction were not out of hand, Alexis set her sights on the more private and exclusive gaming area where she'd found Wheeley before, only to spot an unexpected figure rushing toward her from that direction.

Villar, her first officer on *Mongoose* who'd had to go off with the private ships, nearly got himself shot, coming out of that gaming area, freezing as he saw Alexis and then rushing toward her.

"Belay that, Aiden!" Alexis said as the lad raised his weapon at Villar's approach. "*Oof!*"

The air for any more was knocked out of her as Villar wrapped her in an embrace that took her feet off the ground, then hurriedly releasing her and stepping back, his face red.

"Sorry, sir, I couldn't credit it when I saw you and —"

"Never mind that — is Wheeley in there?"

"Yes, sir, I went to ask him if there was any word of you, or back from New London, when news of ships in-system came and then —" He looked around, puzzled at the spacers turning the casino to ruin. "How are you here? What —"

"Come on, then, I'll explain on the way!" She started for where Wheeley was, filling Villar in as they went, but when they reached the more exclusive gaming area they found it empty.

"He was here, the bastard," Villar said. "I was here to speak with him every time a ship came in, asking if there was word from Penduli of a rescue fleet. Every time he told me, 'No,' and likely had a good laugh over it. Never sent word at all, if I'm any judge."

"He had us all fooled, but he'll answer for it," Alexis said. "Buying up the taken ships and the captured pirates and merchants off our hands — likely sent them on their way as soon as the private ships cleared the halo." She looked around. "Where could he have got to?"

There was a muffled cry from farther back in the gaming area, near the back wall draped in heavy fabric to deaden some of the sound from the main floor.

"The drinks and food come out of there," Villar said, "there must be passages."

Weaving around the tables, they made their way to the back wall and found an entry into the service corridor. They found Wheeley quickly, too, only a hundred or so meters along, but in no condition to answer further for any of his past actions.

The heavy man lay on the floor, face down, the back of his head flattened to mush and a growing pool of blood beneath it.

Beside him on her knees, heavy service tray still in her hands, was the dealer from Wheeley's favorite table.

Afet, Alexis thought, *odd that I remember her name.*

The tray was bent and dented, but had been heavy enough for the job and its back was covered in Wheeley's blood, which spattered the walls and the dealer, Alexis saw as she grew closer.

Afet rocked back and forth, then, as they approached, slowly raised the heavy tray and brought it down on Wheeley's head again.

Alexis motioned for the others to stay back and stepped closer, going to her knees so as to be on the same level as the woman.

"He's done," Alexis said softly.

Afet dropped the tray to clatter to the floor and stared at Alexis as though she'd just then noticed the others were there, which she might well have, as focused on Wheeley's body as she'd been. Her right hand went to her throat and Alexis noted the distinctive pattern of earrings, marking her as one of the slaves Wheeley had brought from Erzurum to work his casino.

"He's done," Alexis repeated, "and we'll have that out of you instanter. Nabb, would you escort her out to the medical station?"

"Aye, sir." Nabb knelt, the new lad, Aiden, recovered, or nearly so, from his wound in taking Ness' frigate, beside him.

"He said he was taking me with him," Afet said. "On his ship."

"Come on now, miss," Nabb held out his hand to assist her in standing, but not too close. Aiden took her other side. "Away from him and never see him again, eh?"

She took Nabb's hand, eyes still on Wheeley's body. "I wouldn't go."

"Right, miss," Nabb said.

"He was really in league with the pirates?" Villar asked when they'd gone.

Alexis nodded. She'd much preferred to have taken Wheeley alive. With Ness dead and all the other pirates, pardoned or not, claiming no knowledge of the deal, it would have been beneficial to have one backing up Skanes' story of the Marchant Company's involvement. She shrugged. There was nothing for it now, and she couldn't very well blame Afet for acting as she had.

"But ... I told him everything, sir ... I did, Malcomson did, all the private ship captains ... thinking he'd send word to New London for a larger force, an official one." Villar looked stricken.

"You had no way of knowing," Alexis assured him. "None of us did."

MONGOOSE WAITED AT ENCLAVE, and Alexis with her, for the other ships to return to Erzurum and return with the next load of rescued spacers. Three ships were sent on to New London, requesting escort and better transport for the men.

That left Alexis with weeks of idleness, during which she hoped, in vain, for a return of the privateers who'd abandoned her on Erzurum.

She didn't blame them, but she did wish to have a word or two of goodbye with Malcomson, for she was fond of the huge Scot, and more than a word with Spensley, if only to see the scars she'd left him and determine if that were enough.

"Most of the lads signed on with the other private ships," Villar told her. "Some with merchants, wanting nothing more to do with adventures, they said."

"I don't blame them," Alexis agreed, accepting a glass of wine from Isom.

One benefit of having just raided Wheeley's casino was the

ability to restock her pantry aboard *Mongoose* properly from the man's stores.

"Parrill is sailing with Malcomson," Villar went on.

Alexis raised an eyebrow at that. The woman she'd taken on as an officer aboard *Mongoose* had been aboard merchantmen before that, and she'd seemed ill-suited to the privateering life.

"There was talk of them being a couple," Villar added.

Alexis' brows raised further and there was a sniff of disdain from Isom.

"And Hacking?" Alexis asked. Her haughty officer had not taken well to life aboard a private ship, but neither did she think he'd take a position aboard some merchant — the man's disdain for such had been vocal.

"Took passage back to New London," Villar said. "Said he'd set up shop in Admiralty's Waiting Room and await a commission, rather than any more of this, er, 'nonsense'."

Alexis nodded. He'd be much happier there, ship or no, she thought.

Of the crew who'd fled Erzurum with Villar and the other private ships, only those who'd come with her from Dalthus, and before that *Nightingale*, had stayed, though even a few of those had taken berths on other ships and moved on.

More time passed and the last of the round-trips back to Erzurum to retrieve the freed slaves was finished.

Mattingly came with the last of them, leaving behind Kannstadt and the other Hanoverese to see about setting Erzurum to rights and returning those slaves taken from other Barbary worlds to their homes.

Alexis had some qualms about that still. She remembered Kannstadt's treatment of Isikli and his family, wondered which influence might now play out in Kannstadt's management of that sad planet — Hanover's or Lieutenant Deckard's.

That thought brought another.

Her leave-taking with the Hanoverese captain back on Erzurum had been, if not emotional, at least fraught with such.

They'd, neither of them, made mention of their own disagreements directly, but Kannstadt had seemed to respond to Alexis near-worried glance from Erzurum's landing field to the town beyond with a frown and nod.

"Have no fear for Erzurum's people. I have much to think on still, but they will be safe," he'd said, then, "I fear I must ask a thing of you, *Kapitän* Carew. For Ian."

Alexis knew without him going further what the request would be — and wondered what Admiralty would think of her delivering such a message to a senior captain and for an officer of a foreign, enemy power.

She sighed.

Bugger them and they shouldn't have joined if they can't take a joke.

"Should I find myself near Captain Ellender, sir, I shall deliver your message and make what arrangements I may for your meeting."

Kannstadt jerked his head in a nod and held out his hand. Alexis took it.

"*Danke.*"

FERRY WORK DONE and Mattingly arrived at Enclave with the last of the New London and Berry March spacers, Alexis could finally see the final totals and she nearly wept with rage at how very nearly so many been left to rot there.

From the ships which fought and died around Erzurum, over fifty thousand men had been taken by the pirates. A staggering number, nearly impossible to believe until one remembered that they'd been taken from crowded, ill-gunned boats after days and weeks of deprivation in the deepest of *darkspace*.

Of those, a bit over five thousand were of the Berry March fleet, and over twenty thousand of New London. The remaining Hanoverese were left behind to await their own rescue fleet, while close to thirty thousand men swelled Enclaves New London settlement to bursting — crammed into icy corridors and rooms intended for a population a third that size, and those already present.

The body heat alone had Enclave's citizens worried the whole place would melt, and the constant dripping made it a not inconceivable concern.

"You'll need to go, Carew," Mattingly said. "There's nothing else for it. Hate to send you off alone, but there's barely enough food here, no matter we're buying every bit that comes in system as it is, and we're seeing little help from the Hannie and French settlements."

The Hanoverese, in fact, had requested that the New London spacers clear the system as quickly as possible, and sent for instructions from their own more populated worlds. The French, as in the attempt to free the Berry Worlds themselves that had started the whole mess, seemed less than eager to take on their erstwhile countrymen from the Berry March fleet. It was as though no one wanted to acknowledge the folly of either Chipley or the Hanoverese admiral involved in this debacle.

They were in some rooms on Enclave's surface where Mattingly had set up offices while overseeing the men there, but Alexis couldn't quite attribute the chill she felt to the place's icy walls.

"Your *Mongoose* is the fastest — maybe faster than those we sent on before," Mattingly finished.

Alexis had to agree with that. Neither the captured merchantmen nor pirates were particularly fast sailors and it was possible *Mongoose* might still overreach them and arrive at Penduli before they did.

"Aye, sir," she said. "Who will sail with me?"

"The wounded, I think," Mattingly said. "Those most in need of a proper station's medical care."

There were enough of those to fill *Mongoose's* spare spaces — the wounded and the Isikli family, who Alexis insisted on carrying on.

She'd promised them a home on Dalthus and she'd see to that. She might put them aboard a merchantman at Penduli, but she wanted to see them safely to a place where there were not so many men who'd come to hate the natives of Erzurum.

"Will, ah, you be —" Alexis started, but Mattingly cut her off.

"No. The conflicts between the men and Enclave's citizens are too frequent — and there's the Hanoverese here. They're less inclined to believe word from one of their formerly captive captains and the Dark knows what they'll get up to or what word will come from Hanover proper." He shook his head and Alexis could tell he was as weary as she was. "I know I said it was best for you to come in with all of us in tow, but —" He shrugged. "We need relief here. Supplies. Ships to bring the men home. And no time."

"Some of the other captains, then?" Alexis asked.

Mattingly rubbed his eyes.

"Need them to help keep the men in line ..." He paused for a long moment. "To be frank, Carew, I'm not sure who I might send that would be of help to you. There's a great deal of talk."

"Talk?"

"Concerns," Mattingly said. "Some of the captains have been talking and the subject of *Hermione* came up. That was a bad bit of business. More than one fellow with Chipley's fleet knew Captain Neals."

Alexis felt her jaw tighten at the mention of the abusive captain she'd served under aboard the ill-fated *Hermione*, that his friends might be coming to the fore now, and after she'd risked so much to free them.

"Yes, sir, but —"

"They're grateful to be free," Mattingly cut her off again, "but they, most of them, think you overstep yourself. Take on too much."

"I see, sir." She swallowed hard. "And you?"

Mattingly looked away. "You were, so far as one can tell, senior at the time. I'll not second-guess your actions."

Alexis nodded. She felt a growing anger, but kept her voice level. "But you'll not support me, either."

Mattingly cleared his throat, rose from his seat and went to a cupboard set into the ice to pull a bottle of wine and pour himself a glass. Alexis noted that she was offered none.

"It's unclear how Admiralty will view the situation. I think —" He drank. "Best perhaps, for everyone, if none of the other captains are put in a position of having to express an opinion. You go, give the admiral at Penduli your report, and then, well, you've had the first and strongest word, yes?"

"Aye, sir," Alexis said, there being no other real response. She rose to leave.

Mattingly's eyes narrowed and his jaw tightened. "Oh, and should our good friend Captain Ellender happen to still be at Penduli, Carew?"

"Sir?"

"Do pass on that there's a fellow captain or six who wishes to have a word with him, will you?"

"*CONNARD,*" Delaine muttered.

"If that means a right bastard, I agree," Villar said.

"Means worse," Isom added, "and not near enough, if you ask me."

"Gentlemen," Alexis admonished. They were three days out of Enclave and well on their way to Penduli. Mattingly had been nearly the whole talk of every meal and she was tired off it. "Enough. Delaine, please — Villar will return home to his Marie with very nearly more words in French that he *cannot* speak to her than what he may."

Skanes, who was aboard more because Mattingly had not known what to do with her than for any other reason, looked up from her plate.

"He's a coward," she said. "As I was."

"Captain Skanes —" Alexis began, but the woman was looking back down at her plate as she had at every meal, and Alexis knew she'd not be drawn out again. Her only words now seemed to be to admonish herself or state her intentions of crying the perfidy of the Marchant Company from every vantage possible upon her return to New London space.

Alexis, despite her own anger, again found herself in the position of, if not defending Mattingly's decision, at least explaining it.

"While I'd like to have a fleet of other captains behind me in support, I've had enough time to think your arriving alone is, at least, better than a fleet *not* in support." She sighed. "I always did know that Captain Neals had his friends and they'd come back to haunt me one day, I suppose."

"Ain't right," Isom said, clearing plates in readiness for dessert.

"This Neals could not have had so many friends, could he?" Villar asked.

"It doesn't take many," Alexis said. "I suppose none of the captains were particularly happy with my actions — especially not with Lieutenant Deckard effectively mutinying against Ellender and forcing him away as he did."

"But you had nothing to do with that, sir," Villar said. "It was Deckard's own decision."

"Yes, but some will wonder. And, wondering, they'll listen to others." She shook her head. "No, much as he's protecting himself and his own position, I do believe Captain Mattingly has done me as much a favor as he felt himself able in sending us home ahead of anyone else."

FIFTY-EIGHT

And so, we sailed off, me mates,
And left that Hell behind.
Came home to Queen and Country,
For both we'd so long pined.

DARKNESS AND SHADOWS SWIRLED AROUND ALEXIS, GROWING EVER *nearer and more defined with each moment.*

She groaned and tried to look away, knowing this for what it was, but even knowledge couldn't defend her from these things — they grew out of something deeper than knowledge and mere facts.

Dark figures rose from the shadows, formed of the very stuff that swirled around her, seeming to be formed of the Dark itself.

Alexis forced herself to face them, as Poulter, the surgeon on Nightingale *who'd first helped her to deal with these dreams — at least in some way other than drinking to insensibility — had advised.*

"A pirate!" she yelled at the first, always the first, stout figure. "Took my ship and held my lads! Killed one of them, and how many others in your roving?" She took a step toward it. "I've no shame in

your death! None! Or if I do, I'll carry it willingly for those saved from you!"

She turned to others, not waiting for the first to fade or step back. At those she recognized, and there were all too many, she yelled specific defiance — more general for those she didn't recognize, but she'd weigh herself down with shame for them too.

Hardest were those who hadn't been enemies, the men aboard her own ships who'd fallen under her orders. Those she couldn't scream defiance at, she could only call them to their duty and remind them of their mates who still lived due to their sacrifice. Tears, not anger, drove these words, and she could only hope that voicing her true regret might give these spirits some comfort.

One, slight and barely her own height, drove her to her knees at its approach and she could feel the wet runnels of her tears down her cheeks.

"You were the best of us all, Sterlyn," Alexis told the shade of Sterlyn Artley. "It was you who truly saved us at Giron, keeping the lads at their guns through that Hell. I — I feel like I stole from you, using it as I did on Erzurum, I —"

Alexis broke off, for the dream was differing now.

Behind the usual shadows were new ones, but not dark.

These sparkled with light as they strode toward her, passing close on either side. They turned featureless heads toward her as they went by and seemed to laugh.

"What is this?" Alexis asked.

This nightmare was for the dead, not the living, as she somehow knew these figures were.

One even gave her a jaunty salute as it passed, soundless mirth echoing in her mind.

But where these sparkling figures walked, the shadows stirred. Their footsteps roiled the very essence of this place, and new figures rose — these darker than any she'd seen before.

From each of the shining, living, figures' footsteps the dead rose to surround Alexis. They huddled about her in misery and pain, each pointing or staring or somehow wordlessly demanding Alexis pay for what she'd done, how she'd wronged them.

"I had to," Alexis whispered, understanding who these were.

The glowing figures of the pardoned pirates moved on out of sight, yet even there more shadows rose in their footsteps.

She'd known it as she offered the pardon, known it as she signed them, yet she'd gone on anyway to free the slaves on Erzurum.

Some of the pirates would go home, to whatever homes awaited them after so many years roving, and live out the rest of their lives in peace — but others would not.

Others would return to their pardoned trade — taking ships, killing crew, looting and raping their way through Fringe world towns and villages.

"It's no more than they'd have done if I hadn't pardoned them!" Alexis cried, shocked by the density of the figures around her. These weren't enemies or her fellows who'd fallen in action — these were innocents who'd pay the price of her decisions. "I couldn't stop them all entire!"

The shadows didn't care, closing in and grasping at her, seeming to rend her with each touch, though her body remained whole.

ALEXIS WOKE, shaking and sweating, bedclothes damp and clammy to the touch.

She swung her legs over her bunk's edge and stood.

Deep breaths.

She followed her own advice, taking in great lungfuls of air, slowly and deliberately as she calmed herself.

There was nothing for it, she knew — no point in thinking on it further. The dream would come no matter how much she rationalized things while awake, and now she knew what new horrors awaited her in sleep.

That she couldn't have stopped those pirates didn't matter, nor that she'd put an end to hundreds aboard the ships or dancing at the end of a rope after the action, nor all the lives who'd come off Erzurum and out from under Ness' hand.

The dream's scales had only the one side for balancing, and cared not at all for the other.

Alexis stood and paced a bit. She longed to call for Delaine and let his comforting bulk keep the dream away the rest of the night, but she couldn't.

Mongoose was properly in commission, at least until they reached Penduli and her own commission met its fate there. While some captains might take their spouses or lovers along on a sail, she'd not become one of them and rub the crews' nose in the comforts they couldn't enjoy.

She made her way to the sideboard and the bottles there.

Oblivion would do as well.

Cap off the bourbon and bottle halfway to her lips she paused, stood still, and lowered it.

No, she'd been down that road and she owed her crew better than a captain who drank herself to senselessness every night, no matter the cause.

She set the bottle back and replaced the cap.

A soft chittering came from the Creature's cage. Not the angry sound the thing usually made, but one that felt like an invitation.

Alexis sighed and made her way there.

She undid the latch carefully and slowly, so as to make no noise. Isom had promised to find how the thing escaped its cage so often, so had come to wake easily at such sounds, even from his berth in her pantry.

The Creature came to her hand in silence and she picked it up.

Back at her bunk she sat and raised the thing so that it hung limply from her grip around its middle and looked it in its dark, beady eyes.

"Look, you," she said, "not a word to anyone about this, right?"

She took the Creature's sniff for agreement.

"Especially to bloody Creasy."

This time she'd almost have sworn the thing sniffed amusement.

She lay back on her bunk, set the Creature on her chest where it curled into a ball and vibrated with its version of a purr as she stroked it.

Alexis closed her eyes and settled into a dreamless sleep.

FIFTY-NINE

THEY WERE TWO DAYS OUT FROM PENDULI AND WORKING THEIR way toward the system, when Alexis found herself too anxious to spend a watch on the quarterdeck. She wandered toward the gundeck, wishing to walk the ship and get a feel of her crew once more before they arrived at Penduli. There'd be little opportunity for such after, she thought — not once Admiralty was through with her.

After they arrived, she'd have to turn *Mongoose* back into some semblance of a civilian ship, pay off the crew as best she was able, and see the vessel protected from Admiralty's greedy hands. That wouldn't endear her to whatever board of inquiry was assembled to look into the matter any more than her other actions, but she could at least see Dansby didn't lose his ship.

That she'd be seeking the man out and possibly killing him for sending her into the Erzurum mess didn't make a difference. Promising to keep his ship safe and slitting his gullet were two different things.

She stopped first at the surgeon's compartment, but the man was out and about the ship, so settled for looking in on the wounded. All who were still alive would likely recover fully once they arrived at

Penduli and the station's medical facilities, save Morgan, from her boat crew, first injured in the crash and carted along so far across Erzurum's swamps. He'd yet to regain consciousness, and the surgeon gave poorer odds for that, for the man had been unconscious for so long.

Alexis laid a hand on his shoulder, certain he could feel her near.

"You take heart, Morgan, and stay with us," she whispered. "Your mates will speak ill of you if you kick off now, after they carried you halfway across Erzurum."

She spoke a word to each of the other injured, those she knew well and those she didn't — though her frequent visits on this sail home let her think she knew them each a little.

That task complete, Alexis made her way up toward the gundeck, thinking to speak to the rest of the crew, or merely wander *Mongoose's* length and feel the ship.

Coming up the companionway she heard voices, hushed, but with angry tones, and slowed her steps. She couldn't make out the words, nor who was speaking, but if there was conflict aboard she wanted to know of it.

She eased down a step, then another. A lull in the argument let her hear the sound of music coming from the gundeck, so whatever the argument was about it didn't affect too much of the crew — most seemed to be having a fine time, finally back aboard ship and off Erzurum's surface.

She thought for a moment whether she should intervene in the argument or merely ease her way back up the ladder. What a captain saw, the captain knew about, and it was sometimes better if the captain could pretend to take no notice. It might be better if she eased away and sent Dockett or Nabb to investigate. ...

"... put a bloody stop to it!" Dockett's voice rang out from the arguing pair.

Well, that settles the way of it, Alexis thought, letting her footsteps *thunk* down the last few steps, and then turning to face the two arguing before the gundeck hatch.

Dockett and Nabb both turned to face her, eyes going wide and, if she was any judge, paler than the typical spacer ought to be.

"Gentlemen," Alexis said. "Is there some trouble?"

The two shared a look, then, both quickly, "Trouble, no, sir, none!"

"I should hope not," she said. "Not from you who've been with me through all this already, and not when the new hands seem to be settling in so well, and us being nearly home." She nodded toward the hatch where the music sounded from. "This isn't about your bets, is it? I thought that was already settled."

"No, sir!" Dockett said. "It's —"

Her bosun cast a glance at the hatchway and Nabb did as well, then they both turned toward her, edging closer as though to hide the way to the gundeck.

There was a roar of laughter from the gundeck hatch, drowning out the music for a moment.

"The lads seem in fine fettle, so what is the matter?" She frowned. "And is that live playing?"

"It is, sir," Nabb said. "The lad Aiden. Got a guitar off the pirates as we left Erzurum, he did."

"Load of twangy bung-twaddle, sir," Dockett said, edging toward the hatch. "I'll put a stop to it."

"There's no need of that," Alexis said. In fact, a bit of music, and the fellowship that came with it, might be just the thing to lift her spirits and drive away the ghosts. "Certainly not. In fact, I might slip in and listen for a mom —"

"*Aye, sir, stoppin' it instanter, sir,*" Dockett said, slipping quickly away and through the hatch while Nabb stepped toward her.

A loud bit of chorus echoed through the companionway before the bosun slammed the hatch with a forceful *clang*.

"*... look me hearties, see me mates? Us lads were not forgotten ...*"

"It's a rough, tune, sir," Nabb said. "You know how the men are. To have an officer, much less the captain —"

Alexis frowned as the men on the gundeck raised their voices to sing over the shouts of the bosun, both coming garbled through the hatch.

"Was that my name?" she asked.

"Name, sir? Couldn't hear it, myself, sir," Nabb said, his own voice echoing in the companionway. "But if you've a moment, sir, there's a thing about your boat and resupply from the new purser —"

Nabb gestured up and forward to where her boat nestled against *Mongoose's* hull.

Alexis sighed. She saw that both Dockett and Nabb were trying to keep her from the gundeck and that only deepened her sadness. She supposed they were right to do it — her days as a midshipman, when she might sit with the lads and share a pint, were over. They deserved their fun without the judgmental eye of an officer looking on.

She followed Nabb to her boat, only half-hearing her coxswains lament on how miserly the purser had been in resupplying it, as though the man thought his temporary warrant on *Mongoose* would somehow become permanent and —

Alexis tuned him out, knowing that, in the end it wouldn't matter. She ran fingertips along the bulkhead, feeling what might be her last ship. In a few short days, *Mongoose* would return to Dansby and she'd face whatever Admiralty might have in store for her.

SIXTY

Alexis' arrival at Penduli Station was quite unlike her arrival there from Giron with the victorious fleet of little ships.

Then she'd been aboard the flagship of an admiral, nearly in tears as the full fleet paid tribute to her crew aboard *Belial* and what they'd accomplished.

Now it was only *Mongoose* arriving, transmitting her written report to the port admiral as they transitioned to normal-space at L4, and enduring the long slog toward the station while awaiting a reply.

That reply did not come before she brought *Mongoose* alongside the station's quay and made fast. Docking tube extended and sealed to the station's airlock, Alexis, flanked by Villar and Delaine, stepped through to find that her report had not exactly been ignored — for she found, waiting for her, not only Penduli's port admiral, but several captains she assumed were senior on station, and none of whom she knew, save one.

"Ellender," she murmured, eyes locked on the man.

"Sir," Villar said.

"*Mon coeur*," Delaine murmured, with just the barest touch of his fingertips to her arm.

Alexis was having none of the restraint their voices urged. She cleared the lock's hatch, shrugging off her officers' attempts to call her back, and strode toward Ellender, ignoring both the other captains and the admiral.

The admiral had her written report. The lost spacers were safe on Enclave — though crowded and on sparse rations, they were in no danger. More and better ships would be sent to retrieve them, and there was nothing in Alexis' next actions that might impede that. She'd be judged on what she'd already done, and there was nothing, she thought, in these next actions that might change that, either.

But before she was taken up, and she suspected the file of Marines behind the admiral and captains were there for that purpose, she had a promise to keep.

"Lieutenant Carew —"

She ignored whoever spoke and stopped a pace away from Ellender who was staring at her with barely disguised hatred.

"Captain Ellender, where is Lieutenant Deckard?"

"I had him hanged and left adrift, as I hope to see you soon," Ellender said. "Admiral Acton, this person was in league with —"

"I read your report, Captain Ellender, as I will hers. There's far too much to —"

"Captain Ellender," Alexis said, overriding the admiral and ignoring his astonished look, "on behalf of my principal, Captain Wendale Kannstadt of the Hanoverese Navy, I name —"

"Sir —" Villar was at her elbow, tugging her to the side.

"Alexis —" Delaine was at her other arm.

"—you coward, abandoner — "

"Carew!" Admiral Acton fairly yelled, but Alexis had attention only for Ellender who'd backed up a step, eyes wide.

"—and murderer, sir! Name your second that we might —"

"Marines! Shut this —"

"—arrange a meeting, sir, or be known craven!"

Rougher hands than Villar's or Delaine's seized her arms and dragged her back a step.

"This is outrageous!" Ellender said.

"Carew! What are you about?" Admiral Acton stepped between her and Ellender now that there was space.

"My duty, sir," Alexis said. She leaned to the side so that she could see Ellender. "Your second, sir? I've need of a name, instanter!"

"Well, undo it!" Acton yelled. "Queen's officers may not duel!"

"I'm acting as second, sir, not —"

"*I do not bloody care!*" Acton yelled. He paused and looked around into the silence that engulfed the quayside.

In addition to their little group, the ships to either side of *Mongoose* had crew and officers out and about, all stopped in their work to watch the drama unfolding. More were coming from ships farther away.

"We'll take this to my offices," Acton said.

ACTON'S OFFICES were quite crowded, as it seemed none of the captains who'd accompanied him to the quay wished to miss the rest of the show.

Alexis sent Villar and Delaine back to the ship to arrange leave for the crew after so much time of deprivation on first Erzurum and then Enclave. They were reluctant to go, but she insisted, both for the sake of *Mongoose's* crew and themselves — she didn't want them tarred with her actions.

"Very well, then," Acton said once they were all settled — it nearly more than Alexis could bear to sit, drink in hand, with Ellender but two seats away. "First, Carew, I'll have you withdraw your challenge and we'll get that settled."

Alexis shook her head. "I will not, sir. I've read the regulations, sir, and there's no prohibition against a serving officer acting as second in a challenge. In fact, sir, it's frequently done."

"Not on behalf of a foreign officer," he said. "Not on behalf of a foreign officer with whom we are still, technically, in state of war, cease-fire be damned!"

"It's not prohibited, sir."

"*That's because such a thing would never bloody happen!*" Acton pounded a fist on his desk. "There are any number of absurd things the regulations don't explicitly prohibit, Carew! That's because we rely on Queen's officers to *not act the bloody fool!*"

"With respect, sir —"

"Yes, that would be quite refreshing."

"Sir, I gave my word to a fellow officer, foreign service notwithstanding, and I will fulfill it. Captain Ellender —" Alexis took a deep breath, wondering what she might say to make Acton see Ellender as she did. "Sir, I have no further words for Captain Ellender until he names his second ... but you may find that the —" She swallowed hard, still astounded at the number. "—twenty-nine thousand one hundred eighty-nine men awaiting transport on Enclave do."

Alexis turned her gaze to Ellender, who'd gone white at her words, though she still addressed the admiral.

"While I do not act as their second, sir, I'm given to understand you'll be faced with more than a few resigned commissions when Captain Ellender's fellow captains arrive." She smiled at Ellender. "Regulations being what they are, sir."

ALEXIS TOOK A DEEP, cleansing breath, possible now that she'd delivered Kannstadt's challenge, little hope there might be of a meeting between the two. She might, at least, send the Hanoverese captain a description of Captain Ellender's face as he hurriedly begged leave of Admiral Acton and rushed from the office. She suspected he might resign his own commission and flee Penduli — if not, well, she'd arrange somehow for word of the man's eventual fate to make it back to Kannstadt.

With Ellender's departure it was as though all of the tension in the office left with him, and the occupants sat in silence for a moment.

"You've brought me a mess, Carew," Acton said, finally.

"I am sorry, sir," Alexis said.

"No doubt. Captain Ellender's report painted the situation back there in the Barbary in quite a different light — made it sound as though there must be only a few men left on the planet, irretrievable, and fleeing with those he had was the best course."

"Of course, sir," Alexis said.

"A mess."

"I'm sorry, sir."

"So you said." Acton scrubbed at his face. "All right, then. We'll form a board of inquiry for this matter —" He nodded to one of his captains. "Sealworth, set it for a week from now, will you? We'll hear from you and your officers first, Carew — and Captain Ellender and his. By the time we're done with that we should have the first of the ships I'll send to Enclave back here and hear from those officers." He sighed. "In the meantime, Carew, your ship is to stay where it is. You and your officers may make use of quarters on station if you wish, but —" He held up a warning finger. "—you stay away from Captain Ellender, hear?"

"Aye, sir. Thank you, sir."

Alexis thought of Skanes aboard *Mongoose* and the word she brought that the Marchant Company, one of the largest in the kingdom, with more than a few political ties had been in league with the pirates.

"Ah, sir, there is another person you may wish to hear testimony from."

Acton stared at her for a moment, then narrowed his eyes. "Has the mess grown larger, Carew?"

"I am sorry, sir."

SIXTY-ONE

ALEXIS CAME AWAKE PEACEFULLY AND EASILY, BUT WITHOUT opening her eyes. She was curled up against Delaine's side — a delight of being housed in Penduli Station's officers' quarters, rather than aboard *Mongoose* — arm and leg thrown over him in certainly not any sort of way that would indicate fear of him disappearing while she slept, no matter how it might appear. The little stings of terror whenever he was out of sight were easing, she was sure.

She pressed her cheek more tightly against him, his chest hair ticking her nose, so she twitched it and ...

Delaine did not, she recalled, have so very much in the way of that.

Alexis opened her eyes to find the bloody Creature curled on Delaine's chest, tail toward her face, and her nose mere centimeters from the thing's —

"Shoo," she whispered.

It ignored her, much as it always did, but began kneading Delaine's chest with its little forepaws.

How was it even here? She'd sent it off with Isom to her own quarters, Delaine's being larger with him being a captain and from a foreign service. The thing would have had to make its way along two hundred meters of corridor and three hatches.

"*Shoo!*"

"Your friend is most comforting, *ma petite*," Delaine whispered. "I do not mind."

"It's not my —"

A buzzing from both their tablets, jumbled with some other items on a nearby table, interrupted them.

"Bugger," Alexis muttered. "I'd hoped to have more time this morning."

Delaine grunted as the Creature rose and hopped to the floor.

"Are you concerned?"

"It's only a board of inquiry, not a court martial — yet." Alexis shrugged. "I did what I did, and I'll not gainsay it. If they don't like how I got our lads home, then they'll make that clear to me, I suppose."

"I am unfamiliar with your Admiralty still," Delaine said. "And *La Baie Marche* under Hanover is nothing to compare. What might they do — if they are to make this displeasure clear?"

Alexis didn't wish to think on that any longer, much less discuss it with Delaine. There was no sense in him worrying along with her about whether there was a noose in her future for usurping the Queen's authority.

Perhaps, at best, I can hope to be cashiered and sent back home to Dalthus.

"Whatever they wish, I suppose," she said with a sigh. "It's best we rise and face them, though."

They rose from the bed. Alexis gathered up her boots from the floor where the Creature was gnawing on one heel, and slid the hatch open to shoo it out with a foot.

"Find your own way back to Isom or don't, you bloody great vermin. If you found your way here, you can — oh!"

A captain in the uniform of the French Republic, was just sliding his own hatch shut across the corridor.

He looked first at Alexis' face, peeping around her hatch as she'd not yet dressed, then down to where her bare leg wrapped around the edge, toes pointed to poke the Creature, which sat to stare up at the French captain with its head cocked to one side.

"*Bon ... jour ... mademoiselle?*" he said, drawing it out a bit doubtfully as the Creature bared teeth at him in a way that had him press his back to his hatch and fumble a bit for the latch to return inside.

"*Bonjour, capitaine,*" Alexis said, prodding the Creature with her toe again in hopes it would dash off to find Isom ... or find Penduli Station more to its liking and take up residence in some curry shop.

"*Qu'est-ce que c'est?*"

"Oh." Alexis prodded the thing again, but it made to nip at her toe, so she withdrew her foot. "Ah ... *le rat?*"

"*C'est gros,*" the captain said.

"Yes, it is," Alexis agreed.

Isom chose that moment to enter the corridor and cry out.

"Boots!"

Alexis' clerk rushed down the corridor, scooped the Creature up into his arms and began alternating excuses to Alexis while coddling and petting the thing.

"Sorry, sir, I don't see how he got out ... thought the crate was latched double before I turned in and ... how he found you, I couldn't say, either." Isom edged away. "I'll just see him safe, shall I?"

Both Alexis and the French captain watched him go out of sight, then shared a look.

She opened her mouth to say something, what she wasn't quite sure, but he spoke first.

"*Fou Bifteck,*" he said with a shake of his head as he walked way.

Alexis almost huffed after him, but slid Delaine's hatch shut instead. She could hear the shower running in the room's small bath compartment.

"Your neighbor thinks I'm crazy," she called to him.

"You are a New Londoner," Delaine said simply.

They showered — each receiving somewhat more assistance from the other than was strictly efficient — and dressed, then left for the board of inquiry. Alexis was nervous, but tried not to show it so as not to worry Delaine.

In the small lobby of the visiting officers' quarters, a clerk stopped them.

"Lieutenant Carew! There's a merchant captain just there — been waiting for you," he said.

"Thank you."

Alexis looked where he pointed and found Commodore Skanes — well, properly Captain Skanes — approaching. She was dressed in her full Marchant Company uniform.

"Lieutenant," she said.

"Captain Skanes." Alexis thought the woman looked as nervous as she herself felt.

"I'd heard your testimony was today," Skanes said, "as is my own. Would you mind terribly if I walked with you?"

"Not at all."

"Thank you."

Skanes fell in with them as they left, heading for the busier, more public corridors of the Naval section. The board of inquiry had been set a compartment on very nearly the opposite side from where all those who might be called as witnesses were being housed.

They stopped for tea and buns from a vendor's stall, setup in the main corridor just outside the visiting officer's quarters and a few steps outside the range of odors from the nearby Naval mess. Alexis didn't think she could stomach anything more and Delaine typically ate only some sort of pastry and a bit of coffee for breakfast.

The vendor had coffee, but not a very good one, if Delaine's expression was to be trusted.

"Not to your liking?" Alexis asked.

"It is as weak as your teas," Delaine said.

"Perhaps some milk and sugar then?" Alexis teased.

Delaine shuddered, and Alexis grinned. She stepped close to him as they walked, their hands occupied with breakfast, but able to press close at least.

Skanes remained silent as they walked, staring ahead, the bun and cup in her hands apparently forgotten, for she'd taken neither bite nor sip of either.

Alexis eyed her with some sympathy. She was, after all, about to destroy her career with the Marchants, and likely her career a'space all entire, for what merchant house would hire a captain who'd said such damning things about an employer?

"You're not eating?" Alexis observed, thinking to prompt the woman into speaking. She'd sought them out for some reason, after all.

"It seems odd to be wearing this uniform on my way to do this, but I couldn't think what else to wear," Skanes said.

It was an odd comment, but Alexis knew what strange places the mind went under stress.

"I mean," Skanes went on. "I'm certainly released from the Company, though they've not said so formally yet — and I'd not sail for them again, in any case — so am I even entitled to wear it? Do you think the captains on the board will think it disingenuous at all? I looked for something else, but couldn't find better, I thought — do you suppose I should mention that?"

"You'll have a fair time just answering their questions, if it's anything like my last court martial," Alexis said, then her face went hot as she realized how that sounded. "Not that I'm any sort of old hand at —"

"I mean," Skanes went on as though Alexis hadn't spoken, "I used to wear this uniform quite proudly, you know? Being a Marchant captain meant something — they'd only take the best, after all, so what did that make me? And now —"

Alexis realized the woman was simply venting her nerves, which, oddly, made Alexis feel a bit better about her own upcoming testimony. She pressed closer to Delaine, chewed the last of her bun, and took a sip of tea with one ear cocked to Skanes in case a comment of support became necessary.

The knowledge she need not pay too close attention to Skanes left Alexis free to think of other things.

The quay corridor alternated between crowded and nearly empty as they moved along, depending on whether a ship or its boats were docked at each lock they passed. Where there was a crowd, it was a steady stream of men and crates from the warehouses and chandleries to the airlocks. More vendor stalls were set up here and there, catering to those crews whose officers would give them a bit of a break during their efforts — or disconsolately moving on to greener pastures when they finally determined they'd chosen poorly and found a crew run by Tartars.

It appeared that was the decision a vendor ahead of them had made, as he took down his sign offering brekkie pies for as little as tuppence for a thin slice.

It seemed an odd choice, though, to close up shop, for she could see the work crew's midshipmen eyeing the stall eagerly. There were three of those supervising the men and midshipmen were legendarily hungry, so she'd have thought the man would stand a decent chance of some business once a few of the crates were shuffled about.

Odder still was that the vendor didn't fully load his cart before moving it, just unlocked the wheels and pushed, leaving a few boxes he'd normally stack aboard in place. Perhaps he was simply moving the cart to a better location to serve the men.

"I suppose I might find a place with one of the very small lines," Skanes went on, and Alexis returned her attention to her. "There's no future in it, of course, save sailing all my days — but it would keep a hull around me and there're worse fates, I suppose."

I could speak to Avrel Dansby for you, she didn't say. *Assuming he survives our next meeting.*

She might, even, if Dansby and Eades could explain how they'd not bothered to warn her about Wheeley and Ness and their pirate band, despite Dansby's being so well-known to them.

It would serve Dansby right to have to take Skanes on as a favor to me for this mess, and him have to deal with her haughtiness.

Yes, she might very well do that. Perhaps write Skanes a letter of recommendation and send her in search of the man.

They paused as a group of spacers crossed the corridor in front of them, pushing a floating pallet loaded with crates of new shot canisters.

The vendor was pushing his cart nearly as hard, then, oddly, let it go to roll forward on its own toward the line of Navy men and their own burdens.

Well, that's —

Even as her mind was wondering at it, Alexis' body was in motion. She couldn't say why — only that the vendor had such an odd look to him. Not nervous, but determined — a far more determined look than selling brekkie pies would call for in even the most difficult environment. But even that was likely some attempt to put a reason to an action she simply took.

Creasy's later claim that she'd actually heard a sharp, angry chitter of warning in the corridor was right out.

"*Cover, lads!*" she yelled.

Alexis took Delaine to the deck with her, and none too gently.

Her left arm flung out to strike his chest, her left knee into the back of his, and then she twisted to drive him down and fall atop him, remnants of tea and coffee splashing them both.

Older hands among the work crew, whether sensing something odd themselves and taking the excuse of her call or simply responding to what could only be an officer's voice, flung themselves down, arms about their heads. One had the sense to slap the controls of the antigrav pallet he hauled and duck behind it as it crashed to the floor.

"What —" Skanes had time to say.

"*Belay that!*" a startled midshipman called.

But over them all was the vendor's cry of, "*Tiocfaidh ár lá!*"

Then the world disappeared in a fiery roar.

SIXTY-TWO

ALEXIS GROANED AND REALIZED SHE WAS WAKING WITH somewhat more reluctance than she could ever remember having in the past. Her head ached and her stomach was none too happy with her either. She didn't remember drinking any great deal the night before — but, then, she likely wouldn't if she was feeling this bad of a morning.

She made to scratch at something tickling her face — and, more, to shove the damn Creature away, for it was surely the cause — but her right arm wouldn't seem to work.

Numb — perhaps Delaine was laying on it, if he were in the same condition she was, they'd not have made it to their more normal positions of her throwing an arm and leg over him while they slept.

She tried with her left, but that was brought up short, twisted in some way in the bedclothes.

She groaned again. Isom would certainly have words for her after she'd left this sort of drinking behind.

"She's waking."

That brought her more fully awake and cut through much of the fuzziness in her head, for the voice hadn't been Delaine's or Isom's and none but those two should be in her rooms.

White light, painfully bright, cut through her vision — at least her left eye's, for the right was stuck closed with whatever gunk had coated it in her sleep. She'd rub that away if she could only raise her arms.

Which she tried again, finding that it was neither Delaine nor bedclothes which had her entangled.

The painful brightness was due to the lights, as well the white ceiling, drapes around the bed, bedclothes, and nearly everything else in what could only be a hospital room — the incessant beeping of some devices making her head throb in time as she noticed them. Her left arm, she could at least identify now, was immobile from a soft cuff around her wrist, though she still couldn't feel her right.

"What?" Her voice croaked and her lips failed to part fully, stuck together and dry.

"Here," the voice said and a face swam into her vision.

"Dansby?"

A cup pressed against her lips and she sipped gratefully at the icy water, even as she wondered at his presence. What was he doing here? What was *she* doing here? The last she remembered was —

Alexis frowned. Dining with Delaine the night before she was to testify before the board — had she been in some sort of accident? Where was Delaine?

"Delaine?" she croaked.

"Your young frog's better off than you," Dansby said. "He's resting nearby. The nurse will go and get him."

"I oughtn't," a man's voice she didn't recognize said. "Oughtn't to have woke her up for you. Doctor said two more days under."

"Go," yet a third voice said, "and don't return until I've gone."

Alexis squinted against the brightness and blurriness until she placed face with name.

"Malcombe Bloody Eades and Avrel Buggering Dansby at my bedside? Who'd I bollox up to deserve this? Where's Delaine?"

"I just told you, Rikki, he's nearby and well."

That was a relief — just the moment's fear that they'd been in some sort of accident and he'd been hurt, that she might have lost him, must have set her blood and heart to racing. Her head throbbed more to the increased beeping in the room.

"Do you see?" the unknown voice asked.

"My good man," Eades said, "you know who I work for, now out. And not a word of this or it will go poorly for you."

There was the sound of a hatch working, but Alexis' thoughts returned to Delaine. He was all right, if Dansby was to be believed — which did focus her on the bit about Dansby being there.

Alexis shook her left arm.

"Arm," she said, weakly.

"Aye, Rikki," he said, setting the cup on a bedside table. "They tied your wing to keep you from pulling at things." His fingers worked at the cuff. "Now you're awake and sensible, there's no call to — *urk!*"

Alexis lunged.

Avrel Dansby at her bloody bedside was closer than she'd ever thought she'd get to the man again. Conspiring with Eades to send her off to the bloody Barbary where his own old fellow Ness was the target, sending her to Wheeley who was involved to his eyebrows in the bloody mess, and all without telling her what to expect.

She might be injured and he might have whatever power had so terrified the band of pirates of him, but she'd beat them and she could take their bogeyman as well.

She couldn't roll and grasp him with her right hand as well, but she got his face with her left. Fingers clawed, she grabbed at him, getting her thumb inside his mouth as he spoke and clamping down with whatever strength she had left. Perhaps, if she could leverage around his teeth she might rip his bloody jaw right off, and his thrice-damned lying tongue with it.

"*'Ikki!*"

Dansby tried to pull back, but she got her grip and twisted. He could bite her, but she didn't think he could bite clear through her thumb before she did more damage to him.

"*Ow, 'uggerin' 'ell!*"

"You lying, *snake!*" Alexis rasped at him, though not loudly, for her mouth was still dry and she felt herself weakening quickly. "You *knew*! Had to have known!"

Eades stepped to Dansby's side.

"A 'it o' 'elp, 'an!" Dansby's head twisted to the side and nearly down to Alexis' bed as she pulled on him.

Alexis very nearly released Dansby to lunge at Eades, for he was as much to blame, but she remembered the Foreign Office man's speed when she'd once struck at him in full health. His bit would have to wait until she was out of hospital.

Eades grasped her wrist and tapped it, deceptively lightly for the shot of pain that ran up her arm, causing her fingers to go limp and unresponsive.

"Much as I'd enjoy seeing you rip his face off, Miss Carew, I'm afraid I can't allow it. We've only woken you because there's a word or two I'd pass along in person before I must leave."

"You bastards!" she said. "Sending me off into that mess without a bit of warning of what to expect!"

Eades sighed, but Dansby stood up, rubbing at his jaw and giving her a wounded look, then his shoulders slumped and he reached out to grasp her limp hand.

Alexis grasped it back, though her fingers were still so numb and weak Dansby might not have realized she was trying to break one of his fingers.

"I swear to you, Rikki, I didn't know," Dansby said.

Alexis gave off trying to will strength into her left hand and glanced at Dansby's face, the look of which shocked her. His normally dapper appearance was rough and haggard — hair out of place, unshaved where it was normally clean and beard ragged where usually well-trimmed. His eyes were red-rimmed and narrowed in what she would almost take for true concern in a normal human being.

"I sent you to Wheeley thinking he'd point you *away* from Ness and his group — point your privateering at some independents, is what I thought," Dansby went on, "and I'd certainly never have expected that bastard to have let himself get caught up in taking fleet spacers. Sweet Dark, the arrogance of him. Thought certain those must have made planetfall on some world never sees a merchant but in a jubilee year and merely needed finding." He took a deep breath. "I *swear it*, Rikki, by everything I hold dear."

The often-smuggler, sometime-pirate, and likely always confidence-man's voice sounded quite sincere to her. She could almost believe him, which was likely an effect of whatever drugs the hospital had put in her.

Eades cleared his throat. "Such a nugget of truth from Mister Dansby is a rare and precious thing. One should grasp it. None of my sources, either, suggested any pirates, much less Ness' band, were at all involved with our spacers. I'd thought the privateering merely a convenient ruse for you to be in the Barbary and agreed Mister Wheeley would do an adept job of steering you away from his own band of scoundrels, who were a greater force than any single private ship could hope to confront."

"I swear it, Rikki," Dansby repeated.

It seemed oddly important to him that she believe him, so she nodded. She could always shoot him once she recovered more if she found out he was lying. Wheeley *had*, when she was able to open the miser's fists on information, pointed them in much the same directions as Skanes, which was to say, nowhere in particular.

"You're both bloody, addle-pated scrubs."

Eades sniffed.

"At times, Rikki, at times."

None of which explained why she was wrapped up in hospital, though.

"What happened?" she asked.

"You don't recall?" Eades asked.

Alexis made to shake her head, then thought better of it at the twinge of pain.

"Last is dinner the night before my testimony — did I —"

"It's five days since then," Eades said. "We ourselves arrived two days ago after hearing rumors of what happened. Word of Captain Ellender's arrival spread and we took ship immediately, thinking you must be involved somehow."

"The board?" Alexis asked.

"All right," Eades said. "The board's not heard you yet. You were attacked on your way to —"

"Attacked?" Her voice was growing raspy again and Dansby took up the cup of water to hold it to her lips once more.

"When someone takes the time to relate events to you, Carew," Eades said with a sniff, "it will often go faster if you don't question every revelation — just assume, for the moment, the teller isn't a bloody nincompoop and will get the whole thing out if you give him time."

Alexis thought he might have got the whole thing out in the time he spent admonishing her, but held her tongue.

"Thank you." Eades began pacing the room. "It's said you had the poor fortune to walk into an attack by separatists — at least if the corridor video of the attack is to be believed. You, your Frenchy fellow, and Captain Skanes were quite close to the blast and —"

"Blast?"

Alexis had thought some sort of bar fight or robbery attempt, but had there been a bomb? And if so, how badly was she hurt — they'd said Delaine was all right, but —

"Where's Delaine?"

Eades sighed.

"Bugger off, old man," Dansby said, "you've never cared about another in your life, so you can't imagine." He pulled out his tablet and tapped at it. "There, Rikki, I've sent him a message you're up — and your man, Isom, as well, for he's been haunting the corridors and driving the staff mad. They'll likely be here in a moment, so I'll tell the rest."

Eades shrugged and stepped away from her bedside.

"Skanes was killed," Dansby said bluntly, "and it was only you throwing your fellow to the deck that kept the two of you from it as well.

"*He's fine*," Dansby stressed as Alexis opened her mouth again. "A nick or two where you weren't enough to cover him, but ... as it was —" He nodded to her right arm. "— you'll recover, but they've said it'll not be an easy road."

Alexis brought her left hand over and felt at her right. It was solidly wrapped, with the ridges of tubing and other medical devices embedded in the covering.

"I'm sure some doctor'll be along soon to tell you, but the gist is you'll keep the arm and it'll function with a bit of work."

"Function," Alexis repeated. She raised her hand, almost fearfully to her head and felt at the bandages over her right eye.

"That'll be all right as well, they say," Dansby told her. "You've not lost the eye, at least."

"Sweet Dark," Alexis muttered.

It was too much to take in.

She'd sailed to the Barbary, engaged pirates, taken a whole bloody planet, and barely made it off the pirate flagship before its fusion plant went up, all with merely a cut or two — only to be blown up in the heart of Naval territory on Penduli Station. It was difficult to credit —

Alexis paused.

"You said, 'It's said.'"

"What?"

"Not you." She nodded at Eades who was across the room studying some device in the corner. "Mister Eades, you are not one to be careless with words — what did you mean by that?"

Eades raised an eyebrow. "Only that the Gaelics off Killarney II have taken responsibility for the blast and renewed demands for New

London to pull out." He shrugged. "Your bad luck they chose to attack here ... at Penduli ... half the kingdom away from Killarney, or any real political target for that matter ... after —" He shrugged. "— nearly three decades of silence on that front ... and right along your route from quarters to the inquiry room. Quite bad luck."

"What do you mean?"

Dansby snorted. "Come, now, Rikki — you know him. I might be a snake, but he's a bloody spider, aye? Sees everything as convoluted as his own webs, and makes up what he can't prove."

Eades shrugged.

"You think this was something else?" Alexis asked.

"Rikki, don't follow him down these paths, he's —"

"There was a time you walked them with me," Eades said.

Dansby laid a hand on Alexis' shoulder and turned to glare at the Foreign Office man. "There was a time I didn't understand the costs," he said. "But I came to know them all too well, didn't I?"

"What are you two on about?" Alexis asked.

Eades shrugged again. "Captain Skanes is dead and her testimony with her. Neither the board nor anyone else will ever hear her testimony regarding her former employers. Luck cuts bad for some and quite well for others, it seems."

"But she told others what she learned," Alexis said. "Her testimony notwithstanding, surely —"

Eades sighed. "Hearsay, slander, libel, defamation *per se*, Miss Carew. Be careful what you repeat of what you've heard, for the ways of silencing you are legion. Only Skanes would have had the facts of what she was told to pass on to you and the other privateers, in conflict with the real state of the Barbary, or what the pirates said to her. Now she is dead and that testimony with her."

Alexis frowned. "Are you saying the Marchan —"

"I am, I assure you, *not* saying such a thing," Eades said. He didn't even bother to look at her, just let his eyes idly scan the room.

"But the pirates themselves would have the knowledge and could testify. Their records, surely —"

Eades sighed. "Alas, piracy and good clerkship do not, in general, have compatible skill-sets. As well, the average pirate would know nothing of such things — only the captains, and they only that certain ships were off-limits. The why would be closely held." Eades sighed again. "Of those pardoned who might have knowledge, I imagine we'll begin hearing of their deaths soon. The Gaelics —" His voice was heavy with sarcasm. "— are nothing if not thorough."

Eades stood and patted Alexis' shoulder as if she were a child, but his voice became deadly serious.

"Of course, you're in no danger from separatists, so it's *best* if you simply put the worry out of your mind and *not speak of it* again. You've no need to worry about it, as you're to be packed off to your home as soon as you may travel." He grinned at Alexis' look. "The inquiry is done, or at least what may be done on Penduli. The board decided it were better to pack the whole review off to higher authorities ... and remove you from the station as quickly as possible."

Home. Injured, but whole, if these two were to be believed, yet with Admiralty's decision still to be made and the outcome still hanging over her head. Regardless, home —

With Delaine? She'd have to see about that — having just got him back, there was no way she'd allow them to be separated so soon.

"So, I must be off," Eades said, then, as though he were some sort of paternal uncle — or a thoroughly shudder-inducing Foreign Office man — he bent over and brushed her cheek with his lips, whispering low, "For yourself and those you love, be seen to accept it was the Gaelics ... for now."

He stood and, without a word to Dansby, left.

Dansby sat and took her hand again. "I should be going too, but I'll sit with you until your young man returns." There was a beep from the machinery above her bed. "Or until you've gone to sleep again, which it appears they've decided you shall."

Alexis struggled against the cool flow of the drug, she couldn't go back to sleep — not until she'd seen Delaine again and made sure with her own eyes that he wasn't injured.

"Who's Kaycie?" she demanded, thinking to keep Dansby talking to her and fight the drugs. "And give me nothing about some girl you wished to bed, for one doesn't set the keys to a ship by that. And Ness said something of regrets."

She'd wondered since he'd first given her the codes to run *Mongoose*, his *Elizabeth*, at such an odd set of phrases to take control of the ship, but hadn't wanted to pry at the time. Now, she thought, he owed her a bit of an answer — and she could always blame the impoliteness of prying on the drugs.

"Are you certain Ness is dead?" he asked instead.

Alexis nodded, setting her head to spinning in an oddly pleasant way. She tried it again.

"He is," she said. "Hard to believe you were ever involved with one such." She giggled, the part of her horrified by that buried deep in the pillowy softness pumping through her veins. "Dansby & Ness ... sounds like a sweets shop."

"A product more sour and bitter, I assure you. Was it a hard go for him?"

Alexis thought of what it must have been like for the pirate leader, pinned to the decking where he could hear the countdown on the fusion plant before it went, hearing the clump of boots through the hull, the clangs and thumps as *Mongoose* worked her way free and he was left behind to his fate, then nothing but silence and the knowledge he'd failed to take his old enemy's ship with him before the fire. She still thought, no matter how quick, there must be an instant in such a case where a man would know he was being consumed.

Her eyelids drooped, but she nodded. "I think it was, quite."

Dansby looked away and took a deep breath. "Good. Then Kaycie was someone who can finally rest easy."

The drugs were taking tighter hold and Alexis' thoughts blurred.

"He kept the ears," Alexis said.

Dansby's eyes widened.

"In a box, with Presgraves' head, he said — said he whispered to her at times."

"So, Presgraves was there when a fusion plant went?" For a wonder, Dansby actually smiled at that, though his eyes were wet. "She'd have liked that." He sobered. "I'm sorry you had to meet him, Rikki, but I'm in your debt for what you settled."

Alexis scowled at him — or one of him, there seemed to be three or more of the man now, something she thought the universe itself might weep at. She fought the drugs, thinking Delaine must come at any moment and not wanting to miss him again.

"What happened between you?" she asked.

Dansby's smile fell. "That's another story, Rikki, for another time, with time enough between us to share a bottle or two."

Alexis' eyelids drooped despite her best efforts.

"I broke your ship," she said to Dansby.

"Rather expected that."

EPILOGUE

O', ease your pulling now, me mates,
And join we happy few.
It's raise a glass to Annalise
And Little Bit Carew.

Lord Cunningham, First Lord of the Admiralty, turned from the window as the others entered. He'd been idly wondering which departments filled the myriad buildings below him — he always did lose track of which was where, generally being able to summon whomever he wished to his own offices atop the central, highest tower. Those windows would likely be darkened in a bit, in any case, as they talked about fleet dispositions and those surfaces were used to display data — much as the walls, ceiling, and the surface of the long table dominating the center of the room could.

Neither were all of those entering of much importance in the coming meeting — it was a wonder to him that the question had risen to this level ... again.

The First Space Lord, Lord Rotherham, would have something to say about it, though with less weight now that the active fighting with

Hanover was at a stop. His bailiwick of strategy and operations was once again in decline with no real shooting going on. Although his twin responsibility for intelligence might come into play, given that the whole mess had started with the damned Foreign Office meddling in things they oughtn't ... again.

Cunningham fought back a grimace at the thought.

Bloody skulking about, he nearly muttered aloud.

Lady Swindmore, Second Space Lord and Chief of Naval Personnel, would certainly have a bit to say, as settling the returned spacers, nearly thirty thousand of their own and some four thousand French of the Berry March at last count, had set her department in a tizzy. As well she would be looking to the disposition of this meeting's cause ... again.

The next three through the door would have little to say, Cunningham thought, though Falkirk, Fourth and overseer of the Sick and Hurt board might put in a word or two — he nearly always did, though the preference of the weaselly little man was to see to the needs and perquisites of his pets, the ships' pursers and port chandlers, leaving the medical side of things to some deputy. Likely he brought some word to pass along from such-and-such subordinate, who was waiting in the anteroom should they wish to hear an opinion regarding the meeting's principal ... again.

The last three would certainly have ... opinions.

Fighting admirals all, at least still in name, for they could take to *darkspace* and command a fleet if they wished, though they were past their prime for such things.

Kinaellen, Admiral of the Fleet and the Red Squadron, Lady Larcbost, though she preferred Admiral of the White if one were to address her, viewing that title as more her own than the one acquired at birth, and Damerel of the Blue Squadron, least among the three and anxious for Kinaellen to retire so that he could take Larcbost's position as she moved to become Admiral of the Fleet.

Between the three, they commanded all of New London's fleets and ships, here in the home system, the Core worlds, all out to the edges of the Fringe, and even beyond, in the case of those Royal Navy ships tasked with exploration.

Tens of thousands of ships, ranging from the most massive liners which never left the Core to the slightest pinnace seeing to the Queen's tariffs and protecting trade between newly settled worlds, and tens of millions of men and women manning those ships, seeing to the ports, and a billion other details that kept what could be considered the mightiest navy to spinward of Old Earth running in fine fettle.

And they were here to speak about a single one of them ... again.

A bloody *lieutenant*, if one could believe it, and that a mere slip of a girl, barely ...

Cunningham stepped to his place at the meeting table and checked the records there.

Twenty. He shook his head in bewilderment. There were admirals five times that age who'd occupied the attention of those in this room for no more time than to approve the promotions list they graced with a hundred others, and this Carew's name had sullied their deliberations twice before already.

The squeaky wheel might get the grease — and this girl had got more than her share of that — but there was also some saying about hammers and which nails stuck up, wasn't there?

Cunningham waited until the others were at their places, then gestured for them to sit, taking his own place at the table's head.

"Is a special meeting really necessary on this, Cunningham?" the Third Space Lord asked.

Cunningham held up one hand. "A moment, Narfolk, and I'll explain." He tapped his tabletop. "Burchett, come in, please."

A moment later the door behind him opened and his First Secretary came in.

"Give them the number, Burchett," Cunningham ordered.

The newcomer cleared his throat and consulted his tablet. "Gentlemen," he said, "ladies, as Secretary to the Admiralty, I have totaled the notes from this incident and prepared a funding bill for Lord

Cunningham to take to Parliament, this being an amount in excess of, shall we say, discretion."

"The number, Burchett," Cunningham said.

"Keeping in mind, my lords, that a full accounting must await arrival of any late-come notes in hand from those farmers on ..." He glanced at his tablet. "Erzrum ... Erseroom ..." He shrugged. "In any case, the natives there are submitting their notes through Hanover, which must —"

"The total, Burchett?"

"Well, and keeping in mind, sirs, the vital work of Lord Falkirk's pursers and chandlers in discounting these notes so much as they are able, and —"

"Two million three-hundred thousand six hundred forty-two pounds," Cunningham said.

Burchett gave him a purse-lipped, scolding glance, then said, "Two million six-hundred thousand two hundred thirty-eight pounds, sir. A fresh packet just arrived this morning."

"Sweet Dark," Damerel muttered. "That's more than Chipley's entire fleet!"

"No, not so much as that, but as much as the ships he lost there!"

"And how many pirates?" Rotherham asked.

"Captured and paid for, sir, or pardoned?" Burchett asked.

Rotherham winced. "Never mind. I'd rather not know either one, I think."

"I told you so," Falkirk, Dameral quckly nodding agreement.

"We did," Dameral said. "Should have hung her after she mutinied."

Lady Larcbost curled her lip at the two. "Only because of your pet."

Dameral puffed air through pursed lips and scowled at her. She might be senior on the lists, but they were all — or nearly — equals here.

"Captain Neals is —"

"A bloody, abusive toad," Larcbost said, "who should never have —"

A beeping drew all eyes to Cunningham's tablet, then followed his to the room's windows where a procession of aircars could be seen approaching the building.

"Oh, blast," Cunningham muttered. "We're in it now, lads."

———

QUEEN ANNALISE, sovereign of New London, did not, as a matter of course, make unexpected visits.

She felt it was unfair to both the visited and her security detail to do so.

In this case, however, as the subject of the meeting she'd learned of touched, however tangentially, on her own prerogatives, she felt it justified.

A glance out her aircar's window to see the chaos of buildings that had become of Admiralty grounds since her grandfather had granted the lands for it was enough to firm her resolve as well. Though no current occupants of the tower's highest levels were personally responsible for the mess, they would act fine as proxies.

Her security detail — or some of it — landed first, on the private pad jutting out from the tower's top floor. They were still a bit more on edge than usual since the war, so Annalise indulged them. The New London Protective Service took its job seriously at all times, though, since there'd been more than one monarch assassinated in the nation's history — and accidents.

As her own aircar landed on the pad, the security force already there fanned out to flank her path to the building's door, as though she were a small child who might rush to the railing and fling herself through the static field and fall.

Not mentioning this or objecting to it was another indulgence, as so many of her detail had been with the family for decades and well-remembered the time forty years before when an avalanche on their favorite ski slope had taken Annalise's parents and older brother without warning — not that there was anything they could have done about an avalanche, or that the only thing to save Annalise from the same fate was the start of a head-cold which kept her indoors at the lodge.

Even with that she'd spent hours in that darkened, buried lodge before rescue.

She'd emerged from that to find that at fifteen years old, she'd gone from the latter in the old adage about monarchial children, "an heir and a spare," to Queen of the Realm — and her security detail had gone from quiet, and sometimes amused, exasperation at her own antics and adolescent attempts to evade them to outright panic.

She'd allowed them their worries and contingency planning ever since, not least because their reports to Parliament in those early months, about how she herself had changed and was no longer playing at escaping them, had gone a long way toward her efforts to avoid a Regency. Advisers she readily accepted, but a Regent, no matter her own age, would have chafed and she'd forced herself to grow up, seemingly overnight, so as to present the very best face to her Parliament.

Her own aircar landed and she stepped out, murmuring thanks to the security officer who offered her a hand — so that she might not slip or stumble and further embarrass his Service by breaking her neck on the eminently flat surface of Admiralty's landing pad.

The door to the tower was already held open and she made her way there, nodding to the Admiralty officials who flanked it and gestured her toward the First Lord's meeting room.

Annalise entered, gave polite and appropriate nods to the "Your Majesty's" cast her way by its now standing occupants, and stepped to the sideboard where refreshments for their meeting had been laid out. She waved away the assistance of the porters who waited on those at the conference table and began filling a small plate with pastry.

Admiralty always did supply itself with the best food — she

thought it had something to do with making up for the deprivations shipboard, now they were all planetside for the remainder of their careers.

"Good morning, my lords," she called out, not turning.

The chorus of "Good morning, Your Majesty," was almost, though not quite, in tune.

"So what amusements do your captains have for me today, my lords?" Annalise asked. She'd always found her Navy's insistence on the masculine form of address a bit ridiculous, especially with Lady Swindmore and Lady Larcbost right there at the table. There'd even been a few women in Cunningham's position, though she mused that "First Lady of Admiralty" as a title might bring to mind those rather gauche Americans who colonized out the other side of Old Earth — as would "First Space Lady" for that matter. And "Second," "Third," or, forfend, "Fifth Space Lady" might be something the Americans would even take offense at, thinking it a slight. They were a prickly lot, refusing to even call their new worlds "colonies" for some reason, and thinking everything the universe did was somehow revolving around them.

"Amusements, Your Majesty?" Cunningham asked.

"Yes," Annalise said, drawing it out a bit as she turned to face them, her face set in just the proper way — her smile like a beautifully tooled sheath around a deadly blade. "Any mutinies of my Navy's ships? Failed invasions of foreign worlds? A captain threatening to shoot the representative of a colonial government, perhaps?" And wasn't her staff *still* having to deal with objections from that official on the Fringe world of Al Jadiq? She took a dainty bite of one of the pastries. "Pardoned a few thousand thieves, murders, and rapists?" She took a breath. "Spent a billion pounds?"

"It's only two million three-hundred thou —" the Secretary to the Admiralty broke off at Annalise's glare and returned his eyes to his tablet, muttering, "So far, Your Majesty."

"Made me the largest slave-holder in the known universe?" the

Queen added, not wanting to leave anything off the list she'd so carefully rehearsed.

"It's a slow week, Your Majesty," Lady Larcbost said into the ensuing silence. "And the principal officer for your amusements is still laid up in ordinary, back at her home, until her wing's healed — I'm certain she'll have something to amuse you with once she's well and has a ship around her again."

Annalise turned her gaze to the woman, who grinned back at her with raised eyebrows. Notwithstanding they were old friends, had played together as children and still met for wine and shopping no less than once a month, despite the demands on their time, this was business and the Queen wished her admirals to understand her position.

It wasn't so much the things this girl -- this Carew -- did, it was the *way* she did them, and that she was still only a lieutenant. She took far too much on herself — more than most captains or even most admirals would dare. And, worst of all, perhaps, at this level, the girl's mad schemes *worked* — something Annalise herself had to admire. And, worse than that — worse than worst of all, to some eyes — what the girl did was *right*.

Annalise might often like to pull a pistol on some Fringe world leader herself, come to that, and Admiralty's inability to find and recall Chipley and his fleet, along with the thousands — her eyes burned and she took a tighter grip on her emotions — *tens of thousands* of her subjects manning those ships, had been like a dagger in her own heart. That so many had suffered so at the hands of pirates on some barbaric world of the Barbary ...

And this girl had got them all home, no matter the cost.

Annalise was used to sometimes being angered by the actions of others, frequently to admiring them, but envy was not a thing she was normally familiar with.

She realized that Larcbost was still grinning and the other admirals and lords were looking hopeful. That wouldn't do at all.

"I'm told there's a song," the Queen said flatly.

Faces, even Larcbost's, fell.

"A song the spacers of my Navy sing, featuring, of all things, their Queen and this lieutenant."

There appeared to be something of immense interest to her Lords of Admiralty on the surface of their conference table, as all eyes were focused there.

"The spacers," Larcbost said, "mean such things with the utmost —"

"And an oddly named pub," Annalise added.

Larcbost joined her fellows in studying the table.

The Queen surveyed her Lords of Admiralty and found their display of contrition satisfactory.

She took another, larger, bite of her pastry — it *was* quite good — and let them stew just a bit longer.

"What do you plan for her?" she asked finally.

Cunningham cleared his throat. "We were just about to begin discussing that when you arrived, Your Majesty."

"Oh, wonderful." Annalise took a much larger bite of pastry and waved the remnants at Their Lords of Admiralty as she chewed, encouraging them to continue and pay her no mind at all.

"Yes," Cunningham said, "of course." He took a deep breath and looked around the table. "Thoughts?"

"Stick her ... somewhere ... she can ... ah ... do ... no further harm?" Lord Narfolk suggested, watching Annalise carefully. "Junior lieutenant on a first-rate, perhaps?"

"I thought we were going to talk about how to keep her in-atmosphere, if not drum her out all entire, as Falkirk suggested?" Rotherham objected. The First Space Lord paid only the scantest attention to politics and was annoyingly open to speaking his mind without regard for consequences. "Perhaps even find some way to let her resign her bloody commission and go home for good and out of our hair. Can't imagine how we're even talking about a single lieutenant ... again."

Lady Larcbost, Admiral of the White, glanced at Annalise, but the Queen made a conscious effort to keep her expression bland. Larcbost sighed, then said, "Rotherham, if the men see this officer ill-treated, there'll be shot-canisters rolling on the decks from Penduli to New London itself."

She looked to Damerel and Kinaellen, finding nods of agreement from her fellows of the Red and Blue squadrons. Damerel might have it in for the girl over his pet, Neals, but he was no fool when it came to the feelings of the common spacer.

"Surely not!" Rotherham said. His outrage was clear in his voice as well as on his face. The rumble of shot canisters rolled on the ship's deck in the dark anonymity of the late watches was a way for them to express their displeasure with something.

Kinaellen, Admiral of the Fleet, steepled his fingers and pressed them to his lips. "The common spacer's a simple man, really. Has to be, and we select for it when we can. Needs to follow orders and be content with conditions most would find intolerable. But with that comes what you might call an over-developed sense of fairness — he'll be content with little, so long as all his fellows have the same little, if you understand — and an utter sense of loyalty. We select for that, or beat it into them if we have to, as well. Loyalty ... to their mates, their ship, the fleet, and —" He gave a nod to Annalise. "— the Queen." He cleared his throat. "In that order, I'm afraid, Your Majesty."

Annalise waved it away, her father had taken a heavy cavalry commission in his younger days and often told stories of his time there. She understood that when the fight was hardest, it was those you served with that you fought for, not Queen and country.

"What's your point?" Rotherham asked.

"You've been too much time away from a ship," Larcbost said. "Her speech to the court after that business with *Hermione?* Refusing clemency if her crew didn't receive it as well?"

"That record was sealed!" Rotherham objected.

Larcbost made a rude noise. "It's the *Fleet*, Rotherham — there might as well have been a live broadcast."

"Then Giron," Damerel continued. "Brawls between spacers and the army are *still* down since that — at least those not entirely for entertainment — and any spacer who can make the claim he was anywhere near the place doesn't pay for a drink if there's a regimental in the pub."

Rotherham opened his mouth to object again, then seemed to wilt in his seat.

"Now this," Damerel said. "She literally led a full third of Chipley's fleet out of bloody bondage. Like some sort of Pied Piper."

"I believe you mean Moses," Larcbost said.

"Do I?" Damerel frowned.

"And don't forget the common citizens," Cunningham said. "The pulpits are full of stories of redemption for those pirates, nevermind they'll likely all return to it. Pubs full of stories of the coin. Morale higher even than after Giron for this is viewed as sticking it to the Hannies and pirates both, somehow."

Larcbost nodded. "Regardless, those spacers will get new berths, and you know the tale's so good they'll drink on it for the next year or more." She eyed Annalise warily, then added. "There's a bloody song, after all." She chuckled. "We'll be lucky if there aren't pictures of the girl with bloody candles and incense aboard half our ships."

"Like as not find the same aboard captured pirates now," Damerel added his own chuckle. "Saint Carew, Patroness of Pardoned Pirates and Scourge of the Unrepentant."

Annalise sniffed, face impassive, and their lordships sobered with a great deal of throat clearing.

"I'm partial to Narfolk's suggestion," Larcbost said after a moment of silence.

Cunningham nodded, with a glance at Annalise. "Yes, a stint as junior lieutenant on a large ship, some boring patrol. She's had far too much time in command and needs seasoning in a proper post."

"It would teach her a bit of respect for authority and procedures," Narfolk said.

Falkirk cleared his throat. "There is the matter of who'll have her."

Several faces fell and Annalise raised an eyebrow.

"What do you mean?" Kinaellen asked.

"Well," Damerel put in for the now silent Falkirk, "one does have to admit she's a certain reputation amongst the officers, as well as the men."

"First Captain Neals, now Captain Ellender —" Falkirk said, finding his voice again.

"Him," Larcbost said.

"Yes, him," Falkirk said. "A fine —"

"Yes, yes," Larcbost said, "I'm sure."

"Regardless, Damerel said, "there does seem to be ... a disturbing pattern."

"That's your concern, Falkirk," Cunningham said, then nodded again. "Does that suit, Your Majesty?"

Annalise raised her eyebrows. "Suit? Oh, I am sorry, Lord Cunningham — I'm certainly not here to *interfere* in your decisions, only to observe and inform myself."

Cunningham pursed his lips and nodded slowly. "Of course, Your Majesty."

Annalise held his eye for a moment, until he looked away to poll the others.

"So, if we're agreed, then, some liner far away from the possibility of further —"

"There'll be a knighthood, of course," Annalise said, popping her last bit of pastry into her mouth.

The assembled Lords of Admiralty turned to watch the Queen chew and swallow.

"It's only to be expected," Annalise said. "It was discussed after Giron, but some were concerned at how the announcement would be taken in the Fringe Worlds. In fact —" Annalise furrowed her brow and touched fingers to her lips. "— I seem to recall the news in the Fringe, even the Naval Gazette, made no mention of the girl's first name at all. Something about rendering honors to a woman offending colonial sensibilities?" She waved her hand dismissively. "Of course, there'll be no risk of that with news of a knighthood — it being a capital offense to alter a Royal Proclamation in any way." She smiled at Cunningham. "You'll remind your captains to make that point to those worlds when the packet's dropped off, won't you, Lord Cunningham?"

"Of course, Your Majesty."

Annalise smiled at the man, then turned her gaze to Larcbost, who was barely bothering to hide her own grin. That wouldn't do at all.

"About that song, Portia ..."

Larcbost's face sobered and she watched her sovereign as a wily cow might eye the Judas goat's approach.

"Majesty?"

"As it mentions me, with the Royal Navy's full love and respect, I'm certain, I do long to hear it."

"Majesty, I'm not entirely sure that would be —"

"When next we have tea, perhaps? You do have such a lovely singing voice." The Queen quickly ran her eyes over the others at the table and pressed her hands together, eyes wide and disingenuous. "Or at Court, when next you *all* attend! Lord Narfolk's baritone would be such a compliment to your soprano — a proper shanty might be just the thing to liven things up. It would be such *fun!*"

Narfolk looked decidedly uncomfortable and Falkirk grimaced outright.

Larcbost cocked her head and took a deep breath. "It's a rather ... rough tune, Your Majesty, spacers being what they are."

Annalise let her face fall in disappointment. "Is it? Oh." She sighed. "Well, perhaps not then ..." She paused just long enough for her admirals to feel a sense of relief, then, "But do, please, all of you be prepared just in case? Perhaps when the fuddier members of the Court have gone off to something else."

She rose, sending them scrambling to their feet as she strode out of the room.

"Well, I'll leave you to your deliberations. I see that you have things well in-hand, and trust you'll find the perfect spot for this lieutenant — suitable to her accomplishments and new status."

THE QUEEN PAUSED on the landing pad to look back at Admiralty, then out over the forest of other buildings to the city beyond.

She thought she'd struck just the right note with their lordships, insisting they keep the girl active in the Service, while ensuring they knew they'd be the ones on the hook should she be less than successful in the future. Rewarding this Carew would also further endear the Queen to the common spacers and reinforce the idea that sending Carew after them had been a Royal idea in the first place, but without saying so outright, which would cause a diplomatic breach with Hanover in these quite delicate times.

Annalise smiled and resumed her walk to her aircar.

Balancing it all was at times rather like trying to dance atop the landing pad's railing — a thin surface of safety, with doom to one side, and a static field trying to push one away. Still, it was satisfying when things went well.

It *would* be interesting to see what the girl got up to next, as she was an absolute magnet for trouble. More interesting would be what the Foreign Office fellow, Eades, found to put her up to.

Annalise had been dubious when the man'd proposed sending someone so young into the heart of the Barbary, but she did have to admit he'd been right ... again. The girl had done far more than bring back word of the missing spacers, after all.

And then, of course, was the impact she was having on the Fringe Fleet and the Fringe Worlds. Just the knighthood would positively throw a fox into the henhouse of the Fringe's regressive ideas, forcing them to acknowledge the girl's accomplishments through their desire to see one of their own do well.

All in all, both she and the kingdom had come out far ahead in the deal. And should the girl ever fail in one of her mad attempts ...

well, that's what lieutenants and junior captains were for, wasn't it? One could always disavow their actions without consequence.

Queen Annalise slipped into her aircar, idly singing a snatch of the new tune she'd learned. She had to admit it was quite catchy.

> *"Alexis, Annalise did send,*
> *To find Her errant spacers,*
> *Little did She know they'd end*
> *Up in the* Randy Whistler."

AUTHOR'S NOTE

Thank you for reading *The Queen's Pardon*, book six in the Alexis Carew series.

I hope you enjoyed it as much as I enjoyed writing it, and if you did like it and would like to further support the series, please consider leaving a review on the purchase site or a review/rating on Goodreads. Reviews are the lifeblood of independent authors and let other readers know if a book might be to their liking.

You might also consider joining my mailing list (http://www.jasutherlandbooks.com/list), if you'd like to be kept aware of the progress of new releases. I send no more than one or two updates a month, and subscribers will receive a free ebook copy of the novella *Planetfall* (a prequel to the series) and the short-story *Wronged* (the first bits of the Spacer, Smuggler, Pirate, Spy series), both set in the Alexis Carew universe, as well as other short works in the series as they come about.

Why would a privateer — and such a manly one as Malcomson — sail on a ship named *Bachelor's Delight*?

Well, the name of that ship was a real privateer, captained by

Edward Davies in the late 17th century (https://en.wikipedi-a.org/wiki/Edward_Davis_(buccaneer))

To the best of my knowledge, though, no one ever called Davis' ship the *Catamite* (and lived, at least).

The pardon Alexis offers the pirates is similar to one issued by King George in 1715, the text of which can be found in:

A General History of the Pyrates From Their firft RISE and SETTLEMENT in the Ifland of Providence, to the prefent Time. With the remarkable Actions and Adventures of the two Female Pyrates Mary Read and Anne Bonny
by Daniel Dafoe (1724)
https://www.gutenberg.org/files/40580/40580-h/40580-h.htm

I do, sometimes, envy authors of past times their liberality of title ... then I compare my laptop to a hand-cut quill and think, "It's a fair trade."

The privateers, other than Alexis (when she's doing it), in both *Privateer* and *The Queen's Pardon* aren't the most noble of creatures when you get right down to it. Not even Malcomson, charming though he might be. Well, this is the reality of privateering — they were not some noble creature, but were one step above pirates themselves. Many of them were, in fact, pirates, enlisted by the Crown to attack enemies instead of friends under the color of authority — much the same as today's civil forfeiture laws, if you'll pardon a single step into the political realm.

Their goal was to make money, and they did it in the same way that pirates did — by targeting merchantmen and weaker foes. When faced with an equal force, there was no profit in a confrontation, so they'd not engage. This isn't, necessarily, a cowardly act, as they were not warships with a sworn duty to the Crown — they were independent businessmen, out for profit.

As Alexis says, "They are what they are," — though Malcomson, at least, admits he owes her a debt which she might collect one day.

Who was Kaycie? Why would Presgraves like that her head, at least, was around for a fusion plant explosion? What *did* Avrel Dansby do to so terrify the pirates of the Barbary?

As he says, those are his stories to tell — or mine to tell for him, rather, which is done in the *Spacer, Smuggler, Pirate, Spy* series. Check it out.

J.A. Sutherland
    Orlando, FL
    October 1, 2018

ALSO BY J.A. SUTHERLAND

To be notified when new releases are available, follow J.A. Sutherland on Facebook (https://www.facebook.com/jasutherlandbooks/), Twitter (https://twitter.com/JASutherlandBks), or subscribe to the author's newsletter (http://www.alexiscarew.com/list).

Alexis Carew

Into the Dark

Mutineer

The Little Ships

HMS Nightingale

Privateer

The Queen's Pardon

Planetfall (prequel)

Dark Artifice

(Writing as Richard Grantham)

Of Dubious Intent

Spacer, Smuggler, Pirate, Spy

Spacer

Smuggler (coming 2019)

Trade Runs

Running Start (coming 2019)

Running Scared (coming 2019)

Running on Empty (coming 2019)

ABOUT THE AUTHOR

J.A. Sutherland spends his time sailing the Bahamas on a 43' 1925 John G. Alden sailboat called Little Bit ...

Yeah ... no. In his dreams.

Reality is a townhouse in Orlando with a 90 pound huskie-wolf mix who won't let him take naps.

When not reading or writing, he spends his time on roadtrips around the Southeast US searching for good barbeque.

Mailing List: http://www.alexiscarew.com/list

To contact the author:
www.alexiscarew.com
sutherland@alexiscarew.com

CPSIA information can be obtained
at www.ICGtesting.com
Printed in the USA
LVHW020826140121
676459LV00001B/14